PRAISE FOR

KAY DAVID

"Multifaceted characters, emotional intensity
and a storyline from today's headlines
make this Kay David romance a winner."
—*Romantic Times* on *The Negotiator*

"*The Commander* has it all—dynamic characters,
fast pacing and emotional ups and downs."
—*Romantic Times*

Dear Reader,

The editors at Harlequin and Silhouette are thrilled to be able to bring you a brand-new featured author program beginning in 2005! Signature Select aims to single out outstanding stories, contemporary themes and oft-requested classics by some of your favorite series authors and present them to you in a variety of formats bound by truly striking covers.

We plan to provide several different types of reading experiences in the new Signature Select program. The Spotlight books will offer a single "big read" by a talented series author, the Collections will present three novellas on a selected theme in one volume, the Sagas will contain sprawling, sometimes multigenerational family tales (often related to a favorite family first introduced in series) and the Miniseries will feature requested, previously published books, with two or, occasionally, three complete stories in one volume. The Signature Select program will offer one book in each of these categories per month, and fans of limited continuity series will also find these continuing stories under the Signature Select umbrella.

In addition, these volumes will bring you bonus features...different in every single book! You may learn more about the author in an extended interview, more about the setting or inspiration for the book, more about subjects related to the theme and, often, a bonus short read will be included.

Watch for new stories from Janelle Denison, Donna Kauffman, Leslie Kelly, Marie Ferrarella, Suzanne Forster, Stephanie Bond, Christine Rimmer and scores more of the brightest talents in romance fiction!

We have an exciting year ahead!

Warm wishes for happy reading,

Marsha Zinberg

Marsha Zinberg
Executive Editor
The Signature Select Program

Signature Select™
MINISERIES

KAY DAVID

the GUARDIANS

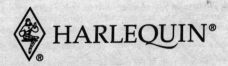

HARLEQUIN®

TORONTO • NEW YORK • LONDON
AMSTERDAM • PARIS • SYDNEY • HAMBURG
STOCKHOLM • ATHENS • TOKYO • MILAN • MADRID
PRAGUE • WARSAW • BUDAPEST • AUCKLAND

ISBN 0-373-21761-7

THE GUARDIANS

Copyright © 2005 by Harlequin Books S.A.

The publisher acknowledges the copyright holder of the individual works as follows:

THE NEGOTIATOR
Copyright © 2001 by Carla Luan.

THE COMMANDER
Copyright © 2001 by Carla Luan.

This edition published by arrangement with Harlequin Books S.A.

® and TM are trademarks of the publisher. Trademarks indicated with ® are registered in the United States Patent and Trademark Office, the Canadian Trade Marks Office and in other countries.

www.eHarlequin.com

Printed in U.S.A.

CONTENTS

THE NEGOTIATOR   9

THE COMMANDER   263

THE NEGOTIATOR

This book is dedicated to the incredibly brave police officers who struggle every day to make the world a safer place. Their jobs are too important and too dangerous for any writer to fully capture the essence of their sacrifices, but I hope these stories somehow express the appreciation I feel for their efforts.

A special acknowledgment to Laura and Paula. Your support and encouragement mean more than I can adequately express. Thank you both for having faith in my abilities and for giving me the opportunity to tell the stories my way.

CHAPTER ONE

LOOKING BACK on it, that night after everything was over, Jennifer Barclay realized with amazement that the morning had started out like any other ordinary day.

She'd had no sense of impending doom, no feeling things were about to go horribly wrong. Not a single clue. If she'd known—if she'd had even the slightest inkling—she would have stayed home in bed.

But she hadn't suspected a thing.

She'd arrived at Westside Elementary at seven-thirty and by four that afternoon, as usual, she was totally exhausted. She loved her job as a fourth-grade teacher, but by May, even she needed a break. With only another five weeks of school, the kids had been wild, and none of them had wanted to concentrate. Their heads were at the coast, a mile down Highway 98, where the white Florida sand and crashing emerald waves were just begging to be enjoyed. Truth be told, Jennifer had had a hard time focusing herself…but for a totally different reason.

She'd had to change her schedule.

Jennifer always visited her mother on Wednesdays and Saturdays, but this afternoon she wouldn't be able to make it to the nursing home. She'd had to arrange an after-school meeting for the children participating in the annual beach cleanup, and the disruption to her usual orderly agenda bothered her a lot. Her friends teased her, but for Jennifer, routine meant everything. During her childhood, no plans had ever been made, much less kept, and now nothing was more important to her than the steady, day-to-day patterns she lived by.

She hurried down the hallway toward her classroom and tried to convince herself to stop worrying. Half the time Nadine Barclay didn't even know who she was, never mind if Jennifer was there or not. Alzheimer's had robbed Jennifer's mother of her family and her memories. Jennifer wanted to be a good daughter to her mother, though. She showed up twice a week whether Nadine knew it not.

Whether Jennifer wanted to or not.

Reaching her classroom, she walked inside and closed the door behind her. In between the last bell and the scheduled meeting, she had exactly five minutes to gulp the diet cola she'd retrieved from the teachers' lounge, but she hadn't even taken her first sip when the door opened. She closed her eyes for just a second, then turned to see who was standing in the doorway.

Ten-year-old Juan Canales smiled shyly at her.

"Juan!" Putting aside her plans to snatch a moment of peace, Jennifer grinned and held up the icy drink. "Come on in. I just went and got a Coke. If you don't tell anyone, I'll share it with you!"

He replaced his indecisive look with one of contained excitement. His family was very poor, and she doubted he and his siblings got enough to eat. Sodas would have been out of the question. The Canales fam-

ily represented the flip side of Destin, the beautiful resort town Westside Elementary served. Juan's mother
cleaned rooms for one of the elegant beach hotels and
his father clipped the bushes surrounding its luxurious
pool. When Jennifer handed the little boy the filled
paper cup, he gripped it with two hands and sipped
slowly.

Jennifer studied Juan surreptitiously as he drank. He
was one of her very best students, and even though she
knew she wasn't supposed to have favorites, Jennifer
had to admit, he was one. Smart, clever and as sweet as
he could be, Juan Canales made Jennifer ache to have
children of her own. He was a perfect example of why
she'd become a teacher, too. He seemed as starved for
information as he was for everything else.

He finished his drink with noisy gusto and she poured
the last of the Coke into his cup with a smile.

"I wasn't all that thirsty," she confided. "I'm glad
you're here to help me."

His eyes rounded with pleasure. "*Muchas gracias*...
uh...thank you very much, Miss Barclay. It really tastes
good."

Within a few minutes, a dozen other ten-year-olds had
arrived, and Jennifer started passing out permission slips.
She walked up and down the aisle between the desks and
spoke. "I have to have these back by next week, signed,
sealed and delivered. You can't participate in the beach
cleanup if I don't have this on record, okay?" Returning
to the front of the room, she stopped beside her desk and
rested one hip on the corner. "We're cleaning up at Blue
Mountain. Does everyone know where that is?"

The question prompted chatter and Jennifer grinned, letting it wash over her. God, she loved her job! The students, their enthusiasm, their joy—they represented everything good in her life. Actually, they represented *everything* in her life. Even her free hours were devoted to the school and if she wasn't visiting her mother, she was here.

Again, sometimes she took ribbing over this. "There's more to living than just work," her best friend Wanda would say. The black woman, who was Nadine's nurse, constantly gave Jennifer a hard time. She was right, of course, but Jennifer had her life organized just as she liked it.

She held up her hands for silence, but before she could speak, she heard a noise in the hallway. Jennifer glanced curiously at the door and the small window in the upper half.

Howard French stood before the glass. The strained expression on the young man's face brought Jennifer to her feet, bells of warning sounding inside her head. He'd been fired from the maintenance staff just last week. What on earth was he doing here now?

Starting toward the door, she thought of how she'd tried to help him. She'd complained after he'd been let go, but it'd been pointless, and she'd known that before she stepped inside Betty Whitmire's office. The school's local board member, Betty hated the simple man. More than once, Jennifer had cringed, hearing Betty's stinging voice down the hall. "If you can't do better than that, French, we'll find someone who can. Mopping the floor isn't brain surgery, you know!"

Jennifer was halfway to the door when Howard burst inside. He stumbled once, then straightened, giving his arm a short jerk. A screaming woman lurched in behind him, her hands on her head in a useless attempt to ease the grip Howard had on her hair. He turned and locked the door behind him, pulling the shade down with his other hand. For a moment, the scene made no sense, no sense at all, then the woman shrieked again, and things became distressingly clear. Disheveled and obviously distraught, Betty Whitmire had an ugly bruise on the side of her face and a rip in the sleeve of her dress. Jennifer's heart stopped, then leapt inside her chest and began to pound, disbelief leaving her mouth dry.

She spoke without thinking. "Howard? My God— what's going on? Wh-what are you doing with Mrs. Whitmire?"

He didn't answer, and Betty's labored breathing was raw and guttural in the shocked hush of the room. Behind Jennifer, one of the children started to sniffle. The sound seemed to bring Howard out of his apparent trance.

"You got to help me, Miss Jennifer," he cried. "I'm in trouble."

Not knowing what else to do, Jennifer took two steps toward the crazed man and his hostage.

"Don't come no further!" he screamed. "Don't do it!"

She wanted to argue, but nothing came out. She was paralyzed, and all she could do was stare as he swung up the barrel of a rifle and pointed it directly at her.

THE DUFFEL BAG was already strained at the seams when Beck Winters threw in one more book, then yanked the zipper closed. He was taking his first vacation in eight years and he wasn't really sure what people did on vacation. He wanted to have plenty to read in case he got bored. He just couldn't stand having time on his hands and nothing to do. His brain would sense the emptiness and before he could stop it, his thoughts would take him places he didn't want to go.

Looking around one more time, he walked out of the bedroom. He was almost to the front door when the telephone rang. As if getting a reprieve, he dropped the bag and raced into the kitchen. "Beck Winters," he answered eagerly.

"We've got a call." Lena McKinney's throaty voice filled the line. The SWAT team's lieutenant, Lena kept the two cells of the group organized and motivated as they covered the Emerald Coast of Florida from just past Pensacola all the way down to Panama City Beach. The fifteen members were close as a family, albeit a dysfunctional one at times.

"I know you're about to leave but Bradley's got the flu and he's whining like a baby. But he couldn't work this one even if he felt okay. We're at Westside Elementary. Get here as fast as you can. We've got a man gone barricade. There are hostages, too."

Beck didn't bother to ask any questions because Lena hung up before he could voice them, just as he'd known she would. If she was there and had called him, the team was already on-site with the perimeter secured and a sniper in place. Now they needed someone to talk. A negotiator. Kicking the duffel aside, Beck ran out the front door without wasting another minute. It'd been planned for a long time, but obviously his vacation would just have to wait.

Thank God…

He hadn't a clue what to do with himself anyway.

"HOWARD…" Jennifer made her voice as soft and non-threatening as she could. "What's going on? Why do you have a gun? Why are you hurting Mrs. Whitmire like that?"

He looked at the woman whose hair he still held. He almost seemed surprised to see her. Jerking his head up, he met Jennifer's gaze, his eyes wide and confused, his hand trembling on the weapon. "She was ugly to me," he said simply.

"That doesn't mean you have to be the same way to her." Jennifer held out her hands. "Put the rifle down, please, Howard. It's scaring the children."

The gun stayed level as he glanced behind her. Jennifer tried not to look down the barrel but she couldn't help herself. She felt her eyes go inexorably to the bore, and for just a second, black dots swam before her. She was a child herself, ten years old, terrified and helpless. Her vision tunneled, bloody images hovering on the edges like the ghosts they were.

Howard's voice yanked her back. "I—I don't care," he said. "N-nobody cares about me so why should I care about them?"

"That's not true, Howard. I care about you and so does everyone—"

"He's insane!" Betty Whitmire cried. Her voice was shrill and discordant, destroying Jennifer's effort for calmness like a train whistle shattering the night's silence. "He grabbed me in the hall and dragged me in here. He's going to kill us all!"

Jennifer stared at her in disbelief, wondering—not for the first time—how on earth the woman had managed to land her position on the school board. Her people skills were nonexistent, and she was totally clueless when it came to the kids. Neither the parents nor teachers respected her, but Jennifer had to admit one thing: Betty was involved. There wasn't a detail about any of the schools she didn't know.

Hearing Betty speak, one of the children started crying in earnest, small terrified sobs escaping. Jennifer turned and tried to look reassuring, but when she saw them, she wanted to cry herself. They'd fled their desks and had instinctively huddled at the back of the room. Cherise was the one sobbing, and Juan was patting her awkwardly on the arm, whispering something to her. His best friend, Julian, hovered nearby, an uncertain expression on his face. Jennifer caught Juan's eye and nodded slightly, hoping her approval would make its way across the room.

Looking at Howard once more, Jennifer spoke above the pounding of her heart. She made her words sound certain and composed, even though she was panicking inside. "Betty, please stay quiet. You're not helping matters. Howard is *not* going to shoot you. Not you, not anyone. Isn't that right, Howard? In fact, he's going to turn you loose right now."

He tightened his grip on Betty's scalp, but then unexpectedly opened his fist. She cried out and fell down, unprepared for the sudden release. From the floor, she shot Jennifer a look of confusion mixed with gratitude, then she scrambled past her on all fours, heading for the children. Jennifer didn't turn but she could hear the chairs scraping and the muffled voices as they moved to accommodate her.

Taking advantage of the confusion, Jennifer forced herself to move an inch nearer the man and the gun, a trickle of sweat forming along her shoulders then drawing a line down her back. She was lucky enough to have a phone in her room, but there was no way she could get to it and dial for help. Howard stood between her and the wall where it hung.

She truly was confident that Howard wouldn't shoot. He just wasn't that kind of man. When the class hamster had died, he'd cried more than any of the kids. If anything, he was too quiet and unassuming…and every time she looked at him, Jennifer saw her brother. Unlike Howard, Danny had been brilliant, but in their eyes lived the same haunted expression. It was filled with confusion, uncertainty and a complete lack of self-confidence. She'd been trying to help the janitor since the day she'd met him. A penance, she knew.

Even still, a thousand thoughts crowded Jennifer's head. Could she grab the gun? Should she even try? What would happen if she didn't? Her forward movement finally registered and Howard yanked the weapon up, tucking the stock under his arm.

"Don't come no closer, Miss Jennifer. I mean it. I'm serious."

Her mouth felt full of beach sand, but she held out her

hands and spoke in an appeasing way. "Okay, okay, I'll stay right here. But talk to me. Tell me what's going on."

The air seemed to go out of his body and he slumped against her desk. The black, empty barrel of the rifle remained pointed at Jennifer's chest. "I'm in trouble," he said again. "Big, big trouble."

Another child started to cry. "Let the kids go, Howard," she whispered. "Let Mrs. Whitmire take them out and then you and I can talk. You can tell me what happened."

He shook his head morosely. "I can't let 'em go," he said. "I can't. It's too late."

"Too late for what?"

He shook his head and said nothing. The bore of the weapon dropped an inch.

"How can I help you if you won't tell me what's going on?" she asked. "Let them go. I'll stay. I promise."

"Won't do no good. Not now. Everbody hates me and they all think I'm stupid. It's too late." He dipped his head and shook it again, the picture of total dejection. "They hate me. All of 'em."

The gun slipped a second inch lower. Jennifer licked her lips, swallowed hard then took a quiet step forward. Another foot and she could touch the barrel, grab it, twist it away from him. She held her breath, trapping it inside her chest and holding it captive, afraid to even breathe. Slowly, so slowly the movement was practically imperceptible, she began to raise her right hand. Howard continued to talk.

"It's all wrong," he mumbled. "All wrong. I'm not that way. I'm a nice person. I really am."

Without any warning, he looked up. Jennifer stopped

instantly, her hand halfway up her side. He didn't even seem to notice. "I'm a nice person," he cried. "I'm nice!"

"I know that," she said soothingly. "I know you are, Howard." Her shoulders tightened, a reflexive action. "But nice people don't point guns. So why don't you hand it over and we'll talk?" She took another step and reached out, her fingers brushing the cold, hard metal of the barrel.

She didn't know what happened first—the ringing phone or Howard's reaction—but an instant later, the opportunity was lost. Wild-eyed, he grabbed her and pulled her close.

"THEY'RE NOT ANSWERING." Beck turned to Lena and shook his head, the phone pressed to his ear. They were inside the War Wagon, a modified Winnebago motor home stocked with the equipment and supplies that would be required during any situation. Parked down the block from the school, he could see the side of the building, an older structure with tilt-out windows facing a worn playground. They were less than a mile from some of the most expensive real estate in Florida, but no one would know it from looking at the school. There was a world of difference between its run-down appearance and the elegant high-rises that dotted the sparkling beaches.

"Are you sure the phone's right there in her classroom? We never had phones inside the rooms when I was in school. Maybe I should drag out the bullhorn."

Lena stared at him, her gray eyes impatient and stormy as usual. "Wake up, Beck. This is the computer age. A lot of the classrooms have their own phones now. Besides that, the guys are already in place in the hallway and they can hear it ringing. It's the right phone."

"Maybe he took 'em somewhere else."

"They're there. A teacher saw the suspect grab a member of the school board who happened to be in the hall and drag her inside a classroom. She's pretty sure she saw a gun, but isn't positive. The responding officers didn't even try to go in. They just called us."

"How many are inside?"

"We don't know yet. Another teacher was having a meeting with some of the students. Fourth graders. Their teacher's name is Jennifer Barclay."

He gripped the phone tightly. He'd faced countless calls like this one since he'd joined the team, but Beck never did it without nervousness sucker punching him in the gut, especially if there were kids involved. He knew too much, he thought all at once. When he was less experienced and more reckless, he hadn't understood what was on the line.

Now he understood all too well.

He forced himself to focus. "Any background info yet?"

"Sarah's working on it, but she hasn't found a lot yet."

Beck nodded. The only nontactical member of the team, Sarah Greenberg served as the information officer. She labored just as hard and was just as sharp as any of the other cops. Her job was to gather any details they might need to resolve a situation. Next to time, information was key.

"Who's in there?"

Lena spoke as she brought a pair of high-powered

binoculars to her eyes. "Cal and Jason are inside at one end of the hallway, and the rest of the gang's at the other end. We don't have much recon yet—can't see inside. The perp pulled the shade on the window in the door and apparently they're nowhere near the only window in the classroom. I've got the floor plans to the school and the guys have those already. Randy's across the street."

"Where?"

She nodded toward the row of the small frame houses opposite the school. "There, the fifth one down with the green shutters, the two-story with the oleanders in front. The owners are gone. Neighbor had a key and she let us in the back door." She handed Beck the glasses. "He's in the upstairs corner window."

Beck stared through the lenses and the head of Randy Tamirisa, the team's countersniper, leapt into focus. He was lying motionless behind his weapon, the sight trained on the school. Beck couldn't see his face, but he didn't need to. Black hair and even blacker eyes, Randy was an enigma to Beck, the exact opposite of most snipers. They'd never gotten along; hotheaded and heavy-handed, Randy didn't have the discipline Beck felt was necessary to be on the team, but Lena disagreed and she was the boss. Randy's perfect shooting range score didn't hurt, either.

"Where's Chase?"

Beside him Lena sighed.

"I know, I know—" He spoke before she could answer him. "Chase is not a member of my cell, and Randy is good, and what's my problem?" He lowered the glasses and looked at the woman beside him.

"And the answer is?" she said dryly.

"I don't trust Randy," he said bluntly, bringing the glasses back to his face. "He's not a team player. He's a hot dog."

"C'mon, Beck. He's been with us a year and he scores one hundred percent every time he's on the range. He's inexperienced but he's done nothing wrong."

"He's done nothing period."

"Give the guy a chance. You were young once, too, you know."

"I was never that young." Without waiting for her reply, he picked up the phone and hit the redial button. It began to ring in his ear as he looked down at his boss. "I don't trust him," he repeated darkly, "and neither should you."

"LET ME ANSWER the phone, Howard, please." His arm was so tightly pressed against her throat, Jennifer could hardly speak. "P-please. I-it could be important."

"Who is it?" he asked illogically.

"I—I don't know." She put her fingers against his sleeve and gently tugged, trying for a little more air. He had on an orange jumpsuit, the uniform of the maintenance people. It smelled like diesel and fear. "Please, Howard."

They stood together in the center of the room. When the phone stopped ringing, the thick tension seemed to hold the vibrations. A moment later, the sound started all over just as it had for the past hour.

"Let me answer it," she whispered. "It might be a parent. Whoever it is won't give up."

"All right...but don't tell 'em anything. Don't tell 'em 'bout me."

They stumbled together toward the telephone, which hung on the wall beside the door. Jennifer's voice was breathless as she answered, and she prayed someone she knew was on the other end. Someone who could tell something was wrong with her even if she couldn't get the words out. "H-hello?"

"This is Officer Beck Winters with the Emerald Coast SWAT team. Who am I speaking with, please?"

Jennifer's heart knocked against her ribs in surprise, then she pulled herself together, fear, shock and relief combining inside her in a crazy mix. "Th-this is Jennifer Barclay."

"Who is it?"

"Is everyone okay in there?"

Howard's voice was harsh in her left ear, the policeman's cool tones were in her right. She answered the policeman and ignored Howard. "W-we're fine."

Howard jerked his arm and Jennifer gasped automatically. "Who is it?" His voice dropped and menace filled it. "You tell me who that is. Right now!"

Jennifer turned slightly and looked into his face. Their eyes were inches apart, and she'd never noticed until this moment that one of his irises was lighter than the other. For some unexplained reason, those mismatched eyes sparked a moment of fear. She spoke quickly. "It's the police. They want to know if everyone's okay."

His reaction was the last one she expected. He stiffened, dropped his arm from her neck and slowly began to back up, shaking his head. The rifle stayed pointed at her.

"Miss Barclay? Jennifer? Talk to me. I need to know what's going on."

Her mind drifting strangely, she imagined what the cop must look like—he had to be a big man, tall and barrel-chested, judging from the depth of his voice. Dark hair, she decided, and a pleasant face, rounded and caring.

"What does he want?" Howard asked again.

Apparently hearing the question, the cop spoke, still composed, still collected. He could have been asking to speak to his own brother. "I need to talk with Mr. French, please, Jennifer. Put him on the line."

Jennifer held the phone out. "He wants to talk with you."

Howard shook his head rapidly, his eyes huge. "No! No way. I'm not talking to them. Uh-uh." He waved the rifle at her and she had to swallow a gasp. "You talk to 'em."

She slowly brought the phone back to her ear. "He doesn't want to speak with you."

"Okay, okay. That's all right for now, but eventually, I'll need to talk to him. If he changes his mind and wants to speak to me, all you have to do is pick up the phone. It's been reprogrammed to ring me automatically. Understand?"

His voice was so reassuring and confident Jennifer felt her shoulders ease just a tad. Here was help, she thought. She added a pair of warm brown eyes to the image of the officer she'd made in her mind. "Y-yes. I—I understand," she answered.

"Good. Now answer my questions and don't say anything else. We don't want to upset him any more than he already is. How many people are there, including you and Howard French? Does he have a weapon? Is anyone hurt? Where are the kids?"

Jennifer glanced at the terrified students, then spoke. "Fifteen. Yes. No. At the back of the room."

"All right." She could hear him writing something down, a pen scratching on paper, then the sound stopped. "I'm going to ask you some more questions but first, no matter what happens, keep those kids where they are, okay? We have to know they're in the same location and staying there. Understand?"

"Yes."

"Okay. Now, does he have a gun?"

"Yes."

"A rifle or pistol?"

"The first." She licked her suddenly dry lips. "A .22."

A second passed, as if he were surprised by her recognition of the weapon. She found herself wishing she didn't know.

"Is he calm?"

"For the moment."

"Scared?"

"Yes."

"Violent?"

"No, absolutely not." She dropped her voice. "Howard isn't like that at all. You don't understand. Something must have happened to upset him. Something really bad—"

"Yes, ma'am, something bad happened. He's come into your classroom, taken hostages and has a weapon."

He didn't give her time to reply. "Our first priority is you and those children, though. We want everyone in there to come out alive and that's our main goal. We want Mr. French to stay cool. We've got nothing but time, okay? But I've got to talk to him. That's paramount. I can't do my job if I can't talk to him."

"Well, I'm sure he'll talk to you as soon as—"

The moment Jennifer spoke, Howard's eyes flew open and his whole body stiffened. With a practiced movement, he brought the rifle to his shoulder and looked through the sight. "Put down the phone!" he screamed. "Put it down right now or I'll shoot!"

CHAPTER TWO

"JENNIFER! Jennifer… Shit!"

Beck slammed down the phone and wiped his brow. The Winnebago's air-conditioning was cranked all the way up but it didn't seem to matter. The ever present humidity, a damp and sticky gift from the nearby Gulf of Mexico, still managed to creep through the sealed windows. He watched an errant breeze kick up a small cloud of dirt at the center of the deserted playground and cursed again. A month later and there wouldn't have been any kids or teachers in that classroom. "I lost 'em."

"Move him to the end of the classroom. I can set a shot if she gets him by the window."

Randy Tamirisa's voice sounded inside Beck's head, coming through the tiny earpiece he wore. The whole team communicated with each other via a complicated system of earphones and wraparound microphones. As Randy spoke, Lena raised her hand to her ear and Beck knew she'd heard the sniper as well.

"It's way too early—"

"Not yet, Randy—"

Lena and Beck spoke at the same time, but Lena immediately hushed him with a hand motion and answered the sniper herself.

"Randy, we're not ready for that yet. Stay cool, all right?"

"There're kids in that room."

Beck bit his tongue.

"I know that," Lena said patiently, "but *I'll* let *you* know when it's time to set the shot, not the other way around."

Silence filled their earphones and Beck knew that was all the answer she'd get from her rebuke. He spoke anyway, pulling his microphone closer as if he and Randy were the only ones hearing the conversation. "I haven't even talked to the suspect yet, Tamirisa. I need to establish communications before you get trigger-happy."

Again, Randy didn't answer.

"I need an acknowledgment, Officer." Beck's voice was icy.

Nothing but an absence of sound, then finally—"Ten-four, *Officer.*"

A pointed stick of pain stabbed Beck between his eyes. He resisted the urge to lift his hand and massage the bridge of his nose. The tension headaches were getting worse with each situation.

Showing no outward sign of discomfort, he picked up the phone with an unhurried movement and redialed the number.

Jennifer Barclay answered after the fifteenth ring. She spoke before Beck could. "He won't talk to you, okay? The only reason he let me answer is because I promised I wouldn't make him talk."

She sounded remarkably collected, and Beck suspected that was for the children's benefit. She didn't want them more scared than they already were, but deep down she had to be terrified. Every hostage was. When someone had total control over your life…you were terrified.

"I understand," Beck answered. "I can work with that. Like I told you before, we've got all the time in the world. There's no hurry. We can wait him out, but ask him this…will he at least listen to me? He doesn't have to answer, okay?"

"Let me see."

Beck heard her put the question to Howard French, then a moment later, she spoke into the phone. "He said he'll listen, but that's all."

"Great. Let me talk with him."

Harsh breathing sounded in Beck's ear. "Howard? I can call you Howard, can't I?"

Silence.

"Listen, Howard, you doing okay in there? Everybody all right? You need anything?" This time, without waiting for an answer, he continued. "I want to help you, Howard. I'm here just for you, but you have to tell us what you want, buddy. We can help you out with almost anything. There's one rule, though, okay?"

Beck's fingers cramped on the phone and he consciously loosened them. "Are you with me?"

Silence.

"You can't hurt any of those kids. That's the rule. You can't hurt them or the teacher or the school board lady, okay? Once you understand that, we can talk and I can help you out, but you have to tell me you understand me."

A rustling sound came over the line, then Jennifer Barclay spoke again. "He said to tell you he won't harm anyone. And I believe him. You won't hurt him, will you?"

Beck looked out the window. It was still light, but the sky had begun to fade into purple, the shadows growing long and dark. He filled his voice with hearty reassurance. "He'll be fine and so will you and the kids. No one's going to get hurt. Our goal is to keep everyone alive, including Mr. French. I promise you that."

"He said I could ask for some sodas. He's thirsty...."

"I'd be happy to bring that in. Tell him to send out one of the kids and we'll send in cans of anything he wants."

He heard another muffled conversation. "Okay... okay...he says that's fine." She spoke once more, but this time in a whisper. "Look, this guy isn't some kind of wild killer, okay? He's a little simple, but he's not going to shoot anyone. He loves the kids and he loved his job and he's just upset because he got fired. Let me work on him a little bit, okay? I think I can talk to him."

Beck closed his eyes. *Everyone was an expert.* "Miss Barclay—Jennifer—the man has a gun. He's assaulted your boss and taken hostages. I understand that you know him and think of him as a friend, but he's dangerous. You need to let us handle this."

"He *isn't* dangerous," she insisted. "He can't even read, for pity's sake. I've been working with him for months. He's confused and upset, all right? I'm telling you—"

He interrupted her gently. "Ma'am, we've got a situation here you're unfamiliar with...but we aren't. It's our business so let us take care of it."

"And just how are you going to accomplish that if he won't talk to you?"

Beck waited a second, then spoke. "We don't negotiate everything, Miss Barclay. Believe me, we have alternative ways of resolving issues."

WHEN SHE WAS TEN, Jennifer's father had taken all of
them to Disney World for a rare family outing. She
didn't want to ride the monster roller coaster, but the
cruel gibing she would have gotten from William Barclay had she refused would have been worse. She hadn't
known the word then, but *sadistic* came to mean a lot
to her as an adult.

She'd looked askance at Danny, but he'd slid his eyes
away from hers and stared off into the distance. He
knew how frightened she was, but what choice did she
have? What choice had *any* of them had? Afterward,
when she'd jumped off the ride, her rubbery legs had
given out and she'd collapsed. It was one of the few
times she'd failed in front of her father, but it'd given
her a taste of what Danny got every day. Her father had
never let her forget the incident.

Her legs felt the same way now.

She walked slowly to the rear of the classroom. Howard's eyes were on her back, and she prayed she
wouldn't fall down. The children surrounded her as she
reached them and kneeled down.

"I want you all to stay back here," she said in a low,
reassuring voice, "and don't say anything. I know you're
scared, but so is Mr. French." She glanced at Betty—no
help there—then again forced her eyes to the children's
faces. "He lost his job last week and he doesn't understand what's going on."

"Who called?"

She looked over at Juan and by the quiet way he spoke, she was sure he knew the answer to his question. "It was the police," she said. "They're outside and they're going to help everybody, including Mr. French. But you guys have to do your part and don't move from here. If you need something, Mrs. Whitmire will help you."

Betty nodded but stayed silent.

Jennifer cleared her throat. "Mr. French has asked the police for some colas and they're going to send some in to us…." She faltered here, not knowing what to do. Which one to send? Which ones to keep? Her gaze fell to Taylor and the answer became clear. The little girl was diabetic; she had to go. Jennifer reached for her. "But…someone has to go get the drinks, so Taylor here is going to help us out."

She put her hand on the child's shoulder. and squeezed, leading her to the front of the room. She didn't explain that the little girl wouldn't be coming back. "You'll be fine," Jennifer whispered. "Don't worry." A moment later, Taylor was gone. Howard locked the door behind her, her tennis shoes slapping as she ran down the hallway.

Jennifer listened to the sound with Beck Winters's words ringing in her mind. *We have alternative ways of resolving issues.* She'd seen enough movies to know what he meant. SWAT teams stormed buildings. People got shot. Hostages were killed. Then she remembered what else he'd said. *No one's going to get hurt…I promise you that.*

She didn't know him, of course, but she believed

him. Unlike her father, he had the voice of a man who would tell the truth, no matter what.

Jennifer turned back to Howard. One way or the other, she had to try. "What's wrong, Howard? Why are you doing this?"

He lifted his dejected gaze to hers. "I lost my job."

"I know. Remember, I tried to help but—"

"They came and took my truck." His expression was dead and lifeless. "How can I get another job without no truck? How can I pay my rent if I don't have a job?" He started shaking his head before she could even speak. "I ain't going back to that shelter place. There's bad people living there."

Jennifer didn't want to be naive; this man had done just what the cop had said—he'd come into her classroom with a gun and taken hostages—but this was Howard, for God's sake. He was a lost soul. Like Danny.

"You're jumping to conclusions, Howard. Thinking the worst possible thing. Remember how we talked about that when you left here? I told you a positive attitude would help you get another position, remember?"

"And you lied." His voice was blunt. "I went ever'where and I had a real positive attitude, but wouldn't nobody hire me. Said they didn't need nobody." He took a ragged breath and stared out the window. The light drifting through was faint and dim. "That's why I came up here," he said. "I wanted to make Miz Whitmire give me my old job."

Jennifer didn't reply but he shook his head as if she had, his hand tightening on the gun at this side. "When she saw me in the hall, she acted all crazy and ever'thing, and started talking trash to me like she always does. Then she saw my gun, and she tried to run off. She crashed into the door and hit her head. That's how she got the bump. I didn't hit her."

"Of course you didn't," she said soothingly.

"I—I reached out to help her up and something went off in my head, like an explosion or something. I grabbed her…then I didn't know what to do with her. That's when I saw I was by your door. I knowed you'd help me."

"And I will, but Howard…what on earth were you doing here with a gun anyway?"

His eyes narrowed. "I was gonna scare 'er. That's all. Just to make her gimme the job back."

"Well, that plan didn't work too well, did it?" She paused, but he didn't answer. "Let the children go, Howard. Let them go and we'll think up a new plan."

He didn't appear to even notice she'd said anything. He raised his hand to his bottom lip and pulled gently, then after a minute, he spoke. "That policeman fellow on the phone—he said he'd help me. Do you think he could make her give me my job again? And make 'em give me my truck, too?"

Her heart fell. He simply didn't grasp the seriousness of what he'd done. "I don't know, Howard."

He stood up and gripped the rifle's barrel with both hands. "You call 'em," he said, nodding his head to the phone. "Tell 'em what I want. You can do it."

BECK GRABBED THE PHONE even before the first ring ended. "Winters."

"This is Jennifer. Did Taylor make it out okay?"

"She's fine, just fine. Her mother is here and they're together. I've got the drinks coming. They'll leave it at the door."

"Are the other parents there?"

Beck glanced down the street. Behind a cordon of officers, the media was gathering, along with the gawkers events like this somehow always attracted. Mixed in the throng, there were worried school officials and moms and dads going crazy. Lena had been down twice to reassure them.

"A few of them, yes," he said. Switching gears, he spoke again. "Let me talk to Howard, Jennifer. That's the only way this is going to get resolved."

"He wants me to ask you something," she said, by way of answering. "He wants to know if you can help him get his old job back."

"Tell him anything's possible," Beck said instantly, "but not until I talk to him. I can't help him if I can't talk to him."

Jennifer's voice was soft as she relayed his message. A second later, she spoke again. "He wants his truck, too," she said. "It was repossessed yesterday. He said if you bring his truck to him, he'll talk to you."

"I'll get the truck and we'll talk. But I want another child, too."

She was starting to sound tense, and just around the edges, a little unraveled. Beck glanced at the countdown clock he'd started when he'd gotten there. They'd been at it almost two hours already. It seemed like he'd just arrived; it seemed like he'd been born there. Catching his eye, beside the clock, were the photos Sarah had obtained. With the phone propped against his shoulder, he shuffled through the mess of papers until he came to the one he wanted. The school picture of Jennifer Barclay.

Sometimes when he watched television, he placed bets with himself. He'd close his eyes, switch channels, and listen to whoever was on the screen. Nine times out of ten, he could guess what they looked like by the way they spoke. He would have lost the farm on this one, though. Jennifer Barclay did not match her voice at all. Her chestnut shoulder-length hair was straight and shiny and her gaze was dark and sad. Except for those eyes, she looked much younger than he would have expected. He'd imagined a woman in her forties, someone with a lot of experience behind her, a person who knew and understood others well.

Flipping through the profiles of the suspect and all the hostages Sarah had gotten along with the photos, Beck found the notes on Jennifer. She lived in Fort Walton Beach, in a small condo complex a few blocks off the beach. She drove a white 1995 Toyota Camry, had no outstanding tickets or warrants and she lived alone.

She'd sounded middle-aged, but Jennifer Barclay was young, pretty and single.

She came back on the line. "Okay, he'll do it. As soon as he sees the truck, he'll send another child out."

The line went dead and Beck grabbed the microphone attached to the headset he wore. "Lena? Did you get all that? You got a line on the truck?"

"We're trying. Sarah knew he'd had a vehicle repossessed so she's contacting the dealership now, but they're closed. It's going to take a while."

Beck nodded, but before he could reply, his ear phone crackled to life.

"Get him to the window to see the damned truck. I want to set my shot."

Beck spoke instantly. "That's premature—"

Lena's voice interrupted. "Beck, we don't have another option. We can't do a chemical assault here, not with those kids, and this guy isn't going to surrender. He's not the type and you know it. We need to be prepared just in case." She spoke to someone nearby, then came back over the headset. "While you were talking to the teacher, I told Randy you'd move the guy."

"This is ridiculous." Beck felt his jaw clench, the pain in his head intensifying, his voice going cold. "What are you doing? Trying to make the ten o'clock news?"

When Lena answered, her tone was as chilly as Beck's. "I don't make command decisions based on the media. If you don't know that by now, you should. You're out of line."

Beck closed his eyes and shook his head. Dammit, what in the hell was he thinking? What in the hell was he *doing?* His head throbbed, and suddenly he felt like the situation was sand slipping through his fingers. Lena had seen what he hadn't in forcing him into taking that vacation. He did need some time off.

But not yet.

"You're right. That was out of line, and I'm sorry," he said stiffly. "But I still think Jennifer's got a point. Howard French doesn't have a sheet and I can get him out of there. Randy should be our last resort, and *you* know *that*."

"What I know is he didn't have a record before, but not now. Cal called in while you were talking. There's been a new development. It's not good."

"What is it?"

"One of the guys found someone in the maintenance shack, out behind the school. We're not sure yet, but it looks like it might be French's supervisor." She took a breath, then spoke. "He's been shot with a .22 rifle."

CHAPTER THREE

BECK'S GUT TIGHTENED. "Damn! Is he dead?"

"He's hanging on but barely."

"Has anyone talked to him?"

"No. He was completely out of it and fading fast. The medics were struggling just to get him to Central before it was too late."

His gaze went to the school, his mind going with it to the woman and children inside. Did Jennifer Barclay know? He answered his own question. Obviously not. She wouldn't be defending Howard French if she knew he'd shot his boss. Would she?

"Get him to the window." Randy spoke bluntly. "It's at the front, away from the kids. If he's looking for the truck, I can get a clean shot."

"And that's it? The decision's made?"

Lena answered. "We're setting the shot, Beck, that's all. I haven't given Randy the green light."

"All right." Beck's words were clipped. "But I think this is premature. I think you're making a mistake, both of you."

"I have to think of the team, Beck. The guys are getting tired and that means they're going to get sloppy and let their guard down. I can't risk a breakout, either. If he starts shooting…"

"I know the drill, Lena, but those kids in there are nine and ten years old. Do you want them living with the sight of a man's brains getting blown out for the rest of their lives?"

"I want them *to* live, Beck. *That's* my only concern and it ought to be yours, too."

"But—"

"If you have a problem with this, we'll discuss it later." She interrupted him, ending the argument sharply. "Right now, act like a team member and do your job. Get the man to the window. When the time comes, *I'll* decide if we shoot or not."

THE CHILDREN were getting restless.

Jennifer had done her best to keep them corralled—without much help from Betty—but they couldn't be expected to huddle in one corner forever. Howard had let them use the bathroom attached to the classroom, but other than that, they hadn't really moved. She glanced down at her watch and was shocked to see the time. It was past eight!

The drinks had helped. A dozen cans had been left outside the classroom. Howard had made Juan retrieve them, then report back to him. Were there police in the hallway? No? Was he sure?

It was hot, too, and that *didn't* help. The air-conditioning had shut down hours ago. It was on an automatic timer, but Jennifer suspected it'd been purposely shut down early. She pushed a sticky strand of hair off her forehead and glanced toward Howard. He was standing by the door. Obviously growing weary, his expression was one of pure dejection, his shoulders slumped, his face shadowed. The gun had never left his side, and she'd given up the idea of grabbing it. It was just too risky.

They'd talked on and off, but he'd refused to say much more than "It's too late." When she'd pressed him, he'd simply shaken his head, and she'd finally moved to the rear of the room to be near the children. Trying to reassure them, she'd sat down and waited for the phone to ring again.

When it did, though, what would happen? They weren't really going to give Howard his truck…or get his job back for him. He wasn't going to just drive away from the school and off into the sunset. Surely, he understood that.

The phone sounded shrilly, startling her even though she'd expected it. Jennifer looked at Howard and he gave her an almost perceptible nod. She jumped up and ran to the front of the room to grab the receiver. "Hello?"

He answered as he did each time he'd called. "Everyone okay in there?"

Jennifer closed her eyes briefly and leaned against the wall. "We're all right," she said. "But getting tired."

"I understand. It's a tough situation, but you're doing a terrific job keeping everyone together." His voice turned lighter. "How 'bout coming to work for us when this is over? I could get you a negotiator's job. Sound good?"

Jennifer shuddered. "No, thank you. That's way more excitement than I want. Ever."

"It's not all that thrilling. Mainly I sit here, then I talk but no one really listens, and when it's finally settled, I do paperwork. The next day, we do it all over again."

"Sounds like my job."

He chuckled. "Yeah, I guess it does at that. You like being a teacher?"

"I love it," she answered, surprised by his question. It seemed like a strange time to be talking like this, but it made sense in a weird kind of way. He was trying to keep her relaxed. "The kids are fantastic and I feel as if I'm doing something worthwhile. Most days, that is."

"You are doing something worthwhile—all the time—but especially right now. You're holding this thing together, Jennifer, and you really are doing a great job."

For just a second, she almost felt she was somewhere else, in a different time and place. The warmth of his praise eased her fear. "Thanks."

His raspy voice went serious. "So now…you have to help me some more. The truck's finally on the way. Put Howard on the phone so I can tell him."

"I'll try."

Jennifer turned and looked in Howard's direction. He was staring into the distance, his mind obviously not in the present. "Howard?" she asked gently. "Howard? Please come talk to the officer."

He didn't respond at all. She rested the phone's receiver on a shelf and walked to where he stood. Her stomach in knots, she ignored her fright and spoke firmly, as if talking to one of the children. "Howard, you need to come talk to Officer Winters. He's on the phone and he has something to tell you."

"You tell me."

"No. You need to hear this yourself."

To her total surprise, he nodded once, then lumbered across the room and picked up the phone. She hurried behind him. He held the receiver to his ear but didn't say anything.

A moment later, he turned and handed her the phone. Jennifer spoke. "Yes?"

"I told him the truck's on the way. In the meantime, you're going to have to do something else, too."

"What?"

Instead of answering, he waited a moment, the seconds ticking by almost audibly. Once again, Jennifer found herself imaging the man behind the voice. His words carried the same timbre of authority her father's always had—academies taught you how to do that, she suspected, military or police, it made no difference— but absent from Beck Winters's tones was the overlay of cruelty her father's voice had always possessed. Winters had children of his own, she decided, and was a good father. Patient. Kind. Loving. Emotions and actions that had been empty words to her father. With a start, she realized she was connecting with Beck Winters, this stranger, on a level she seldom did with men.

"You have to get him to stand by the window. I won't bring the truck down the street until that point."

She felt a flicker of unease. "Why?"

"Because that's how we do things. These are negotiations, and he gets nothing for free. When he sees the truck, then he has to talk to me and release another child. You've got to get him to do this."

Her mouth went dry. "I understand but…"

Beck's voice dropped, and she felt as if he were standing right beside her, his warm eyes on hers. "Jennifer…how else can he see the truck? This is the only way."

Her chest eased a tad and she took a deep breath. He was right, of course.

"It's going to be fine, Jennifer. He trusts you, and I know you can get him to that window. Once he's there, then…then we'll start to talk and I can influence him." He fell silent. "I *have* to be able to talk directly to this guy, Jennifer. The most dangerous hostage takers are the ones who won't talk to me. If I can't get some kind of conversation going with him, this is going to end badly. I can almost guarantee that, especially with Howard's history."

"His history? What do you mean? He's never done anything like this before."

The officer answered quickly. "He's male, he's urban, he has below average intelligence. These are people who turn to violence as an answer. It's not the boss at the steel plant, it's not the manager at the oil company. It's the worker, Jennifer. The poor slob at the bottom who has no control over his life." He paused. "He has nothing to lose. He thinks it's hopeless anyway."

"I understand how you could read it that way, but you don't know him the way I do—"

"And you don't know everything *I* know." He bit off the words, as if he'd said more than he'd planned. "Just help me out, okay? Are the kids still at the back of the room?"

"Yes."

"It's imperative you keep them back there. I'll bring

the truck down the street as soon as I see Howard at the window. You just get him over there."

"Okay."

She started to hang up, but before she could put the receiver down, she heard his voice say her name. She brought the phone back to her ear. "Yes?"

Static rippled over the line, faint and barely discernable. The noise made her wonder if they were being recorded. "Be careful, Jennifer. Just…be careful."

She started to answer, then realized he was gone. Hanging up the phone, she looked over at Howard and said a silent prayer.

BECK WIPED HIS FACE and looked over at Lena. "Is the truck here yet?"

"There's a traffic tie-up on Highway 98. One Q-Tip rammed another. Surprise, surprise. The road's blocked in both directions, but Dispatch said they'd have it moving in just a few minutes. It should get here anytime."

Beck shook his head. Everyone on the force called the older local residents "Q-Tips" because they all had white hair and wore tennis shoes to match. Florida had its share of elderly drivers, but Beck wasn't sure they were any worse than the tourists who drank too much then got on the road. At least the older people drove slowly.

Lena ducked her head toward the building. "How are they doing? The teacher holding up?"

"She's the only reason there hasn't been gunfire yet. She's keeping French appeased and the kids quiet."

He stared out the window of the motor home into the dusk. They'd cut the electricity to the school and the building had fallen into darkness as soon as the summer sun had dipped behind them, rimming the school in gold. Occasionally he saw the beam of a flashlight near the rear of the room. Beck wasn't surprised to see the teacher was prepared. Classrooms were supposed to have emergency supplies in case of hurricanes, but people forgot, and batteries went bad. Not in Miss Barclay's class, though. He'd bet money she had the correct number of bandages and aspirin as well.

Lena sank into a chair by his side, her fingers going to the shuffle of papers beside the phone. She picked out Jennifer's photo, studying it intently. Without looking at him, she spoke. "She's pretty."

"I hadn't noticed."

Lena's head came up. "Right."

He flicked his eyes toward the picture, but immediately returned his gaze to the school. He didn't need the fuzzy image anymore—Jennifer's face was planted firmly in his brain. Too firmly, in fact. It'd be a while before he was able to get those brown eyes out of his mind, no matter how this all ended. They sat without talking for a few minutes, then Lena spoke once more. "Did you tell her to get him to the window?"

"Yeah."

"What'd she say?"

He turned and looked at her. "I didn't explain why—"

"Of course not."

He turned back. "She'll do it."

Lena leaned forward and put her hand on his arm. "Beck, listen. I know you don't agree, but we can't let this go on forever—"

Lena had taken off her headset and had been using a radio. It came to life with garbled speech. She pushed the button on the side and barked, "What is it?"

"The truck's here." Lincoln Hood, one of the entry men, spoke, the noise of the crowd behind him filtering into the radio's microphone along with his voice. "I'm switching places with the driver right now, then I'll bring it down the street when you're ready."

"Go slow, Linc," Tamirisa said immediately. "Less than five miles an hour, okay?"

"No problem."

Beck resisted looking at Lena. She stood and paced the tiny aisle. "Listen, Randy—French is going to be facing the window, looking down the street. Are you sure it's going to be a cold shot? If it isn't, I don't want you taking it. Not with those kids in there."

When he'd been younger and gung ho, the euphemisms had meant something to Beck. They'd made him feel as if he were part of a secret club that ordinary cops didn't belong to; now the words made him feel tired and old. Why didn't she just say what she meant?

Can you kill the guy with one shot?

"It'll be so cold, *you'll* freeze." Randy's cocky answer spilled into the room with arrogance. "Hear that, *Officer* Winters?"

"That's enough. I'm not giving you the green light yet," she snapped. "The man's promised Beck he'll talk so let's see how it goes down first." She turned and motioned for Beck to pick up the phone. "Beck's calling now to get him in place. On my word, Linc, you go. If necessary, *if necessary,* I'll give you the code, Randy,

otherwise, standard ops are in effect. Heads up, everyone. This is it."

JENNIFER JUMPED when the phone rang. She grabbed
the receiver. "Yes?"

"Everyone okay?"

"We're fine."

"Then it's time. We've got the truck and we're bringing it down the street. You need to get Howard to the
window."

Although it was just as calm and reassuring as always,
his voice sounded different. The tension was getting to
him, too, Jennifer thought. How could he do this day
after day? What kind of man would want this crazy life?

"All right," she said. "We're going right now—"

"Not you!" Beck's voice went up, then he spoke
again, in a more reasonable tone. "That's not necessary. Use this time to calm the children. Go back to
where they are and wait there."

The suggestion seemed perfectly reasonable.

"Okay," she answered.

"Let me talk to him first."

Holding the receiver at her side, she turned to Howard. He was standing right beside her, the rifle cradled
in his arms, crossed before his chest. "They want you
at the window, Howard. Your truck is here. But Officer
Winters needs to talk to you first."

"No." He shook his head. "Not going," he mumbled.
"Won't talk."

"Howard…" She put a warning in her voice, and the
students at the back of the room lifted their heads as one.

They knew that tone. "You asked for your truck," she said. "And it's here now. You have to be reasonable about this, or Officer Winters isn't going to help you." She held the receiver out to him. "Talk to him. He wants to help you."

"No."

She found patience from somewhere deep inside her. "Why not?"

"Don't want to."

"All right, then. Forget talking to him. Just go to the window and look out. Right now. No more messing around."

He glanced at her, but there was no other warning.

He simply grabbed her and she screamed without thinking. From the back of the room, one of the children cried out. Jennifer dropped the phone. Then Howard dragged her roughly toward the window.

"OH, SHIT!"

"Jennifer!"

"What's going on?" Beck spoke again, overriding Randy's curse. "Randy? Can you see them?"

"He's heading to the window, but...I'm not sure... wait, wait a minute...he's coming to the window. Goddammit—"

Beck leapt from his desk and peered out into the night. It was completely dark now and the outline of the window was nothing more than a square of blackness. He fumbled for the night vision binoculars that had been sitting on the desk but Lena had already grabbed them and brought them to her eyes. "Tamirisa? What's going on? Can you see?"

"He's coming to the window and he's got the teacher with him. Oh, man…I don't frigging believe this!"

"What? What is it?"

"A kid…a little boy…he's just run up to both of them—" His voice turned deep. "Don't do it, you son of a bitch, don't do it—" Randy's voice broke off abruptly.

Beck yanked the binoculars out of Lena's hands but before he could even focus, the horrible sound of glass shattering split the humid night air. A second later, a scream followed, the kind of scream he knew would be replayed in his dreams for months to come. When it stopped, Beck heard nothing beyond the beating of his heart.

Another second passed, then that stopped, too.

CHAPTER FOUR

JENNIFER HAD ALWAYS heard time slowed in a moment of crisis.

Not true.

One minute she was standing beside the window, Howard's hand painfully gripping her arm, and the next instant Juan's sturdy ten-year-old frame was flying through the air to knock her unexpectedly to the ground. In less time than could be counted, the two of them pitched to the linoleum, a shower of breaking glass somehow accompanying their fall. Jennifer could think of only one thing: the child in her arms. She had to protect him.

The impact between the hard floor and her shoulder sent pain streaking up her arm then down her spine, but she barely felt it. She forced it away so she could deal with everything else. Raining glass, screaming children, a strange *pop* she couldn't identify at all.

Jennifer lifted her head and stared at Howard. He was standing, exactly where they'd been a second before, but something wasn't right. A small red circle had appeared at the base of his throat. Above this spot, their gazes collided violently then he began to sway. A second later, his mouth became a silent O of surprised betrayal. The rest of his face simply collapsed—a balloon with the air suddenly released. He fell to the floor beside them, and as he landed with a heavy, dull thud, the back of his head disappeared in an exploding red mist.

Jennifer screamed and covered Juan's face with both her hands, but the movement was useless. The child had seen it just as she had—the moment of Howard's death.

She told herself to move, to get up, to do *something* but the odor of cordite hung in the air, sharp and biting, pinning her down. She wanted to gag, but she couldn't do that, either. She couldn't do anything. *He'd promised,* was all she could think. *He'd promised no one would be hurt....*

Juan's urgent voice, crying out in Spanish from somewhere beneath her, finally jarred her. "Señorita Barclay? *¿Qué pasa? ¿Cómo está usted?* Are you okay?"

She rolled off the child and he jumped up, his shocked gaze going instantly to Howard. He covered his mouth with his hand and pointed toward the man, still clutching his rifle. *"¡M-madre de Dios!"*

Jennifer scrambled to her feet. Maybe he wasn't really dead. Maybe it wasn't too late. Maybe she could do something.... Before she could think of what, the door to the classroom opened with a loud bang. Adrenaline surged and she grabbed Juan again. Shoving him behind her red-flecked skirt, she faced the door.

Men spilled into the room. They were dressed in black, a barrage of noise and brutal action coming with them as they surged inside. They divided by some pre-arranged, silent signal; one group fanned across the classroom, obviously searching for more danger. Their guns held out before them, they quickly covered every corner and empty space. A second, smaller group raced toward Jennifer and Juan while a third team rushed to the back where the children were screaming.

"Are you all right? You weren't hit, were you? The kids okay?"

A black-garbed figure paused at Jennifer's feet, putting a hand on Howard's neck. Only when she spoke, quickly but with composure, did Jennifer realize the officer was a woman. "W-we're fine," Jennifer answered.

Standing up, the woman nodded then pulled Juan from behind Jennifer and pushed him toward a man waiting behind her. Holding Howard's rifle, he quickly turned away from the body to lead Juan to the back of the room.

"I-is he?"

Though lean and muscular, the woman in black had soft gray eyes and a sweet face. She looked out of place, especially when she said calmly, "He's dead."

A thick fog descended over Jennifer, blanketing all her emotions but two. Disbelief and betrayal. "He's dead," she repeated numbly.

The woman nodded again, then barked an order to the men surrounding them. To Jennifer, what she said didn't even register but it was obviously an all-clear sign. The words passed through the group like a wave, and in its wake, another figure pushed to the front.

In a daze, Jennifer stared as the man approached. Everything was over—the damage had been done— why now, she thought almost trancelike. Why did time stop now?

He was huge, well over six feet, his chest a blur of black as he moved, his legs so long they covered the distance between the door and the window in three strides. Adults always looked bigger in the classroom where everything was reduced in scale, but this man absolutely towered over the child-size desks and bookcases. Reaching Jennifer's side, he ripped off a black helmet to reveal thick blond hair. It was plastered to his scalp, but the pale strands gleamed, and she realized—illogically at that moment—that the lights were back on. He was intimidating and all at once, she understood the true definition of *authority*. It was none of this, however, that made her feel the clock had stopped.

His eyes did that.

In the fluorescent glare overhead, his cold blue stare leapt out at her. She might have thought the color unnatural, it was so disturbing, but she knew immediately it wasn't. No one in their right mind would actually buy contacts that shade. The color was too unnerving, too strange.

His eerie gaze swept over her bloody clothing then came to a stop on her face. She forced herself into stillness and looked directly at him. When he spoke her name, she recognized his voice.

She knew without asking that this was Beck Winters.

SHE WAS COVERED in blood and bits and pieces of something else Beck noted but didn't need to analyze. For one inane moment, he wanted to pull her into his arms and tell her everything was going to be all right, but he'd be lying if he did. It wouldn't be all right. Not for a very long time—if ever. Not for her, not for the kids, certainly not for Howard French. For the survivors, a hostage incident didn't end when the team busted in.

In fact, Jennifer Barclay's wide brown eyes told him shock had inched its way in, leeching the color from her face and forcing into her eyes the kind of glazed disbelief he'd seen too many times. She'd been stronger than most, but that was over.

It was a mistake of monumental proportions and he knew it, but Beck decided he didn't care. He reached out for her.

She stepped back so quickly she almost slipped and fell. Grabbing the windowsill behind her, her eyes blazing, she spoke from between gritted teeth. "You bastard!"

Immediately Beck's mask fell into place. Her words weren't what he'd expected, but different people reacted in different ways. He'd once rescued a woman who'd slapped him as he'd carried her out under fire. Jennifer Barclay's anger was a coping technique. She'd been holding her emotions in check for hours and now she was going to erupt.

At him.

Beck took a step away from her and held up his hands, palms out. "Calm down, Miss Barclay, please.... It's over now. You're safe—"

She blinked, and he saw some measure of relief in her expression, something that seemed to loosen for a moment, but she put the response behind her so fast, he almost missed it. Her voice was low but scathing as she lashed out at him. "You lied to me! You promised— *promised*—no one would be hurt." She flicked her eyes downward to where Howard lay. "He's dead!

"You don't understand—"

"You're damned right I don't understand!" She pushed a strand of hair away from her eyes. They were red and rimmed with exhaustion, her face contorted with the obvious anguish she was feeling. "He wouldn't have killed anyone—"

"He raised his gun at that child."

"He wasn't going to shoot! He was trying to stop Juan from grabbing the gun—"

"That's not how it looked to us."

"But he wouldn't have shot! He wouldn't have done that."

"How can you be sure?"

"I know him, that's how!" Her gaze filled with angry tears. "My God, I told him to go that window and then you shot him! What happened? I can't believe this…."

Beck watched the emotions cross her face. She made no attempt to hide them, but it wouldn't have mattered if she had. He understood better than she did what she was feeling.

I feel guilty because I couldn't stop this.

I feel guilty because I survived.

I feel guilty because I helped.

Before he could say more, Lena broke in. Introducing herself formally, she put her hand on Jennifer's arm and spoke gently. "Miss Barclay, why don't you come with me now? We'll get you cleaned up, then we need to talk to you. Everyone in the room will have to speak to an officer and give their version of what happened."

Jennifer turned her back to Beck and answered Lena

quickly, her voice filled with dismay. "Of course…but not the kids—"

She wanted to protect them above all, Beck realized. That was the only thing that mattered to her.

"I'm afraid they'll have to. It's standard, but it's necessary, too. Especially after a shooting."

"My God, I don't believe this…. My students…"

"I know, I know." Lena's attitude was sympathetic and calm. "I've already spoken to Mrs. Whitmire. Our information officer called Dr. Church, the school counselor, and she arrived some time ago. She's with the kids right now, and so is our department psychologist, Dr. Worley. You should talk to the doctors, too. Not just tonight but in the coming days as well."

Jennifer Barclay's full lips were drawn in a narrow line across the bottom of her face. Beck could see traces of pale-pink lipstick she'd put on earlier that day. When her life had been normal. "I don't need to do that."

"You will."

Her gaze shot to Beck as he spoke. Her look was controlled and measured. "What makes you think I'll need help?"

"No one goes through something like this without needing to talk about it later. If you don't, you'll pay for it in ways you can't even imagine."

"I don't have to imagine anything, Mr. Winters." She held out her hands, palms forward, mimicking his earlier action. The smooth skin was sticky with blood and her fingers trembled even as she spoke. "Thanks to you, I've gone through the real thing. I think I'll be able to handle the instant replays on my own."

IT WAS AFTER midnight when they finished. The questions had been endless, and Jennifer had described the situation so many times, she almost felt as if she were telling a story. A story that had happened to someone else, not her. Dr. Church had counseled every one of children and had tried to talk to Jennifer, too. She'd nodded and told the woman she'd call, but she wouldn't. There'd been a police psychologist, too. Another "professional."

Pointless. Simply pointless.

Jennifer would go home, take a hot bath and get into bed. That's what would help her, not talking with some half-baked psychologist. Maybe she'd call Wanda, too. If the other woman had heard what happened—and who wouldn't?—she'd be worried sick.

The press had been satisfied with Betty Whitmire's histrionics and thankfully had left thirty minutes before. Jennifer trudged through the now dark and empty parking lot to her car. She was glad she didn't have to face the cameras and microphones because she didn't think she could. Nothing seemed real to her. How could it? One man she'd known was dead and another was wounded. A second wash of shock came over as she recalled Lieutenant McKinney's words during the debriefing.

"Mr. French said nothing to you about shooting Robert Dalmart? Nothing at all?"

"No. I—I had no idea...."

It must have been an accident. Howard wouldn't have shot down Robert like some kind of animal. The police lieutenant had told Jennifer that Robert would probably survive, but he'd been injured badly.

The rush of a passing truck caught her attention and Jennifer glanced up in time to catch the white oval of the driver's face. Where was he going? How could he pass by so casually? Didn't he know lives had just been ruined?

She knew she was being ridiculous, but she didn't care. Howard French had been shot before her very eyes. A man who had reminded her of her brother. A man who had trusted her. A man she only wanted to help, but had led to his death instead.

In the back of her mind, a silent voice countered her words. *He'd promised no one would be hurt.*

She reached her car and pulled out her keys but they wouldn't go into the lock. Something was wrong. She struggled with them for a moment, then her hand began to shake and she dropped the ring, somewhere underneath the car door. It was the final straw. She laid her head against the roof of the vehicle and began to cry.

"Can I help?"

Jennifer turned at once. The body armor was gone, but its absence didn't diminish Beck Winters's size. In fact, he looked even taller and more commanding, looming over her car and staring down at her with his strange, cold eyes. A ripple of anger went through her, but she was too exhausted to even acknowledge it.

"I—I dropped my keys," she said stupidly.

He knelt down, patted the ground beside her feet, then stood. She held out her hand, but he reached past her and slipped the key in. The sound of the door unlocking was unnaturally loud.

"Thank you," she said.

"You're welcome."

There was nothing else to say, but neither of them moved. After a moment, he broke the silence. "Look, I know it's hard to understand what happened back there and I sympathize because this man was your friend, but the team has to save lives—first and foremost. Surely you understand that."

"I told Lieutenant McKinney what I understood," she said. "I don't think you and I need to go over it again."

"Of course," he said stiffly. "I just thought…"

The medic had checked Jennifer and pronounced her all right, but she wondered briefly if he hadn't missed an unseen injury. A painful stab flared in her chest as the cop before her spoke.

"No, you didn't think," she snapped back. "That's the problem with men like you. You put on your uniforms and grab your guns and run out the door to fight. The people left behind are the ones who have to pick up the pieces, but you never consider them!"

As soon as the words were out her mouth, Jennifer regretted them. They weren't fair and she knew it—they came from a place deep in her past that had nothing to do with the man standing before her—but she was beyond caring. She was completely drained and empty of all logic and reason. She opened her mouth to say so but he stopped her.

"You're right," he said. "But you're wrong, too. The ones left behind do have to pick up the pieces, but I *always* think about them. Believe me, Miss Barclay, they're the reason I do what I do. Seeing someone killed in a situation like this is the *last* thing I want."

He was telling the truth; she could see it in those strange, clear eyes.

"Then what happened in there tonight?" Her voice cracked. "Why was Howard shot?"

"He raised the gun and we thought he was going to shoot the boy," he said raggedly. "Having a sniper in place is standard operating procedure and when he perceived imminent danger to the child, he took the shot."

Something in his voice alerted her. She jerked her head up and stared into the blue ice of his gaze, her stomach churning with the gut feeling that came from hearing the truth mixed with a lie. She wasn't getting the whole story.

She shook her head slowly and stared at him. "I don't believe you. I want the truth. Something went wrong, didn't it? *You* didn't want him killed, did you?"

"Let me take you home," he said gently. "I can call a uniform and catch a ride back up here to get my car. You're in no shape to drive to Fort Walton."

"I'm a teacher, Officer Winters. Diversions don't work with me."

"I'm not trying to divert you. I'm trying to help you. You're wrung out, and you need to get home and take care of yourself."

"So I won't bother you anymore with my questions?"

"No." He paused and took a breath. Was he stalling as he searched for a more satisfying explanation or simply exhausted as she was? "So you won't torture yourself with what-ifs," he said finally. "You did everything you could back there and we did, too. It was a bad end, yes, but it wasn't our fault...or yours."

"He didn't need to be killed," she said stubbornly.

He shocked her by his answer. "Maybe, but we'll never know for sure. Only one thing's certain. We can't go back and play it a different way. We have to take what happened and deal with it."

"Then just tell me the truth. Tell me what really happened—what *I* did—then let me deal with *that*."

From beneath his matted hair, he stared at her, his eyes almost glowing. For a second she caught a fleeting glimpse of something in their cold depths, but she wasn't sure. She was so tired she was imagining it. She had to be.

"I'm sorry." He shook his head, his expression closing against itself. "But I can't tell you more. You'll have to be satisfied with that."

THE MESSAGE LIGHT on her answering machine was blinking furiously when Jennifer finally reached her condo. She hit the play button and closed her eyes.

"I heard about the shooting, and I'm real worried. You call me as soon as you get in. I don't care what time it is, you just call."

Wanda's Southern accent filled the small living room. Normally Jennifer would have picked up the phone and called immediately, but she couldn't make her fingers reach for the receiver. They were as tired as the rest of her, and what little energy she had left, she wanted to use getting clean. She peeled off her clothing, right there in the middle of the den, and walked into the kitchen. Retrieving a paper sack from the pantry, she dropped everything in it and rolled the edges tightly together. Tomorrow she'd burn them.

Naked and shivering in the air-conditioning, she opened the refrigerator. The strongest drink she could find was a bottle of Coors left over from a pizza party some time back. She grabbed it, opened the bottle, and downed the beer. She didn't lower the bottle until it was empty, then she stumbled into her bathroom and opened the shower door. When she stepped out twenty minutes later, her skin was red and raw—whether from the heat of the steaming water or the scrubbing she didn't know.

Her stomach in knots, she knew the only way she could get to sleep was to eat something first. Somewhere between scrambling the eggs and getting the grape jelly out of the refrigerator, she began to cry. The tears ran down her cheeks, but she just ignored them. They weren't going to stop and there was nothing she could do about it so she let them come.

God, how had it happened? One minute she'd been standing beside Howard and the next she'd ordered him to go to that window. No wonder he'd grabbed her— she'd scared him half to death. Then Beck had finished him off.

And she'd trusted him!

He'd sounded so sympathetic over the phone, so caring and warm. In reality, he reminded her of a photograph she'd seen in a sixth-grade world history textbook of a Nordic trapper. He had the same cold, blond looks and size, plus a face like a stony mask. All that was missing were the dogs and sled.

The ringing phone startled her out of her thoughts and her heart thudded in answer against her chest. It took a second for her to regain her composure. Would she ever hear a phone sound again and not jump? Wanda's worried voice could be heard on the answering machine, her drawl even thicker than usual.

"Are you there, girl? What's going on—"

"I'm here, Wanda." Clutching her robe, Jennifer grabbed the phone. "I just got in. I—I'm fine."

"Praise the Lord! I've been worried sick. I heard about what happened at the school, and…well, good grief, honey, are you okay?"

That was all it took. Jennifer began to sob again and several minutes filled with Wanda's "That's okay, now, darlin'" and "C'mon, sugar" passed before her tears subsided. When she hiccuped to a stop, she explained what had happened.

"Oh, my God!" Wanda's concern echoed over the line. She didn't know him but she'd listened to Jennifer's Howard stories time and time again. "And they killed him?"

"Y-yes. Right in front of us. It was terrible, Wanda. I—I can't believe it actually happened. And I helped!"

"But, honey, he might have murdered every one of y'all."

"Wanda! You've heard me talk about him! Do you really think he would have shot us?"

"He shot that poor other man."

"It must have been an accident! Howard wouldn't have just walked up and done it in cold blood. He wasn't like that."

"But you said he raised the gun when Juan ran over."

"He did but he was trying to keep it away from Juan. When he saw Howard dragging me to the window, Juan thought I was in danger. He ran over to grab the gun."

"Are you sure? Absolutely positive?"

In the background, Jennifer could hear canned laughter coming from Wanda's television. She lived alone and when she was home, it was on.

"How do you know Howard was just keepin' that gun away from the boy?" Wanda continued, cutting off Jennifer's potential answer. "He could have been bringin' it up to shoot. You don't know! You just don't know."

"No." Jennifer replied immediately. "I'm sure he wasn't—"

"Why? What makes you so sure? Haven't you ever been wrong before, Jennifer? I certainly have and I can't imagine that you haven't been in all your thirty-six years."

Despite her Southern ways, Wanda never minced words. Jennifer swallowed, her throat tight. "I have been wrong before, certainly."

"We never know what's in another person's mind, sugar." The nurse's voice softened. "We just don't know. You could be mistaken. Howard French was a strange duck. He coulda been liftin' that rifle to shoot that poor little boy. You better think long and hard before you set what you think in stone."

They talked a few more minutes after that, Wanda reassuring Jennifer her mother was fine. "We turned off the TV so she wouldn't hear all the news. She seemed pretty foggy today, but you never know what's soakin' in and what isn't."

"Thanks for watching out for her."

"Oh, honey, you're welcome. You just don't worry about her. I know you won't listen to me, but you take care of yourself…and if you wanna talk some more, you call me, hear?"

Walking to the balcony off her living room a few minutes later, Jennifer stood and looked at the sky. There was no moon and only the twinkling lights from a few houses here and there alleviated the dark. She wasn't close enough to the beach to hear the ocean, but if she leaned all the way to the left at one end of the narrow patio, she could catch a glimpse of the water. She did so now, but all she saw was blackness.

We never know what's in another person's mind.

Wanda was right. You couldn't tell for sure what someone else was thinking, but some things you just knew. And Jennifer knew—for sure—that Howard French would never have shot Juan Canales in cold blood. She just knew.

Beck Winters had made a terrible mistake.

And she'd helped him.

"GO AHEAD," her father taunted. "Do it. Do it."

Holding her breath, her ten-year-old lungs about to burst, Jennifer watched in horror as Danny peered up at the twenty-five-foot pole. Her brother's fingers tightened on the rope, and his eyes grew even larger.

"You aren't man enough to do it, are you?" William Barclay's voice was as sharp as his words, cruel and unforgiving. "You can't do anything right. You can't even climb a pole! Hell, kid, your scrawny little sister can make it up that damned stick. Why the hell can't you?

You can't do anything but mess around with that damn paintbrush of yours!"

Jennifer opened her mouth to cry out, but her warning was trapped, somewhere deep inside her. She managed to make some kind of sound, and her brother glanced in her direction. That's when his face changed into Howard's.

Jennifer tried to scream, but still no sound came. She lifted her fingers to her mouth and understood why. Her lips were sewn shut.

Horrified, she jerked her head in her father's direction, knowing without asking, he'd been the one to make her silent. But her father wasn't there anymore. Betty Whitmire stood where he'd been.

"It doesn't take a brain surgeon!" she cried. "Just mop the floors, French. Mop the floors!" Standing at Betty's side was Dr. Church and another woman. She didn't immediately recognize her, but Jennifer knew who she was anyway. Dr. Worley, the police psychologist. As Jennifer watched, they turned, very slowly and deliberately, until their backs were to what was happening.

Jennifer whipped her head around to where Howard stood. The rope had changed into a mop, but as she watched, Howard lifted it and fired. The bullet came out in slow motion and finally, when it hit the target, Jennifer was able to scream.

Betty had turned into Danny. "Help me," he cried, clutching his chest. "Help me, Jennifer! You're the only one who can…."

Gasping for breath, she called out Danny's name then she woke up, choking. For one terrifying second a stabbing pain burned in her own chest. Clenching her nightgown with both hands, she rose up on her knees, tangling herself in the covers she'd been fighting, swaying and almost falling. Then suddenly it was over. Her mind took control of her body, and she gasped, cold, sweet air rushing painfully into her lungs.

Covered in sweat, Jennifer collapsed on the bed and began to cry.

CHAPTER FIVE

THE CEMETERY was ringed with oleanders. Their emerald branches swayed in the Saturday morning breeze as Beck leaned against his car and waited for Jennifer. Howard French's autopsy had been cursory, the funeral scheduled quickly. In the crowd surrounding the grave site, Beck spotted Jennifer easily. Her chestnut hair had a mind of its own; strands had already escaped the knot at the back of her head and they too, were moving in the wind.

He crossed his arms and told himself he had no business being there, waiting for her. Just like he'd had no business talking to her in the school parking lot after the incident. It wasn't against the rules, but getting involved with victims was never a good idea. He needed a certain perspective on every case and growing close to someone involved made that task hard.

This situation was even tougher though, because Jennifer Barclay wanted more answers than he could give. Like most civilians, she didn't understand he couldn't tell her more. He couldn't tell her he hadn't wanted Randy to shoot. And he couldn't tell her about the fight they'd had afterward. The team was just that—a team—and both he and Randy had to keep their mouths shut. Lena had promised Beck an informal investigation and he felt damned lucky to get that. It meant she'd pull him and Randy into a room and grill them until she dressed down either one or both of them severely. But the results would never be public.

Regardless of all that, he'd come to Lawndale at 10:00 a.m. on the dot, knowing Jennifer Barclay would be there, and knowing, too, he wanted to see her, just one more time. He didn't understand why the need was so strong, but it was there, and he couldn't ignore it. Something about her was different, and he wanted to figure it out. Figure *her* out.

He waited patiently and half an hour later, the mourners around the casket began to move away. There was no limousine to carry off grieving family members. French had had no family.

Jennifer picked her way across the lush green grass. She was wearing a dark-navy dress and was having a hard time walking, because her heels were sinking into the lawn. She seemed smaller than he remembered, less self-assured. Maybe because she wasn't surrounded by the authority her classroom gave her.

A woman walked with her, talking as they moved through the headstones. Dressed as somberly as Jennifer, she had an expression of concern on her face and glanced at Jennifer with almost every step they took. She was trying to convince Jennifer of something; Beck could read body language as easily as he could listen to and understand a conversation and he wondered what she wanted. As they came closer to Beck, she put her hand on Jennifer's arm and pulled her to a stop.

He strained to catch their words. One or two floated toward him on the wind.

"…come stay with me…"

"…absolutely not…"

"…can't sleep, can't eat…"

Obviously disagreeing, Jennifer shook her head vehemently at the woman, and that's when she saw Beck. Her body stiffened and the graceful arch of her back went ramrod straight. Their gazes met across the verdant lawn, the marble angels watching to see what would happen next.

Beck wondered as well. She looked as if she wanted to run the other way, to escape as fast as she could but he was leaning against *her* car. If she wanted to go home, she had to come to where he stood.

She said something to her companion and the other woman turned her head in Beck's direction. She scrutinized him, then nodded once. She didn't smile, but he felt no animosity in her frank appraisal, only curiosity and something he couldn't quite interpret. She hugged Jennifer tightly, rubbing circles on her back before releasing her to walk away. Beck hadn't a clue who she was, but she clearly cared a great deal about Jennifer.

When she got to the car, he could see Jennifer had been crying. Her brown eyes were teary and a bit of mascara was smeared beneath her thick lower lashes on the right side.

Without thinking, he reached out and rubbed his thumb on the spot. She blinked in surprise but otherwise stood still.

"Mascara," he explained.

She lifted her hand and with the back of one slim finger touched the same place he had. "I don't know why I bother. It inevitably ends up where it shouldn't."

"My ex-wife always blamed me for that," he said gruffly.

"Did you make her cry?"

She wasn't going to make it easy for him. Beck nodded slowly. "Sometimes."

As if thinking about his answer, she stared past him to watch the line of cars disappear, then she faced him once more. He could see now, in the ribbons of sun streaming through the trees, that her eyes were more than sad. They were filled with exhaustion, deep shadows ringing them with the puffy look that came from not sleeping. She appeared thinner, too. He'd assumed it was the dress, but all at once he wasn't sure.

"Why are you here, Officer Winters?" she asked. "What are you doing?"

"It's Beck," he said. "My first name is Beck."

She didn't reply so he reached into his shirt pocket and removed a business card. He held it out to her, but she took so long to accept it he thought for a minute she was going to refuse. Finally her fingers curled around the card, brushing his hand with a softness he wanted to ignore.

If she recognized the name, she gave no indication. After reading the card she looked up at him. "Dr. Maria Worley?"

"She's our police psychologist, the one who came after the incident. I want her to visit your classroom next week along with me. I know it's almost the end of the school year, but I don't think those kids should leave without seeing her at least one more time."

"Dr. Church already mentioned this to me." She tried to hand back the card but he kept his arms crossed. She fingered the square a bit more, then gave up and stuffed it into the pocket of her dress. "She's very competent. She doesn't need assistance."

"I agree, but we spoke and she decided that Dr. Worley might help. She specializes in this kind of trauma. Dr. Church felt a little overwhelmed, especially since she knew Howard, too."

Her voice revealed her skepticism, but she nodded wearily. "Well, if that's what Dr. Church wants…"

"It is. Betty Whitmire thinks it would be a good idea, too."

Jennifer's expression shifted instantly. "Betty Whitmire wouldn't know a good idea if it bit her on the butt. She's incompetent, tactless and part of the reason all this happened. She shouldn't have fired Howard. He was a good worker."

Her candor surprised him and he chuckled. "Don't like your boss?"

"I hold her responsible. Just as I do you."

His amusement evaporated under the heat of her words. "That's fine," he said evenly. "I'm accountable for my actions."

"Including Howard's death?"

"I didn't pull the trigger. That's not how it works."

"Then tell me how it *does* work." Her eyes flared, the conversation taking on an animosity he hadn't anticipated but should have. "Tell me how I managed to get Howard to that window—for you—and then he was killed. Tell me how you aren't responsible for that."

"I can't."

"You can't what? Tell me the truth or be held accountable?"

"Either."

"But you lied to me."

"And I would again," he said harshly. "That's what I do for a living, Jennifer. I lie to people to make them do what I want them to. So I can save lives."

Disgust and frustration fought their way across her once smooth brow, but before she could say anything more, the roar of a backhoe stopped her. She turned to look and he followed her gaze. The workers had lowered the metal casket and were covering it with dirt.

The sight clearly drained her anger. She faced him once more.

"But there's more to it than just that, isn't there? And you won't tell me the rest, will you?"

Beck felt a tug at the boundaries that divided his work from his emotions. Dixie, his ex-wife, had never asked...because she'd never cared. This was different, though. Jennifer cared almost more than she should.

He kept the struggle from his voice. "You were there, Jennifer. You don't need my interpretation. You *saw* what happened."

She made a low, rueful sound. "And Wanda says I can't even trust that."

"Wanda?"

She nodded behind her. "The woman who was with

me. Wanda LaFleur. She's my mother's nurse. And my best friend."

"Your mother's sick?"

"She's at Seacrest. She has Alzheimer's."

"I'm sorry to hear that."

Jennifer nodded but said nothing. The cemetery was only a few blocks from the beach, and the seagulls soared overhead, their raucous calls breaking the silence between them. Now Beck understood what he'd seen earlier. Jennifer and Wanda LaFleur were friends, but Wanda was a nurse as well, and she was trying to get Jennifer to take care of herself. She wasn't sleeping well or eating right. The thought coalesced in his mind with everything else he'd learned, and all at once, with crystalline clarity he understood who Jennifer Barclay was.

She put everyone else first and if there was anything left, then she gave it to herself.

She wouldn't seek help on her own. People like her didn't. He had to try anyway.

"You need to talk to Dr. Worley, along with your students. She's an excellent listener and she'll understand what you're going through. She understands post-traumatic stress."

Jennifer's dark eyes flashed. "I appreciate your concern, but I'm not 'going through' anything, including post-traumatic stress."

"No nightmares or insomnia? No depression? Howard French was your friend. You might have experienced some of those things even if you hadn't seen him shot."

She regarded him silently, with an iciness he might

have worn himself. He bore the chilly stare better than most, probably because he knew the pain it could hide.

"The doc's a good shrink," he said finally.

"Is that the voice of experience?"

He gave her a level look. He could cloak his feelings, too. "Would it make any difference if it was?"

"I don't know." Her expression thawed slightly. "I'm sorry, I didn't mean to pry. I—I'm upset, that's all." She waved her hand toward the grave. "The funeral and everything…"

"It's okay," he answered. "I'm being pushy, too." He stopped because he didn't know what else to say. How could he tell her what he really thought? *I think you're beautiful and intriguing, and I don't want to see you hurt more than you already are?*

"I'm simply trying to help," he said. "That's all."

"And I appreciate it," she answered stiffly. "But I don't need your assistance. I've been taking care of myself for a long time. I can handle this, too."

JENNIFER DROVE to the nursing home with her windows down. It was sweltering outside and the dark linen dress she'd worn to the funeral felt sticky and limp. Underneath the sleeveless shift, however, a coldness had seeped into her body and refused to leave. She didn't know whether she should shiver or wipe her brow.

Beck Winters left her feeling that way.

Had he saved lives or simply ended Howard's?

She'd almost fainted when she'd seen him leaning on her car. For the past few days, she'd thought about him a lot. In the middle of a math lesson, his image would pop into her mind. While reading aloud to the class, she'd suddenly recall his eyes. She knew these interruptions were just her brain's way of dealing with everything that had happened: It was far easier to think of Beck Winters than it was to remember the blood. But she had to wonder why her psyche had picked him, of all people. It couldn't be because she was interested in him. Absolutely not.

She hadn't dated anyone seriously since Andy McCall. She desperately wanted to be married and to have a family of her own, and he'd seemed like the perfect choice. A fellow teacher, Andy had been the kind of man she'd always wanted, or so she thought: stable, responsible, totally unlike her father. When he'd proposed, though, she'd turned him down. Something important was missing from their relationship. Something vital, even though she couldn't name it.

She pulled into the driveway of the nursing home and parked. The breeze was slightly cooler here—closer to the bay—but the emotional riot going on in her head didn't take note. In fact, she felt even warmer as her thoughts returned without permission to the man who'd waited for her at the cemetery.

She hadn't thought it possible, but his eyes had looked even bluer in the daylight, almost electric. And in their depths, she'd seen a hint of something that piqued her interest. It wasn't sympathy. After her brother's death, she'd developed a finely tuned radar for that emotion. No, this was something else and she wasn't sure what. Reaching into her pocket she pulled out the card he'd given her and laid it on the dash.

Dr. Maria Worley Psychologist. The address was for a commercial building near the center of town, close to the bridge that spanned Highway 98 as it crossed from Destin to Fort Walton.

Jennifer stared at the business card a moment longer, then she grabbed her purse and got out of the car, leaving the card to curl in the humid heat. No matter what had been in Beck's eyes, she wasn't going to a therapist to deal with Howard's death. She knew firsthand they simply did no good.

A few minutes later, Jennifer entered the glass doors of the nursing home. Walking briskly to the brightly painted wing that housed the ambulatory patients, she nodded to the security gaurd and several of the nurses as she passed. Her mother had been in Seacrest for five years and Jennifer knew everyone. The facility was always spotless and the staff really cared about their patients. They didn't just line the halls with wheelchairs; they planned activities and even gave certain patients small tasks like feeding Smoky, the home's fat gray Persian.

When Jennifer entered her mother's room, she found it empty.

Her heart skipped a beat, and she hurried over to the nurses' station in search of Wanda.

One of the aides saw Jennifer and smiled. "Your mom's outside," she said, tilting her head toward the patio just beyond the window. "It's such a nice morning, we thought she might enjoy the breeze. She's having a very good day."

Jennifer's pulse slowed. "And Wanda?"

"She's with a doctor. I'll tell her you're here."

Jennifer murmured her thanks then turned to go through the nearby double doors. She stopped at the last minute and looked at her mother through the glass.

She was sitting in a glider, her profile sharp and lean, her silver hair pulled back and coiled in one of Wanda's elaborate French braids. She wore a double-knit pant-suit with flared legs and an elastic waist. She refused to wear anything else, and Jennifer had to haunt second-hand shops to even find them for her. She often wondered if Nadine liked them because she'd worn them in the seventies, before Danny's death—when things had been perfect, if only in Nadine's mind. She looked healthy and was physically fit but her mind never seemed to be in the present. Sometimes she was thirty and Danny was a little boy, Jennifer not even born yet. Other days, Nadine was older and Jennifer a toddler. The days were scarce where her mother lived in a world that had known Danny but lost him.

Jennifer understood completely. For a while, she'd done the very same thing.

Pushing through the doors, she crossed the patio and came to where her mother sat. "Hi, Mom," she said. "How are you?"

Nadine Barclay looked up at her daughter and smiled sweetly. "Oh, you look so pretty! Are you a new nurse?"

With a sigh, Jennifer sat down in a nearby chair. "No, Mom, it's me, remember? Jennifer. I'm your daughter."

It hurt each time she had to remind her mother of who she was, but what else could she do?

"Jennifer?" Nadine said uncertainly.

"That's right." Jennifer nodded. "Your daughter."

"Jennifer…" She brightened suddenly. "Have you seen Danny? How is he?"

They went through this on Nadine's good days. When she understood who Jennifer was, she always asked about Danny. At first, Jennifer had wondered why Nadine never asked about her, but over time, the painful torture had ceased to matter. There were too many other things to worry about.

"He's fine, Mom," Jennifer answered automatically. "He's gonna come see you next week."

"Oh, good!"

Nadine smiled with satisfaction and pushed the glider back into motion, saying nothing else. A lot of times their visits went this way. After greeting each other, they'd sit for half an hour in silence, each lost in thought, then Jennifer would rouse herself and leave, feeling vaguely guilty that she hadn't tried to engage her mother more. She made a vow today to try harder.

"I saw Mr. Winters again," Jennifer said. "You remember me telling you about him? He was the policeman at school the other day?"

Nadine's eyes rounded briefly. "Policeman? Did he have on a uniform?"

Her mother hated the sight of any man in a uniform. She'd get terribly upset. Wanda had to keep her in her room when the UPS man made his deliveries. It would have been funny if Jennifer hadn't understood the reason her mother felt this way. She not only understood, she shared the feeling. A quick glimpse of a uniformed man, especially in fatigues, and her throat would swell up and she'd be a terrified ten-year-old again—a little girl whose father had been in the Navy Special Ops.

Jennifer wasn't sure her mother would perceive Beck's black T-shirt and pants as a uniform but she avoided answering the question all the same. It was simpler that way. "He's a member of the SWAT team. I told you about him."

"Oh, yes…" Nadine resumed her rocking.

"He gave me a business card, from a psychologist he knows. She works for the police and he wants me to talk to her. He said she could help me."

"That's nice, honey."

Jennifer glanced at her mother. Nadine hadn't understood a word of what she'd said. When Jennifer had told her mother about the hostage incident, she'd looked up to find Nadine sleeping soundly.

"I'm not going," she said, almost to herself. "Those kinds of doctors never do anything, and besides, I'm handling the situation just fine."

"Yeah, sure you are. That's why you aren't sleeping and you look like a scarecrow!"

Jennifer didn't even turn around. "If you're going to join our conversation, the least you can do is sit down."

Wanda's rubber shoes squeaked as she crossed the covered patio and came to Jennifer's side. "That's all I have to say."

Jennifer arched her eyebrows and stared at her friend. She'd changed clothes, replacing her dark dress with pink cotton pants and a bright top. The cheerful colors made her skin look even smoother than it normally did. "Really? That'd be a first!"

They grinned at each other, then Wanda dragged a chair across the tiled floor and plopped down in it. "Well, actually, I do have some more to say—"

"Of course you do."

"Don't go interrupting me. It's important."

"I'm sure it is. Everything you have to say is important."

"Well, you bet it is! Miss Nadine, you know that's so, don't you?"

The older woman smiled vacantly. "Yes, dear, that's true."

Wanda looked at Jennifer. "See there? Your momma knows how smart I am."

Jennifer couldn't help but smile. "Of course she thinks you're smart. Sometimes she thinks I'm Barbara Walters, too."

"That's okay. There's worse people she could accuse you of being." Wanda leaned over and patted Nadine's leg, then turned back to Jennifer. "What I was going to say before I was so rudely interrupted is that Officer Winters is right. Why not visit this psychologist? She might help."

Jennifer rolled her eyes.

"Hey! This is me! Wanda. You've already told me you're not sleeping and it's more than obvious you aren't eating, either. You're skin and bones."

Deep inside, Jennifer heard a begging teenaged voice, which she ignored. "You know my feelings on this, Wanda. My brother saw a therapist for years. What good did it do him?"

"Your brother has nothing to do with this."

Jennifer sighed. "I know, I know, but I can't stop

thinking about him. Betty Whitmire talked to Howard just like my dad always did to Danny. *'Why didn't you catch that ball? It was thrown right at you! Your sister would have caught it!'*" In a higher tone, she spoke again. "*'Why can't you clean up this toilet? Any fool could see it's still dirty! Do that one again, Mr. French!'*"

Wanda just shook her head. "You are going to drive yourself crazy over this, girl. Howard French was a criminal! Your brother died trying to prove something to your jackass of a father. There was no connection. The fact is, this goes way past the doctor, honey."

"What do you mean?"

Wanda's voice turned gentle. "Beck Winters is trying to help you because he likes you."

Jennifer shook her head. Wanda was forever trying to link her to someone; she wanted her married off with babies on the way. Jennifer wanted the same thing, but she wanted to find the right someone first. "You've been tending to your patients too long. I think you're the one losing your mind."

Now it was Wanda's turn to be stubborn. "You are wrong, wrong, wrong."

"Wrong." Nadine repeated. "You're wrong."

"See there! Your momma knows."

"You're both nuts," Jennifer replied. "The man's a total stranger. For God's sake, Wanda, you didn't even meet him. How on earth could you say what you just did?"

"I didn't have to meet him. He waited for you in ninety-degree heat for more than half an hour. For what? To give you a business card? C'mon, girl. Use your brain for something besides those damned kids you're always trying to teach."

Jennifer blinked, Beck's image swimming before her. "That's his job," she said. "He was just doing his job."

"No. He was doing his job when he tried to get Howard French out of that classroom."

"And that's the best reason in the world not to have anything to do with him…even if he was interested," she added.

Wanda simply shook her head.

"You don't understand, Wanda. The least he could do is explain what really happened. I'm sure there's more to the situation than I was told about, and I want to know what it was."

"Why? Do you just want him to admit a mistake was made? He wouldn't do that, even if it was so."

"I need to know the truth. It's important!"

"Well, if something else went on, that's his business, not yours. He knew what he was doing, Jennifer. It's his job. And he doesn't have to defend it to you." Wanda leaned closer. "And I'll say it again. He didn't drive out to that funeral and stand in that heat just to hand you that card. Think about it. You're a smart girl. You can figure out the real reason."

CHAPTER SIX

WANDA'S implication was stupid. Just plain stupid.

Even if Beck were interested in Jennifer—which he wasn't—and even if he hadn't been involved with Howard's death—which he was—there was no way she'd even remotely consider him. Jennifer wanted a peaceful, calm life. Orderly and planned. Beck obviously lived the exact opposite way. With a job like his, it was inevitable. Always on call, constantly facing chaos and violence. She shuddered, her crazy childhood coming back to her in a flash. Her father always running off in the middle of the night to somewhere strange, none of them knowing where he was. Her mother all upset.

No. Jennifer wanted nothing to do with a man like that.

As she worried over the conversation, a noise sounded behind her. Her heart in her throat, Jennifer whirled around. Beck Winters stood in the doorway.

They stared at each other across the classroom. She'd been expecting him; he was there to talk to the kids, but as she met his gaze, Jennifer felt as if she'd made a terrible mistake in allowing his visit. Could he read minds? Could he tell what she'd been thinking? She told herself she was being absurd, but the intensity in his eyes had her wondering. Breaking the eye contact, Jennifer looked at the woman standing beside him.

Jennifer vaguely remembered meeting her that night, but she'd been too shocked to really notice the police psychologist. Petite and well dressed, Maria Worley looked to be in her midthirties. She had dark hair and lively eyes. As she and Beck came closer all Jennifer could think was she didn't look like a psychologist. That made no sense, of course, therapists didn't look a certain way, but her open and friendly manner surprised Jennifer.

They shook hands and made conversation, but moments later the students began to stream into the classroom. Grateful for the ensuing confusion Jennifer watched the kids tumble in and grab their seats. Through it all, she could feel Beck's stare like a hand against her back.

Finally the children sat down and settled in, and Jennifer began to speak. "We have guests today. Officer Beck Winters and Dr. Maria Worley. As I mentioned before, they're going to talk to us about what happened with Mr. French and take any questions you may have."

Jennifer stopped and took a deep breath. She didn't even know if she was making sense or not she was so conscious of Beck's presence. It felt as though they were connected by some invisible bond. She didn't like the feeling, but what could she do? Forcing herself to focus, she said, "I want you to feel free to talk to our visitors about anything, anything at all, okay?"

Her pulse still jumping, she walked to the back of the classroom. Beck rose and began to address the rapt and silent group.

Jennifer could tell what people really thought by the way they talked to her students. If they didn't respect the kids, they talked down to them. If they felt uncomfortable in the classroom, they often did the opposite and talked over their heads. Beck did neither. He struck exactly the right chord when he told them who he was and began to speak. The debriefing they'd gone through right after the incident had helped, but in the time since, the questions and issues had been simmering. She hadn't realized how much until now.

The first question came from Cherise. The little blonde held up her hand in a tentative way, her eyes darting to Jennifer instead of Beck. Jennifer smiled encouragingly as Beck answered the child. "You have a question?"

Jennifer could see her gather herself. "My mom said he was dead, but is he really? Mr. French, I mean?"

Beck nodded, a serious expression on his face, his electric blue eyes thoughtful. "Your mom is right. Mr. French died. We're very upset that it ended that way, but bad things happen when guns are involved."

Three more hands popped up, and he pointed to Juan. "You first. Go ahead."

Juan spoke softly, but as soon as he did, Jennifer's heart broke. "Are his friends mad?"

Beck frowned. "I'm afraid I don't understand. You mean, Mr. French's friends?"

The little boy nodded. There weren't gangs in Destin as there were in the larger cities, but even still, the kids knew about them. Jennifer started to explain then Beck's expression cleared as he realized what was going on.

"I'm sure Mr. French had friends who are sad he died, but they aren't going to come to the school, I can promise you that. You're safe and it's not going to happen again. He acted alone...." Beck stopped, his gaze searching the children's faces. "Do you understand what I'm saying? I mean he wasn't part of any group. What he did, he did by himself because he was upset and angry. Sometimes people do things like that when they're confused."

Julian put up his hand, speaking at the same time. "But it could happen again, couldn't it? Somebody else could get a gun and come in here and start shooting and everything—"

"They could, but they won't," Beck said firmly. "What happened is a rare thing. Think about it. In all the years that the school has been here, has anything like this happened before?"

The kids all shook their heads and more than one or two seemed to relax and ease back in their chairs. Jennifer stared in amazement; Beck handled them like a pro, and she wouldn't have done half as well herself. By the time he brought Maria to the front of the room, the students were ready to deal with the deeper emotional issues.

As they'd already arranged, Jennifer and Beck slipped out into the hall. The psychologist had told Jennifer she wanted to see the children alone at first, then possibly later with her in the room.

Walking quickly, Jennifer led Beck to one of the courtyards outside. He held the door open for her, and Jennifer brushed past him, catching just a whiff of a spicy aftershave. His chest seemed to be a mile wide, and by the time she reached the bench in the center of the little patio, she was having a hard time breathing.

She sat down, again feeling the strange connection to him, but trying to ignore it. She pretended instead to concentrate on the beauty of the garden. She often came here to calm herself. Each year a different class took over the care and tending of the small plot, and this year's gardeners had obviously been studying vines. In the humid air of the early afternoon, the sweet scent of Carolina jasmine was mixed with honeysuckle. Normally, just smelling the flowers would make her feel better, but today it didn't work its usual magic. The silence felt too heavy, and she had to break it. She spoke nervously.

"You were very good back there," she said, inclining her head toward the building. "You have an excellent feel for what the kids need to hear. Sometimes people tell them too much and other people don't quite know what to say. It gets complicated, I guess, but—" She realized she was babbling and stopped abruptly.

He seemed surprised by her compliment, and for just a second, she could have sworn the blue ice of his eyes thawed.

"I like kids," he said. "They're innocent and I don't see much of that in my work."

She couldn't help herself. She had to ask. "Do you have children of your own?"

"No. My ex-wife didn't want a family and she didn't stick around long enough for me to convince her otherwise. We were only married two years." He lifted his foot and rested it on the bench, draping his arm across his bended knee as he looked at her. "How 'bout you?"

"I've never been married," she said. "But someday, I'd like a family. A big one." She often thought of having a houseful of children and dogs and noise and confusion. What would it be like?

"Do you have lots of brothers and sisters?"

"I had one brother, but he's no longer alive."

"I'm sorry."

"It happened a long time ago." She paused, the remembrance too painful. "A lifetime ago." Searching for a different topic so he wouldn't ask any more questions, she spoke again quickly. "Have you always been a negotiator?"

He looked at her with those strange eyes and she could tell he knew exactly what she was doing. He answered anyway. "No," he said, shaking his head. "I used to be one of the tact group. I was a front entry man."

When she frowned in confusion, he explained. "It's another position on the SWAT team. I'd be the first guy inside when we'd have to do an assault."

She thought of Howard and his rifle. "That sounds dangerous."

"Not any more so than the rest of the positions but it definitely had its bad points." An unreadable expression crossed his face. "I lasted five years, then I had to get out. I was going to quit the team, but Lena wouldn't let me. She sent me back to school for more training and I came out a negotiator."

Jennifer studied his profile, then something clicked and she understood what she was seeing. She encountered the same emotion in the mirror every morning. It was guilt. A warm rush of sympathy came over her, and despite not wanting it at all, she felt the bond between them tighten even more.

"What happened?" she asked softly. "Why'd you want out?"

His mouth, usually full and generous, she realized all at once, narrowed into a slash. "It's not something I talk about," he said coldly.

"I—I'm sorry," she said quickly. "I just thought…"

He straightened his back and stood. "It's a boring story, that's all. You don't really want to hear it." He nodded toward the classroom. "Why don't you tell me why you became a teacher instead? That would be much more interesting."

"I've always loved children." She answered automatically while the rest of her was wondered what he was hiding. Obviously she'd hit a nerve as sensitive to him as Danny's death was to her. "I like helping them learn."

"And why here? Are you from Destin?"

"I'm not from anywhere. My dad was in the navy, and one of his last stops was Hulbert Field. When he came home and said 'We're moving' again, I refused. I was seventeen and we'd lived in twenty different houses. I got a job and an apartment and settled in and finished school. I haven't left since."

"Where is he now? Still traveling?"

"My father died ten years ago from a heart attack, and Mom came back here and bought a house. She'd loved the area as much as I did and had hated to go. She stayed in her home until about five years ago, then when she couldn't really look after herself anymore, I got her a place at Seacrest."

"You've been on your own for a long time."

She met his gaze. "I was on my own before they moved."

He nodded and started to sit down again, but he froze in midmotion, his hand going to his beeper. Snatching the black box from his belt, he stared at it intently, then raised his head. "I've got to go," he said. "Can you get Dr. Worley a cab when she finishes?"

"Of course." Jennifer jumped to her feet. "But what's going on? Is something wrong?"

He'd already turned and was striding toward the door. "It's a call for the team." As if that explained everything, he said nothing more and a second later he was gone.

Standing alone in the courtyard, Jennifer watched the door swing shut, then a stark memory flooded her; the image of her mother watching her father leave.

"When will you be back?" she'd asked tearfully.

"When it's over," was all he'd said.

Her mother had cried herself to sleep every night until he'd returned. Three months later.

"God told him to do it."

Beck stared down at the woman before him. She was a tiny thing, no more than five feet tall and no more than forty years old. Her face had the wrinkled appearance of a dried prune, though. There wasn't an inch of skin the sun hadn't aged into a leatherlike surface. She was way too young to look as she did, but the hard, dark tan, and her anxiety, added an extra ten years. Every few minutes she'd jerk her head over her shoulder to stare at her apartment.

"God told him, huh?"

She nodded, her hair flying as she turned back to face Beck. "He talks to God a lot. He's only fifteen but he's very religious. This morning, when he called me at work, he said 'Mother, God told me you're a sinner and I should make you pay. I'm following his orders.'"

Beck glanced back toward the weathered apartment building. It held only four units, each one with an identical door facing the street and a small rectangular window to its left. The bottom half of the windows were blocked with small air conditioners. "Then what happened?"

"I heard him start to trash the place. Glass breakin' everywhere, things a-crashin'. I screamed at him to stop, but it was too late. He'd already ripped the phone out of the wall, I guess. The line went dead. When I got here, he wouldn't let me in and that's when I called the police."

"And what time did he call you, Mrs. Stone?"

"About two or three, I think."

They were standing beside a cruiser in the hot afternoon sun. The War Wagon was parked down the street with Bradley Thompson, the assistant commander, inside, coordinating everything. Beck had come outside to talk to the mother.

"And there are no weapons in the house, right?" He'd already been briefed, but it never hurt to double-check.

"I don't believe in guns. And I'd know if he'd brought one in. I got an eye for that kinda thing."

The woman worried a cheap silver ring with her fingers, twisting it around and around.

Beck spoke gently. "Where's your husband, Mrs. Stone?"

In the bright light, her gaze dropped to the street, then she spoke with defeat. "He's up at Raiford. He won't be home for a while."

Beck knew what she meant without further explanation. Raiford, a small town near Jacksonville, was the home of the Union Correctional Institution. Among others, it housed Florida's Death Row inmates. Obviously Mr. Stone had not been a model citizen. Beck felt a weary stab behind his eyes as he placed his hand on her shoulder and squeezed reassuringly.

"We appreciate your help, Mrs. Stone. Why don't you let Officer Greenberg get you some coffee, and I'll try to talk to your son."

Waiting nearby for Beck's signal, Sarah started forward to lead the woman away. She started to go with the information officer, but she stopped at the rear of the vehicle and squinted back at Beck, a hand above her eyes to shade them. Heat rolled over them in waves. Her voice turned thready as it rode one toward him. "You—you won't hurt 'em, will you? He's just a kid."

"Absolutely not," Beck said automatically. "Our goal is to get him out of there, that's all." He hadn't finished the sentence when Jennifer's face replaced the mother's worried countenance. "It'll be all right," he said and prayed he was telling the truth.

She started to cry as she left, her thin shoulders shaking. Sarah put an arm around her and bent her head to listen as the woman sobbed.

Beck watched them leave, his own head beginning to pound as his cell phone rang. He grabbed it off his belt. "Winters."

"Things okay down there?" Lena sounded almost as anxious the woman who'd just left. She wanted to be at every site and monitor every event, but she'd sent Beck and the Alpha Team with Thompson this time. As the team's specialist in security, she'd taken a dignitary protection assignment at the Civic Center for the state's local senator who was speaking that evening.

"It's fine," Beck answered. "Just an upset kid who's trashing his mother's apartment. The arriving officers didn't think he had any weapons but they couldn't get him to come out so they called us. We can't get him to answer the phone—looks like he destroyed it or the line, so I'm gonna bullhorn him in a minute. If that doesn't work, I'll throw in a cell phone. No weapons, nobody hurt…just a little misunderstanding."

"Good." She sounded relieved. "Call me back if it heats up. I can be there in five."

A second later, Beck crossed the street and stood behind the car of the patrol officer who'd first arrived on the scene. It was the closest vehicle and offered the best protection. He lifted the bullhorn to his mouth and spoke, hating it as his voice boomed across the pavement. He preferred to use a phone. "Stephen? Stephen Stone? Can you hear me? This is Officer Beck Winters."

Beside Beck stood Lincoln Hood and Edward Ventor, two of the three front entry men. The rear men, Cal and Jason, were already stationed at the back door of the apartment.

The blinds above the air conditioner twitched and the two men at Beck's side tensed, their weapons at the ready. Beck spoke into his headset. "He's at the window, everyone. Heads up."

The blinds moved again, separating enough for Beck to see a face. A young, scared face.

He raised the bullhorn to his mouth once more. "Stephen, I want you to come outside right now with your hands over your head. When you get out here, lie down on the sidewalk. No one will hurt you. We're here to help, buddy. But you have to come out first."

The blinds dropped back down.

Sarah's voice came over Beck's headset. "I've got the neighbor here, Beck. The woman who lives in the apartment on the right-hand side. If you don't want to risk a direct assault through the back door, then Cal and Jason can go into her unit and break through the connecting wall."

"Can they get in her place without him seeing them?"

"I think so," she answered quickly. "I've got the floor plans to the units. There are no windows in the back, just the door."

"Okay," Beck answered. "Keep the neighbor here and stay cool. I don't think it's that serious yet, but you might have a good plan—"

"Shit, man, look at that!" Beside him Linc Hood pointed to the door. "I think he's coming out."

The front door was covered by a screen, making it hard to see exactly what was going on. With no hesitation, the men beside him lifted their weapons. Beck tensed. "Stephen, if you're coming out, then do it. Come out and lie down. But don't do anything else."

The screen door opened wider and a kid stepped out into the glaring sun. He was skinny, his face scarred by acne, limp dark hair falling over one eye. Sometime during his rampage, he'd hurt himself. There was a cut running down one arm, blood staining the edge of his T-shirt. Hardly a seasoned criminal.

But everyone held their breath as he stood on the sidewalk. You never knew, Beck thought, you just never knew. A second later, the kid dropped to the concrete, facedown. Lincoln and Ed immediately ran to the young boy's side. They had him cuffed and dragged to his feet within a few moments, but not before Beck had time to notice the teenager's shoulders jerking and shaking just as his mother's had a few minutes earlier.

He was crying.

Once Beck would have felt the satisfaction of knowing the incident was over and no one had gotten hurt, but all he could think about was how easily it could have ended a much different way.

And then he thought of Jennifer.

Pushing her out of his mind, Beck headed toward the youngster. "You okay?" he asked.

The teen raised his head, but he wouldn't look Beck in the eyes. If Beck had seen him on the street, he wouldn't have thought him twelve, much less fifteen. He looked pitiful and terrified all at the same time, and Beck couldn't help but feel sorry for him.

"I'm all right," he mumbled.

Beck nodded to the two men and they led the boy

away. As they reached the patrol car, Mrs. Stone ran up to them and threw her arms around her son.

He watched for a moment, then Beck joined the knot of men who'd already begun to gather near the War Wagon. After such a simple incident, the debriefing wouldn't take long and in anticipation, some of them were already shedding the heavy, hot Kevlar they were forced to wear. As Beck removed his own vest and helmet, Bradley Thompson separated himself from the group and came up to where Beck stood, extending one beefy hand. The assistant commander of the team had been a military policeman and he still carried himself with the regal bearing most MP's possessed.

"Good job, Beck," he boomed. "Zero casualties and one successful mission! Excellent."

Randy Tamirisa came to where they stood. "Yeah, Officer Winters. Excellent job!" His black eyes narrowed. "You're a real miracle worker getting a fifteen-year-old kid to surrender!"

A few of the men standing nearby chuckled. They didn't hear the undercurrent of challenge in the younger man's voice. They functioned as part of a team and that kind of razzing was expected. Beck knew better, though. Randy wasn't teasing.

But Beck also knew better than to encourage the countersniper. If he said nothing at all, the younger man would get even more frustrated. With an almost perverse pleasure, Beck pointedly ignored him. "Thanks, Bradley," he answered, pumping the man's hand once then dropping it. "It was a good effort on everyone's part."

"Yeah, but kinda boring, wasn't it?" Randy patted the

stock of his weapon. "I didn't get to do my part like I did last week. You guys need to try a little less hard."

The rest of the men shifted uneasily. This time Randy's voice held an obviously disrespectful tone.

"That's the goal, Randy," Beck answered coolly. "We don't want to use you any more than we have to. I'd think you feel the same way as a member of this team."

The younger man jutted out his jaw, his black eyes glinting in the hot sunshine. "I don't need you telling me how to feel, Officer Winters. You telling me how to do my job is bad enough."

Beck's pent-up frustration with the younger man got the best of him. "I wouldn't have to if you did it right."

The black-garbed sniper took two steps and thrust himself into Beck's face. "I do my job better than anyone else on this sorry-ass team," he growled. "And I don't appreciate you saying otherwise."

Beck stayed exactly where he was, noting with satisfaction the younger man had to crane his head to look at him and express the empty threat.

"You're full of shit," he said softly. "I'd trade any one of these men for two of you. They have experience and brains—you've got dick."

Just as Beck had known, his words were all it took. Dropping his weapon, the younger man raised a fist and took a wild swing. Beck calmly blocked the blow with the side of his hand. Before Randy could do anything else, Beck folded his fingers over the sniper's fist and squeezed hard. His knuckles cracking, Randy let out an agonized grunt and his eyes narrowed in a squint of pain. He couldn't do anything but go along as Beck dragged him closer and pushed his face into Randy's.

"You're a menace to this team and the civilians who need us." Beck's voice was a cold roll of thunder. "Get a grip on your emotions, or I'll see that you're out of here."

IT WAS Sunday afternoon. Jennifer had gone to church, washed all her laundry, read the paper…and there was nothing else to do. Usually she had her day all mapped out in advance, but as she moved restlessly about the condo, the walls seemed to move in on her, and everything she'd planned seemed pointless and dull. She thought briefly of walking down to the beach, but dismissed the idea. The churning emerald water, rolling in and rolling out, wouldn't work its usual magic and calm her; she knew that without even thinking twice.

Impulsively grabbing her car keys, she stabbed her feet into a pair of sandals and headed out the door, not even bothering to change clothes. For once, her shorts would just have to serve. Twenty minutes later, she was pulling into the parking lot at Seacrest.

The Sunday staff was smaller. Wanda, one of the senior nurses, never worked that day. Not quite knowing why she was there herself, Jennifer went inside the nursing home and made her way to her mother's room. She opened the door slowly. It was a little past two and she expected just what she saw. Her mother lying in bed.

Jennifer slipped inside and sat down in the plump cushioned chair that rested in one corner. For a long time, she stared at her mother as she slept. Her face looked lovely, the skin smooth and marblelike, her hair spread over the pillow like strands of woven silver. Gradually Jennifer felt the morning's tension ease from her body. She gave in to the feeling, not understanding, but accepting it. After a little while, she began to talk.

"I don't know what to do, Mom," she said, feeling a little foolish, but not letting that stop her. "I saw Beck Winters again on Friday and I don't understand it."

Her mother murmured in her sleep, as if encouraging Jennifer.

"He's not the kind of man I want in my life. Not at all. In fact, as we were talking, his beeper went off and he ran out the door on a call. It reminded me so much of when Daddy used to leave and how you hated that. I asked Beck where he was going and he didn't even answer me.

"But…I keep thinking about him! It's driving me nuts. I've never been obsessed with a man in my life, but for some stupid reason, I just can't quit thinking of him. He's so tall and well, dammit, he *is* good-looking. I think that's part of it. I've never actually been close to a man that overwhelming.

"And his eyes, my God, those eyes…" Jennifer shuttered her own gaze as she thought about Beck. "I've never seen that shade of blue before. There's something almost hypnotic about it." She glanced at the motionless figure on the bed. "But it's more than just how he looks, Mom. It's a lot more. He was so kind to the children and so considerate. How can one man be two different people?"

Nadine didn't answer, of course, and Jennifer didn't expect her to. Sometimes there weren't answers, she was learning.

Which brought her full circle. The more she thought about it, the more uncertain Jennifer became. What if Beck had been right? What if Howard *had* shot Juan? How would Jennifer be feeling right now if that precious little boy had died?

Jennifer's eyes went back to her mother. As she watched, Nadine raised her hand to her face. Tucking it under her cheek, she turned on her side and started snoring softly. Jennifer stood then stepped next to the bed and bent over to kiss her. She spoke softly. "I love you, Mom."

By the time she got home, she felt strangely better. Not completely calm, but not as anxious as she had been, either. She went out to her balcony then sat down to watch the sun set.

In her mind, Beck Winters sat beside her. She didn't like the image, but it wouldn't go away.

CHAPTER SEVEN

THE PARTY ON Friday night at Betty Whitmire's house had been planned since the beginning of the semester, and she saw no reason to cancel it. "We want to end the school year well," she'd announced pompously. "I'd appreciate a good turnout."

Jennifer didn't need the reminder. Betty might irritate her, but with everything else that had happened, Jennifer was actually looking forward to tonight's event. She needed to get out and mingle. To forget. Every time she went to sleep, her rest was interrupted by the same horrible nightmare. And during the day, she kept thinking of Beck—the man she wasn't interested in.

Worst of all, last week, waiting in line to check out at Delchamps she'd had a flashback to the moment Howard had died. Someone behind her had dropped a jar of mustard. The yellow goo had gone everywhere, but Jennifer hardly noticed. It was the sound that set her off. And for just one second, her lungs quit working. She gasped, catching herself at the very last moment from actually dropping to the floor. The teenager behind the grocery store's register stared at her strangely, but Jennifer simply abandoned her cart and dashed from the store. She didn't care what anyone thought. All she wanted was escape. Careening into the parking lot, she'd thought her heart was going to explode it was pounding so hard.

When she'd climbed into her car, she'd immediately spotted Maria Worley's card and in a fit of frustration, she'd crumpled it up and tossed it out the window.

With a conscious effort, she put the problem behind her and focused on the present. She was going to a party and she wanted to have a good time. Walking up the sidewalk leading to Betty's house, Jennifer felt her white dress wrap itself around her legs, whipping back and forth in the fresh, evening breeze. Betty lived in Sandestin, near the bay, and her home was her pride and joy. Gracious and perfectly maintained, the house was a reflection of the others surrounding it. Sandestin was one of the nicest neighborhoods in the area.

Betty greeted Jennifer at the door, the perfect hostess as always. She smiled and pulled Jennifer inside. "Oh, don't you look darling," she said, her eyes sweeping over Jennifer's haltered sundress. "So casual, too! Just the right touch for a pool party…."

Jennifer didn't need a dictionary to translate. Betty's gold lamé jumpsuit offered the most obvious clue. Jennifer smiled anyway, determined to have a good time. "I'm glad you approve," she replied. "It's already so hot, I thought this might be the most comfortable."

"And a smart choice it is, young lady!" Betty's husband came into the marbled entry and smiled warmly at Jennifer.

How the two of them managed to stay married, Jennifer had no idea. A well-respected local physician,

Waylon Whitmire was one of the kindest men she knew. He held out both his hands then took hers and kissed her on one cheek.

"You look as beautiful as always, my dear," he said. His eyes crinkled and he shook his head. "I was awfully sorry to hear about what happened in your classroom. I hope you're doing all right."

"I'm fine," Jennifer lied, "but thank you for asking. That's very sweet of you."

"Oh, he's not just being concerned, Jennifer!" Betty raised one eyebrow and eyed her sharply. "He's being professional. When you go through what you and I did, you have to be careful, you know. I spoke at length with Dr. Worley and she says we might very well experience PTSD." She leaned closer. "That's Post-Traumatic Stress Disorder. The symptoms include insomnia and depression, or you can have nightmares. You can even have flashbacks—"

"I know what PTSD is, Betty." Jennifer tried to keep her voice polite.

"Well, that's good. Because I've arranged for you to see Dr. Worley. In fact, I've decided to make your interview with her part of your year-end evaluation for this school year. The district will pay for it, of course."

Jennifer's jaw actually dropped. She could feel it, along with a flood of dismay. "Are you kidding?"

"Absolutely not," Betty replied. "Dr. Worley understands what we experienced." She lowered her voice. "You have to *deal* with these things, Jennifer. You can't ignore them."

Jennifer began to sputter. "I—I don't think talking to

a shrink should impact my job evaluation, Betty! Th-that's not fair."

"Please, Jennifer!" Betty patted her on the arm. "Surely you know me too well to think that! I'm not *basing* your evaluation on your little talk with the doctor. Good heavens, I won't even know what the two of you discuss." She wiggled her fingers in the direction of her husband. "Doctor-patient confidentiality, you know. I just want you to have a chat with her, that's all. She's a wonderful listener and it will do you a world of good."

"But, Betty—"

Ignoring Jennifer's look of dismay, Betty glanced into the mirror hanging at Jennifer's back. When her expression returned to Jennifer's, she smiled vacantly. "Why don't you run along inside and join everyone and we'll talk about it on Monday. Just have fun this evening."

Waylon's sympathetic gaze raked Jennifer's face as Betty clutched his arm and dragged him with her to the door to greet their next guests. Jennifer stared after them for a moment longer, then she turned with a sick feeling in the pit of her stomach. Having fun was the last thing that was going to happen to her now. What on earth did Betty think she was doing? Making her way into the Whitmires' elegant living room, Jennifer shook her head. Betty meddled in everything and that's why she'd run for the school board. She wasn't really malicious, or at least, Jennifer didn't think she was. Clueless was more likely.

Either way it didn't matter. The results were the same.

But there was nothing she could do about it tonight, Jennifer decided. On Monday morning, they could fight over it. Spying Cindy, the teacher whose class-room was opposite hers, Jennifer nodded and headed toward the covered outdoor patio where the other woman stood. Maybe she could salvage something from the evening. If nothing else, they could gossip and drink and eat the delicious hors d'oeuvres Betty always provided.

Jennifer was halfway across the room when she saw him.

Beck stood head and shoulders above everyone else in the crowd, his blond hair shining under the low-level lights. He was completely alone, standing near the bar, with a drink in his hand. And he was watching her.

All at once she turned into a column of wood and be-came incapable of moving. As if he knew she couldn't escape him, he started slowly toward her, his eyes never leaving hers. She felt like a mouse being stalked by a lion. As he cut through the party-goers, her pulse began to sound loudly in her ears, competing against the chat-ter of the guests and the music playing somewhere in the back of the house. By the time he reached her side, Jennifer was sure he could hear her thumping heart.

He had on navy slacks and a white shirt, and his hair was slicked back, off his face. "Surprised to see me?"

She had to swallow twice before she could answer him. "I—I— Yes," she finally managed to say. "I am surprised. Betty invited you?"

He nodded. "When I brought Dr. Worley to the school last Friday. She said she wanted to 'reward' us."

"Us? Is the doctor here, too?"

"I'm not sure. But she invited Lena—you remember

her?—too." He lifted his drink to the patio outside. "She's around here somewhere. She's got her date in tow."

Jennifer nodded, the gist of the conversation flowing by her unheeded by any attention. "How was your call?" she asked. "The one you had to go to after you spoke to the class?"

"Just fine." His answer was quick and his tone matched it. *Don't ask anymore,* he seemed to say.

She hardened her heart as she looked up at him, but it didn't seem to matter. He still got to her. He was, without a doubt, one of the best-looking men she'd ever met, but there was more to Beck than just that, and finally she realized what it was. He was magnetic. There was no other word for it. She didn't want to like him. She hated what he did and how he lived his life...but she couldn't have walked away from him any more than she could have stopped the sun from shining. Simply standing beside him, she could feel an actual physical pull toward him. She fought it with everything she had in her and even took a step back from him.

"I was on my way to visit with a friend outside. I'll just head that way, I guess...." She let her words die out.

His eyes searched her face as he answered, but at the same time, he stepped to one side. "Of course, I won't keep you." Then their gazes met, and suddenly, once more, Jennifer couldn't move.

For a long moment, they just stared at each other. She might have doubted it before, but she no longer could: Beck felt the unseen cord that linked them, just as she did. Those blue eyes reflected the knowledge back at her. The revelation made her shiver.

"Maybe later we could share a drink?"

She didn't say a word—she couldn't. She just nodded.

"I'll find you," he said.

"Okay…"

She forced movement into her legs, made herself start to walk off, but without any warning, he reached out and put his hand on her arm. His fingers were hot, not just warm, and the heat burned through her bare skin and went straight into her bones. She almost flinched, but the feeling seemed like such a contradiction, she thought she might be imagining it. How could a man who looked so cold and forbidding have such a blistering touch?

He gazed down at her. "Don't try to get away without talking to me, now. I'm a cop…I'll find you."

He was teasing her, she knew, and waiting for a smile or a reaction, but Jennifer could give neither to him. She could do nothing but nod.

And maybe that *was* the reaction, she thought as she crossed the room.

Whatever he asked, Beck left her no answer but yes.

BECK WATCHED Jennifer head toward a set of double doors that opened on to the patio. Just as she reached them, she paused and looked back over her shoulder. He lifted his drink in a silent promise, and she nodded, as though she understood his message. *I'll be waiting.*

It was more than just a promise, he thought, watching her slim, bare back depart. No catastrophe he could imagine would keep him from finding her later. When she'd walked into the room, her white sundress baring tanned arms and legs, her chestnut hair gleaming, he'd been unable to catch his breath, along with every other man in the room, he was sure. He'd thought before that she was pretty, thought she was attractive, but he hadn't seen her like *this*.

She was sexy. Sensual. Incredibly desirable.

He was still staring out to the patio when Lena appeared at his side.

"What are you doing, Winters? Stargazing?"

Beck pulled his attention away from the doors. Lena's right hand was linked with the man standing next to her, her date, Nate Allen. The police chief of Pensacola, Nate nodded briefly at Beck, then stared down at Lena. All the men teased her about Nate's infatuation. He doted on her and she hardly seemed to notice. A few years before, she'd been about to marry, but it hadn't worked out. Every time Beck saw her with someone, he knew her heart was still in the past and it pained him.

"I was talking to Jennifer Barclay," Beck answered.

He waited for a smart-aleck remark, but Lena merely nodded vaguely. "Nice lady. Seems sharp." She appeared distracted, her mind somewhere far beyond Betty Whitmire's living room.

Bending toward her, Nate spoke. "Would you like a drink, sweetheart?"

"Yes," she answered quickly. "A glass of cola would be great."

He nodded then looked at Beck and raised one eyebrow. "May I get you something, too, Beck?" His voice was polite as ever, but underneath the veneer Beck sensed the same tension that was in Lena's eyes. Had Nate asked her to marry him and been turned down again?

Beck raised the bottle of imported beer he'd taken when he arrived. "I'm fine."

Nate nodded curtly, then vanished into the throng. Beck watched him disappear, just as he'd watched Jennifer. Beside him, Lena did the same. For a few seconds, they stood together silently, then Beck noticed what she was doing. She was removing then replacing the tiny gold ring Nate had given her at Christmas. On. Off. On. Off. She wore it on her right hand—it was not an engagement ring—but it looked as though she wouldn't be wearing it at all soon.

"Everything okay?"

She looked up at him in surprise as he spoke. "Of course. Everything's perfect. Why wouldn't it be?"

"I don't know. You just seem a little tense."

"It's fine...*I'm* fine." As though the words were spoken for her own benefit as much as his, she nodded her head in emphasis. "It's going great."

She was trying too hard to convince him, and suddenly she seemed to realize it. Her expression shifted, and she seemed to switch gears. Beck could almost hear them grinding as she went to safer ground.

"I heard you and Randy had a problem," she said. "At the Stone call-out."

"Yes, we did. You should have been there. He's a bomb waiting to go off."

"That's funny. Bradley used just about those same words to describe you to me. He said you almost came to blows."

"Randy was shooting off his mouth. I'm getting tired of it."

"I am, too," she said, surprising him. "He's more hotheaded and impulsive than I'd first thought, but it's my job to worry about the team, not yours."

"He's going to get someone hurt," Beck said darkly.

He could have said more, but he broke off and looked toward the patio doors. Lena's gaze continued to drill his profile. He could feel it.

"You need a vacation," she said, her voice flat. "I want you to go ahead and take off like you were planning to before the Westside situation. Next week."

"I can't."

"Of course you can—"

"I can't." He interrupted bluntly. "I've got a seminar down in Panama City already scheduled. I was going to do it when I came back. I don't have enough time to leave and do that, too. I can't take off now. Maybe later."

He could still feel her scrutiny, but he refused to look down. Finally, she sighed heavily. "All right. But I'm not fooling, Beck. You need a vacation. You're getting the thousand-yard stare in your eyes, and I don't like it. I want you out of here in the next month. One way or the other."

JENNIFER WAS RECLINING in a lounge chair by the edge of the pool when Beck found her an hour later. Partially hidden by the drooping fronds of a huge sago palm, she'd thought—hoped?—he wouldn't spot her, but no such luck. He prowled around the circumference of the turquoise water, until he came to where she sat. The light from the swimming pool bathed their faces with a flickering glow. Beyond the edge of the yard, the darkness of the bay shimmered endlessly.

She looked up at him. "You're not mixing and mingling?"

He took the lounge chair next to hers and stretched out, the steel-and-mesh frame creaking beneath his weight. His feet, covered in soft leather loafers, hung over the end a good six inches. "I met everyone," he said. "They seem like nice people...."

She heard the hesitation in his voice, read it and supplied the unspoken ending to his sentence. "But all they wanted to do was talk about what happened."

He nodded slowly. "That just about sums it up."

"Not exactly party talk."

He stared into the water, his voice meditative. "You'd think I'd be used to it by now, wouldn't you? When the team gets together, it's always shop talk, but I guess I thought it might be different tonight."

His remarks surprised her. All her father had ever talked about was his work. It had consumed him, and she'd always made the assumption that men who thrived on adrenaline were like that. But Beck *didn't* want to talk about his job?

"They're just interested, that's all, You're someone different," she explained. "We've all worked together for years so when someone new turns up, everyone wants to talk to him. And, well..."

He waited.

"Besides that..."

He laughed as she hesitated again. "What? Don't tell me teachers are cop groupies."

She laughed, too. "Maybe, but frankly, we have a lot of unmarried women at Westside. I'm sure no one missed their chance to check you out."

He shook his head in a rueful gesture. "And here I thought it was my charm and personality they were after."

She smiled back in the darkness and spoke without thinking, something that was beginning to be a habit, she decided. "You *are* charming. I'm sure that had something to do with it."

She immediately felt awkward in the aftermath of the compliment, but it didn't seem to bother Beck. In fact, he shifted in his chair and stared at her. "I didn't think you held that high an opinion of me."

Folding the edge of her skirt between her fingers, she fussed with the fabric as she thought of what to say. It was hard to organize her thoughts. Beck's proximity threw a net of confusion over her that she just couldn't seem to escape. "Maybe I spoke too quickly that day," she said finally. "The day Howard died... All I had was your voice. I was in shock when it was over and—"

"You don't have to explain."

"But I want to," she answered, looking over at him. "I need to. You sounded so kind and caring over the phone. You were a real lifeline for me. That's why I was so shocked when—when it ended as it did. I had imagined you as someone much different."

He sat up and locked his laser beam gaze on hers. "I am the person you heard, Jennifer. I care more than you can possibly understand even if I don't always show it the way you think I should. Don't judge me by what happened that day."

His words were a rumble on the humid air, and for just a second, she almost expected lightning as well. "I don't have anything else to go on," she answered.

"Then let me give you something. Let me show you how I'm different. Get to know me better."

Her stomach flipped over. "I don't think that would be a good idea."

"Why not?"

"I just don't."

He reached out and took her hand in his, and again, the heat was instantaneous. She almost snatched her fingers back, but at the very last moment, managed to resist the impulse. He raised his eyes and met her gaze. "What are you so afraid of?"

She did pull her hand away then. "I'm not afraid of anything," she answered. "I don't think it'd work."

"Tell me what I could do to change that."

"I can't think of anything."

"Do you date at all?"

She flushed. "Of course I date."

"So if I were someone else, you'd say yes? We could go out, maybe have some dinner then get to know each other better and after that we'd decide if we wanted to take it further. But since I'm me, you've made that decision already. Is that it?"

She spoke hotly, feeling trapped. "Do you negotiate everything?"

He laughed then and leaned closer to her, dropping his voice as the darkness wrapped them together more intimately than she would have thought possible. She fought back a shiver.

"This isn't negotiating, Jennifer. When I decide to do that, you won't even know it's happened until it's over."

As his blue eyes locked on hers, his implication became clear, and her face flamed even more.

"C'mon," he said. "I promise I won't bite."

He might not bite, but he was still dangerous and she knew it. Men like Beck needed excitement, tension, stress in their lives, and she wanted none of that in hers. She labored hard to keep her existence as ordered and tranquil as she could and getting involved with a man like him would disrupt everything she'd worked for since she'd left her father's house. No matter how intriguing he might be. No matter how hot his touch.

"I'm sorry," she said firmly. "But you'll have to take my word on this. It wouldn't work."

CHAPTER EIGHT

THE FOLLOWING Wednesday, Beck walked out of Maria Worley's office and into sunshine so hot and bright, it momentarily blinded him. He slipped on his sunglasses and glanced at his watch, thinking about the meeting he'd just had. SWAT team members regularly presented lectures to the various nearby police departments. The information helped the other officers with potential problems and kept them all in touch, a good thing if they had to work together to resolve a situation. When his topic involved psychological issues, Beck always spoke with Maria as part of his preparation. The woman was smart, and her recommendations never failed to be helpful.

Ignoring the sweltering late-afternoon heat, Beck stared back at the building. He should have been asking the good doctor for dating advice instead. Jennifer's rejection had stung more than he'd expected. He wasn't the kind of guy who thought women should swoon at his feet, but Beck generally didn't have them refuse his first offer straight out.

He understood her reasons, of course. Jennifer was holding on to a ton of anger. He suspected part of it came from somewhere in her past, and he could do nothing about that. The rest sprung directly from the incident with Howard French. She might not blame Beck anymore, but she had questions and she didn't trust him. He wanted to try to erase that doubt from her mind and assure her everything possible had been done to keep Howard alive. Beck didn't know if he could do that, though.

For one thing, he wasn't so sure he believed it *was* the truth. For another, it didn't matter. It was over and done with, and Beck never looked back. It did no good.

Still, he'd wanted to try and she'd rejected him.

After she'd turned Beck down, Jennifer had explained Betty Whitmire's plans. He'd wanted so badly to pull her into his arms, he'd almost been able to feel her curves beneath his hands, but he'd held back. He told himself now it was possible her rebuff had more to do with that situation than it had to do with him. She was upset, right? How could she think about a date when she was worried about talking to Maria?

"Why don't you want to talk with Dr. Worley?" he'd asked.

Jennifer had crossed her arms and regarded him with dark eyes. "I don't believe in psychologists," she'd answered. "My brother saw one for quite a while before his death, and it didn't help him at all."

The mention of her brother sharpened Beck's attention. He considered asking her once more what had happened, but something told him she wouldn't tell him the details until she was ready. "Maybe he wasn't a good doctor."

Her glare chilled. "That goes without saying."

"Maria's good at her job," he persisted. "In fact, she's excellent."

Jennifer didn't answer. He hesitated, then reluctantly gave in to the silent urging he was hearing in his head. How could he hold back if what he knew might help the woman standing in front of him?

"Do you remember asking me a while back if I'd seen Maria personally?"

"Yes..."

"Well, I have. It's not something I like to recall, but the fact is a few years ago we lost several men during a standoff. Every one of the guys on the team had to go see her. Some of them didn't want to, but Lena made it mandatory, and it turns out she was right to do so. We were all suffering from the same thing. Blocking out what had happened, having flashbacks, feeling angry. Avoiding thinking about the problem altogether." He stopped. There was no way he could explain everything—he didn't even want to—so he kept it simple. "It was bad."

Jennifer's expression shifted slightly. "What happened? How did—how did these guys die?"

"You don't want to know."

His reply upset her; he could see that immediately from the look on her face, but the memories of that night were still painful and routinely he had to repress them, putting them far into the darker recesses of his mind. There was no answer anyway. None that made sense.

"That was when I almost left the force." Trying too late to soften the hardness of his earlier answer, he spoke again. "I think I told you already. Lena refused my resignation and sent me to negotiating school instead."

Despite her obvious frustration at his reticence, Jennifer raised her hand in a comforting gesture, as if she were about to put her fingers on his arm, but at the last minute, she didn't. She pulled them back, and he suffered the loss even though he hadn't felt her touch to begin with.

"I'm sorry," was all she said.

"I am, too," he answered. "Especially for the three officers who died." *And the four little kids.* The images shifted slightly—they never left—and he focused on Jennifer once more. "I believe in Maria. She helped me."

The momentary sympathy that had warmed her dark-brown eyes slowly disappeared. "I'm glad, but I don't think she'd do anything for me. I don't need help, anyway."

She was hurting and didn't even know it. Maria *could* help her. Then he realized how futile it would be to try to persuade Jennifer. She'd made up her mind and he wasn't going to change it, just like he wasn't going to get her to go out with him. Shortly after that, she'd left the party, and he'd watched her walk away without saying another word.

The traffic whizzed along Highway 98 and Beck stood by, looking at his watch one more time. She ought to be coming soon or she was going to be late. Maria hadn't told him, of course, but he'd charmed—then tricked—Sher, the receptionist, into telling him the time of Jennifer's appointment. But she obviously wasn't going to keep the booking Betty Whitmire had made. Disappointment rose inside him. He knew it was pointless, but he'd wanted one more chance.

Beck waited a few more minutes, then he started down the palm-lined sidewalk. His apartment was only a few blocks over, the headquarters of the team down the street in the opposite direction. He'd walked to Maria's, leaving his car at home. As he waited for the light to change, he looked idly around, then stopped. Jennifer stood at the door he'd just left.

She looked angry and upset, and as he stared, she raised one hand and tugged at her dress. She stood in the sunshine a moment longer, then she pushed on the door and went inside.

A BLAST OF FRIGID AIR hit Jennifer as she opened the glass doors of the building that housed Maria Worley's offices. She'd rather be anywhere else on earth than here, in this doctor's office, but Betty hadn't left her a choice.

"You really need to talk to her," the woman had insisted. "I've had two sessions with her myself and she's a lovely person. I want you to do this, Jennifer. For me, please…"

That had been two days ago, on the Monday after the party. Sitting across from Betty's massive desk, Jennifer had wanted to refuse. She'd started to say no, willing to suffer the consequences, whatever they might be, but something in Betty's expression had stopped her. By the time Jennifer had left she'd convinced herself she'd imagined it but for just that one second Betty had actually appeared to care. Jennifer had given in and agreed, but now she was regretting the capitulation more than ever.

Making her way to the seventh floor and then through the maze of suites, she opened the door to the one marked Dr. Maria Worley and stepped inside. The receptionist, who sat at one end behind a small, white desk, looked up as Jennifer approached. "I'm Jennifer Barclay," she said, her stomach fluttering. "I have a three o'clock appointment."

The woman smiled warmly. "Oh, yes, Miss Barclay, the doctor's expecting you. I'll let her know you're here."

Jennifer turned and headed toward a blue couch on the other side of the room, but before she could sit down, the door opposite her opened and Maria Worley stuck her head out. "Jennifer—come on in. I'm glad to see you made it."

As if I had a choice, she thought.

Jennifer greeted the dark-haired woman then followed her down a short hallway to her inner office, a bright, open area with a wall of windows facing south. They weren't directly on the waterfront, but the building towered over the smaller beach houses and condos in front of it, so the view was spectacular. For as far as she could see, emerald green waves rolled in and out, a stretch of pristine white sand stopping their progress with foamy precision. In the distance, past the waves, a parade of sailboats and fishing rigs dotted the horizon, their serpentine line leading backward to the marina just down the road.

It was a peaceful, calm scene, and Jennifer wondered at once if that was why Maria Worley had picked the office. Did she think it would bring serenity to her confused and upset clients? The contrast made Jennifer remember Danny's doctor. A cold, reserved man who'd expressed no opinions of his own, the psychologist had reminded her of a dead fish when she'd visited him once with Danny. His office, in shades of gray and black, had been so stark and bleak it'd scared her. Judging solely by her decor, Maria Worley was a very different kind of doctor.

But that still didn't mean Jennifer wanted to talk to her.

Confronted with two chairs and a couch, Jennifer nervously took one of the plump armchairs and sat down, putting her purse at her feet. To her surprise, Maria took the sofa, sitting back comfortably on its floral-patterned cushions and even slipping off her shoes to tuck her legs underneath her. They could have been two friends settling in for a chat, only Jennifer knew better. She crossed her arms and waited for Maria to speak.

"You don't want to be here, do you?" The psychologist smiled, her expression taking some of the edge off her bluntness.

"No, I don't." If she was going to be that direct, Jennifer could be, too. "I only came because Betty insisted."

"I know. I told her coerced therapy was never a good idea, but you know Betty…." Maria grinned again. "She has a mind of her own so I just let her make the appointment then counted on having a free hour." She clasped her hands behind her head and leaned back. "Looks like I won't be hitting that sale down at the mall after all, huh?"

The doctor's refreshing openness and almost conspiratorial attitude did just what it was supposed to—lowered Jennifer's emotional barrier. She knew exactly what Maria Worley was doing, but she was so good at it, Jennifer couldn't help herself. She grinned in return. "I could leave now and we could both go."

"That'd be fine with me," Maria laughed. "Reluctant

clients are not happy campers. Betty didn't accept my opinion, though."

"She doesn't accept anyone's, but her own. She's not a good listener."

Maria lowered her arms, clasped her hands in her lap and looked at Jennifer. "Do you think Howard French felt that way about her, too? That she didn't listen to him?"

Jennifer shook her head at the frank question. "I don't know, but probably. Betty wasn't kind to Howard. In fact, she was downright mean. The way she talked to him reminded me of my father."

"Why is that?"

Again, Jennifer realized what was happening. She was actually talking, and she hadn't wanted to do that at all. But Maria Worley wasn't like a doctor. She seemed genuinely interested.

"He was a cruel, sadistic person and he belittled everyone he came in contact with. Betty's not *that* bad, but there was just something about the way she spoke to Howard." Jennifer shuddered. "It brought back so many memories."

Maria waited calmly, and Jennifer kept going before she could stop herself. "He gave my brother an especially hard time, and I guess that's one of the reasons Howard's death affected me so much. They were a lot alike, my brother and Howard, and I had wanted to help him, too."

"Help him, too?"

Jennifer glanced up. "My brother died in an accident when I was a child."

"I'm sorry to hear that. How old was he? How old were you?"

"He was sixteen. I was ten."

Something in Jennifer's attitude must have come through. "Were you present when it happened?"

Jennifer closed her eyes then opened them after a minute. "I was standing right beside him…and I didn't do a thing."

"Are you saying you think you could have prevented what happened?"

"Of course."

"Are you sure?"

The doctor's words reminded Jennifer of Wanda's. She looked up and met the woman's dark eyes. "I always thought I could."

The doctor nodded. "Children do that."

Jennifer's tongue stuck to the roof of her mouth. She felt as though she'd bitten into a biscuit made only of flour. She finally managed to speak. "Children do what?"

"Feel responsible," Maria answered. "Look at the kids in your classroom. Think of the last one whose parents divorced, and I bet you'll see what I'm talking about. Unless they're reassured repeatedly, they always believe the divorce is their fault, no matter what."

Jennifer sat in silence. There was nothing to say.

"So it's completely understandable you'd feel that way about your brother." Maria shrugged casually. "But I'm sure you know that's not the case. You wouldn't be the terrific teacher Beck told me you are without seeing that for the fallacy it is."

Jennifer nodded slowly. *Of course. You're right.* The words wedged themselves in her still-dry throat and refused to come out. None of this was news to her, but she'd never applied the theory to herself.

"Look, you really don't have to stay here if you'd rather not. I'll tell Betty we met and leave it at that." Maria swung her feet to the floor. "Whatever you want."

Jennifer stared at the woman. She had a kind face and as she waited patiently for Jennifer to answer, she wondered how many tears had been shed in this office by someone sitting in the very chair where Jennifer now was. How did Maria Worley absorb them without drowning? How did she deal with the pain? What would she say that could help?

Could she end Jennifer's nightmares?

The decision was an impulsive one, but it felt exactly right. "I think I'd rather stay."

Maria smiled warmly and settled back into the couch. "Then I'm all yours. Let's talk...."

FORTY-FIVE MINUTES LATER, the doors to the office building opened and Jennifer came outside. The sun was just beginning to head westward, and in the pale-yellow streaks that heralded its exit, her skin turned to gold. She wore a navy blue jumper—nothing like the white sundress from the party—but the simple lines seemed made for her, elegant and classy. Beck stared at her for a few seconds, almost unable to move, then he realized she was walking down the street toward her Toyota. If he didn't hustle, he'd miss her. He jumped up from the bench where he'd been waiting and crossed the street to cut her off.

Her eyes widened when she saw him and she stopped abruptly. "Beck! What are you doing here?"

He thought about lying, but couldn't, and that surprised him so much for a moment, he was actually at a loss for words. "I knew you had an appointment," he said finally, opting for the simple truth and nothing more. "I wanted to see how it went for you."

She started to answer, but he interrupted, speaking quickly before she could think up an excuse to dash away. "There's a juice vendor down the street. Walk down that way with me and have something. We'll talk."

"Beck, I don't—"

He ignored her protest and took her elbow instead. "It's not a date," he said. "A fruit smoothie after work doesn't count."

She looked up at him and he could see she'd been crying. And suddenly it hit him. He was attracted to Jennifer—had been since the moment he'd seen her—but now it was more than just that.

"I'd like to hear what the doc had to say." Rubbing the inside of her elbow with his thumb, he felt the silk of her skin. "We'll have something to drink and you can tell me."

She pulled her arm away, then nervously reached up to touch her hair. The dark curls were piled haphazardly on top of her head with longer ringlets hanging down around her face. "There's nothing *to* tell," she said. "I talked to her about my nightmares. And we discussed my family, spoke some about Betty. I had a problem the other day at the grocery store. I guess you'd call it a flashback, and I told her about that." She shook her head. "It was boring stuff, really. You wouldn't want to hear it."

"Try me."

She seemed tempted for a moment, then she shook her head again and even took a step back. "I'm sorry, I really can't. Today's Wednesday. I always visit my mother on Wednesdays."

She said the words so precisely he understood immediately. Her life was ruled by a schedule, by bells, by teaching plans. She didn't like disruptions or changes and all the hints he'd seen of this before now made sense. Another piece of the puzzle fell into place.

"C'mon. Five minutes," he said. "That's all. Then we'll drive to Seacrest with my red lights flashing, how's that?"

She looked alarmed, her brown eyes rounding. "We?"

"I've got some free time. I'd love to meet your mother."

"Oh, no. I don't think—"

"Jennifer…"

She fell silent.

"Let me be friendly, please." He looked down at her and this time he did lie. "That's all I want. Just to be your friend."

She didn't know what to say. He could see the conflict cross her expression.

"I think you could use one," he said. "And I know I could."

She seemed to consider his answer, then she nodded slowly. "All right. Five minutes, and that's it. I have to leave."

They walked down the sidewalk toward the yellow-and-white-striped umbrella that marked the juice stand,

Beck wondering with each step what it would take to earn her trust. What had been a vague suspicion before turned into a more concrete notion. There was more to her lack of trust than the incident with Howard French. It went back a lot further than that and way beyond Beck. What was the problem?

Esther, the older woman working the stand, grinned at him as she filled their orders. Leaning over the counter, she nodded toward Jennifer. "Very nice, Mr. Beck. I'm glad you've found yourself a lady friend. You treat her good, now."

Beck glanced over at Jennifer and smiled. "I will if she'll let me, Esther."

Jennifer's blush deepened.

Paying the woman behind the cart, Beck steered Jennifer to a shaded table a few feet away, then pulled out her chair. When he pushed it in, he couldn't help but stare at the back of her neck. Shorter tendrils of her chestnut hair lay along the curved line of her spine, and all at once he imagined pressing his mouth along its ridge. *Get a grip,* he told himself, then he ignored the advice. The spot would be warm and tender and taste slightly salty.

Jennifer spoke first. "You come here a lot?"

He grinned widely. "I stop on my way to work every morning. Esther's always giving me advice of some kind."

"You live nearby?"

"Just down the block. I have an apartment close to the beach. I like to do a little surf fishing now and then, so it's nice to be around the water."

She asked the questions with determination, as if she

were bound to make pleasant conversation and nothing deeper, then disappear after the allotted five minutes. "Are you from Destin?"

"No," he answered slowly, just as determined to draw the time out. "I grew up in the north, near Rochester, New York. Hated the cold and the snow and the sleet, and as soon as I could I headed south. I wandered around for a while, and ended up here."

"Is that when you joined the SWAT team?"

He shook his head. "I was a street cop for a long time, then I met Lena at a guy's retirement party. She convinced me I'd be good for the team and that I'd enjoy the work. I got my training and joined up shortly after that."

She put her elbows on the table, trying to seem casual, but failing. "Is it hard? What you do?"

The ocean breeze grabbed one of her curls and sent it flying into her eyes. She lifted her hand, but he beat her to it, reaching across the table and pulling the strand away first. He rubbed it between his thumb and finger for just a second before tucking it behind her ear. The curl felt as soft and silky as her skin.

He put away the sensation and thought about her question. "It's not the easiest thing in the world, but I enjoy helping people and saving lives." He paused. "I know you still have questions about what happened at the school, but I believe in my work. I hope that's not why you won't see me."

She followed his fingers with her own, securing the curl better. Her perfume was light and airy and smelled of lilacs as it drifted over to him. "I *do* still have some questions, but it goes beyond that."

He leaned across the plastic tabletop, dropping all pretense of a casual conversation. "Then tell me. Why won't you give me a chance?"

She licked her lips. They were lined with the same soft-pink shade he'd noticed that first day. "I have my life organized," she said slowly. "It's just the way I like it. Calm, serene, planned. Every day I know what I'm going to do and I do it. That's how I want it. You live a totally different way, Beck."

Her words only reinforced the realization he'd had moments before; she had to have her life ordered. He understood the need, but why did that prevent her from seeing him? "And?" he said.

She lifted her gaze. "And I don't want to get involved with someone who lives the way you must. Because of my father's work, our lives were filled with total confusion when I was growing up, confusion and secrets, too many secrets. When I got old enough to handle things on my own, I promised myself I wouldn't live that way again. Ever. It's too crazy."

A seagull cried out overhead and Beck shook his head. "Life *is* crazy, Jennifer. You can't hide and pretend otherwise."

"I'm not hiding!" she said hotly.

"Then go out with me," he said. "Live a little. Vary your routine and see your mother at six instead of five." He reached across the table and took her hands in his. "I promise you…the universe will keep spinning and you won't fall off the planet. Life will go on if your plans are changed."

As soon as he'd said the words, Beck knew he'd

made a mistake. Her expression went chilly and she pulled her fingers away. Pushing her chair back until the metal legs screeched against the concrete sidewalk, she rose angrily. Before she could speak, though, a woman approached the table. Beck hadn't heard her coming, and afterward, he cursed himself for being so unaware. If he'd known what was about to happen, he could have reacted faster. As it was, he had no forewarning to rely upon, only instinct. She was well dressed and posed no physical threat, but Beck stood immediately. Something was wrong.

With an expression of pure anger, she glared angrily at Jennifer. "I'm having you fired," she snarled furiously. "You're the worst excuse for a teacher I've ever seen and I'm going to make sure this whole town knows it!"

CHAPTER NINE

"NANCY!" Jennifer retreated a step involuntarily, her chair scraping the sidewalk again, even more loudly this time. "Wh-what's wrong? What are you talking about?"

Nancy Thomas, the mother of one of Jennifer's students, continued to stare at Jennifer with a venomous expression. "You're what's wrong!" she cried. "What kind of teacher are you to let this happen?"

"What are you talking about?" Jennifer sent a helpless glance in Beck's direction. "I don't understand.... Please calm yourself!"

"You almost got my baby killed. Don't go telling me to calm down! You let a man with a gun come into your classroom. How could you? You're supposed to protect those poor children."

Jennifer stared at the distraught woman, her heart knocking against her ribs as she searched her brain for a way to reply. A single parent, Nancy worked long hours for a local brokerage firm and traveled constantly. Her ex-husband devoted an equal amount of time to his dental practice. Matthew spent more time with a housekeeper than he did with his parents.

"Nancy, please..."

Jennifer started around the table, but Beck intercepted her, putting himself protectively between her and Nancy Thomas.

"Let's just all cool down here," he said pleasantly. His voice was affable but at the same time, Jennifer couldn't help but see that his blue eyes were assessing the other woman intently. "Nancy, is it? Nancy with an *I* or with a *y?*"

She looked at him blankly, thrown off base by his question. "With a *y*. Who are you?"

"I'm Beck Winters. I'm a friend of Jennifer's but I happen to work with the Emerald Coast SWAT team."

"Then you're just as guilty as she is!" Nancy said loudly. "My child was in that classroom. He saw someone get killed! What kind of place is this? How did that idiot get inside, and why wasn't he arrested before this happened? What kind of cop are you?"

Beck spoke in a low and reasonable voice. "I don't think you understand the situation—"

"I understand it all right. I understand my child was in harm's way and you did what cops always do. You shot first and asked questions later."

The unfairness of her accusation was too much to bear. It didn't matter that the stinging words were awfully close to Jennifer's own feelings, Nancy Thomas had no right to attack Beck, none whatsoever. He'd done the best he could, and responding angrily, Jennifer began to defend him. "You don't know what you're saying, Nancy. Officer Winters did everything he could to—"

Nancy swung around and faced her furiously.

"Don't you dare stand up for him. You should have stopped this whole thing before it happened. Why didn't you—"

"That's enough!" Beck's voice rumbled across the outdoor area. A group of older people standing near one of the flower beds turned and looked. "Lower your voice, ma'am, and collect yourself."

She started to speak again, then all at once, she collapsed. Beck had no choice but to catch her. She would have fallen otherwise. He wrapped his huge arms around her, and she let out a sob, clinging to him tightly, crying in earnest now.

"I—I was out of town," she hiccuped. "My ex called and told me what happened, but I couldn't come back. Matthew could have been killed and I wasn't even here! I—I can't believe it!"

A wave of sympathy replaced Jennifer's anger. She understood now, understood Nancy completely. Unable to return, she'd felt helpless. Her guilt had been building all this time.

"It's okay," Beck murmured. "It's all right." Looking over Nancy's head into Jennifer's eyes, Beck nodded toward a chair. Jennifer scrambled to bring it closer and when she'd done so, Beck eased his way toward it. Gently he lowered Nancy Thomas's trembling form into the seat.

"But your son is okay." He spoke in a kind voice and looked directly into her eyes. "Your son is perfectly fine, and even if you had been here, you wouldn't have been able to do anything for him. Not at that moment."

"B-but he saw someone k-killed! It's just too horrible!" She jerked her eyes to Jennifer's face. "Why didn't you stop him—"

"Whoa, whoa…"

Just as it had been when he'd talked to Jennifer over the phone that horrible day, Beck's voice was firm but compassionate as he interrupted Nancy Thomas. Hearing those calming tones, everything rushed back and all at once Jennifer turned faint, suddenly feeling as weak and strange as she had last week in the grocery store. She sensed the color leave her face and she, too, sat down.

Beck was focused on the upset woman, but he glanced at Jennifer. Seeing her obvious distress, he gave her a reassuring look with those startling blue eyes. Everything would be all right, they said, and she didn't have to do anything but let him handle it.

He turned back to Nancy. "Miss Barclay did everything she could in that classroom to avert disaster. In fact, if she hadn't been there, no telling what would have happened. You owe her a debt of gratitude, not a hard time." He stopped and sent another glance in Jennifer's direction. The words were directed to the woman in front of him, but Jennifer understood who he was really speaking to. "She did the right thing every step of the way," he said. "I helped, but she saved lives, and we should all be grateful."

Beck's praise warmed something deep inside her, and even as she fought the sensation, Jennifer felt the last bit of her resistance melt under his approving look. How could she be embarrassed and ridiculously pleased at the same time? To cover her confusion, she looked back at Nancy, who wore a doubting expression of uncertainty.

Jennifer took one of the woman's hands in hers. "Nancy, please, if I'd known you were gone, I would have called you. Betty never told me. I had no idea. Matthew didn't say anything, either."

Her anger deflating under Jennifer's sympathy, Nancy Thomas's eyes filled with tears of remorse. "I was in London. There was an emergency and I ran out to catch a flight that morning. I didn't even kiss Matthew goodbye before I left. I was on my way to the school when I saw you sitting here. I stopped the car. I was just so upset and scared and..." She took a deep, ragged breath, glancing at Beck and then Jennifer. "I—I'm sorry, Jennifer, really sorry. I guess I just went crazy with the thought of what could have happened."

"I understand." Her stomach quaking, Jennifer nodded. She looked at Beck and spoke again. "Believe me, I understand."

"GIVE ME YOUR KEYS."

They were walking down the sidewalk a half hour later, heading for Jennifer's car. "I'm going to drive you to Seacrest," Beck said. "You have no business behind the wheel as upset as you are."

"I'm fine, really."

He lifted his eyebrows. "That shade of white is your normal color?" He shook his head. "I don't think so, Jennifer. Let me drive."

She answered as they reached her car, her keys in her hand. "But I'm okay," she insisted. "Perfectly all right."

He didn't bother to answer. Instead, he reached over, took her hand in his, and pried open her fingers. It didn't take much effort. She was clearly shaken and didn't have the energy to resist him. "You're upset," he said. "And rightfully so. Let me drive you over there, then I'll catch a taxi back to the station. I don't want to see you have an accident."

She didn't say a word; she simply stood there, beside her car, her hand cradled in his. "Are you sure?"

He squeezed her fingers gently. "I wouldn't have offered if I wasn't."

Her eyes filled suddenly and she shook her head. "I can't believe that! Poor Nancy. She must have felt so horrible when she heard the news."

A single tear escaped her right eye and Beck lifted his finger to stop it. Beneath his palm, her sun-warmed skin was smooth and soft. The sensation made him hungry for more, but he satisfied himself with this meager taste, afraid he'd scare her off if he brought her as close to him as he wanted. She was feeling unsure of herself and no one could understand that better than him. Flashbacks, nightmares? He'd suspected as much, but having her confess to the problems made them more real. They were clear signs of PTSD. Instead of worrying about herself, though, she was concerned for a woman who'd just tried to assault her. Suddenly he wanted to wrap Jennifer up in a blanket and protect her from everything... including herself.

"You handled yourself well back there." He shook his head in amazement. "I think she might have decked you, if I hadn't been there."

"I know," she said. "But I understand, too. If my child had been in that classroom, I would have been just as upset."

He rubbed his thumb gently over her cheek. "But you did everything you could. And the kids did fine because of you. You have nothing to regret, if that's what you're thinking. You handled that situation better than a lot of cops would have, believe me."

Her eyes shimmered. "Are you telling me the truth?"

"Why would I lie?"

She reached up and put her hand on his wrist. Her grip was surprisingly strong. "You told me once you'd lie to save lives. Why not lie to make me feel better?"

"This is different. And you'll just have to trust that I'm telling the truth."

She blinked, her long, curled eyelashes lowering then sweeping up again. Small beads of moisture dotted her upper lip as the dying sun beat down on them. "I don't have a lot of experience with trust."

He tightened his fingers along her jaw. "Then maybe it's time to get some."

JENNIFER SAT in the seat beside Beck as he maneuvered the Toyota out of the parking spot and into the stream of traffic. It was a small car and he filled the front seat, just as he did most of the places he occupied. It was more than his physical size, although that was definitely a factor. He filled it with his presence, his strength, his attitude. Jennifer glanced over at him, her eyes going to his capable hands as they gripped the steering wheel. Jennifer's cheek felt hot from his caress. What would it feel like to have those hands touch her more intimately?

She closed her eyes and leaned her head against the headrest of the car, grateful all at once that Beck had insisted on driving. She felt drained and exhausted. Seeing Maria Worley had been her biggest worry this morning, but now that seemed like a lifetime ago, and petty, as well. The talk with Maria had actually proven to be the best part of Jennifer's day!

Beck had cooled Nancy's anger almost instantly. Thinking back on the situation, Jennifer marveled at the way he'd handled the woman. Firm yet gentle. It was easy to see how he could calm someone even more upset and angry, and all at once, her eyes were opened as they'd never been before. She couldn't help but wonder how things would have ended if Howard had actually talked to Beck instead of using her, then she put the thought aside. What good would it do to dwell on it now?

They arrived at the nursing home a short ten minutes later. Beck pulled the car into the nearest shaded parking spot and killed the engine, the scent of honeysuckle and salty sea air riding the summer breeze into the open windows of the car. As the motor ticked down, Jennifer turned in the seat to look at him.

"Thank you," she said simply.

"You're welcome," he said. "But for what?"

"For doing what you did back there. For taking care of things."

He tipped an imaginary hat. "Just doing my duty, ma'am."

"I'm serious," she said. "I really do appreciate it. I think about the negatives of what you do, the secrets, the danger, the unsettled nature of it all, but if you hadn't been there, I'm not sure how I would have dealt with Nancy."

He reached across the seat and put his hand on her shoulder. In the shaded light of where they sat, his eyes almost glowed, and for a passing second, she had the ridiculous thought that he might be about to kiss her. She stiffened while deep down inside she knew she wanted nothing more.

"Does this mean you'll go out with me?"

"You're relentless, aren't you?"

"I never give up," he agreed. "And now you owe me. I saved you from a pretty dramatic moment. From the viewpoint of a negotiator, I deserve something in return."

He waited, her unspoken answer hanging between them.

"Well?" he said.

He was right, but if she admitted that, she'd admit more, if only to herself. And she wasn't ready for more just yet. "I'll consider the possibility," she said.

He ran the back of one finger over her cheek, then dropped his hand. "I guess right now that's the best I can hope for."

IT WAS PAST six o'clock and the halls of the nursing home were almost empty, the smell of pot roast and mashed potatoes a clue as to where everyone was. Jennifer led Beck to the nurses' station and leaned over the counter to pick up the phone and call a cab. He reached out and stopped her at the very last minute.

"I really would like to meet your mother," he said. "Would it upset her to see a stranger?"

Jennifer hesitated, then put the phone back down. "I

don't think so. If you had on your uniform, that'd be another story."

He tilted his head quizzically and she explained.

When she finished, he nodded, his expression thoughtful. "No offense, but your father must have really been a bastard."

Jennifer smiled grimly. "That just about sums it up. He punished my mother by withholding his affection, but he saved his cruelest taunts for my brother. He pretty much ignored me."

"I want to know more about Danny."

Something tightened inside her. "There's nothing to tell—"

He reached out and put his fingers across her lips. "Don't ever try to lie to a liar," he said quietly. "We always know."

Her breath stopped, but she found herself nodding. There was nothing else she could do with his touch on her mouth and his eyes boring into hers.

"This isn't the time or the place, but I want to know." He took his finger away. "Fair warning."

Concentrating on Beck, Jennifer failed to notice Wanda's arrival. Only after the nurse coughed, ever so delicately, did Jennifer realize she was standing right beside her. She came to with a start.

"W-Wanda! I didn't see you," she stuttered.

"I noticed," she answered dryly. Looking up at Beck, she extended her hand. "I'm Wanda LaFleur…and you're Beck Winters."

"That's right." He took her hand carefully in his and shook it once. Jennifer was surprised. Most men his size squeezed and pumped, but Beck wasn't like most men.

"Are we having an old folks' breakout?" Wanda asked, raising one eyebrow. "Somebody call in the SWAT team over the mashed potatoes again?"

Beck laughed. "Not that I know of." He glanced down at Jennifer and his blue eyes seemed warm all at once. She told herself it was the lighting over the desk. "I brought Jennifer to see her mom. I didn't want her endangering the citizens of Destin."

Wanda put her hands on her hips. "You speedin' again, girl? I thought we talked about that."

Jennifer shook her head. "You wouldn't believe it if I tried to explain. Let's just save it for later."

"Okay." Her black eyes turned serious. "Might be better anyway. Your mama's not having too good a day. In fact," she looked up at Beck, "I'm not really sure this would be the time for a new visitor. She's pretty confused."

Beck nodded. "I understand completely." Again he looked at Jennifer. "Why don't I just wait out here? When you finish, we can decide what to do later."

Feeling Wanda's eyes on her face, Jennifer answered quickly. "No, no. Please don't hang around just for me. I might be a while. Why don't you go ahead and call a cab?"

"I'll wait."

His answer held no room for argument, and Jennifer couldn't help herself; a warm flush of anticipation came over her at the thought of what *later* might bring. "Okay," she answered.

"Good." Without any further warning, he bent down

and brushed her cheek with his lips, then turned and walked away.

Jennifer stood silently in a state of shock. The kiss was totally casual, something you'd expect from a friend or a cousin, but she felt it hit her in three places at once. Her cheek at his touch. Her mind at his actions. Her heart at his sweetness. He really did care.

Under her breath, Wanda spoke beside her. "Whoo-eee… That is one hunk of a man, honey." She glanced sideways at Jennifer and grinned. "What trick are you trying to pull telling me you're not interested? You look like you just got hit by a truck."

"I feel like I did, too."

Wanda took her by the arm and led her down the hallway. "Then go with it, baby. Just go with it."

THINKING OF JENNIFER, Beck headed for the blue plaid sofa in one corner of the waiting room. He probably shouldn't have kissed her like that, but it had seemed like the right thing to do. She'd looked so upset, so overwhelmed by everything that had happened to her, he'd wanted to let her know she didn't have to carry it all on her shoulders. He didn't know if the message got through or not, but he could still smell her perfume and still feel the softness of her cheek beneath his lips. It'd been worth it for that if nothing else.

Crossing a small area rug, he walked to the couch, but he didn't get a chance to sit. The beeper at his belt began to vibrate and sound just as he lowered himself to the cushions. It only took one look at the readout to know he had a problem, and he sprang up immediately. The flashing code, in bright-red numbers, told it all.

Priority One. Priority One. An address followed.

He didn't take the time to try to find Jennifer. He couldn't. A message like that meant every member of the team was needed and needed immediately. He hit the corridor running, the startled nurse's aide looking up as he streaked past the desk. "Tell Jennifer Barclay I had to leave," he yelled, throwing the words over his shoulder and not even looking back. "I'll call her as soon as I can."

Digging into his pocket for his key ring, he ran along the sidewalk. By the time he reached the parking lot, he realized his problem.

He didn't have his keys because he didn't have his truck. The realization didn't stop him; it couldn't. Someone's life was in danger, maybe more than just one "someone's." He sprinted toward the Toyota, clutching Jennifer's key chain, and two seconds later, he was in her car, speeding away from the nursing home.

JENNIFER CLOSED the door behind her as she entered her mother's room. She was exhausted and completely drained, but she was here. It was Wednesday and she was here.

The lights were dim and low, the only sound coming from the television set located on the wall above the bathroom entrance. Her mother was already asleep. When Jennifer and Beck had arrived, she'd been upset and worried over everything that had happened, but now she was even more unnerved. Wanda had explained as they'd walked down the corridor about the bad day Nadine had had.

"I don't know exactly how to tell you this," the nurse had said, "but we lost your mama for a while today. She was nowhere to be found."

Jennifer had stopped so fast, her heels had streaked the polished linoleum floor. "What?"

"It's true," Wanda said, shaking her head and sighing. "I can't believe it, but she was somewhere other than her bedroom or the patio, and we still don't know where. We were gettin' frantic, then here she came, ambling down the hallway tryin' to see what all the fuss was about. I damned near had a heart attack, Jennifer. I don't know how I could have called you and told you that, especially on top of everything else."

Jennifer closed her eyes, the hall swimming for just a minute. When she opened them again, Wanda looked so miserable, Jennifer ended up consoling her. "Oh, Wanda, it's not your fault. You can't watch her every second of the day."

Regret filled her dark eyes. "But I'm supposed to. That's what you pay us for."

"Where do you think she went?"

"I have no idea, but not off the grounds, I'm sure. She couldn't have. She wasn't gone ten minutes."

Jennifer patted Wanda's arm. "Did you ask her where she'd been?"

"Oh, yeah, we asked."

"And?"

"She said she'd been to visit your brother. Said Danny had called and she'd gone to see him."

For the third time that day, Jennifer felt her world shake a little, a small temor but one she couldn't ignore. "Oh, Wanda…"

"I know, honey, I know."

Jennifer shook her head. "What are we going to do?"

"We're not going to do anything, except keep a closer eye on her." Her accent deepened and her voice went soft. "She's getting worse, baby. She's having more days than not when she's losing everything. I haven't wanted to say anything, but you might need to consider moving her to the more restricted wing of the home. They *can* watch her closer over there, you know."

"I don't want to do that." Jennifer looked at her friend in dismay. She didn't bother to list all the reasons why. Money. Time. Effort. She only voiced the most important one. "It'd upset her so. She loves you and she has her routine established with everyone else…."

Wanda interrupted with a shake of her head. "Sweetheart, she didn't have a clue who *I* was this morning and she's never done that before."

Not knowing what to say, Jennifer stared at Wanda with dismay. Nadine always knew Wanda, even when she didn't recognize Jennifer. This *was* troubling.

Wanda gave her a quick hug, then Jennifer had gone inside. Walking to the edge of her mother's bed now, Jennifer looked down and cursed herself for the sudden rush of resentment that overcame her.

She was an awful person and a terrible daughter.

She didn't want to be there. She didn't want to have to face this problem—a mother who didn't know who she was or even where she was—and she didn't want to deal with all the dilemmas that came with it.

She didn't want any of it.

Her nice orderly life was falling apart, and even the solution that popped into her head was an answer that made no sense. How could she want what added the most to her crazy state of mind?

It made no sense, absolutely none, but all that was comforting Jennifer, the *one* thing that made her feel better, was the knowledge that Beck was down the hall waiting for her, his arms a refuge she could take at any time.

CHAPTER TEN

"WHAT HAVE WE GOT?" They were in the War Wagon, Beck struggling into his vest as he made his way to the back where Lena sat.

"A domestic violence with multiple weapons." She glanced in his direction as he spoke, then focused on the fax coming through the machine. "Caught the call from the Panama City Beach guys. Apparently the suspect is a frequent client of theirs. He's been in and out of county for petty stuff, but this is the first time it's been this serious. He's high on something and he's inside, waving a knife in one hand and a gun in the other. We can't tell if the wife is a hostage or what."

Beck peered out the window of the motor home toward the tiny beachfront shack about a hundred yards from where they were parked. In the growing dusk, it was hard to see the details, but he didn't need too much light; he knew the neighborhood. The single street ran perpendicular to the beach, and the houses along its rutted path were mostly frame, all run-down, and completely worthless compared to the land they sat on. Lena had already killed the power to the homes so the stretch of road was empty and quiet, but at the end, he caught a flash of white motion now and again—the phosphorescence of the waves crashing on the sandy beach.

In her usual concise way, Lena gave him more details, outlining the positions of the rest of the team and explaining what had happened. A frantic 911 from the neighbors had brought the beat cops out, but when they'd tried to approach the residence, numerous shots had been fired, inside and outside the house. Nodding his head at the narrative, Beck picked up the phone and dialed the number she had handed him.

No answer. He dialed again, an empty ringing sounding in his ear as Lena spoke.

"Where were you when you caught the call?"

"I was at Seacrest."

"Seacrest? The old folks' home?"

He disconnected the line, then punched the redial almost immediately. "I think the proper term is *retirement facility.*"

She shook her head impatiently. "Whatever. What were you doing there?"

"I was with Jennifer Barclay. We were visiting her mother."

He started to say more, but all of his instincts went on sudden alert as the phone was answered. No one spoke, but he heard a small sound, almost nothing but enough to trigger his attention. "Hello? Hello?" More silence was his only answer. His stomach roiled as he remembered the last time this had happened, when Howard French had refused to speak with him. Beck swallowed to get past the memory. "This is Beck Winters with the Emerald Coast SWAT team. Who am I talking to, please?"

He glanced at Lena. She had raised one eyebrow as if to say "What's the deal?" He shrugged his shoulders and scribbled on a notepad. "No answer."

She nodded her silent acknowledgment. They couldn't risk a conversation being overheard without knowing who had answered the phone. She wrote something on the pad and shoved it toward him. "Any background noise?"

Beck pressed the receiver closer to his ear and closed his eyes, concentrating. There might have been something…he caught just a hint of a breath, the fleeting impression that someone was there, but it was nothing more than that. He could have just as easily imagined it. He opened his eyes and shook his head. He didn't want to lose the open line and had no idea if anyone was even listening, but he began to talk, a rambling introduction with questions interspersed, hoping against hope one would elicit a response from the person on the other end.

"I'm with the Emerald Coast SWAT team," he repeated, "and we're here to help you and help whoever's in there with you. We understand you had a little problem tonight and we don't want anyone getting hurt so we came out to see what's going on. Are you there..?" He rummaged through the notes he'd taken while Lena had explained the situation. "Are you there, Fred?"

No answer. Beck remembered Jennifer as she'd looked just after the hostage incident. He wasn't about to end another one that way this soon. He gripped the phone tighter and stared at the notes, using his standard opening ploy—saying something about the perp's name. People always responded when you talked about their name. Nothing was more personal.

"Fred, I see your last name is Mikeouski. I had a buddy in college named Mikeouski. He was from Long Island. You wouldn't be from there, would you?" He made his voice friendly. "That'd be a hoot, wouldn't it? His first name was T.C. Well, I mean his *name* was Thomas Charleston, but he couldn't stand that so we called him T.C. He's not your cousin or anything, is he?" *Answer me,* he wanted to scream. *Just say something so I know you're in there and you haven't blown your wife to kingdom come.*

The name trick didn't work. Beck stared at the man's house. Near the northwest corner, by one tire of a weary-looking pickup truck, a quick movement grabbed his attention. Beck tensed before he realized what he was seeing, then he spoke quickly. "Hey, Fred. I see your dog in the yard. Damn, he's a great-looking retriever. You a hunter, Fred? Ducks? Deer? What?" Cradling the phone between his shoulder and jaw, he picked up the binoculars on the desk and trained them on the truck. There *was* a gun rack across the back window but it held a fishing rod. "I bet you like to fish better than hunt, huh? You got a boat somewhere? You take the dog out with you? Those retrievers do love the water, don't they?"

He took a deep breath and prayed for an answer. Anything. A grunt would have worked, but nothing came down the telephone line. Not even a buzz. He could tell he was still connected, but that was all. Lena caught his eye and just shook her head. In situations like this, there was nothing they could do, but hang on. Thank God, there weren't any children inside.

Beck closed his eyes, rested his elbows on the desk and started to talk again. "When I was kid I had a dog like that. Boy, did that dog love to hunt. I named him Bojangles, kinda dumb name, maybe, but I was just a kid and I'd heard the song so…"

Two hours later, he was going hoarse and running out of even inane things to say. Lena had written him so many notes they had piled up over the desk like snow and were drifting to the floor. Finally, she handed him this one.

This is dragging on too long. Front window. Right side.

He nodded at the cryptic message and continued to speak. Sometimes the only thing they had left was to shake the guy up. Breaking out a window was one of the simplest options. The unexpected noise and destruction was the diversion that convinced some folks to talk…or walk.

But it didn't this time.

The sound of fracturing glass came over the phone line, but it came by itself. No cursing, no call of surprise. Nothing. Beck looked up at Lena and shook his head when she stepped back into the wagon. Pulling a piece of paper toward him, he scribbled furiously. *Mirrors?*

She pulled her microphone closer and spoke. A few seconds later, Beck watched as a long pole was inserted through the now open window. At the end of the rod was a mirror. Beck continued to talk. He didn't think he was making sense now. No one would after this length of time.

Lena pressed her earphone closer, then her expression changed abruptly and she spoke out loud, her voice disbelieving. "Dammit to hell! Are you sure, Hood? Absolutely sure?"

Beck fell silent, his throat stinging.

A second later, she ripped off her headset and stared wearily at him. Outside, the team started in. They weren't doing an assault, but merely a cautionary entry. Swarming over the porch, they called out, then crashed through the door.

"Tell me…." he said painfully, knowing already.

She looked out the window and didn't speak.

He lowered the phone, but still held on to it. He couldn't hang up. He couldn't break the connection. His fingers refused to make the move. Covering the mouthpiece with his hand, he spoke again, his voice so hoarse it was hard to understand. "Both of them?"

With her back to him, she nodded once.

He cursed loudly, then threw down the receiver. Racing outside, he stumbled in the darkness toward the house, knowing all the time speed no longer mattered.

And it hadn't for some time.

He careened into the living room. Most of the team were near the back door where a man's body was on the floor. Death had already claimed him, rigor mortis stiffening his legs and arms, his face pasty and grey. He'd been dead for hours, probably shot himself right after the beat cops had come. A familiar clutch of dismay swept over Beck, but the groaning burden of failure didn't really hit until his eyes searched further.

He saw the phone first, then he saw her. Sprawled on the floor, the woman looked as if she'd been trying to get away from her dying husband. Beck assessed the situation without even thinking hard. The man had attacked her, then shot himself…only she didn't die—at first. Her hand was wrapped around the phone cord. She was the one who'd answered. Beck's eyes followed the coiled line to the receiver lying near her ear. She'd been listening to him until the end, but she hadn't been able to answer Beck's stupid questions or even call for help.

Her husband had slit her throat.

HAD HE GONE for a walk?

Jennifer came back into the waiting room and when she didn't see Beck right away, she assumed he'd gotten bored. She took a quick tour around the wing that housed her mother, but he was nowhere around so pushing open the double glass doors, she stepped outside. The air was dense and salty, the forerunner of fog. She made her way through it slowly, taking the winding gravel path that circled the home. Five minutes later she was back where she started and still no sign of Beck.

Hesitating in front of the building, Jennifer actually shook her head at the thought that barged into her brain like an unwanted guest. He wouldn't have, she argued with herself. He wouldn't have just left. He would have found her first and told her. Or at the very least, he would have told Pamela. The nurse's aide had been at the station just around the corner from the waiting room the whole time. It wouldn't have taken two minutes to tell her if he'd had an emergency.

Her feet moved without instructions from her brain, but when she found herself in the parking lot, all Jennifer could do was stare blankly at the empty space where her car had been. No, she thought illogically, this can't be. He wouldn't have.

But the facts were before her. No car. No Beck. No "later."

She couldn't bear the onslaught of disappointment that came over her. If she did acknowledge it, then she admitted to herself she was falling for Beck, and she couldn't do that. So instead she got angry. A red flush started at the base of her neck and worked its hot way up her throat to her cheeks. It was still heating her face when she slammed back into the home a few minutes later.

Wanda's startled eyes met Jennifer's over the curved Formica of the nurse's station. "Whoa, girl! What's up with you?"

"He left me," she said between clenched teeth. "Beck took my car and left me."

Wanda frowned, three dark lines dividing her forehead. "Are you sure? I didn't see him leave."

"Well, unless he's invisible as well as invincible, he's gone and so is my car." She put her hands on her hips and shook her head, muttering, "Is Pamela around? Maybe he said something to her…."

"Well, he must have gotten a call. I can't imagine—"

"Are you talking about that man who was with you?" Drawing Jennifer's attention, the aide stepped into the hallway from the linen closet, shutting the door behind her and speaking. "He *did* have to leave. He asked me to tell you, but I've been busy in Mrs. Becker's room. He said he'd call you."

"What happened?"

The young girl shook her head. "I dunno. But he ran out in a big hurry."

Jennifer's earlier disappointment mushroomed. "He got a call."

Wanda came from around the station to stare at Jennifer. Her expression was sympathetic, but pragmatic. "The man's a cop. What do you expect?"

Wanda was right, but Jennifer's regret was so overwhelming she couldn't stand it. She answered unreasonably, knowing her reply sounded foolish. "The least he could have done was find me first."

"Oh, good grief! Come on! What if he'd taken that kind of time before showing up at your school? You woulda been countin' the minutes with that gun at your throat!"

"How long would it take to find me?"

"Too long," Wanda answered. "And you know it." She shook her head, her black hair shining under the lights over the desk. "You're acting like one of your kids! Just give me a minute and I'll drive you home."

She started to say thanks, then Jennifer hesitated. Beck didn't know where she lived, or have her phone number. It was unlisted. How would he return her car? She looked at the aid with a frown. "Did he say he'd come back here or…?"

The girl shook her head. "All he said was he'd call you. That's it."

Facing Wanda again, Jennifer made her up mind. "I think I'll stay here. He doesn't have my number or address. He'll probably come back and get me as soon as he can."

"You sure? Those things take time, you know."

Jennifer looked out the window before answering.

The fog had rolled in. Curling over the tiled floor, it reached for the patio chairs with a wet and heavy hand. "I'll wait," she said, a sudden quiet confidence replacing her earlier disappointment. "He'll come back."

IT WAS WAY past midnight when Beck could finally leave. Fleeing the chaos inside the house, he walked to the dusty yard outside the War Wagon and dialed the nursing home's number. The woman on duty told him Jennifer had left hours ago in a cab. He closed his cell phone with a snap and shut his eyes, rubbing his forehead wearily. His headache was almost blinding and had been since he'd walked inside the house. Crossing swords with Randy hadn't helped, either. The sniper had strutted into the death-filled home and made his usual smart-aleck comments. Beck's fist had been drawn back and ready to strike when Lena had walked in unexpectedly.

Something wet and cold touched Beck's fingertips without any warning. His eyes shot open, and he looked down, into the sorrowful gaze of the golden retriever he'd seen earlier. The dog's tail wagged slowly as their eyes connected, then all at once, the animal dropped his head. With a whine more like a sigh, he slouched to the ground, putting his nose on his paws in a gesture of pure dejection.

Beck felt the same way.

He turned and headed for Jennifer's white Toyota, and twenty minutes later, he pulled up outside her condo, remembering her address from Sarah's information. Locating the proper unit, he saw only darkness. She'd probably gone to bed hours before, even more strongly convinced that she wanted nothing to do with him.

He stepped out of the car, exhaustion dragging his steps, and made his way up to the second floor, pausing just outside the door. Nothing but silence and mist surrounded him, the vapor light above the parking lot giving an eerie yellow glow to the fog-shrouded grounds. He wanted to knock on the door, have her open it and pull him inside, into her warmth and understanding and love, but that was a fantasy, and he knew it. His only course of action was to slip her key through her mailbox slot then leave. He started to bend down to do exactly that when he heard a noise from inside. The back light from the peephole went dark, then a second later, the door flew open.

Jennifer stood before him. She had on a long white T-shirt embroidered with little pink hearts. From somewhere behind her, a lamp shone, throwing the light forward to outline her body beneath the cotton. Beck took what he thought would be a quick look but it lasted a lot longer than he planned. She spoke while his eyes were still on her curves.

"Beck! My God, where have you been? I waited hours at Seacrest for you, but you never came back. I've been so wor—" She broke off at once. Her expression was peeved and her words annoyed, but behind the tension was just what she'd been about to confess to: worry. Her concern, even if she didn't want him to know it, warmed him with a rush of sudden pleasure.

"I had a call," he answered. "I asked the aide—"

"She told me, but—"

"I didn't have the time to find you, Jennifer. I'm sorry, but I had to go and go fast. That's just the way it is."

To cover up her anxiety, she tried to maintain her act, giving her head an impatient toss, her chestnut hair down and full around the curves of her face. It didn't wash with Beck, though. He understood her too well and instead of reacting to her pretense, he found himself responding to the scent of lilacs as it drifted over to where he stood. The fragrance, that sweet, innocent smell, did him in. He grabbed the doorway with his hands in a gesture of absolute weariness and she reached out.

"Are you okay?" she asked softly. Her hands curled around his. "You look like hell."

"That's because I feel like it," he answered. "I know it's late and I know you're furious with me but can we talk?"

She was immediately torn, indecision battling with her obvious sympathy. She wanted to let him in, but she just wasn't sure. Of herself or of him, he couldn't tell.

"I had a really shitty night." He looked directly into her eyes and didn't blink. "I need a drink...and I need to talk. That's all I want."

She hesitated for a minute more, then she stepped aside. When he walked into her living room, she spoke from behind him. "I have some beer. Would that be all right?"

"That would be perfect," he answered. Sitting down heavily on her sofa, he closed his eyes, the dreamy image of the watercolor on the opposite wall mixing with the smell of her perfume. Settling into the cushions, he felt something loosen in his chest.

He was almost asleep when she returned a moment

later. Opening his eyes, he watched as she set a cold amber bottle on the table beside him. He reached out, circling her wrist with his fingers, and their eyes met again. "I'm sorry about tonight."

"I understand," she answered. "I was mad at first, especially after I waited and waited and you didn't come back, but it couldn't be helped, I guess."

"Believe me, I wish like hell I hadn't gone, but I didn't have a choice. And I'm truly sorry I had to strand you like that. I couldn't take the time to do anything else, though."

The dark well of her gaze seemed endless. He wanted to fall into it and disappear.

She nodded at his answer. "Was it bad? What happened, I mean?"

I talked to a dead woman for over an hour. I guess some people might call that bad....

Sensing his hesitation, she spoke. "If you don't want to tell me…"

"I don't," he answered, "but I need to. Holding this one inside would kill me. I can't do it."

Taking one step, she started toward the chair near the sofa, but stopped short when he didn't release her wrist.

"Come over here," he said. "Sit by me."

Without a word, she did as he asked. The cushions moved with her weight when she turned to face him. "Tell me." Her voice was soft and gentle.

"We did everything we could, but it wasn't enough. It was a murder-suicide. A man and his wife." He closed his eyes again and described what had happened, leaving out some of the gorier details.

He rubbed his forehead angrily. "The whole damn thing was so pointless! I talked for two hours and she was already dead—or dying—and I didn't have a clue." He turned and met Jennifer's horrified gaze. "I didn't even know," he said hoarsely. "I didn't know she was there."

Her eyes welled up and she reached out for him, to bring him to her and give him the comfort he needed so badly. He couldn't have resisted had it cost him his very life, and when he fell into her embrace and buried his face in the sweet curve of her neck, it seemed as if they'd done this very thing a thousand times.

Except for the way his body reacted.

He held her a few seconds more, then he raised his head. Their eyes locked, and he knew he had to kiss her. Nothing else could have possibly happened next. It was ordained. He drew her close and covered her lips with his.

HIS LIPS WERE soft and warm, and Jennifer responded without any thought. She didn't have a choice. Her body took command of her senses and even though she knew she was making a very big mistake, she gave in to the order and kissed Beck back. It didn't matter that he'd stranded her. It didn't matter that she hated his job. It didn't matter that she wanted nothing to do with him.

Nothing mattered but kissing him.

Pressing her mouth against his, she wrapped her arms around his neck and tightened her grip. Beneath her fingers, his blond hair was tangled and damp. He tasted like the fog outside: salty from the sea where it had risen. Feeling her reaction, he pulled her roughly toward him, and deepened his kiss with an almost desperate urgency.

His hands spanned her back and through the thin material of her nightgown, his touch was just as hot and compelling as she'd imagined it would be. Her breasts pressed into his black T-shirt, and through it she caught more of his heat. His body felt as if it were burning from some internal flame.

Her brain tried to intrude, tried to get her to stop, but she ignored the command and continued to kiss him, parting her lips and teasing his tongue with hers. Beck murmured into her open mouth, saying her name over and over, then his lips left hers and trailed down her neck. His beard scratched her, but she didn't care, didn't feel anything but the pleasure building deep inside her.

He brought his hand around and cupped her breast, teasing her nipple until the blazing drive inside her grew even stronger. The feeling shocked her. She couldn't call it desire or even lust. This wasn't anything remotely like those two emotions—it was a genuine need that had to be met regardless of the cost to her heart and soul.

He seemed to experience the same thing at the very same time. Beneath her hands, she felt his body tense, and under her fingers, his muscles grew tight, everything about him turning taut and hard. For a heartbeat longer, he stayed as he was, his mouth on her skin, his hand against her breast, then he tore his lips from her neck and raised his eyes to hers. His gaze was tortured and full of so much pain, she could barely stand to look into the icy blue depths.

"We've got to stop," he said hoarsely. "If we don't, there's no going back."

CHAPTER ELEVEN

HER LIPS WERE FULL and red in the soft light of the lamp, her dark gaze seductive.

"If I carry you into that bedroom behind me and we start to make love, a line gets crossed," he said. "I'm not sure you're ready for that."

"You're not sure *I'm* ready?"

"That's what I said."

"What about you?" she shot back. "Are you ready?"

He searched her eyes. They'd been filled with heat. Now suddenly they were chilly again. He spoke carefully. "You're a beautiful woman, Jennifer. And I want to make love to you."

She blushed, her skin glowing with an apricot tinge. "But…"

"There are no buts," he said. "I want to make love to you, period. When that happens, I don't want you waking up the next morning asking yourself what kind of mistake you've made. And I think you'd do that now. You're not the kind of woman who falls into bed with a guy and doesn't look back."

"How do you know that?"

He didn't answer. All he did was stare at her.

Disentangling herself from his embrace, she stood

slowly and walked to the sliding glass door that made up the back wall of her living room. Easing it open, she allowed the night air in, the dampness bringing a chill. The silence built, and Beck didn't know how to break it. Finally, she did it for him.

"You're right." Pivoting, she faced him once more, her arms crossed over her chest, her expression tight. "I *would* feel that way in the morning so maybe you should leave."

He walked to her, and she looked up at him, tilting her neck to frown into his eyes. He couldn't stop himself from reaching out and taking her face between his hands. "When you reach the point where you don't feel that way anymore, I want to know."

"When?" She arched one eyebrow. "Don't you mean *if?*"

He didn't answer right away. Instead, he leaned down and kissed her again, his mouth pressing against hers until she swayed slightly under the onslaught. He'd never tasted a woman so enticing, one who made him want her so much that it hurt. To pull back was torture, but he did, and she blinked as they separated once more.

"I mean when," he answered in a rasping voice. "Otherwise I'd be doomed."

He walked out of her condo and didn't look back. He couldn't. One more glimpse of her half-lidded eyes or swollen mouth and he'd return to pull her into his arms, his pretty little speech nothing but words. He'd been a fool to even go inside in the first place, but he'd felt so completely wiped out, he'd thought it would help him— to see her, to talk to her, to smell her perfume. Instead, those very things had made him realize how much he wanted her. Walking rapidly down the street, he hailed the first cab he saw, and ten minutes later Beck climbed out in front of the station.

When Lena came in at seven the next morning, he was still there. She stared at him in shock, her eyes going over his unshaven face and wrinkled clothes. "Beck! What on earth are you doing here? Didn't you go home last night?"

"No." He concentrated on the paperwork in front of him. His vision was fuzzy, and his mouth tasted like something from the sewer, probably because of the motor oil-like coffee he'd been swigging all night. Taking another sip from the mug in front of him, he scribbled something on the form he was filling out. "I didn't go home last night. I went to Jennifer's. And then I came here. What's your problem with that?"

She blinked at his brusqueness but her gaze went steely, and she sat down in the chair beside his desk, dropping her briefcase on the floor by her feet. "I don't have a problem with you seeing Jennifer Barclay. I might wonder how it affects your ability to deal with the incident, but you seem to have moved on so I guess it's not an issue. My problem with you is your inability to judge your own readiness. What if the phone rang right now and we caught a call? Could you go out and be effective? I don't think so."

"I'd be as effective right now as I was last night," he answered bitterly. "What difference would it make?"

She stared at him for a minute, then pursed her lips. "That's it," she said. "You're going on vacation. Right now."

"I can't—"

"Don't even try," she said, interrupting him. "There's nothing you can say that will change my mind. I want you out of here. And that's an order."

Beck's hands went into fists. "You don't understand—"

"Oh, really? What part don't I understand? The part where you're exhausted and don't even know it? Or the part where you've lost all patience with Randy and have no tolerance around him? Maybe you mean the part where you're feeling sorry for yourself because of last night? Which one is it, Beck? Tell me."

He stared at her through bleary eyes.

She rose and grabbed her briefcase. "Get out, Beck. And I don't mean out of the station. I want you to leave town. For at least a week. You need a change of scenery."

"No." He stood as well. Towering over her, he shook his head stubbornly. "I'm not leaving town."

They glared at each other, a standoff in the making.

"And your reason is…?" she demanded.

His brain felt as unclear as his eyesight; he was exhausted and dispirited, but he knew one thing. He didn't want to abandon Jennifer. When she'd told him about her meeting with Maria, he'd felt a surge of protectiveness that surprised him. Now, with the memory of the kiss they'd shared still burning in his mind and the way she'd defended him to Nancy Thomas still ringing in his ears, he felt an even stronger bond. He didn't want to leave town, or her, for an hour, much less a week.

"Why isn't important," he answered. He crossed his

arms. "I'll go home, but I'm staying here in Destin. And not for a week, either. Three days. That's it."

Lena stared at him with incredulous eyes. "This isn't a standoff, Beck! You don't have a choice so don't try that negotiating shit with me!"

He started to argue, to offer an alternative plan, then he thought about it. Lena *was* his boss; whatever she said, he needed to do. But he couldn't. It was just that simple.

He made his expression contrite and held up his hands in a sign of defeat. "You're absolutely right, Lena. I'm sorry. I'll do it. I'll get my crap and go to the house right now and pack. I'll take off in the morning...." Turning to his desk, he began to shuffle the papers strewn across its scarred wooden surface.

She watched him go through the motions, then after a minute, she put her hand on his arm, as he'd known she would. He raised his face wearing what he hoped was an innocent expression.

"Beck, look, just get out of the station, okay? If you don't want to take a trip, I understand. But you need a break. We all do after last night, but you most of all. You're losing your perspective."

He'd gotten what he wanted, but he didn't like her tone. "What do you mean?"

"That fight with Randy—it was pointless. I know there's a problem with him, he's wild and uncontrollable. You've made me aware of it, but decking him wouldn't have helped, and you would know that if you had some balance in your life."

He clenched his jaw. "The guy's not a team player, Lena. What does he have to do before you see that?"

"We're discussing *your* problems here, Beck. Not Randy's." She frowned at him with an unflinching expression. "You got me to do exactly what you planned. Go home. But don't come back for a week."

THE BEACH WAS lonely and deserted. Snowy white sand stretched for miles in either direction and as far as Jennifer could see, the expanse was empty. Everyone had departed an hour ago leaving her behind with her thoughts, but, earlier, she and three parents had supervised more than a dozen kids. They'd spent the whole day, running up and down the water's edge, picking up trash and looking for shells. The annual cleanup was really an excuse to give the students some fun time; Destin kept its beaches pristine. There was rarely any kind of debris to be seen, other than an occasional drink can or the scattered flotsam dumped from a ship cruising near shore.

That was one of the reasons Jennifer loved the area. Always clean, always uncluttered, the beaches and clear green water offered the exact parallel to what she sought in her life. Until now.

Her feet sinking into the clingy sand, she stared at the horizon and wondered what was happening to her. Beck's kiss had turned her upside down and inside out. She'd had her share of lovers, some better than others, but she'd never been kissed like that before. His mouth had molded to hers as if they'd been made for each other, the fit so perfect and right, she'd been astonished. That wasn't what had stolen her breath and stopped her heart, however. No, what had done that was him pulling back when she hadn't been able to do so herself.

Had he known? Could he tell? His words rang in her mind. *When you reach the point where you don't feel that way anymore, I want to know.*

Shading her eyes with her hand, she looked into the brilliant sunset that hovered over the water, the streaks of purple, gold and red etching their way into her mind as sharply as the emotions that had attacked her when he'd spoken. Disappointment. Frustration. Acceptance.

He was right, of course. If they'd made love, she *would* have chastised herself later. They'd only known each other three weeks! She *didn't* sleep with strangers. It was not only dangerous, it just didn't feel right. She wanted love and a family, a white picket fence and a secure little life. All the things she'd not had as a child…and all the things Beck couldn't give her, either.

An unexpected memory rose to the forefront of her thoughts. Her father's birthday was coming up and he'd called the night before. He'd been out for more than a month and when the phone rang late that night, her mother had gone rigid in her chair. She'd looked at Jennifer with alarm and told her to answer it. Her own heart kicking up a notch, Jennifer had barely been able to hear him, the line scratchy and filled with echoes. She'd handed the receiver to her mother, and she'd begun to speak to him, her face wreathed in a smile Jennifer simply didn't understand. After she'd hung up, she'd said, "Your daddy's coming home tomorrow. We'll bake him a chocolate cake and decorate it to surprise him."

The next morning, they'd driven to the PX and bought the special kind of bitter chocolate he liked, then spent the rest of the day on the elaborate confection. It'd been hot and sticky, Jennifer remembered, the windows of their small on-base bungalow open wide to catch what little cool air they could, the Gulf Coast humidity making their clothes cling and their hair curl.

Then they'd waited. And waited. And waited some more. A week later, her mother had thrown the cake in the trash can, untouched.

Four days after that, he'd called and said "something had happened." Jennifer never forgot the look on her mother's face. A curtain of disappointment and hurt came over her that didn't leave for a long time, even after he returned.

Wasn't something like that ahead for any woman who fell in love with Beck? He wasn't her father, of course, yet Beck's life was worlds away from what she really wanted. Where was the cottage, the kids, the station wagon?

But his lips… They'd felt so good! And his hands… She closed her eyes briefly and considered what they could do to her. After a quick, forbidden image, she put the idea aside. She couldn't even begin to imagine what making love with him would feel like.

She shook herself mentally, her feet taking her farther down the beach, the clear, warm water lapping at her toes. She'd just felt sorry for him, that's all. He'd had an unbelievably bad night and she'd let her sympathy get the better of her. The agonized look in his eyes, the guilt he'd taken on—anyone would have responded as she did. She'd only wanted to comfort him and she'd done it the best way she knew how.

"Who are you trying to kid?" she said out loud to a seagull strutting nearby. "Comfort him? What a crock!"

The bird bobbed his head up and down, his white-and-grey feathers ruffling in the evening breeze as he let out a loud squawk. He agreed with her, obviously. She was a fool and an idiot; a fool for thinking more about the kiss and an idiot for hoping her life would stay unchanged should she get involved with Beck.

She watched the sun ease closer to the shoreline, the last crimson rays tinting the surf with gold, then she made a wide arc in the sand, heading back to where she'd started. She'd grab a pizza, go home and watch a movie. That's what she usually did on Thursday night, and that's what she'd do tonight. She had to put Beck and his kiss behind her. They had no future together, and it was time she quit acting silly and accepted that. The thought calmed her and as she walked down the hard-packed beach, she knew she was making the right decision. She *had* to get her life on track. That was the only thing she could depend on.

She reached the wooden stairs linking the shore to the parking lot a few minutes later. In the evening breeze, the tall grasses beneath the open steps whispered and swayed among the dunes. She breathed deeply of their calm, soothing scent, then she picked up the tennis shoes she'd left by the bottom stair and grabbed the handrail. She felt better now that her decision was made.

Then she started up the stairs. Beck met her halfway down.

JENNIFER'S FACE was shadowed as she stared up at him, but he could tell she was surprised to see him by the way she spoke. "Beck! What are you doing here?"

He stopped as he reached the stair where she stood. "I'm not stalking you, I promise. I knew about the cleanup and hoped you'd still be here." He took a deep breath and met her puzzled stare. "I came to apologize, Jennifer. I've been told I'm losing my perspective and after I thought about it a bit, I decided that might be right. So I'm sorry I showed up at your house at midnight and I'm sorry for everything else. Can you forgive me?"

"There's nothing to forgive. I should have understood the situation better, anyway." She smiled, but then her expression faded and filled with concern. "What's wrong, Beck? You look as if you just lost your best friend."

He lifted his head and stared out the water. He couldn't remember the last time he'd been to the beach and the gentle call of the surf lured him closer. "Come walk with me, and I'll tell you."

She thought about it for a moment, then she answered quickly, as if she were afraid she might try to change her own mind. "All right."

Beck took her hand in his and they started down the sand. Ten full minutes passed before he began to speak. Anyone else would have wanted to break the quiet, but not Jennifer, he noticed. She was comfortable with silence.

"Lena kicked me out," he said. "She told me to take a week off and not come back to the station for a while."

Jennifer's eyebrows lifted. "Oh, my gosh! Why?"

"She thinks I need a vacation."

"Do you?"

There was barely enough light to see her eyes now, but he could hear the compassion in her voice. "Yeah," he answered, "I think I do, but I don't want to."

"You don't want to go or you don't want to need one?"

"Both," he said slowly. "I can't stand the idea of 'needing' time off—"

"But, Beck, everyone requires a break now and then. And with your work…"

He nodded. "I know, I know. And I've actually made guys on my team do the same thing, but it didn't feel right when Lena told me I had to. But besides that, I don't want to leave town."

"Why not?"

He stopped and turned to meet her eyes. They were still holding hands, and as he looked at her, he covered her fingers with all of his. "I don't want to leave you."

"I—I don't understand…." The words were spoken, but her gaze, still on his, said something entirely different.

She wasn't ready to acknowledge their growing closeness.

"I'm not sure I do, either," he answered, going along with her. "But it's the way I feel."

The waves rushed along the shore beside them, the growing darkness surrounding them. She said nothing.

"Look, Jennifer, I've gone through some of the same things you're experiencing—the nightmares, the flash-backs, the anger—and it's not good stuff, especially if you're alone. I want to be here for you."

"You can't stop them—"

"I know." He tightened his grip and gently squeezed her hand. "But I want to be here in case you need me. It's just how I feel so don't ask me to change my mind."

"And if you're wrong?"

"It wouldn't be the first time. I'd live."

She didn't answer. She simply stared at him, and a moment later, they started walking again, the white, powdery sand slipping beneath their feet. They seemed to cross an invisible bridge. Ten yards down the beach, he spoke again. "Tell me about your brother."

"I don't think—"

"Just tell me," he said, looking off toward the horizon. "I want to hear the story."

They walked a few more yards, the sandpipers scurrying ahead of them, skipping over the waves and pecking at the sand in search of food.

"I was ten when he died," she said slowly. "I saw it happen."

"Damn. That must have been tough."

She nodded. "Seeing someone die is not something you forget…but I guess you know that."

"It's never easy, but it's different if you love the person."

She stayed silent for a few seconds, then began to speak again. "We were living at Hulbert Field, in Fort Walton, and my father had just returned from a four-month mission. We had no idea where he'd been, as always. While he'd been gone, though, my brother turned sixteen, and he'd been making some of the decisions around the house…stuff my mom would ask him about." She shook her head. "None of the problems were earth-shattering. I think she mainly asked his help to boost his self-confidence."

"Did it work?"

"Oh, yes. He seemed really happy there for a while. Then Dad came home."

"What happened?"

She kicked at the surf as a wave came close. Her toe-nails were painted pink. "Dad did his usual thing. Started taunting him, teasing him, calling him names. Said Danny wasn't a real man and he was kidding himself if he thought he was." Looking out over the water, her gaze didn't see the sunset, he was sure.

"He took us to the training field one afternoon. You know, where they do the running and the tower climbing...all the stuff the new recruits have to go through. I could scamper through it like a monkey. I loved sports and did well at almost all of them. Danny was just the opposite. He was artistic. He didn't have a shred of athletic ability, but he loved to draw and paint. He did fantastic watercolors. I have one hanging on the wall opposite my couch."

Beck nodded. "I saw it."

She smiled sadly. "He wasn't yet fifteen when he painted that. He was so very talented...but it ended that day. Dad teased him unmercifully." She deepened her voice. "'You think you're a man? Shit, boy, you don't even know the meaning of the word. Your sister can climb that pole a hundred times faster and she's just a ten-year-old girl! Don't even try 'cause you won't make it.'

"Danny took the bait, of course. I knew I should try to stop him, but I was afraid of Dad, too, and Danny was determined to make Dad shut up once and for all." Her voice wavered just a bit. "It was hotter than hell and he was wearing an old Rolling Stones T-shirt. He'd sweated completely through it. He looked over at me, then walked to the pole and started to climb."

She took a deep breath, held it then let it out slowly.

"He did pretty good at first. He made it past halfway, almost to the top. Then he looked down."

Her tone became matter-of-fact. "He fell fifteen feet and broke his neck. He landed right beside me."

Beck felt himself flinch inwardly. The pain she was hiding behind her attitude was just as fresh and raw as it had been back then. "God, Jennifer…"

She acknowledged his sympathy with a nod. "It was terrible. My mother was completely wiped out. I think she started down the path to where she is right now because of it. She has more than just Alzheimer's. It's complicated so I generally don't explain everything."

"And you?"

"I blamed my father." She glanced up. "And I still do. Danny would never have died if it hadn't been for him."

They walked farther down the beach, the salt spray stinging their faces, the wind picking up. No wonder she wanted her life to be calm and peaceful. She linked everything bad that had happened to her to her father and his job. There was more to it than that, though. She blamed herself just as much.

Guilt. It was a powerful emotion and Beck understood that fact intimately. It motivated him, too.

She spoke after a while. "I've told you all my secrets. Now it's your turn. Tell me about your ex-wife."

The question surprised him, and he felt a spurt of hope because she cared enough to ask. He told himself he was acting stupid, but the feeling remained.

"It was not a match made in heaven," he answered after a few steps. "Dixie had her share of quirks and I had mine. They weren't the same and didn't quite mesh."

"But you loved her once?"

"Of course," he answered. "Desperately. Then I figured out why and it scared the hell out of me."

She looked up and raised an eyebrow, the unvoiced question obvious.

"I rescued her," he said. "She was a hooker, working Front Street, and I felt sorry for her. I married her to get her out of the life, then it went to hell pretty fast after that. We had nothing in common."

They'd covered a few more yards as he'd spoken, but Jennifer stopped as he finished speaking. She didn't appear shocked by his revelation about Dixie, but she didn't look happy, either.

"Is that what's going on here?" Her face glowed in the aftermath of the last ray of sun. Beside them, the surf picked up its pace, the foamy waves coming in a little faster. "Are you rescuing me? Because if you are, we'd better quit this right now. I don't need someone to take care of me."

She was so beautiful, he felt his gut tighten. "Are you sure?"

Her eyes flared. "Of course, I'm sure. I've been on my—"

"On your own for years, I know. And so have I," he answered. "But I'd still like someone to meet me at the door and kiss me hello." He paused and held back the urge to gather her into his arms. "We all need to be rescued one way or the other, Jennifer. That's just part of life."

BY THE TIME they made their way back to their parked cars, Jennifer didn't know what to think. Her heart was in more turmoil than it had been a few days before. Something about Beck was drawing her closer and closer, and it scared her so much, she didn't know what to do. She was fighting the attraction, but it was a losing battle, and she knew it.

They stopped beside the cars. Jennifer's back was to the Toyota's door and Beck stood before her, his arms on either side of her shoulders, trapping her as she leaned against the automobile. They were surrounded by the isolation, the old beach road empty this late in the day. Beyond the dunes, the waves had begun to rise with the late tide, their noisy arrival filling the empty silence.

She knew he was going to kiss her again. She could tell by the way he was looking at her. His eyes were hungry, and with a start, she realized her own probably held the same kind of need. She put her hands on his chest and started to stop him, but she was too late, and he told her so.

"It's pointless," he said. "Don't even try to tell me it's not going to happen."

She shook her head. "Beck—"

He lowered his head, talking to her as he did so, his breath warm and tantalizing. "I'm going to kiss you, Jennifer. And you're going to kiss me back."

He pressed his mouth against hers and she gave in to the sensation of the kiss, of the touch, of the smell. She wanted him so badly, she couldn't even fight it. What she had told him was certainly true; she didn't need rescuing, but right now, she definitely needed this kiss. Her mouth opened to his and he slid his tongue inside, gently insistent, his hands tightening on her back.

With the empty sky overhead and the velvet night enveloping them, Jennifer felt her world tilt and slide. There was nothing to hang on to except Beck, and she clutched his shirt, his muscular back hard and tight beneath her fingers. The heat of his body traveled the full length of hers, the obvious strength of his desire making itself known. He groaned and whispered her name.

The kiss went on until Jennifer pulled back, her heart thumping so hard against her ribs it was almost as loud as the roar of the surf behind them. "I—I don't think this would please the school board," she said breathlessly. "I can see the headlines now. Schoolteacher Caught Making Out With Cop At Local Beach. Betty already thinks I'm a nutcase. This would seal the deal for sure."

"Do you really care what she thinks?"

His eyes were bright, even in the darkness.

Jennifer met their stark expression and slowly shook her head. "No…I don't actually think I do now that you ask."

"Then kiss me again." His voice was a low rumble and where it touched her skin, it lingered. "Make me think you really mean that."

Nodding slowly, she fell into his gaze, then she did what he wanted. She moved closer and tangled her hands behind his neck. A second later, she kissed him again.

CHAPTER TWELVE

JENNIFER DIDN'T KNOW how it happened, but Beck drove off smiling. Somehow, he'd managed to get her to agree to dinner the following Saturday. She told herself over and over that it was just a meal, nothing more, but by Wednesday, she was a nervous wreck. That evening, she visited the nursing home, as usual, and had a long conversation with her mother. Actually, Nadine sat by blankly while Jennifer talked, only it didn't seem to help.

Her students added to the confusion, too. They were absolutely wild as the school year drew to a close. On Thursday, the last day of classes, everything was chaos. Jennifer spent most of the day having fun with the kids. The nightmare they'd been through seemed far behind them until Juan approached Jennifer late that afternoon. He was hiding something behind his back but as he drew close he brought his hands around with a shy look and held out a carefully wrapped package to her.

"It's from my *mamá*." His voice was so low she could barely hear it.

"Oh, Juan!" A lot of the children brought her presents at the end of the year, but this one represented a real sacrifice. The family had so little. "This truly wasn't necessary."

"Yes, it is." His expression reflected his seriousness. "Open it and I will explain."

She did as he directed, slowly undoing the ribbon and peeling back the tissue paper both of which had been folded precisely. The small white box was heavy.

Nestled inside on a bed of cotton a silver cross winked up at her. Six inches long and maybe three inches across, its gleaming surface was decorated with small symbols, also made of silver. Jennifer didn't know what they meant, but she recognized the value of the piece immediately. What had the Canaleses done without to buy her this? Her eyes filled with tears.

"Oh my, Juan! This is so beautiful!" She reached out without thinking and wrapped her arms around the little boy.

He responded by putting his own around her neck then dropped them quickly, clearly embarrassed. "I-it's a *milagro,*" he stammered to cover up his chagrin.

Jennifer knew enough Spanish to recognize the word. "A miracle?"

He nodded. "My family knows a miracle took place the day Mr. French came into our classroom. You covered me up after the shooting began. You saved my life. My *mamá* wanted to give you this. The symbols on the cross represent different parts of your body. It will keep you safe and healthy, too."

A lump came into Jennifer's throat. "I don't know what to say, Juan. You're the one who was brave that day, not me."

"No, no. I wasn't brave." He shook his head. "I was scared."

Their eyes met over the shining silver. "So was I," she said. "So was I."

Jennifer felt her vision blur again then she reached out once more and hugged him tightly. A second later, he ran off and joined the other children.

At 7:00 p.m. Saturday, she was standing nervously on her balcony, trying to calm herself with a glass of white wine. The minute she saw Beck's truck pull into the parking lot, she grabbed her purse and shawl and ran out the front door, throwing the lock behind her. If he came up those stairs and they started kissing, she was afraid they wouldn't even make it to dinner and that wasn't what she wanted to happen. Or so she told herself.

They met on the sidewalk downstairs. Beck's slow perusal of her sleeveless knit sheath made her wish she'd picked something less attractive. His eyes burned through the fabric and touched her body so intimately it felt as though she'd left the dress off completely.

"Very nice," he said slowly. "You look good in black...but then I haven't seen you look bad in anything yet."

Heat suffused her body and made its way to her face. His compliment was nice, but in reality the praise should have been going in the opposite direction. With his navy herringbone slacks and a collarless white shirt, he looked so downright sexy, she was twice as glad she'd met him downstairs. His blond hair was slicked back, but one strand fell down over his forehead. The almost white shade of the curl made his tan seem even darker, but as always, his eyes were what captured her attention. Their intensity pulled her gaze like a flame she couldn't avoid, even though she knew it'd burn her.

He led her down to his truck and helped her climb inside. She was in such a fog she didn't even know what their small talk covered, but twenty minutes later, they pulled up in front of the Marina Café. Following the tall redhead who led them through the elegant restaurant, Jennifer felt beautiful and alluring and desirable and she knew exactly why. It was because of Beck. Every woman in the restaurant stopped and stared at him. His presence and aura of sexuality made it impossible for them to do anything else.

They took a table near the back, beside a bank of windows that looked out over the harbor. The slips were lined up outside the glass, just off the deck, so close Jennifer felt she could reach out and touch them. Every spot held a boat, some small, some big, but all impressive, their paint gleaming in the late-evening sun, the water lapping at their sleek white hulls. Tall, weathered pilings divided the openings, and on top of almost every pole sat a huge, grey pelican.

As soon as they were settled, the waiter appeared and took their drink orders. Beck looked over at her and smiled. "Thank you for coming with me tonight. I guess my powers of persuasion haven't completely failed me."

"I don't think they'd ever do that." She played nervously with the napkin beside her plate. "Your arguments are hard to resist."

He reached across the table and took her hand in his, stilling her fingers. "I'm glad to hear that. But not everyone agrees, you know."

"You mean the criminals you arrest after they give up?"

"Yeah. They usually aren't too thrilled with the situation. Sometimes they blame me." He shrugged. "That's the way it goes, though. As long as they don't come out shooting, I don't mind."

Her throat started to tighten, but she forced herself to relax. "Does that happen often?"

"Me getting shot at?"

She nodded tersely.

"Actually, no. We've caught some pretty bad situations lately, but a vast majority of the time, SWAT calls are answered and resolved without any shots exchanged. You just don't hear about it. The TV cameras show the bloody, disastrous ones instead. Ratings, I guess."

Jennifer shivered lightly. "I don't understand. Why would someone want to watch stuff like that?"

"Because they've never experienced it," he answered in a matter-of-fact way. "They think of it as entertainment. They don't appreciate that they're seeing real people get hurt. To them, it's just happening on the screen and nowhere else."

She met his gaze over the flickering candle that sat on the table. "But it *is* real. Howard French was a person who lived and died. *I'm* real. And my, God, the children, they're real."

"You're preaching to the choir." His jaw went tight, and she could hear the emotion behind his words. "I know all that."

She forced herself to pull back and relax. They were here for dinner, nothing more. They didn't have to solve the problems of the world. Beck seemed to think the same thing at the same time, and when the waiter brought their drinks then left, he raised his glass to hers and tapped the rim. "To a nice dinner and good friends," he said with a smile. *"Salut."*

The crystal rims rang as she brought her drink to his. They drank in silence then watched an immaculate yacht glide through the harbor waters.

"I wouldn't mind having a boat like that some day," Beck said thoughtfully. "Stand at the wheel, sail around the world, forget about everything…"

She looked across the white tablecloth in surprise. This was a side of him she'd never seen before. Where was the driven, focused cop? "You'd quit the force?"

He waited a second before answering. "If you'd asked me that five years ago, I would have said no way. Now, I'm not so sure."

Intrigued, she leaned closer, resting her chin in the cup of her hand. "Why is that? What made you change your mind?"

"Well, at first, you're in love with the idea of being a cop. You have to be, otherwise, you wouldn't make it. Getting into a police academy isn't easy—only about two out of every one hundred applicants make it. For a SWAT team, it's tougher." His gaze went down to his drink. "After you're accepted and actually going through the training, all you can do is worry about finishing it. You only have time for studying and pleasing the FTO—the field training officer. If you're lucky enough to pass, then the good part comes."

"And that is?"

"The job. It's great. You try to improve all the time, you think you're helping folks, you bend over backward to do things by the book and live right. Every day's a challenge. Nothing matters but the job." He took a sip of his drink and met her look. "That's when I got married, and it was the worst possible time."

"The worst time? But I'd think—"

"I know, I know. That's what I thought, too. That it'd be the best, but I was gone all hours of the night and day, and Dixie hated it. We fought over my time away and then we didn't even fight. She just left. After that, things shifted for me."

"What do you mean?"

"I started wondering if I was doing the right thing. That's when I wanted to quit but went into SWAT, instead. I enjoyed it a lot until I saw how wrong it could go, how totally screwed up the runs could get, even more so than on the regular squad." He shook his head. "The potential for disaster is always greater with a specialized team. Bad things happen. Really bad things. That's why the members are so important."

Something in his voice clued her in, and the hair rose on the back of her neck. She tensed. "Like people getting killed?"

"Yes," he said evenly. "Like people getting killed."

She wanted to press him. Was he thinking of Howard or the time he'd mentioned before when he'd gone into therapy with Maria? Jennifer started to ask, but at that very second, the waiter reappeared. "May I tell you about our specials this evening?"

After the man left, the moment was gone. Beck

seemed to sense what she was about to ask, and he took the conversation in a different direction. She thought of returning to the issue, but what was the point? She told herself it didn't matter, and the rest of the meal, they chatted about inconsequential things. By the time dessert was served, Jennifer found herself relaxing once more. Beck was an easy person to talk to, entertaining and complex. Unlike a lot of men she'd gone out with, he didn't talk just about himself. They discussed the state of the world, religion and money. It was remarkable how much they agreed on.

The arrival of a large party, noisy and bent on celebrating, brought their conversation to a temporary halt. She and Beck watched as a dozen or so people circled around a nearby table. They'd brought balloons and flowers and everything else they needed to commemorate the birthday of their matriarch. The obviously pleased gray-haired woman walked slowly down the aisle toward them, and Jennifer felt a flash of sorrow. She would have liked to do that sort of thing for her own mother, but the noise and people and confusion would never have worked for Nadine. Instead of being happy, she would have been scared.

One of the younger members of the party, undoubtedly a grandchild, ran up to the older woman and pulled out her chair. Dark-haired with flashing eyes and a quick smile, the little boy was precious, dressed to the nines in a suit and so delighted to be helping his grandmother that he could hardly stand still. His exuberance and shining black hair immediately brought Juan to her mind. Jennifer smiled then caught Beck's eye, the thought flashing into her head that he'd make a terrific father.

And that's when it happened.

The child yanked on the red balloon they'd tied to the grandmother's chair. The bright sphere dipped, then unexpectedly popped.

Jennifer's vision tunneled without any warning. The harbor, the restaurant, even Beck's face grew small then disappeared. She knew what was going on, but there was nothing she could do to stop it. The progression was inevitable. Fighting a swamping wave of dizziness, she tried anyway and pushed back from the table, rising unsteadily to her feet.

The movement only made things worse.

Gripping the edge of the table, Jennifer swayed, and everything else—all the rest of her senses—started to fade. The only remaining sensation she had was a flash of heat that rolled over her, starting at the top of her head and streaking its way to her feet. It felt as if a flame was rippling down her. She broke into a sweat, but strangely she shivered.

A moment later, Beck's blue gaze, full of alarm and shock, came into focus then disappeared for good. The next thing she saw was Howard's terrified face, then a mist of red. The foglike cloud spread into a fine rain and hit her, the drops staining her dress and face with crimson. She tried to brush it off, but the damning evidence coated her hands and refused to leave.

She stared at her fingertips, then moaned and crumpled to the floor.

THE WHOLE THING took only a second. Beck understood the look on Jennifer's face even before she knew what was occurring, but he was still too late. Throwing his chair behind him, he jumped up and ran to her side of the table where he knelt down beside her.

She was out cold. He swept her into his arms, then strode quickly to the rear of the restaurant with her limp and almost weightless body in his embrace. A private dining room spanned the whole back area. They disappeared into the empty area so fast he was sure only the waiter actually saw what happened. He took one look, then ran toward the front of the restaurant.

The redhead who'd led Beck and Jennifer to their table earlier in the evening appeared a few moments after that. There was concern in her voice. "Is she all right? Can I do anything?"

"She'll be fine," Beck said. "Bring me a wet towel and some ice. Some brandy, too."

The woman hurried away and Beck gently placed Jennifer on the carpeted floor, pulling a cushion from a nearby chair to put under her neck. Her face was ghostly, her lipsticked mouth a slash of dark pink against the ivory skin. Beneath the thin lids of her eyes, he could see movement, rapid and anxious. Her breathing was shallow as well, her chest rising and falling far too swiftly. She moaned and turned her head against the damask seat cushion.

"It's okay," he whispered. "It's okay, Jennifer."

The hostess appeared a moment later and handed Beck what he'd needed. With quick, efficient movements, he bathed Jennifer's face, then wrapped the towel around some of the ice and put it behind her neck.

"Do you want me to call an ambulance?" the woman asked.

"No, no." Beck didn't look up. "That's not necessary. She's okay, just give us a bit of time here."

"Of course, take all you need. And please call us if we can do anything else."

He heard her move away and then they were alone again.

"Jennifer? Jennifer, can you hear me?" He took another ice cube from the bowl and eased it over Jennifer's forehead.

She groaned and her eyelids fluttered.

"C'mon now. Wake up. It's time to come back."

Slowly she opened her eyes. Her gaze was still unfocused and vague, but as he watched, she became more aware and remembrance filled her expression. As if yanked by a string, she sat up abruptly, her eyes wild and frightened as she reached out for him, her chest heaving with alarm. "Beck!"

He put his arms around her. "It's okay, honey. It's okay." Rubbing her back with wide circles, he tried to calm her trembling. "Slow down. Breathe. You're all right."

She continued to shake in his embrace, then all at once she started to sway again, even though she was sitting. He pulled back and lowered her head to her knees, his hand on the back of her neck. "Breathe in," he commanded. "Breathe!"

In a moment, he felt her spine expand. "Let it out slowly." She followed his orders. "Once more," he said. After three more deep breaths, she lifted her head and stared at him. Her skin still looked clammy, but two spots of color now dotted her cheeks.

"My God…" She shook her head slowly. "Wh-what happened?"

"A balloon popped. Do you remember?"

"No." She spoke slowly, a dazed look on her face as she brought her hand to her hair and pushed it back off her forehead. "I don't. I remember we were eating and talking and then…"

"The family came in," he prompted.

She stared at him, her eyes narrowing in concentration. "A family?"

He nodded. "Lots of people with an older woman. A little boy ran up…"

Her hand went to her throat. "Oh, my God, I remember now. He reminded me of Juan, and then the sound. It scared me…the noise of the balloon. I heard it, and then all of a sudden—" She broke off and stared at him, her mouth falling open.

"You had a flashback."

She nodded and began to cry softly as he put his arms around her once more. "I—I saw Howard," she whispered against his neck. "It was h-horrible. There was blood and it wouldn't come off me…."

"Shhh. Shhh…" He held on tight, her body trembling against his, her tears staining his shirt. "I'm here. It's okay."

She hiccuped into silence and Beck rocked back on his heels to reach behind him, one arm still around her. He gave her the glass of brandy. "Drink this."

She lifted the crystal tumbler in hands that were still unsteady. Two sips later she grimaced and set it down. "I can't believe this happened. I felt badly that day at the grocery store, but it was nothing compared to this. God, I feel so foolish."

"Don't." He stared at her with a frown. "It's perfectly understandable for someone who went through what you did. Didn't Maria tell you that?"

"Yes, but—"

"Yes, but, nothing. You didn't do anything wrong."

She nodded, then took another sip of brandy. When she raised her gaze to his, her brown eyes were full of tears. "Beck, can you hold me again? Just a little while longer?"

He smiled gently and opened his arms. "Actually, yes, I think I can arrange to do just that."

DESPITE WHAT Beck had said, Jennifer still felt foolish. While he paid their bill, she waited for him outside, on the walkway by the marina, and cringed as she remembered more of the incident. What had everyone in the elegant restaurant thought when she'd cried out then collapsed? She couldn't imagine.

The door opened and Beck walked out. Coming toward her, he smiled reassuringly. "You doing okay?"

"I'm a little shaky but I'll make it."

He nodded. "Let's walk to the end of the dock and get you some sea air."

They headed toward the pilings that marked the end of the pier. On either side of them, water slapped the hulls of the boats with an almost hypnotic rhythm. Jennifer took a deep breath. The salty air did feel good as it entered her lungs, clear and sharp.

He kept the conversation light—just what she

needed—until they reached the railing that stopped their progress. Looking down at the water, Jennifer shook her head. "I'm so sorry, Beck. Did I...did I embarrass you back there?"

He laughed deeply, the sound echoing over the calm dark water that stretched before them. "Jennifer! C'mon, I'm a cop. You could take off all your clothes and dance a jig and I wouldn't be embarrassed. Hell, there's nothing you can do or say I haven't seen before."

She laughed, too. "Well, that may be true, but I'm sure most of your dates don't end that way. With the woman screaming then fainting."

He leaned one elbow against the railing then reached out with his other hand and trailed a finger down her arm. She tried not to shiver. "Sure they do," he said easily. "But it usually happens later...in my bedroom."

He grinned then, and she couldn't help but return the expression, his humor relaxing her and making the moment less awkward.

Slowly he leaned toward her. "It's all right," he said. "I've been there myself."

"Will it end?"

"Yes, it will," he answered. "If you stick with Maria and work through the problem. If you push the memories deeper and try to ignore them, then no." A silver-white sailboat glided by in ghostly silence, the water's surface barely broken by its passage. "I've tried it both ways so I know."

Jennifer couldn't help herself. She lifted her hand to his face and gently traced the line of his jaw with her finger. "Tell me what happened to you," she said softly. "I need to know."

He captured her fingers and brought them to his lips. For a long moment, he held her hand there, his mouth warming her skin. When he released her, it was only so he could pull her into his arms. Looking down at her with his pale, blue glaze, he stared for a second, then closed his eyes. "I went into a house with three other cops. I had the lead. We were trying to serve a high-risk arrest warrant on a repeat sexual offender. That's all we knew." He swallowed. "He wasn't supposed to be violent and Intelligence had told us he had no arms, no weapons...but they were wrong. He had a modified Uzi and he opened it up the minute we broke in. Somehow—God only knows how—he missed me and got the rest of the team. Every one of them. Then he turned around and shot the four kids he'd lured into his living room."

"Oh, my God." He'd told the story without any emotion, in a cold, hard way almost as if he were reading it from a script. The realization came to her that this was probably the only way he *could* recount what had happened, and her heart broke as if he'd cried instead. She asked the question gently. "Did you arrest him—"

"I shot him." His jaw clenched. "I wish he could have died more than once."

He met her eyes. The look that passed between them was quick, but the feeling it created was so strong it stole her pulse. They were different in so many ways she couldn't count them, but they were alike, too. They shared too much to ignore and she was a fool for thinking he was like her father. Beck was nothing like the man she'd grown up avoiding. She raised her hands and pulled Beck's face down to hers. The kiss was long and deep and said everything she didn't have the words for. When they broke apart, he spoke in a husky voice.

"Come home with me."

She looked into his blue eyes and nodded once.

BECK PUT THE KEY into the lock of his apartment door and turned it slowly, his eyes on Jennifer's face. She was still pale, still shaky, but she'd seemed determined enough when he'd asked her to return home with him. Now, he wasn't so sure. She tugged nervously at the gold necklace around her neck and spoke.

"So this is it, huh?"

Without speaking, he nodded and pushed the door open. She preceded him into the entry, her high heels tapping on the tile foyer until she stopped at the edge of the carpet that marked the living room's boundary. "How long have you lived here?"

He took her shawl from her outstretched hand and draped it over a nearby bar stool. "A few years," he answered. "It's close to the station, and the beach, too."

"It looks new." She turned. "No pictures on the walls? No plants? No dog?"

"I'm not a very responsible person. I'd kill a plant and probably starve a dog." He shrugged. "My hours are a good excuse for a lot of things." He put his hands on her shoulders and looked down into her eyes. In the single lamp's light, they were huge and soulful. "I didn't bring you here to tell you all my shortcomings," he said. "I had something else in mind...."

Her tongue slipped out and moistened her lips. "I know that."

She looked so impossibly kissable Beck didn't bother to try to resist. He lowered his head to hers and proceeded to kiss her. With a tiny, almost imperceptible moan, she responded, her breath as sweet and heady as the brandy she'd sipped earlier.

Drawing her close, Beck moved his hands to her shoulders then down, following the curve of her spine with his fingers. Her dress went into a V between her shoulders and he let his touch linger there. Her skin was so warm it made him think of lazy days on a sailboat, just the two of them, somewhere tropical and remote. He cupped her buttocks, and she pressed herself into him.

His lips followed the line of her neck, teasing her skin with more kisses, his tongue laving a path as he went. She even tasted like sun on a beach, he thought illogically. Hot and captivating. By the time he reached the curve where her shoulder met her neck, he could hardly stand it. Turning her around slowly, he began to kiss the nape of her neck, his fingers finding the top of her dress. The sound of her zipper was soft, but her sigh was even fainter as the back of the garment fell open and he slipped his hands inside.

CHAPTER THIRTEEN

JENNIFER CAUGHT her dress with her hands as it slipped off her shoulders and fell forward. Beck was behind her, kissing her, soft little touches of his mouth against her bare skin. She groaned and closed her eyes, letting the sensation of his touch, his smell, his presence envelope her completely.

She'd never wanted a man as much as she wanted him.

Each time his lips found a new place on her body, a small flame built, her craving for more growing even stronger. He was connecting all the blazes with his tongue and his hands. Sooner or later, the fires would merge and consume her. She knew this as surely as she knew how wrong it was for her to let him continue, but she couldn't stop him…and she couldn't stop herself, either.

She leaned against him as his fingers inched forward then played their way over her bare skin between her bra and panties. The touch was exquisite when he trailed one finger along her rib cage, then nibbled on her neck. A moment later, the flat of his hand encompassed the whole of her abdomen, his palm spreading over her skin with the same searing heat she'd experienced before. When he ran his thumb inside the top of her panties, she actually felt weak.

He murmured against her skin, his mouth lifting for only a second. "You are so incredibly beautiful. And I want you so much."

As his deep voice rumbled, she stared through a half-lidded gaze across his living room. Their reflection in the glass of the patio doors barely registered, but what she saw was enough. The erotic pose—Beck behind, his mouth pressed to her neck, her dress halfway down—made her sway with desire.

Through this fog of heat and touch, she gazed at the window, and slowly, so slowly she hardly noticed at first, something else registered, something so outside the realm of where they were and what they were doing she didn't even make sense of it at first. She closed her eyes against the sight; she wanted nothing to interrupt them. Not reality, not her problems, not his job. She only wanted him, but compelled by an insistence she couldn't ignore, she looked again.

In one corner of the glass his bedroom and a closet door were reflected. Hanging over the top of the door was a lightweight jacket and a pair of pants, both black and neatly pressed. All she could see of the jacket was the back and from that she caught the curving *S* and the slash of a *T*. On the doorknob dangled a bulletproof vest and beside it sat his helmet and boots.

All the components of his SWAT uniform.

She told herself she was acting ridiculous; Beck was kind and loving and considerate—everything her father had never been. She was thinking too much about this. *Close your eyes and kiss him, that's all you have to do. Let him make love to you and forget about it.*

But she couldn't. She couldn't just *make love*. To Jennifer, that action meant commitment and a life with Beck would hold the same pitfalls, even if he wasn't the same man.

She stiffened, and Beck's hands stilled in instant response.

"What's wrong?" he asked.

She swallowed, her throat as tight and constricted as if she were choking. "N-nothing," she fibbed.

He pulled back and slowly turned her around to face him. "I told you once never to lie to a liar. It's pointless." The blue gaze scorched her. "What's wrong, Jennifer?"

With shaking hands she pulled her dress up to cover herself. "I—I don't think I'm ready. That's all."

His eyes widened for a moment with an incredulous expression, but he shuttered it quickly, his voice as neutral as if he were talking someone off a ledge. "What changed? You were certainly ready a second before."

The answer ran through head. *I saw your uniform and remembered who I'm really with.* But she couldn't tell him that. He'd think she was an even bigger nut than she'd already demonstrated.

She held herself with awkward tension and stared at him. "I changed my mind," she said. "That's my prerogative, isn't it?

His face reflected his hurt, but he nodded once like the gentlemen he was. "Of course it is. I'll get your shawl and take you home. Turn around so I can zip your dress."

She did as he instructed, and when he finished, he lifted his gaze. His puzzled expression cleared as his eyes went to the same thing she'd seen.

He looked back to her. "It's my uniform, isn't it?"

"It's not the uniform itself," she answered. "It's what's behind it. You know that."

"And you're going to let that stand between us?"

"I have to."

"No, you don't *have to*." His words were chips of ice. "You're making the choice. You and you alone."

THE NEXT FEW DAYS were torture for Beck. A dozen times he picked up the phone to call Jennifer and a dozen times he put it back down. She was the one who'd stopped things. When she was ready, she could call him. Maybe he was being harsh, but she had to make the decision, not him.

Standing on the shoreline in the early-morning sun, Beck crammed his hands into his pockets and stared out over the water. His rod and reel were anchored in the sand at his feet, the line playing out then coming back with the wash of the tide. He wasn't really fishing—the gear was just an excuse to come down to the beach and do something. He'd hoped it might get Jennifer off his mind, but he'd been wrong. It'd take something stronger than a fishing pole and a bucket of bait to get rid of those thoughts.

The line grew taut and Beck watched it for a minute. Deciding there really was something taking the bait, he picked up the rod and gently played it out a bit more, the spool twisting smoothly. Whatever was on the other end swam out farther and took the hook with it, the slack in the line disappearing as the crank handle turned against Beck's palm. With only half his attention, he went through the motions of slowly bringing the fish in, his finger on the line guide, his mind still on Jennifer.

When they'd gone out this past weekend, something had happened between the two of them. Something he couldn't ignore. Up to this point, he'd been attracted, sure, even thought once or twice that he might be falling for her, but now he knew the truth. Nothing was going to dislodge her from the place she'd carved for herself inside his heart. When he'd carried her pale form from the Marina's dining room, he'd been snagged as surely as whatever was on his line. Just remembering the expression in her eyes when she'd asked him to hold her was all it took for him to feel the same wash of need and desire again. The kiss they'd shared later and the anticipation of making love with her had sealed his feelings even more. Jennifer was someone he could love.

Just as quickly, though, he remembered those same brown eyes after she'd spotted his uniform. He'd cursed himself a hundred times for leaving the damn thing out. He'd known how she felt about it—she'd told him, but he just hadn't remembered. It wasn't the uniform itself, of course, it was what it symbolized. She'd wanted to discuss Howard, too. He'd sensed that when they'd talked over drinks, but he'd dodged the issue one more time. Would that always hang over them?

She had a major problem with his job, that much was for sure. But he was falling in love with her and that was just as obvious, at least to him.

What in the hell was he supposed to do?

He reeled the line into the shallow water, then tucked the rod under his arm to snag the floundering amberjack.

The yellow scales were bright in the dawn's breaking light. The fish was a small one and with a deft flick of his wrist he freed the barb from its gills, set it back into the water, then watched as it flashed away, free once more.

His thoughts stayed hooked and tangled.

NADINE DIDN'T REALLY like to leave the safety of Sea-crest, but at least once a month, Jennifer and Wanda took her on an excursion. Wanda insisted it was good for the older woman to experience different settings, even if she didn't appear to appreciate the outings. It wasn't the best place in the world to bring her mother, but Jennifer had been unable to think of anything better and they ended up at the outlet mall the weekend following her date with Beck. The sprawling complex covered hundreds of elegant shops, and in the center, a group of restaurants served a dozen different cuisines, as well as snacks and drinks.

Jennifer hardly noticed where they were. Her mind had been a sieve the past week, confused thoughts and anxieties passing through her brain with barely enough time for her to think about them before they disap-peared. Her nightmares had returned, too, but thank God she hadn't had another panic attack. She'd seen Maria twice, the therapist instructing her on how to handle the problem if it happened again and commiser-ating with her about the incident in the restaurant.

But what really had Jennifer upset had nothing to do with any of that.

It was Beck. The man was trapped inside her head and nothing she could do would budge him. She'd played their kiss over a thousand times, reenacting the ending with just as many changes. She'd really wanted to make love with him, but she'd stopped it from happening.

And she had the strong suspicion, she'd made an awful mistake. He'd been absolutely right. She needed to move from the past and live her own life.

As they strolled along the covered walkway with Nadine between them, Wanda glanced in Jennifer's direction. "You never said much about your date. How did it go?"

Torn with indecision, Jennifer looked at her friend. She'd wanted to call Wanda all week and cry on her shoulder, but something had held her back. As she caught her friend's caring glance, Jennifer realized what that something was. She knew exactly what Wanda was going to tell her and she was afraid to hear it. She had to talk about it, though. If she didn't, she might explode.

Jennifer took a deep breath and explained it all, including the panic attack. "He was really sweet and kind and after it was all over, he took me back to his place."

Wanda had been frowning as she listened to the details of what had happened, but she smiled when Jennifer mentioned Beck's home. "God, girl, why didn't you start with that little detail instead?"

Jennifer shook her head. "It was a disaster."

"Oh, no! What happened?"

"He kissed me," Jennifer answered. "And I kissed him back. It was…incredible."

"An incredible kiss and it was disaster? I need details to understand that."

"It was too incredible for details," Jennifer answered. "Just trust me on the point, okay?"

"Well, at least tell me what happened next. You can't leave me hanging like this."

Jennifer looked away. A family of tourists were ahead of them, complete with sunglasses, stroller and video camera. They stopped before a jewelry store window, and the mother and father rolled the baby carriage back and forth as they looked into the window. Grandmother stepped back and filmed the event. Jennifer spoke softly. "I stopped it before it went any further."

"Are you crazy?" Wanda's voice rose and the mother of the group ahead glanced back curiously. "Why'd you go and do that?"

"Because I can't have a relationship with him, that's why. All I've been thinking about are—" She stopped abruptly, her eyes going to her mother's face. Nadine was staring into the distance, totally unaware of her surroundings.

"Yes?" Wanda asked gently.

Jennifer forced herself to relax. "—are the reasons I don't need to get involved with him." She held up her hand and folded her fingers down one at a time. "His life is bizarre. I don't trust him. He's unpredictable and he keeps secrets." She stopped and dropped her hand. "Want more?"

Wanda didn't answer. She held up her own hand in response and mimicked Jennifer's movements. "He's as handsome as the devil. He's smart and kind and has a well-paying, steady job. He's nuts about you. Do *I* need to go on? That's more reasons than you had. I win." She shook her head and stared at Jennifer with a disbelieving expression. "What's wrong with you? Most of us spend our lives lookin' for a man like him and you're standing here thinkin' up reasons not to like him. I don't believe it."

They passed an expensive leather shop then a candy store before Jennifer could answer. "I can't do it," she answered. "I just can't do it."

Wanda stopped their progress by putting her hand on Jennifer's arm. Nadine moved ahead of them to stare into a window display of beach towels and swimsuits. "What are you so damned afraid of?" Her black eyes bored into Jennifer's. "The man is good and he'd be good *for* you. It's past time you start to live, Jennifer. Why don't you want to do that?"

"I do," she said immediately. "But he's not the one to do it with."

Wanda put her hands on her hips and shook her head. "Ever since you met him, you've said that, but I don't understand why. So what if he's a cop? So what if his life might interfere with your ordered little plans? What's more important? Living or planning to live?" Her forehead wrinkled and she pointed at Nadine, three steps ahead of them. "Look at your mama up there. That could be you or me tomorrow. We could get hit by a truck and it'd all be over. We could be dead or worse— be like her. Your life is yours to live, *right now.* Don't spend your life waiting for the perfect man or the perfect time. That's never going to happen, because perfect doesn't exist." She dropped her hand and shook her head, her eyes almost sorrowful as they met Jennifer's. "You're insane if you let this guy get away."

They spent the rest of the afternoon meandering

through the shops, but Jennifer couldn't remember which ones they'd gone in when she got home that night. Wanda's words refused to leave her alone.

And Beck's presence haunted her dreams.

BECK WAS STARING out the window at the baking asphalt in the parking lot when Lena came into the squad room on Thursday evening and sat down beside his desk. He'd been back at work for two whole weeks, but his heart wasn't in it. Lena looked as if she had the same problem. She had dark circles under her eyes and a worried air about her.

He leaned back in his chair, the springs creaking. "Are you okay? You look like *you* need a vacation."

She smiled briefly at his attempt at humor, then shook her head. "I'm tired," she said. "I had a seminar in Pensacola last night and I didn't get home until after midnight. I was supposed to pick up Nate at the airport and didn't make it. He wasn't happy."

"What are you doing here then? Go find him and make up."

"It's not that easy, Beck. You don't understand…."

Beck made a sympathetic sound in the back of his throat, but he wasn't really paying attention. He was thinking of Jennifer. Only when Lena spoke sharply did he realize she'd been talking about something for quite some time.

He grinned at her sheepishly. "I'm sorry, Lena, but I wasn't listening. What did you say?"

She looked at him strangely. "My God, you are on another planet. I just gave you news that ought to have you jumping up and down and instead you didn't even hear me."

"Well, tell me again."

"I just put Randy on probation."

He stared at her in amazement. "Are you shi—"

She interrupted him. "This is a heads up, Beck. He's not happy and he's looking for someone to blame. If I were you, I'd lay low for a while and watch my back."

"I appreciate the warning, but I'm more interested in hearing why. What finally brought you to this point?"

She looked at him steadily. "I think you know the answer to that question."

He returned her look then nodded slowly. Last week the team had had a party at the home of Bradley Thompson. The cookout around the sergeant's home had been relaxed and pleasant until Randy had shown up. Drunk and obnoxious when he'd arrived, things had only gotten worse as the party had progressed. Linc had finally driven the young sniper home to sleep it off.

"I talked to him on Monday about what happened at Bradley's. He apologized and said he didn't know what got into him." Her face took on an expression of regret. "I told him that wasn't good enough. We have to be ready to roll twenty-four hours a day. Blowing off some steam is one thing, but passed out drunk is something else. He couldn't have worked if we'd gotten a call. It would have taken more than a day to get that much alcohol out of his bloodstream. His hands would have been worthless. I put him on probation. If he screws up again, he's out. I just thought you might want to know." She stood up slowly, then looked down at Beck. "He said it wasn't really his fault and that you were behind my decision. He's loaded for bear, Beck. Be careful out there, okay?"

Beck nodded once, then the phone rang and Lena left the office. With one hand, he picked up the report he'd been reading and with the other he reached for the phone. "Winters," he said into the receiver, his attention on the papers he held.

"Beck? This is Jennifer."

"Jennifer!" A rush of feeling hit him at the sound of her voice. He'd given up hope that she would call, and now here she was, sounding as if she'd made up her mind about something important and wasn't going to be deterred. "How are you?"

"I'm fine," she said. "Just fine. How's it been going since we had dinner?"

The small talk was curious considering her tone, but he went with it. "Not that easy. I was getting into sleeping late. I could've handled that some more." *Especially if you'd been beside me,* he thought unexpectedly.

"That's good…." She stopped, her words drifting into silence. He waited patiently and finally she spoke again. "Listen, Beck, I'm calling to say…well, to say I'm sorry. About the other night, the last time we were together."

"There's nothing to be sorry for."

"Then why do I feel so awful?"

"I don't know why, but I'd be willing to take a guess."

"And that would be…"

Gathering his thoughts, he hesitated for a bit. "Maybe because you didn't really want to stop. Maybe you wished you'd let things go on to their natural conclusion."

"Is that how *you* feel?"

"You know that's how I feel," he said. "You didn't have to call to find that out."

She paused, and the soft, even measure of her breathing came over the phone. "You could be right. Whatever the reason, I've been doing a lot of thinking about it, and I—I'd like to show you how I really feel about things. I'd like another chance if you're interested."

The image of her silky tanned legs, her shining hair, her full, sensual lips came to him instantly, but an even stronger impression—a realization, actually—overlaid those physical attributes, as wonderful as they were. No matter what happened between them in the future, she had become a part of him he didn't want to lose. It was a scary thought, but there was nothing he could do about it.

His answer was simple. "I'm interested."

"Could I cook dinner for you Saturday night?"

"I can't think of anything I'd like better."

She laughed at his heartfelt expression, a self-conscious note in the sound that made her even more appealing. "Just one other thing," she said. "I'd like to cook it at your place. Do you mind?"

It seemed an odd request, but he didn't care. "Of course, I don't mind. But I'll warn you now. I'm pretty low in the pots and pans department."

"It doesn't matter," she answered. "I'll put everything together at my place and just heat it up over there. I…well, it's kind of hard to explain, but I wanted to come over there."

As she spoke again, further comprehension came

over him. She had something she wanted to prove to herself, and maybe to him, too, although that wasn't necessary. "I understand," he answered. "And it's not a problem, so don't worry about it."

"See you at seven?"

"See you at seven."

Beck hung up the phone, leaned back in his chair and stared out the squad room window. In the hot morning light, the palm trees seemed to shimmer. He stared at them but thought of Jennifer. What had changed her mind?

Whatever it was, for the moment, it didn't matter. Glancing down at his desk, he saw the stopwatch he used for calls. Impulsively, he picked it up and set it for 7:00 p.m. on Saturday, the green digital numbers changing the minute he touched the button, their countdown beginning. He felt each tick echo in his pulse. Forty-eight hours and counting.

CHAPTER FOURTEEN

JENNIFER HAD MADE her special shrimp dish a thousand times. It was her favorite company entree, but this time something had definitely gone wrong. She stared in dismay at the lumpy cheese sauce, then with a groan, she lifted the pot and dumped it—sauce and all—in the sink. She'd just have to start over. Again.

Reassembling the ingredients, she shook her head over her cooking disaster and stared at her recipe. She knew exactly where the problem lay—it was with the cook. She was rattled and distracted. Making the decision to call Beck had been a big one for her, and she still wasn't sure she was doing the right thing. Talking to Wanda had helped, then she'd discussed the topic with Maria during one of their sessions, too. Strangely enough, it was her mother who'd given her the courage to finally telephone him.

Her eyes focused, her mind almost there, Nadine had listened carefully the previous Wednesday as Jennifer talked about Beck.

"It sounds as if you like him," her mother said timidly. "Is he really a nice boy, Jennifer?"

She'd smiled over the *boy* part. Beck was a man— that was more than clear. "He's wonderful," she answered. "And he's been very supportive. I think you'd like him, too."

"I'm sure I would if you do." Nadine smiled so sweetly it stole Jennifer's breath. "Falling in love with someone is very important, you know. You have to be careful about who holds your heart."

Jennifer left the nursing home with those words ringing in her mind. The next day, she'd picked up the phone and called Beck. Now here she was, burning her cheese sauce and getting nervous.

Concentrating harder, she grabbed the chunk of Asiago and began to grate again.

WHEN HE OPENED the door, Beck wasn't prepared. He'd expected Jennifer to be on the other side—the stopwatch had beeped a few minutes before—but actually seeing her at his door, waiting just for him, was almost unnerving. He'd faced guns and irate husbands, hostage situations and suicide takers but none of them had made him as nervous as he was right now. Maybe he'd thought she would back out or maybe he'd decided he'd dreamed her phone call. Whatever it was, as she stood there and smiled at him, his heartbeat suddenly accelerated, kicking inside his chest as if a .45 were pointed at him.

In an effort to distract himself, he looked at the dress she wore. It was simple, a white sleeveless thing. Her legs were bare, and their tanned perfection didn't help his jitters at all. It worked the opposite way, in fact, so he fastened on the details. She had on sandals, but she'd changed her polish. This time her toenails were red and so was her lipstick. He found himself wondering if that signified something important.

He hoped it did.

She spoke warily, her smile tentative. "May I come in? Or is something wrong?"

"God, yes. I'm sorry...." Feeling like a fool, he opened the door wider and stepped aside, waving his arm toward the entry. "Please, come in. Whatever you're carrying smells outstanding."

"I hope it tastes that way, too." She eased past him and headed toward the small walk-through kitchen, talking over her shoulder. "It'll be a miracle if it's worth eating. I'm going to chill it while I finish making the salads."

Closing the door, Beck hurried to catch up with her. By the time she'd set the dish inside his almost empty refrigerator, he was standing right behind her. "I'm sure it'll be terrific. Anything short of a Hot Pocket is gourmet to me."

She turned to reply and bumped into him with a tiny, "Oh."

He hadn't meant to be so close—or had he? As Beck raised his hands to steady her, he wasn't sure. Either way, when he touched her, his fingers sliding against the bare satin of her arm, something happened between them.

If someone had asked him later to describe that moment, Beck would not have been able to do it. He didn't have the words in his vocabulary. All he knew was that he had to kiss Jennifer. It sounded unbelievable—and it felt that way, too—but he recognized the power of the urge for what it was. Nothing could have kept him from her. Nothing. Lowering his head to hers, he put his mouth against her lips and everything else fell into place. His hands on her hips, her fingers against his chest, their bodies one against the other.

Dropping the lettuce to the counter, she stiffened in surprise. But almost immediately she moved closer to him, her arms going up to link around his neck, her firm curves molding to his hips and thighs with an obvious response. She was perfect and he marveled at the way they fit together. From the very first moment he'd seen her, Beck had felt a connection with Jennifer and now, as she kissed him so freely, he experienced the strength of that invisible attachment. He didn't understand it and had no idea where it came from, but it was as real as the room in which they stood. He'd heard of two people being made for each other and scoffed.

He would never do that again.

They held the embrace for a few more minutes, then Beck pulled back and looked down at her. He wanted to lift her up, carry her to his bedroom and make love to her. He didn't want dinner, he didn't want dessert. He didn't want to open the chilled bottle of Chablis she'd asked him to buy. All he wanted was her, but he couldn't say that. Jennifer was different from the other women he'd dated. She was too smart and too beautiful and too elegant to drag into the bedroom without making sure everything was as flawless as she was. He'd almost done that before and it'd been a disaster. He wanted to do it right this time. She deserved the very best he could give her and rushing to bed wouldn't be it.

She met his gaze with her dark-brown eyes, then she

brought her hands forward and placed them on either side of his face. Her touch was light and delicate and he could hardly bear to feel it because it made him ache for more. With her fingertips barely brushing his skin, a silent spark of anticipation flared between them. It was swift and electrical.

"Let's skip dinner," she said in a husky voice. "Suddenly something else sounds like a lot more fun."

SHE'D NEVER BEEN so direct with a man in her life; it was totally out of character for Jennifer. But feeling the blue heat of Beck's gaze and reading the desire behind the attraction they both obviously felt, nothing else made sense. She wanted him as much as he wanted her, and she'd done enough thinking about it. She wanted action. Whether it was the right thing or not, she didn't care. She'd already decided.

He smiled slowly, an expression that went straight into her heart and warmed her even more—something she'd have thought impossible at this point.

"I agree completely," he said. "But I have to ask—you're sure?"

"I'm here, aren't I?"

"Yes, but—"

She moved her fingers to his lips and silenced him gently. "Don't ask me anymore," she instructed softly. "Just kiss me, okay?"

He did as she requested, and once again, his lips covered hers. The moment seemed to last an eternity but maybe she just wanted it to feel that way. Without taking his mouth away, he bent down and swept her into his arms. In a dozen long strides they were in his bedroom. He set her down beside the bed, his hands going to the back of her dress. With his eyes never leaving hers, he slowly eased the zipper down. The air-conditioning in the apartment suddenly kicked on and cold air from the vent overhead skimmed over her bare skin. Jennifer shivered once, the juxtaposition of the chill to Beck's heated touch almost more than she could handle.

He left her dress hanging on her shoulders, then lifted his hands to his shirt and started to unbutton it. She wanted to do it herself, but Jennifer couldn't move. She watched as the shirt fell open to reveal his tanned and muscular chest. She'd never been with someone so imposing, so overpowering. If her knees hadn't been against the bed, she might have backed up to increase the distance between them. Beck seemed to take all the space in the room and compress it into something flammable. Only when he shrugged out of his shirt did her paralysis end. Her hands went to his bare skin and she spread her palms over his chest. She almost snatched her hands away, his body was so hot, but she left them there, unable to pull herself away. Under her touch, she was amazed to feel his heart thumping almost as fast as her own.

She lifted her eyes to his and his blue gaze, so cold in the past, was burning. "Turn around," he said hoarsely. "Let me take off your dress."

Once again, she did exactly as he said, and when the ivory sheath fell to the floor, she pivoted in the circle of his arms to face him.

Gently reaching out, he traced the swell of her right breast, taking a slow, torturous route before he slipped his finger into the valley of her cleavage. Her pulse leapt. How could he touch her so simply and make her feel as if she were about to explode? He brought his hand up and let the finger lightly flicker over her other side, then he reached out with both hands and cupped the weight of her breasts, his thumbs scorching her nipples through the lace of her bra. She caught her breath in her throat and froze.

She felt dizzy and disoriented and completely undone. As they sunk toward the bed, their arms wrapped around each other, she put her hands against his back and encountered the strength of his muscles. Only then—when her touch registered—did she finally understand what was going on.

Beck made her feel safe. He was so tall and so strong, she felt protected from any danger. No one had ever done this for her before and she opened herself up to him with a sigh of release.

He sensed her acquiescence. Shedding the rest of his clothes and removing what was left of hers, his hands danced over her bare skin with a faster, more urgent need. She responded in kind, her fingers exploring the ridges and cords of his arms and legs and back. Each place she touched felt the same; rock solid and hard.

Only his mouth was soft and tender. Everywhere he could, he was kissing her, his lips drawing a crazy quilt pattern of desire that grew with every second. His hands quickly followed and with each feathered caress, he brought her closer and closer to the brink of a climax. No longer able to control herself, she pressed against him and urged him into a faster pace. But she didn't need to tell him; he read her body as easily as he did everything else. He reached into the bedside table, then she heard the foil tear as he took out a condom. A moment later, he slipped inside her with gentle care and built the rhythm into the kind of frenzied tempo they both needed. With the part of her brain that wasn't on fire, Jennifer noted this in amazement. How did he know how to please her so well? How could he tell what to do and when to do it?

She only wondered for a moment. His powerful thrusts sent her mind spinning into an abyss of pleasure. For what seemed like a very long time, she stayed there, untethered by anything but the thrill of the building heat between them. It was more incredible than she'd even imagined. She couldn't have envisaged the feeling because nothing in her past had come even close. The explosion of her climax was just as astounding. Totally unprepared, she let the sensual wave carry her off.

When she drifted back down, she had a single thought. It came from a place deep within her, but Jennifer knew—as all women do—that the impression was as real as the bed she was lying in.

Nothing in her life would ever be the same again.

SHE WOKE UP in the middle of the night. For one short second, Jennifer didn't know where she was and she panicked, a dark sweep of anxiety and fear washing over her in a haze of black and red. Before the fear could overwhelm her, she brought herself to calmness—just as Maria had taught her—and the jittery confusion fled. Her breathing slowed and her heartbeat did as well.

She felt proud of herself. The bad dreams had almost stopped, and she hadn't had a real panic attack since the night she'd been with Beck at the restaurant. Maria had really helped.

But the man beside her had helped even more. Jennifer turned her head and looked at Beck's chiseled profile in the darkness.

He was extraordinary. That's the only word she could think of to describe him. Patient and kind, he'd insisted she see Maria, then he'd gone on to help her even more. Now they were lovers, and in her heart, Jennifer acknowledged she wanted to go beyond that. She could see him as the father of the children she'd always longed for, as the man who mowed the yard inside the picket fence. Refusing to allow any negative thoughts to destroy the growing image, she let herself play with it for a little while longer. He'd go with her to visit Nadine, he'd attend all the school parties with her, they'd go shopping and to the movies and out to eat. They'd be a couple. They'd be a family.

Easing slowly from beneath his arm, Jennifer rose from the bed and grabbed the shirt Beck had been wearing. She slipped into it and stared down at him, telling herself she was nuts for letting the fantasy build. She couldn't stop, though. As his chest rose and fell, she stared at him with longing. Was there any way this relationship could work? Or was she being ridiculous?

She padded through the darkness of his apartment and into the kitchen. She'd left on the light above the cooktop. The dim illumination served to build the shadows more than anything else, but with it as her guide, she opened the refrigerator and saw the casserole, still tempting even though it was cold. Suddenly she was ravenous. She reached into the oval dish and plucked out a shrimp. Just as she stuck it into her mouth, a noise sounded behind her. Her hand at her lips, she turned.

"Am I going to have to arrest you for burglary?" Beck stood at the doorway to the kitchen, his huge form filling the entry as he spoke. "I believe that dish was made for two—and here you are snitching the shrimp out of it."

She grinned and swallowed, putting on a mock expression of guilt. "I guess you caught me." Reaching over, she snagged another shrimp and held it out to him. "If I share, would you go easy on me?"

He took one step into the kitchen then took the shrimp from her fingers and tossed it into his mouth. "My God, that's wonderful," he said as he chewed. "Can we have it for breakfast?"

"Why not eat it right now?" she countered playfully. "We could call it a midnight snack."

He acted as if he were considering her offer, then slowly he shook his head. "I don't think so. I've got something better in mind."

Before she could answer, he took another step and whisked her into his arms. They didn't even make it to the bedroom this time.

BECK DIDN'T WANT to release Jennifer. Not for a minute, not forever... Despite his protests, though, she slid from his arms a little later and disappeared into the bathroom, closing the door behind her, the sound of running water coming on right after. He immediately felt cold and alone. His reaction should have surprised him—but it didn't. There was no other way he could feel considering the past few hours. If he'd thought she'd gotten under his skin before, he'd had no idea what he was really in for. Jennifer shared his passion, and each touch, each kiss, each look had sealed his feelings for her even more. There had to be a way he could convince her they should be together—forever. He didn't know what it would be, but Beck stared at the line of light seeping under the bathroom door and vowed to find a way. Now that they'd reached this point, he wouldn't let her go. He *couldn't* let her go. He wanted to think she might agree.

A loud pounding on his front door jerked Beck from his reverie. Glancing toward the clock with a frown, he read the time. It was two in the morning! What in the hell? He grabbed his pants, thrust his legs into them and headed for the door, a thousand possibilities going through his mind, none of them making any sense. Sometimes when they caught a call, Bradley Thompson would swing by and pick him up, but Beck got a phone call first or at the least a page. Whoever was beating on the door was impatient and angry, too—adjectives that definitely didn't fit the able assistant commander.

"Hang on, hang on. I'm coming!" Beck crossed the living room to the small hallway closet and unlocked it swiftly, removing his service revolver from the top shelf where he kept it. He checked the weapon once then crammed it into the back waistband of his slacks. He didn't know who was on the other side, but with Jennifer around, he wasn't about to take any chances. Two strides later, he threw open the front door then stared in shock, a sweep of anger hitting him like a wave from the Gulf.

JENNIFER TURNED OFF the bathroom light, opened the door and headed back into the bedroom. She was at the edge of the bed when she realized it was empty, and grinned. Beck must have returned to the shrimp. Calling out his name, she started into the living room, then stopped abruptly, the sound of loud voices in the entry halting her footsteps and filling her with concern. Whoever was talking was more than just upset, she realized belatedly. He was furious and from the tone of his voice prepared to do something about it.

"This is all your fault, Winters! You've screwed me, and I'm not going to put up with it. Your bullshit has gotten me in enough trouble!"

The rage in the other man's voice was deep and penetrating, and Jennifer felt it all the way to her toes. She hadn't heard that kind of undisguised fury since she'd left her father's home.

"Randy, this isn't the time or the place. If you have a problem with me, let's work it out at the station. I'd be happy to talk to you about it then—"

"I'm sure you would!" The voice was slurred, but the emotion wasn't. It was all too clear and Jennifer shivered. "You got Lena on your side up there and all the rest of your asshole buddies! They'd stick up for you and look down their noses at me, like they always do. Uh-uh, Winters. It's you and me, right here, right now."

Jennifer froze against the wall. The man was obviously one of the SWAT team members. She thought of what Beck had called him. *Randy*... Then she remembered. Randy Tamirisa. He was the sniper. She'd read his name in the newspapers and had heard Beck speak of him before.

Randy Tamirisa was the man who'd shot Howard.

Beck spoke again. His tone was neutral and unengaged, but now that she knew him better, she could hear, beneath the professional attitude, something deeper he was trying hard to hold back.

"Don't do something you're gonna regret, Randy. You're drunk and out of line. You don't know what you're doing."

"I know exactly what I'm doing, you son of a bitch. Just like I knew what I was doing when I took that shot at the school."

Something told her she didn't want to hear what was coming next, but Jennifer was trapped. In more ways than one.

"You *didn't* know what you were doing then and you don't know now." Some of the emotion Beck had been concealing seeped out, his voice going deep and husky. "Don't blame me because you're feeling guilty now! You took that shot without Lena's approval and you shouldn't have."

Jennifer gasped softly, then held her breath in her lungs, her pulse suddenly pounding as shock and disbelief washed over her in a dizzying wave. God, why hadn't Beck told her about this? Before she could think about it more, the sniper spoke again.

"I did my job. That idiot was gonna shoot someone."

"You didn't know that for sure." Beck was now openly angry. "You're trigger-happy, Tamirisa, and that's the only truth we need to talk about here. You have no business on the team."

"Get real, Winters. You're jealous. I was man enough to take the shot, and that's something you'll never be. You're a desk jockey, you're not even a real SWAT man. You're telling Lena shit about me just to screw me over."

Jennifer heard the sound of shuffling and a dull thud, the noise a body makes as it hits an immovable object. It didn't take much imagination to realize what had happened. Beck had obviously grabbed the other man and pushed him. The wall she was leaning against vibrated in response.

Beck's voice was tight, barely in control, as he spoke again. "I'm not the first man through the door anymore, but I'll tell you one thing—you made the mistake that day, buddy. You and you alone. That perp didn't need to die. It could have been resolved."

Jennifer closed her eyes and swayed, the whole ugly scene turning her inside out. Howard's face swam in her vision. Something had told her there was more to the story, but Beck had convinced her otherwise. He'd made it sound like the team had done the right thing when all along he'd thought otherwise. Why in heaven's name hadn't he just told her the truth? The obvious answer came swiftly: he couldn't have. It didn't work that way and she was incredibly blind not to have realized that fact before now. His job would *never* permit the whole truth between them.

The man spoke again, his words coming out strangled. "I didn't kill that bastard, Winters. You did! If you'd done *your* job right, he'd have come out and no one woulda gotten shot."

Another thud rattled the wall, a groan of pain echoing right behind it. A dragging sound came next, then the noise of the front door opening. A thump, another moan, then Beck's voice, more angry and intense than Jennifer had ever heard it.

"Go home and sober up and take your goddamn lies with you."

The slamming door shook the entire apartment, but that wasn't the reason Jennifer was trembling.

Moments later, Beck was walking toward her. But he took one look at her face and stopped short. She knew why, too. She was shocked and horrified and sick to her stomach, each and every emotion written in her expression. They'd just made love and in her mind if nowhere else, she'd committed herself to him. Now she knew the facts, and they were just what she'd been afraid of. Nothing in Beck's world made any sense. She and the people she worked with held meetings, had lunches, argued and complained. Beck's co-workers showed up in the middle of the night, stressed out and drunk, to fight over someone else's death!

How long would it be before the inevitable happened? When would Beck be the one out of control? It would happen sooner or later, she knew, and then once again, her life would be where it had started. Her escape all those years ago meaningless.

With bile rising in her throat, Jennifer realized the

truth that had come crashing through that door along with Randy Tamirisa. There could be no future between her and Beck. The chaos and confusion of his existence was something she'd never be able to handle. She'd known this at first, but she'd put it aside because she'd fallen in love with him.

Beck's life was insane, and if Jennifer had ever thought she could be with him...then she was crazy, too.

CHAPTER FIFTEEN

CURSING SOUNDLY, Beck held out his hand and came closer to Jennifer. Her eyes were enormous and filled with a betrayal that cut straight into his heart. "Jennifer, sweetheart…"

"Stop right there." Her voice held no room for argument, and he did as she instructed. "Don't come another step. I mean it."

Automatically, he went into his negotiating mode. He nodded slowly, his expression neutral. "Of course. I'll stop. Just let me explain—"

"No!" Her one-word answer was violent and vehement. "There's nothing to explain. I heard all I needed to hear."

"But it wasn't the truth—"

"You don't even know what that is." She shuffled backward from him, her fingers locked on the shirt she wore, her knuckles as white as her face. "You said you did everything you could when Howard was killed."

"And that's still the case."

"But not the full story…"

"I didn't want him to die—"

She shook her head. "You know what? I believe you!

You're a good man and I know you well enough now to know you didn't want that—"

"Then why—"

Her eyes flared wide. "Because I can't live with this craziness. I wanted to know what happened that day and I begged you to tell me. But even when we got to know each other better, you didn't come clean! It's not that, though. It's—"

He didn't let her finish. In a flash, he closed the distance between them. Her back against the bedroom door, Jennifer had nowhere to go, and all she could do was look up at him helplessly as he trapped her, his hands on the wall at either side of her head.

"What did you expect, Jennifer? Did you want to hear every little detail? Even if I'd wanted to give them to you, what's the point? Dammit it to hell, I see death and violence everywhere I go. Is that really what you want to hear about when we're together?"

"It's more than that!" she cried. "My father ruined our lives with his secrets and lies and upheaval. It was constant. We never knew what was going on, with him or in our own lives, and I said I'd never live that way again."

"Well, here's a news flash, Jennifer. Life isn't always tied up in neat little bundles that you can stick in numbered boxes. Howard French was killed because our sniper thought he was going to shoot Juan Canales. I disagreed. I thought Tamirisa should have waited. But I could have been wrong. And if I had been, and Juan had died, what would you have thought of me then?"

Angrily he shook his head and didn't wait for her to

answer. "Don't you understand, Jennifer? Life is always going to be full of questions and unanswered problems. Nothing is certain, hell, our *existence* isn't even certain."

"But you could have told me you didn't agree with the sniper. We could have at least talked about it. That would have helped me."

"I am a member of the team." He spoke each word distinctly as he dropped his arms and stepped back. "And I owe that team all the loyalty I can muster. Our lives depend on each other, and if we screw up, it's our problem to deal with. Ours and no one else's. I didn't explain what happened because you wouldn't have understood, just like you don't understand now. You see everything through the filter of your past even when it doesn't apply."

Her face shuttered, the expression going cold and distant. "What are you saying?"

"I'm saying I'm not your father—"

"I know that—"

"Then realize what it means! I'm a different man but because of our jobs, there are going to be similarities. He kept secrets because he had to and so do I. But there's a damn good reason for that, and if you gave it some thought, you might begin to figure out why."

She blinked slowly, then turned her head and stared into the darkness of his living room. Her throat moved as she swallowed, then she faced him once again. Her eyes glimmered with unshed tears. The hurt and distrust behind her gaze cut so deeply, he felt a physical pain. He wanted to start over, to try to explain better, but she stopped him.

"I understand all I need to. Living that way ruined my mother's life and ended my brother's. I won't let it do the same to me."

Once more, Beck began to reply, but the worst thing that *could* happen, did happen. The beeper on his waistband went off. He glanced down and cursed. Another priority call. When he lifted his head, Jennifer simply looked at him.

"I have to leave—"

"You always have to leave." Her voice was almost sad, and Beck heard the goodbye in the words, even though she didn't say it. His chest went tight.

"Stay here," he pleaded. "We can talk about this some more when I get back."

She shook her head, her dark hair brushing her shoulders with a weary whisper. "I won't be here when you come home. There's nothing else to say."

SHE DRESSED in silence behind the bathroom door and when she came out, Beck had left, as she'd expected. There was a hastily scribbled note on the floor of the living room that began "Dear Jennifer..." but she didn't bother to read it. It wouldn't matter anyway. Nothing he could say would change the situation. His life couldn't be hers. Ever. Numbly, she left the apartment and went to her car, getting inside and driving off without a clue as to where she was headed. Only when she pulled up in front of Seacrest did she understand where she'd driven.

Climbing out of the car, she made her way through the empty parking lot and up to the double glass doors.

Like most of its occupants, the building seemed to be sleeping. The lights were muted, the halls were empty and even the ever present music was turned down so low it was almost silent. Jennifer walked past the abandoned reception desk and started down the hallway to her mother's room. When she passed the nurses' station, she saw the aide who manned the desk. The woman had her back to Jennifer and was pouring herself a cup of coffee. Jennifer went by without saying a word then she entered her mother's room still not knowing why she was there.

The revelation came to her without any warning. Seacrest was where she came when she got upset. It wasn't the hardship she'd always thought it was. It was the exact opposite. Being with her mother brought Jennifer peace when the outside world overwhelmed her. The realization astonished her, but Jennifer couldn't deny it. Visiting Nadine wasn't a burden—it was a gift—for both of them.

Nadine was asleep, but as Jennifer approached the bed, her mother's eyes opened. She smiled gently. "Jennifer, come in, sweetheart…."

Jennifer's heartbeat fluttered as Nadine spoke her name. She knew her. The awareness in her mother's eyes felt so good to Jennifer, she almost hated to acknowledge it. Who knew when it would happen again? Or even *if* it would. Inevitably there would be a time when that was no longer a possibility at all. She walked closer to the bed and dropped a kiss on Nadine's forehead. Beneath Jennifer's lips, her mother's skin felt as thin and fragile as the single wing of a moth.

"Hi, Mom. I didn't mean to wake you up. I'm sorry."

"It's okay." Nadine smiled again. "I was having a dream about your father."

Jennifer wearily shook her head and sat down on the chair beside the bed. "A nightmare, you mean?"

"Oh no, it was a wonderful dream. We were both young and so much in love it hurt. Kinda like you and your young man are."

Startled by her mother's words, Jennifer looked at her sharply. She wasn't sure what surprised her the most. Her mother's lucidity, her reference to Beck, or the explanation of the dream. She picked one at random. "You think we're in love?"

"You told me you were the other day. That hasn't changed, has it?"

"I—I don't know."

Her mother sat up, her hair shining in the light drifting in from the hallway. "You look upset. Did you have a fight?"

Miserably, Jennifer nodded.

"Tell me about it, darling."

"I'm not sure I can. It's complicated."

Nadine nodded slowly. "Love usually is. It certainly was that way between your father and me."

Jennifer held her breath. Her mother was making so much sense, it scared her. She'd had clear moments in the past, but they hadn't had a conversation like this in more than a month and even then, Nadine hadn't been this coherent. Jennifer asked the question and prayed there would be an answer that made sense. "What do you mean, Mom?"

She shook her head, the strands of silver whispering against the bed linens. "He wasn't a nice man," she said. "But I loved him so much it hurt. I think I hated our life because he wouldn't give me all of it."

Disappointment came over Jennifer. Nadine *wasn't* thinking straight.

Her mother turned to look at her more closely. "You don't understand what I'm saying, do you?"

"No, Mom. I don't think I do."

She seemed to struggle to find the right words, her forehead wrinkling. "I was always despondent whenever he had to leave. And when he came home, I wanted to know all the details, but he wouldn't tell me. I pushed him so much he got bitter and resentful, then angry. That's the man you knew. When he was younger he wasn't that way. He had changed by the time you were born." She picked at the sheet. "I think that's why Danny was so confused. His father had been one man, then slowly he became someone else. That's not something a child can understand. But I didn't, either. Not until later. I didn't know he was trying to protect me...." Her eyes fluttered down.

As she'd spoken, Jennifer had pulled the chair closer. She spoke urgently. "Mom? Tell me more, please... Mom?"

"I'm sleepy," Nadine answered in a fretful voice. Opening her eyes once more, she looked at Jennifer suspiciously. "What kind of nurse are you to come in here and wake me up? Leave me alone, young lady."

Jennifer's shoulders slumped in dismay. Nadine had been there—really been there—for what? Twenty seconds, maybe less? Jennifer's frustration bloomed. She had questions to ask, things she needed to know. What had Nadine meant about Jennifer's father trying to protect her? Protect her from what? Jennifer wanted to reach over and shake her sleeping mother, but that was pointless, and she knew it. Without any warning, the futility and disappointment of the night suddenly swept over her. Like an avalanche off a mountain, blinding and unstoppable, all her emotions exploded at once, and there was nothing Jennifer could do but hurt. She laid her head on her mother's bed and began to weep.

BY THE TIME she got home, Jennifer was drained. It was almost 5:00 a.m., and she could hardly see she was so exhausted. Staying up all night was for college students. A mature, responsible woman had no business crawling into her apartment in the same clothes she'd put on the day before. This wasn't how it was supposed to be, she thought wearily, unlocking the door and stepping inside. Was the fantasy just that? Would she never have the stable life, the children, the home, the husband she wanted?

She felt bruised and battered, her body aching as much as her mind. Her tears threatened to begin again, but she held them in. By the time she threw back the covers and climbed into bed, she was shivering with fatigue. The feeling was as much mental as it was physical, but when she closed her eyes, sleep refused to come, just as she'd known it would. She almost welcomed the insomnia, though; who knew what kind of nightmares she'd have.

Surrendering to the inevitable, she plumped the pillows behind her back and reached for the remote control. The bluish light of the television bathed the room and bed with faint illumination, the voice of the Channel Seven reporter coming along with the picture. Jennifer always watched the show when she was getting dressed. She shook her head, then found herself focusing on the set, the newswoman's expression and excited hand gestures more agitated than usual. In the background, a modest, low-rise commercial building filled the screen. Jennifer recognized it immediately. The office housed the salon where she got her hair cut. The reporter spoke with staccato rapidity.

"I'm standing in front of the Renaissance Center in downtown Destin. Earlier this morning, police were dispatched to this location following an automatic alarm call. Shortly after they arrived, shots were fired at the officers.

"The Emerald Coast SWAT team is on-site. This structure contains a beauty salon, a drugstore and a demolition firm. The armed man inside is threatening to blow up the building, using material he located in the demolition company's offices."

Jennifer's mouth dropped open with horrified disbelief. This was the call Beck had gotten—it had to be! She threw off the blanket and crawled to the foot of the bed closer to where the television set rested on the dresser. The voice of the Channel Seven anchor broke in.

"Ginger, do you know if there's anyone else in the building right now?"

The reporter put a hand to her ear. "We're just not

sure, Jamie. There could be people trapped inside, but the only persons we've actually witnessed running to the back door area were SWAT members protecting one man who went inside. We believe him to be the negotiator. We're assuming he's talking to the alleged gunman and trying to get him out of there. The media representative for the team, Sarah Greenberg, has refused to comment on the situation."

"Oh, my God…" Jennifer whispered the words, but the room seemed to hold them and magnify their sound, along with her fear. "Oh, God…oh, God…" Her prayer dissolved into silence, her tight throat making it impossible to say more.

"Exactly what kind of material is in the construction office?"

The reporter nodded her head as she heard the anchor's question, her expression avid with anticipation of a bigger story. "We don't know exactly, Jamie. We contacted the owner of the firm, Anderson Destruction, and he confirmed a job had been canceled at the last minute on Friday. Because of that, he took some type of explosive material to the office for, as he put it, 'safe keeping.' Regardless of how this ends, charges may be filed against the firm."

"So it's possible this situation could turn deadly?"

The woman nodded vigorously. "Absolutely, Jamie. In fact, they've cleared and barricaded a square block around where we're standing now. We'll stay in touch and keep our viewers as informed as we can."

Now only inches from the television set, Jennifer reached out toward the screen, her fingers touching the front of the building behind the reporter. "Oh, please…" she breathed. "Keep him safe, please… keep him safe…"

"We'll get back to you, Ginger."

The woman nodded once and turned, then all at once, behind her, a loud explosion rippled through one side of the office. The windows at that end disintegrated, instantly sending glass and debris flying through the air. A corner of the roof lifted, then crashed violently back down, bits and pieces of tile and mortar, brick and metal becoming deadly missiles as they sailed through the dust-filled air. The reporter ducked and so did the cameraman, each of them falling to the ground before the collapsing building. With the sound of terror filling the airwaves, the camera focused on the sidewalk for a only second, then the picture went blurry and finally totally black.

Jennifer began to scream.

CHAPTER SIXTEEN

THE LAST THOUGHT Beck had was of Jennifer.

Staring at the crazed man on the other side of the hall-way, his hand clutching the package of explosives, his gaze wild and disoriented, Beck didn't think of the danger he was facing or even the imminent possibility of his own death. All he thought of was Jennifer. Brown eyes, chestnut hair, the face of an angel.

She was everything he'd always wanted in a woman and he'd never meet anyone else he could care for more.

But there would always be problems between the two of them. That was the nature of his work and nothing would change it. He couldn't tell her what he saw every day, even if he wanted to. It was too bloody, too violent, too horrible to share. Most of the time, he didn't even want to think of it himself.

She'd been right. They had no future…but not for the reasons she thought. The real truth was even more simple, as it usually was. They would never have a life together because he couldn't put her through that kind of agony—regardless of what she wanted. She deserved better. She deserved a husband who came home at night without blood on his clothes and death on his mind. She just deserved better.

A second later, Beck was flying through the air in silent agony, the blast stealing his hearing, a huge sliver of glass slicing him across the forehead. Pain radiated down his face and into his jaw, then the sting of blood hit his eyes. He landed with an excruciating thump, the air jarred from his lungs to be replaced by a searing heat.

He held on a moment more—long enough to feel the torture of a nearby flame, long enough to blink away the blood and see the fire—then the darkness came and Beck welcomed it.

"IS HE IN THERE? That's all I want to know! Just tell me if he's in there!"

Jennifer knew she sounded crazy, but she didn't care. Nothing mattered except for Beck. Lena McKinney stared at her with red-rimmed eyes and a harried expression. In one hand, she clutched a radio, in the other she held a handkerchief. As Jennifer watched, the woman brought the square of cloth up and swiped it over her face. Heat and flames were still coming from the building behind them, adding to the humidity and rising temperature of the early summer dawn.

"I can't tell you yet," she said. "All I can say is that we're working through the problem. Please get back behind the yellow tape, Miss Barclay, and as soon as we know something, I'll tell you, I promise." She turned and started to walk away.

"Wait—please! You don't understand," Jennifer cried. "I have to know. We're—".

The exhausted lieutenant stopped. Taking two steps back to where she'd been, she reached out and put her hand on Jennifer's arm, halting her flow of anguished words with a touch. "I *do* understand," she said in a level voice. Her gray stare held enough compassion to convince Jennifer. "I know how Beck feels about you, okay? And I'm guessing you feel the same way. I promise you, I will keep you informed."

Miserably, Jennifer stood by and watched Lena hurry away. The scene was filled with chaos, fire trucks and police cars crowding every empty spot, people running in all directions. An arriving ambulance added to the confusion, its siren blaring, the red and blue lights on top streaking across the parking lot. Jennifer waited a moment longer, then she cursed and plunged into the disorder, running toward the ambulance without another thought.

They could arrest her if they wanted to, but she was going to find Beck first.

By the time she reached the ambulance, the two attendants had already leapt from the vehicle and dashed to the rear. Throwing open the doors, they pulled out various pieces of equipment then turned and jogged toward the building. Jennifer followed right behind them, dodging cops and firemen. The three of them reached the front door, or what was left of it, Jennifer already covered in a thin layer of soot and mist from the fire hoses still pointed toward the walls.

Nothing could have prepared her for the sight of the building's interior. As they entered the central atrium, the view to the south wasn't the wall that had been there, but the rear parking lot instead. The back of the building was completely gone. Bricks and drywall were crumpled up in piles of wet, soggy mounds, interspersed with shards of glass and metal. Electrical wires hung like snakes from what remained of the ceiling.

Jennifer's reaction was swift and immediate. In a flash, she was back at the school and seeing Howard's crumpled body. The men in black, the carnage, the whole horrible scene brought the taste of bile into her throat and up even farther. She could feel Juan's weight and smell the fear. For a moment, the feelings were overwhelming. She trembled under the onslaught and swayed, the nausea threatening to overtake her, blackness hovering on the edge of her vision.

Then with a strength she didn't know she had, she pushed through the images and breathed deeply. Three more breaths and they started to fade. Two more and they were gone.

But wasn't reality worse? She stared out over the confusion with shock. No one could survive this kind of destruction and if Beck had been anywhere near... Fighting hysteria, she pushed the thought away and concentrated instead on the building. The corner that housed the beauty salon had taken the brunt of the explosion. One of the red leather chairs was upside down, its upholstery shredded. Another one had survived the blast, but was twisted where it sat. Two of the shampoo bowls had shattered along with all of the mirrors. An errant morning breeze fueled by an incongruent ray of sunshine came through an open hole where the roof had been hours before. A group of men, dressed in black, huddled near an overturned desk. One of them saw the ambulance attendants and cried out. "Over here!"

His voice shook Jennifer out of her daze. She bull-dozed past the two medics and ran toward the men, cry-ing out as she went. "Beck? Beck?"

The team looked up as one, but she didn't see their faces. All she saw was the figure they were surround-ing, the man lying on the ground. He was covered in dirt, one leg at an impossible angle, his face a bloody pulp. His stillness told her the story; she didn't have to look longer to know he was dead.

She went weak then, her legs going out from be-neath her, her stomach turning to water. Refusing to ac-cept the truth her eyes were telling her, she cried out again, Beck's name sounding more like a moan than anything else.

She fell to her knees in the rubble just as one of the men stepped forward and spoke her name. His face was blackened, a horrible slash across one side of his fore-head, a bloody handkerchief tied like a headband around it. She raised her stare to his, and only then—when she met the electric blue of his eyes—did she realize who he was.

For one stunned moment, they stared at each other, then Beck gathered her into his arms and she began to cry in earnest.

BECK WINCED as the medic cleaned the cut above his eye. Turning his head, he looked at Jennifer. Sitting be-side him, inside the ambulance, she stared back, her face the color of the sheets on the gurney, her clothing black with soot. He wanted to scream at her for being there but he couldn't. He was too shocked by her appearance and the look in her eyes. If he didn't know any better, he might think she loved him.

But she didn't. She couldn't.

"That's enough." Beck growled at the attendant and shook his head away from the man's ministrations. "It'll be fine."

"I don't think so," he replied. "You need stitches. We'll transport you."

"Leave us alone." The eyes of the two men clashed under the glare of the lights in the vehicle, then the medic shrugged and disappeared. He wasn't going to argue. Beck turned to Jennifer. "You don't have any business here," he said bluntly. "It's too dangerous. How'd you even get inside anyway?"

"I followed the medics," she said. "No one noticed."

"Well, you shouldn't have. You could have been hurt."

She ignored his admonition. "The man…who was on the floor…"

"He's dead." Beck raised his hand to the bandage that covered one side of his forehead and winced. He spoke in short, clipped sentences, giving her the least amount of explanation he could. "He broke into the building to steal drugs then when the alarm went off and the beat cops came, it all went to hell. We couldn't reach him by phone because we didn't know where he was, and he didn't respond to the bullhorn. I went in with the team and when he saw us, he panicked. He grabbed something from that demolition office and set it off. At the very last minute, he pitched it toward the back of the building or there would have been less left of him than there was."

Her eyes took up half her face. "Why weren't you killed?"

"I was standing on the other side of the hallway because he wouldn't let me get any closer. I had two seconds' warning so I jumped behind a metal desk in the reception area. It took the brunt of the explosion and protected me when the ceiling fell in." He shook his head, then wished he hadn't. Pain rippled down his hairline and through his jaw. The aching stab wasn't as sharp as the one building inside his chest so he acted as if he didn't feel it. "Go home. You don't belong here."

His brusqueness didn't seem to faze her. "You aren't getting rid of me that easily, Beck. Don't even try."

He gave her a hostile look, but she didn't back down. She wasn't going to leave…so he had to. Pushing himself to the end of the stretcher, Beck threw his legs out the rear of the ambulance and stood. His surroundings shifted, so he closed his eyes and grabbed the handle of the door. When he opened his eyes again, Jennifer was beside him, gripping his arm and trying to steady him. It was like an ant holding up an elephant. In any other circumstances, he might have found it amusing.

He simply looked down at her. "Get out of here, Jennifer."

Her eyes took on a determined glint. "Look, I know we have our differences but when I got home and flipped on the television and saw this building…" Her throat moved as she swallowed, and in the light pouring from the van beside them, he could see her gaze begin to glimmer. "I—I—"

She was so beautiful, he couldn't stand it. He broke

in before she could finish and before he could say some-thing he'd regret. "Save it."

"Please, Beck. Just let me...."

"It's over, Jennifer." He softened his voice and lifted up one grimy hand to touch her face. Then he stopped. He was covered in blood and dirt and God only knew what else. Staring at his fingers, he shook his head. He couldn't let himself caress her. Or love her. What she'd said in his apartment, every word, was the truth, and the only truth there was. He couldn't share his job with her; she didn't need to hear about the violence and bloody gore. And she wanted to know everything about him. That was how she loved a person. There was only one way to resolve the problem.

He dropped his hand and stepped away from her. "Go home, Jennifer. Go home and take care of yourself and have a good life."

He memorized every detail of her face, then he walked away.

JENNIFER STOOD numbly in the parking lot and watched Beck leave. He couldn't do that, could he? Tell her just to go home and have a nice life? How could she if he wasn't going to be in it?

He went back into the blackened rubble of the build-ing and she kept her eyes on him until he disappeared. Overhead, in the dawning pink-and-gold sky, a few white wispy clouds drifted by. They looked so peaceful against the still smoldering husk, the image didn't even make sense. Finally, she walked away, too.

"SO THAT'S IT? You just left it at that?"

"There was nothing else *to* do." Jennifer glanced across the table at Wanda and shrugged. They were at AJ's, a local bar, and it was happy hour, but neither of them was very happy. Wanda obviously couldn't believe what she was hearing, and Jennifer was still in a state of shock. Four days had passed and she hadn't heard one word from Beck. And she wouldn't, she was sure. He'd been devastatingly clear about how he felt. He didn't want her around. Since then all she'd done was go back and forth between her apartment and Seacrest to visit her mother. Every day, hoping against hope, Jennifer had prayed Nadine would talk to her about Beck again, but her mother refused to emerge from the hazy confusion where she lived. The conversation they'd shared now seemed like a dream. Jennifer continued to talk to her, though, and drew some measure of comfort from it.

"Didn't you call him? Didn't you ask him?"

Interrupting Jennifer's thoughts, Wanda poked her straw in her drink with more energy than was needed. "The man must have had a good reason to send you packing…."

"Better than me telling him it'd never work out?" Jennifer shook her head miserably. "I think that was sufficient."

"But you changed your mind!"

"No, I didn't."

"Then why'd you go to the Renaissance Center?"

"I thought he was dead! I was terrified something had happened to him, and I had to go up there and see for myself. But no matter what, he's still going to lead that life and I can't stand it. The chaos, the confusion, the secrets. No way! I have dreams and that isn't one of them."

Wanda leaned back on her bar stool and nodded. "Yes, I can understand your point. You're obviously much, much happier now that he's not a part of your future. I can appreciate that, of course…"

Jennifer wanted to wail, but out of respect for the man on the stool next to her, she kept her voice low and moaned instead. "It doesn't matter one way or the other. He doesn't want me. He told me to go home and have a nice life. If that's not a kiss-off, then I don't know what is."

"He didn't mean it."

Reaching for her drink, Jennifer stopped, her hand still in the air. Wanda's words made her realize something she'd never thought of before, but thinking of it now, she knew how true it was. "Of course he means it. Beck doesn't say things he doesn't mean."

"Then you have to figure out why he said it."

"I think that's pretty obvious—"

"No, it's not." She leaned closer to the bar and then even closer to Jennifer. "The man loves you. You know that and I know that. Why would he tell you to go home and have a nice life?"

Jennifer couldn't get past the first few words. "He loves me? He's never said—"

"He didn't have to say it," Wanda answered impatiently.

"Then what makes you so sure he feels that way?"

"Think about it, Jennifer. You wouldn't sleep with a man you didn't love. And you wouldn't let yourself fall for him, unless it was safe. Safe as in 'he loves you, too.'" She held her hands out above the bar. "You love him. He loves you. All you need to do now is figure out why he pushed you away. Address that problem and everything's solved."

"There's more to it than that."

Wanda's dark eyes met Jennifer's. "There's always more when it comes to love. You just have to decide if it's worth the trouble or not."

"What about Howard?"

"What about him? You know Beck did the right thing, and you know he couldn't have told you all the details. You've understood that for a long time."

Wanda was right, and Jennifer nodded slowly. Seeing Beck walk out of that building had made her understand the point even better, though. Howard very well could have killed her or even worse, one of the children. He'd had a gun and he'd been irrational. Beck and his team had risked their lives to make sure that didn't happen, and all she'd done was question him. What on earth had made her think she'd known better?

She lifted her eyes and met Wanda's gaze. "You're right," she said simply. "But he doesn't want me now."

"So? Change his mind, if that's what you want. But do you really want it? I'm wondering because all I'm hearing are excuses." She put her hand on Jennifer's arm. "Are you just flat out scared?"

The question echoed in Jennifer's mind. Was she scared? The answer came swiftly.

She wasn't scared. She was terrified. All her life she'd searched for a calm and perfect life—what she thought was the opposite of her mother and father's marriage—and in the process she'd been pretty damn successful in keeping everything at bay, including love. But perfection didn't exist. Or did it? Wasn't Beck Winters as close as she'd ever found?

"You have to take a chance and go to him," Wanda said softly. "Tell him how you really feel. Tell him you love him. If he still doesn't want you, then you can accept that it's over. Otherwise, you'll always wonder if you tried hard enough."

JENNIFER MADE her way from the front of the station to the offices in the back. She was nervous and anxious, but Wanda, as usual, had delivered excellent advice. Jennifer had to give it her best shot otherwise she'd never know. She reached the office where she expected to see Beck, her hands wet and anxious, her chest so tight she could hardly breathe. But Lena was sitting at the desk, not Beck. The lieutenant looked momentarily nonplussed to see Jennifer, but she stood quickly and smiled. "Miss Barclay! How are you?"

"I'm fine," she answered nervously. "I was looking for Beck. I thought this was his office."

Lena's face took on an unexpected expression Jennifer couldn't decipher. "Well, it is…that is, it was." She stopped and shook her head. "Don't you know?"

A nervous flutter landed in Jennifer's stomach. "Know what?"

Lena hesitated then tilted her head to the chair beside the desk. "Why don't you sit down?"

Jennifer did as the woman suggested, a feeling of

panic building up inside her. "Is everything okay? Beck's not hurt or…"

Lena looked puzzled. "He's fine, just fine, but I would have thought he'd tell you—"

"We had a fight," Jennifer said simply. "At the Renaissance Center the other day. He told me to leave, and I haven't spoken to him since."

"Oh, I'm sorry. I didn't know. I just assumed you two were…"

"I was. He wasn't."

Lena's gray eyes darkened sympathetically. "Men can be confusing, can't they? And now he's gone and done something even more unexpected and didn't even tell you."

"What?"

"He quit the team."

Jennifer's jaw actually dropped open in shock. "He what?"

"He left. Gave me his resignation last night. I really hate to lose him, but I'm not surprised." Lena fiddled with a pencil on her desk then sat back and looked at Jennifer. "He's the best man I've ever worked with, but we all have our limits, and he's reached his. It's better to leave before you cross that line."

Through her disbelief, Jennifer's curiosity rose. "Cross that line? What do mean?"

"Did he ever mention Randy Tamirisa?"

"The sniper…" Jennifer nodded. "He came to Beck's apartment a few nights ago—" She stopped and looked out the window of the office then back to Lena. "What's he got to do with all this?"

"He and Beck did not get along and I had to put Randy on probation. He went to Beck's place because he felt Beck had been behind his problem. The truth is, no one's behind his trouble but himself. Randy came to the line and didn't even know it. Thank goodness he's checked into a rehab center. They'll get him back on track." She looked regretful for a moment. "When your job takes over your life, you lose your perspective and when you lose that, you don't make good decisions. It's not important if you make widgets but if you're a cop and you have a gun in your hand, perspective is the only thing that keeps you alive."

"You think Beck was about to lose his?"

"I didn't, but he did."

"Why?"

Lena dropped the pencil and smiled softly. "Maybe you should turn around and ask him that question yourself."

SHE HAD ON a sleeveless dress, a lilac color, and her hair was piled up on top of her head with just a few strands hanging down around her face. He'd never seen Jennifer look more beautiful. And it broke his heart.

"Beck!" She spoke his name as she jumped to her feet.

He nodded but couldn't say much beyond her name. "Jennifer."

Lena rose as well, her gaze going from one to the other, before breaking the tension-filled silence. "I've got some work to do down the hall. If you two will excuse me…"

Lena eased around Beck, then disappeared into the hallway, softly closing the door behind her.

"What are you doing here, Jennifer?"

"I came to see you."

"Why?"

"Tell me first why you quit the team."

"I can't." He moved toward the chair Lena had vacated, but he didn't sit. He put his hands on the back of it and dug in, his fingers indenting the cracked and frayed leather.

"Can't or won't?"

"Does it matter?"

"It does to me."

He sat down, the springs of the leather desk chair creaking as they took his weight. "I don't really know," he answered, the truth hurting as he verbalized it for the very first time. "I just felt it was something I needed to do."

"Did I have anything to do with that decision?"

Did she? He lost himself for a moment in her eyes, then he shook his head. He'd told her the truth; he wasn't really sure why he'd chosen to leave, but it'd felt right and for once, he'd simply done what he thought he should without questioning his motives. "I decided this on my own…." he answered. "But maybe you did."

She looked puzzled, then he continued, the reasons forming only as the words took shape. "I think I just decided it was time to move on," he said thoughtfully. "We all reach a point in our life, if we're smart, when we know it's best to change gears. I don't want to be one of those old cops who can't turn loose of the badge. You see them in the coffee shops, still telling their tales, pretending it all still matters. There's got to be more to life than that but I won't know unless I look for it." He shook his head. "Maybe I'll come back and maybe I won't. I don't know yet, but I do know it's time for a break. You made me realize that and I guess I should thank you."

He leaned back and stared at her. "So that's my sad story. You tell me why you're here now."

She moved around and took the chair beside the desk. Folding her hands she placed them in her lap, then she looked up at him and took a deep breath. "The reason I'm here is that..." She faltered, her tongue slipping out to moisten her lips. "I wanted to tell you I think I was wrong. I understand now why you did some of the things you did. And why you couldn't tell me everything. I'm sorry I was so dense before."

The cold spot that had been inside his heart since he'd turned her away suddenly began to warm. He shut down the process. This wasn't what he thought it was, he warned himself.

"All my life I've wanted straight lines and written rules. I wanted schedules and order and bells to tell me when to do things. Instead of leaving myself open to new possibilities, I've closed doors. That was wrong and I've come to realize why." She stood up to move closer to him. When he saw the look in her eyes, he rose, too.

She tilted her head back and stared at him. "I was scared...and I still am. But I love you, Beck. And that means accepting you and your life as it is, tumultuous or not. You were right when you said I'm living in the past. My parents' mistakes don't have to be mine and they definitely aren't yours. I've known that all along, but knowing the truth and accepting it are two different things."

Stunned into silence, all Beck could do was gaze down at her. It seemed impossible that this was happening.

Starting to say so, he reached out for her and put his hands on her shoulders. She was trembling.

"I really do love you," she said before he could speak. "Do you think there's any possibility—"

"I love you, too," he said roughly. "I've loved you from the minute I saw you inside that school. You were so brave and so beautiful I couldn't believe it. Without even knowing what kind of woman you were, I knew I loved you, right then and there."

She reached up and gripped his hands, her hold ferocious, her expression fierce. "Then why didn't you tell me? Why did you send me away the other night?"

"I sent you away because I believe you should get what you want…and more. You, out of every woman I've ever met, deserve a husband who can come home every night, physically and mentally. I wasn't sure I could give you that, and I wanted it for you as much as you wanted it for yourself."

Her eyes filled with tears and they spilled over. "I want *you*," she said simply. "You're that man, whether you fit the description or not, it doesn't matter. The only thing that counts is whether or not you want me, too."

He crushed her to him in a hug that stole their breaths.

"I've never wanted anything else." He pulled back so he could look at her. "Will you marry me, Jennifer?"

She smiled through her tears. "You name the day and I'll pick the place."

EPILOGUE

SEACREST HAD NEVER looked lovelier. In the late-evening breeze, the water off the bay rippled with small whitecaps. Several rows of folding chairs had been lined up and down a bright-red carpet leading out from the nearby gazebo. Betty and her husband, all the teachers and the entire Emerald Coast SWAT team, both cells, were sitting and chatting. Someone had threaded white satin ribbons and small pink roses through the fretwork of the gazebo, and as Jennifer stared at their fluttering ends and soft petals, she knew who. Wanda. The nurse stood expectantly at the entrance of the gazebo and smiled back at Jennifer. Beside her, in a gleaming wheelchair, Nadine waved gaily in her direction as well.

Jennifer felt her throat close up. The last thing her mother had asked before they'd wheeled her toward the minister waiting to lead the vows was "Where's Danny?"

"He's watching from the back, Mom," she'd answered. "I saw him just a while ago."

"Oh, good!" Nadine had smiled, her soft, fragile skin even more translucent in the late summer sun. "I'll see him later."

"Absolutely," Jennifer had said.

She put the thought where it belonged and turned her eyes to Beck. Standing on the other side of the carpet from Wanda, he looked back at Jennifer and smiled. Then he held out his hand and she began to walk toward him.

THE COMMANDER

No author ever writes in a vacuum.
I always turn to many experts for help, too many, in fact,
to list here. Heartfelt thanks to everyone, but the following
three need special mention.

To Patricia Brown for generously sharing her
medical expertise regarding gunshot wounds. Thanks for the
help, but most of all, thanks for being such a great friend.

To Dr. Ron Grabowski for helping me with my anatomy
questions. You're a rare breed—someone who cares
and cares deeply. Thank you for everything.

To Caimee Schoenbaechler, one of my three beautiful,
intelligent nieces, for editing my Spanish. I wish I'd had you
with me in Argentina. People would have understood me
a heck of a lot better had you been my interpreter!

PROLOGUE

Somewhere off the coast of Cuba

THERE WAS no moon, thank God.

Andres Casimiro stared into the endless black of the water and counted the only blessing he had. If there'd been light, he'd be a dead man by now.

Easing the throttle of the boat, he slowed the vessel and cut the engine. The gentle sound of slapping waves replaced the throb of the motor, and he took a breath of something that felt like relief. No moonlight, no noise...he might have a chance.

In the still, hot quiet, he looked down at the chart on the table beside the wheel and checked his location again. His gaze traveled past the spot that marked his current position, and he drew a mental line from his home now—Miami—to the place he'd grown up—Havana: 198 nautical miles from one to the other. It should have been much farther, he thought. They were worlds apart. He shook his head to dislodge the thought. All he had to do right now was wait. Wait and *not* think.

Andres had never been a patient man, but in this instance, the waiting would be easier than the thinking anyway. He *had* to make his mind as empty as the sea beneath him to get through this. If he couldn't, the next few hours would be his last.

The minutes ticked by slowly. After a while, he lowered his arm to hide the light and pressed his watch to read the dial—1:00 a.m. Despite his best efforts to the contrary, a surge of disappointment—so strong it felt more like grief—washed over him. He and Lena would have been in Cancun by now, the wedding ceremony long behind them, the I do's said and sealed with a kiss. They would be settling into the villa on the beach. He'd reserved the last one on the Point, where no one ever came. He'd wanted the privacy, the intimacy of it. When he'd told Lena about the special house, she'd smiled in that secret way of hers and said one word. "Perfect."

He wondered what one word she had for him right now. It wasn't *perfect,* he was sure.

A tiny beam broke the darkness, unexpectedly radiant against the inky night before it winked out. Andres's heart bucked as if someone had punched him, and he fumbled the flashlight he'd been holding, dropping it to the deck. With a curse, he fell to his knees and patted the wooden planks. His fingers found the flashlight and he jumped up and flicked it once, then again. He thought he heard a splash, but he wasn't sure.

He started the countdown in his mind. They'd agreed on every thirty seconds. *One thousand one,* he began silently, *one thousand two...*

The numbers echoed in his mind, each digit accompanied by the same mantra. *Forgive me, Lena. I didn't have a choice.... Forgive me....*

He'd been completely unprepared for the phone call he'd gotten early that morning. Mateo's voice, coming over the tinny line, was the last one Andres had expected to hear only a few hours before his wedding. His best friend, Mateo Aznar had helped the eighteen-year-old Andres escape Cuba twenty-four years before and had served since as the sole source of information Andres had on the island. A former cop but now working for the Justice Department, Andres passed the intelligence on, most of it centering on one organization—the Red Tide. A drug cartel that purported to be freedom fighters, they had no good intentions.

"You've got to come," Mateo had gasped. "They've found out about everything. The radio, the lines, everything. If you can't get me out, they'll kill me."

Andres's breath had stopped. "But how did they—?"

"I have my suspicions."

"The same as mine?"

They hadn't wanted to say the name—in Cuba, there were ears everywhere. Andres wasn't sure Destin was any better.

"*Sí,*" Mateo had replied. "I'm certain it's him."

"Do you have any proof?"

"I've got records of the payments. I think it's good enough together with what you know of his 'friends.'"

They'd gone on to what was needed, talking in a code they'd already developed. Within hours, Andres had been on a plane to Miami, then at the dock, renting the boat. He loved Lena desperately and the decision had torn him apart. But it was the only one he could make. When this was all over, he'd go back to her. He'd tell her what he could and pray she'd understand. Deep down, he knew she wouldn't, but to get through the night, he had to believe in the lie.

One thousand twenty-nine, one thousand thirty... Holding the flashlight above his head, Andres switched it on once more. His eyes searched the water. He'd anchored well offshore, but Mateo should have been visible by now. A movement to the right caught Andres's eye. Was it him? His palms pressing into the railing, Andres peered over the side of the boat.

If he hadn't been so focused, he might have seen them.

As it was, when the white-hot flash of the spotlight blinded him, Andres was astonished. The huge cutter loomed as suddenly as if the boat had been dropped from above. When his vision returned, shocked and in a panic, he shot his gaze back to the water. Twenty yards off the bow of his own vessel, he spotted Mateo, floundering in the waves. Before he could cry out, the larger boat angled between the two men.

"Put your hands up and prepare to be boarded. Drop any weapons *now!*" The warning was given in Spanish, through a bullhorn from the deck of the ship. "*¿Comprende?*"

Instead of answering, Andres screamed into the night. "Hurry, Mateo, hurry! You can make it! Swim faster! I'll come get you!"

The water was choppy and rough, but Andres's and Mateo's eyes connected over the waves. In that instant, that split second, Andres knew he'd done the right thing. Leaving Lena at the altar, giving up the only woman he'd ever loved... How could he have lived with himself otherwise? He revved the engine then maneuvered the tiny boat around the cutter and headed toward his friend.

He reached Mateo just as an onslaught of bullets peppered the water. A searing pain streaked down Andres's arm as he took a direct hit, but the wound was nothing compared to the agony he felt as Mateo screamed and began to flail about in the now crimson waves.

"Goddammit, no! No!" Andres gunned the boat and cut past the spot, turning the craft as tightly as he dared to fly back once more. He searched the waves with desperate eyes, placing himself between the huge ship and where Mateo had been, but there was nothing to see.

Mateo was gone.

Andres screamed a useless curse and wasted a few more dangerous moments searching the water. With no other choice, he spun the boat around and disappeared into the darkness. Gunfire followed his wake, but it couldn't reach him. His craft was fast and small, and the cutter didn't have a chance.

He made it to Miami a few hours later. He'd sacrificed love for loyalty, a wife for a friend.

Now he had neither. It'd take him a lifetime to forget. And forever to forgive.

CHAPTER ONE

Destin, Florida
Two years later

LENA MCKINNEY stepped onto the red-carpeted aisle of the flower-filled church, the solemn strains of the "Wedding March" drifting above the crowded pews.

All the guests were watching her and she knew what they were thinking—little Lena McKinney was *finally* getting married...after all this time! Her tomboy years were behind her, and now she was a woman. From beneath her lacy veil she smiled with silent satisfaction, then all at once, the realization hit her.

Other than the veil, she wore nothing. She was completely naked.

A wave of humiliation swamped her as she dropped her bouquet and tried to cover herself. Her actions were pointless, though. Everyone had already seen. Everyone already knew.

With a startled exclamation, Lena woke up and pushed herself out of the tangled sheets of her bed. She glanced at the clock on the nightstand, her heart still pounding from the dream—5:00 a.m. What in the hell was she doing? She had to get up in another hour, and now she'd never go back to sleep. She never did after the dream.

She collapsed against her pillows, muttering a curse then immediately chastising herself. Her poor mother was probably turning over in her grave. That's what came from eating, breathing and drinking your work, Lena thought guiltily. She was starting to sound like the testosterone-charged cops she worked with 24/7.

No excuse, her mother's ghost said with a hopeless sigh. You're *supposed* to be a lady, try acting like one for a change.

Lena stared at the stained ceiling above her bed. At least her mother hadn't been alive to see the Disaster, which was how Lena always thought of the aborted wedding.

The beautiful sanctuary, the silken gown, the wonderful music...every detail coordinated down to her bouquet of white freesias and apricot roses. They'd waited for as long as they could, her father holding her hand in the tiny room off the narthex, then they'd sent out Bering, the eldest of her four brothers. He'd explained as much as possible, and the guests had gone home. Lena had been worried, then incredulous, both emotions finally exploding into a bitter anger the next day when Andres had shown up and given her his lame excuses.

Get a grip, she told herself furiously. It was past history. Dead and gone. Andres had moved on and so had she. Stationed in Miami, he was climbing the ladder at the Justice Department, going up so fast he was nothing but a blur. She hadn't been standing still, either. In charge of the Emerald Coast SWAT team, Lena held a position of authority and power, too. Two cells of top-flight officers worked under her command.

Moaning with disgust over the dream and at herself for having it, Lena sat up and put her feet on the floor.

A front had blown in last night and the stained concrete was cold and hard, the icy feeling instantly traveling up her legs. The scene outside the uncovered windows added to the chill, a gray and stormy Floridian sea churning on the beach only a hundred yards away. Above the waves, the October sky looked just as forbidding. Dark, heavy clouds hovered over the horizon, their swirling depths promising rain later.

One of the panes of glass rattled loudly, and propelled by the sound, Lena turned to go to the kitchen. The pipes sang, the shingles leaked, and half the time the heater refused to work. She didn't care. She had memories of her mother here, and of good summers, laughing and chasing her brothers over the dunes. Her father had tried to buy her a condo last summer in the new high-rise going up off Inlet Beach. The units were "only" three hundred thousand, he'd said. A bargain at preconstruction rates. She'd turned him down, and he'd gotten angry, not understanding.

In the kitchen, she flipped on the television set, reaching for the door of the refrigerator at the same time. Bleary-eyed, she grabbed the last diet cola and a boiled egg left over from a few days before. The breakfast of champions. Her planned stop at the grocery store yesterday had been put on hold, as a lot of her plans were, when the team had gotten a late-afternoon callout. The situation had dragged on forever, and they hadn't cleaned up the mess until after two that morning. But that's what SWAT team work was like. You stayed until the end, no matter how long it took to come.

No one had been hurt, though. That was always her goal: everyone gets out alive.

She popped open the cold drink, then took a long

swallow before beginning to peel the egg, dropping the bits of shell into the sink. "Everyone gets out alive," she repeated out loud. "Hostages, victims...even jilted brides."

The ringing phone startled her and Lena fumbled with the egg. She caught it right before it slid into the disposal, then grabbed the receiver. "McKinney here."

Sarah Greenberg's soft voice sounded, and Lena relaxed the muscles she'd tightened automatically on hearing the phone. Sarah was the SWAT team's information officer, and her calls didn't usually signify an emergency. "Sarah! You're calling awfully early. What's up? Everything okay?"

"We're fine," the young woman answered.

Lena sipped her cola. "Did Beck tell you about last night?" A former negotiator, Beck Winters had left the SWAT team a while back but Lena had promised him a desk job and he'd returned.

Before Sarah could answer, Lena launched into an explanation. "Panama City Beach had a warrant they were trying to serve. It went downhill fast, but—" She realized suddenly that Sarah had gone silent. Usually the young cop had plenty to contribute but for some reason, she hadn't said a word. Lena frowned. "Sarah?"

A pause—this one lasting long enough to make Lena really nervous—then Sarah spoke. "We got a fax this morning ordering a special dignitary detail for next week. I thought you might want to know about it right away so you could... um...prepare for it."

"I'll be in the office in an hour," Lena said slowly. "It couldn't wait until then?"

"I thought you might want to know about this one before you got here...so you wouldn't be surprised."

Lena waited a minute, but Sarah said nothing more and finally Lena spoke again, this time somewhat impatiently. "Well, are you going to tell me or do I have to guess?"

"It's for the guy from Justice in Miami." Sarah sounded almost shaky. "You know, the one they're sending to open the new office? There've been death threats called in. They think an attempt might be made on his life."

She should have known, Lena told herself later. She should have seen it coming. But it was only after Sarah said "Miami" that Lena's mind kicked into gear. "No... oh, no... Shit..."

"I'm sorry, Lena. But it's Andres Casimiro. He's coming to Destin and he needs protection."

"IS THIS THE FULL REPORT?" Andres raised his gaze to Carmen San Vicente, his assistant. They were in the director's private jet, fifteen thousand feet above the Florida Panhandle. Andres hadn't taken the time to look out the window and see the turquoise waters beneath him, but he'd buzzed the captain a moment before and asked for the ETA. The man had said ten minutes and Andres had felt his gut respond accordingly. Now he was glaring at Carmen and she had no idea she wasn't responsible for his expression. He was thinking of the same thing he'd been thinking of for the past week—every day, every hour, every minute—since he'd known he was coming back to Destin.

Lena.

Carmen answered, but Andres's mind had already gone elsewhere. He hadn't spoken to Lena since the night he'd returned to Destin following Mateo's death. The meeting had been disastrous, of course. He'd told her what he could—that a special mission had come up, that he'd had no choice but to miss their wedding.

She'd stared him in the eye and said just what he'd expected, her voice calm and controlled. "I'm a cop, Andres. I would have understood if you'd told me."

With his heart cracking in two, he'd met her accusing stare. It had held equal shares of pain and anger, and he'd felt both just as deeply. "I couldn't tell you, Lena. Not this time."

She'd looked as if she wanted to believe him, but a moment later she'd closed her expression. "Then we have nothing more to discuss." Pulling off the diamond he'd given her, she'd handed him the ring and turned away. "Please leave."

He'd done what she asked because he hadn't had another choice. And he still didn't. To begin with, she would never believe him, and if she did accept his suspicions—by some miracle—it would almost be worse. The news would completely destroy her.

Lena's father had arranged Mateo Aznar's death. He'd wanted to kill Andres, as well.

Andres had had his suspicions before the wedding, but for Lena's sake, he'd kept them to himself. He'd waited and watched, collected the tiny scraps of evidence he could, the main one being a local drug dealer named Pablo Escada, who had kept Phillip McKinney's law office on retainer. The Panamanian immigrant was in the Union Correctional Institution for the moment, but he hadn't shut down his business. Andres couldn't prove the connection but he knew—he *knew*—Escada was hooked up with the Red Tide. He had to be. The organization funneled all the drugs that came through the area.

And Phillip was connected to Escada.

For months after the murder, Andres had devoted every minute of his time trying to document Phillip's involvement, but he'd ended up with nothing. He'd been unable to find a shred of data, an iota of validation, to link the wily old attorney with the terrorists.

After a while, Andres had to let it go and accept what appeared to be the truth: things had gone terribly wrong that night and the Red Tide had acted on their own. Mateo had been wrong about the money coming from Phillip's office.

"I brought everything that was in the folder." Carmen's voice held an anxious flutter. "Are you missing something?"

Andres finally heard her apologetic tone. He shook his head. "I'm sorry. I didn't mean to bark at you. I'm a little preoccupied—"

"It's okay," she answered in an accommodating way. "I understand. Really, I do. It's impossible to get anything done when you have to travel all the time." She reached up and tucked a strand of dark hair behind one ear then her eyes warmed hopefully as Andres's gaze met hers. "Would you like to work this evening? I could come to your hotel room after dinner tonight and we could finish this then."

"No," he said, shaking his head. "We'll cover the final details right before the meeting in the morning. It's not necessary to take you away from your kids *and* make you work overtime, too."

Andres watched her hide her disappointment by turning away to fuss with some files in her hands. With her shining hair and olive skin, she had the kind of beauty for which Miami's women were famous. Years before, she'd befriended his aunt Isabel, and the older woman, more of a mother to him than his own had been, had convinced him to hire Carmen when she'd needed a job. She was smart and ambitious, a single mom with two children she was putting through private school.

She'd finally gotten him into bed the month before.

He'd known the minute it started, he was making a big mistake. He'd tried to tell her, to back away and bow out gracefully, but she'd put her fingers across his mouth and stopped him from saying more. When her lips had left his and gone lower, he'd said nothing else, allowing her hot eyes and slow touch to comfort him. But he should never have given in. It'd been unfair to her.

Carmen started toward the front of the plane, then stopped at the bulkhead and turned, as though just remembering something. "Did you get your vest?"

He stared at her blankly. "My vest?"

"The director left a bulletproof vest for you to wear when you get off the plane. He told me he'd have my head if you weren't wearing it when you arrived."

Andres dismissed her words with a wave of his hand. It was a very Latin gesture; as a child, he'd seen his Cuban father make the same one a thousand times.

"I *promised* him," she said.

"You shouldn't have. They're hot and heavy and totally useless. I never wore one when I was a cop and I'm not going to start now." He went back to the files spread before him.

"And did the Red Tide have money on your head while you were a cop?"

"Drop it, Carmen. I don't have the time or the patience."

Ignoring him, she came back down the aisle and rested on the arm of the seat opposite his. "*Por favor,* Andres, those guys are terrorists. They're bad—"

"They're leftover Communists and rejects from the islands who sell drugs. Don't be confused about this, Carmen." He narrowed his gaze. "They're criminals and nothing more. If I let scum like that scare me, then I don't deserve to be in this job."

"They've threatened to kill you."

"So what? They've done the same before and nothing has happened. We've ordered security at the airport. Let the Emerald Coast SWAT team handle this."

He turned his eyes out the window of the plane. Destin was almost in view. What would Lena say to him? How would she react after all this time?

Carmen started to argue more, but the captain's voice came over the intercom. "Two minutes to landing, folks. Everyone buckle up."

"I'll get the vest for you right now." She tried one last time. "You can slip it on before we land—"

"No." He slammed his files shut and pulled on his seat belt. "No one's going to be shooting at anybody. Not the Red Tide. Not anybody. Not today."

Carmen shook her head then sat down abruptly in the seat in front of him, the sound of her own seat belt an angry click as she buckled herself in.

But Andres hardly noticed. Once again, he wasn't thinking about his assistant or the Red Tide or even the man he'd suspected all those years ago of backing them. His thoughts were centered on the only thing he really cared about in Destin.

Lena McKinney.

The woman he'd never stopped loving.

LENA STOOD beneath the overhang of Terminal A, her eyes scanning the buildings around her as the breeze tugged at her hair and pulled on her jacket. The sky was so blue, it almost glowed. Strong winds straight from the Gulf had blown away last week's storm clouds and now it was clear, the sunshine warming the temperature to a balmy seventy degrees, the quick change typical for Destin's weather. A salty tang hung over the blackened tarmac, as well. The airport was blocks from the beach, but the sea was always close in Destin. Even if it wasn't in sight, you could either hear it or smell it.

Her earphone crackled suddenly and Lena put her fingers against the small black piece of plastic all the team members wore in order to communicate with each other. The words sounded faintly in her ear. Andres's plane would be landing within minutes.

She lifted her gaze to the cloudless expanse. The aircraft was not yet in sight, but she could feel its nearness deep inside her. Ever since Sarah had given her the news, Lena had hovered between craziness and calm acceptance. One minute she'd tell herself she could handle Andres's appearance. He no longer meant anything to her, anything at all. The next minute lunacy would take over and she'd start to recall everything about him—his black eyes, his heavy-lidded looks, the Latin sighs.

Standing on the asphalt, she told herself there was only one way this meeting would go. He'd arrive, she'd say a cool hello, then she'd concentrate on her job and nothing else. Keeping him safe was all she had to worry about and nothing could interfere with that goal.

Everyone gets out alive.

To maintain her calmness, she focused on her preparations. The airport was tiny and that made things simple. Their primary concern would be the deplaning. Passengers didn't always go through jetways here;

sometimes after the aircraft landed, they walked down exterior stairways. He'd be the most vulnerable right then. That was why she would go out and meet him personally. Her chest went tight at the thought, but she took a deep breath and concentrated on the details.

She'd put Ryan Lukas, their main sniper, on the center roof and his counterpart from the other team, Chase Mitchell, on the rear building. Peter Douglas and John Fletcher, the two rear entry men from Team Beta were manning security at the entrances inside and out. Cal Hamilton and Jason Field, the rear guys from Alpha were providing undercover surveillance inside the waiting lounges. She'd ordered dogs and handlers into the parking garage as a final extra precaution. The remaining team members she'd scattered about the airport, leaving only a skeleton crew in town under the control of her second in command, Bradley Thompson. Maybe she'd gone overboard, but she didn't want to examine that thought too closely, so she told herself if nothing else, it was good training for the day when someone really important might show up.

The low, thrumming sound of a jet interrupted the expectant silence. When Lena spotted its blue-and-white logo, she reached up and adjusted her headset to bring the microphone closer to her mouth. "Heads up, everyone. Package approaching."

Her voice was level and constant. *It's just another job,* she told herself. Another situation, another callout, nothing more. Andres was coming to meet with the head of the new D.E.A. branch office that was opening in Destin. According to Sarah, he'd be in and out in one day. She'd see him for a total of ten minutes, coming and going, and that was it.

Everyone gets out alive.

The plane came into view and a few seconds later, the wheels touched down, their screaming protest louder than Lena was accustomed to from inside the terminal. In a matter of minutes, the jet reached the end of the blackened asphalt, then turned slowly and began to taxi toward her. Lena's gaze went over the area one more time, checking and rechecking. Everyone on the field had gone through security, but a sudden edginess brushed against her. She didn't believe in omens but all at once her instincts were screaming too loud to ignore. She concentrated a moment more, then her gaze homed in on the porthole in the aft section of the arriving plane, pinpointing the source of her discomfort. Her unease was coming from *inside* the aircraft, not out.

A face stared at her through the thick glass of the window. She caught only an impression—dark hair and a black suit—but it was enough. She knew it was Andres. The engines whined loudly and the plane ended up alongside the waiting stairway. A moment later, the noise from the turbines died, leaving only silence.

Lena walked into the bright sunshine and headed for the stairs.

CHAPTER TWO

ANDRES ROSE from his seat, nervous energy propelling him into the aisle before the jet had even stopped moving. Pacing the tiny walkway, he waited for the flight attendant to open the door, willing the man to hurry up, but without obvious results. A rush of humid air and sunshine flooded the cabin as the uniformed steward finally drew the door back.

He told himself he was prepared.

But he wasn't.

Lena stepped inside and Andres's heart stopped. He could actually feel it thump once then quit. A moment later, it started again, but for a second, he hadn't been sure it would.

Her whiplike body filled the black SWAT uniform with unmistakable familiarity. She'd never had a voluptuous figure, but what she did have was perfect. She was fit and trim without an ounce of extra anything. Her brown hair, still shiny and smooth, was tinged with streaks of blond and cut shorter than he remembered. Her gray eyes weren't as stormy as they'd been the last time he'd seen her, but there was something in her gaze that stabbed him, the pain unexpectedly pointed and physical.

"Andres." She said his name with aloofness. "Welcome to Destin."

"Thank you, Lena. It's good to see you—"

She didn't let him finish, her brisk response impersonal and distant. "We need to do this fast, Andres. The longer we take, the more opportunity for trouble there is." Tilting her head, she indicated the stairs behind her. "I'll go down first. You follow me. Scott will get your back. Everyone else comes off after you're clear."

He knew it was foolish but Andres found himself wanting something else from her, something...more. The realization bothered him, but he put it aside and looked at the man behind her. He was young but had the hard air of a seasoned cop. Wearing the same uniform as Lena, black and tight, he acknowledged Andres with a quick bob of his head as Lena spoke again, her voice even more clipped and cold.

"You've got on the vest?"

"No," he said brusquely. "The vest is not necessary."

"We're not deplaning until you have it on."

"You're wasting my time."

"No," she answered in a no-nonsense way. "You're wasting it yourself." Her eyes flicked over his shoulder and she spoke to Carmen, figuring out her status instantly. "Do you know where his Kevlar vest is?" Carmen apparently nodded, and Lena continued. "Go get it, please."

Her manner brought forth another flash of irritation. She always did it by the book, no matter what. He glanced down at his watch then looked back up at her. "I have to be downtown in fifteen minutes."

Carmen appeared at Lena's side and handed her a small black bag. Without even looking at it, Lena handed the pack over to him. "Then put this on, and we'll leave."

He glared at her and she glared back, but a moment later, he snatched the bag from her hands and pulled out the black sleeveless garment. His eyes remained on her face as he ripped off his tie and began to unbutton his jacket. "This is ridiculous." When he was upset a trace of Spanish inflection always came into his voice. He heard it now. "You've made the area safe, no? Why should I do this?"

"Because I'm not perfect," she told him calmly. "And neither are the men who work for me. We've swept the terminal and have people in place, but you never know. Someone could have slipped through."

He pulled off his black silk coat and shrugged into the Kevlar, the fabric stiff against his white, starched shirt. In the closeness of the cabin, he could smell her soap...or was he imagining it?

"I'm trusting you to have done your job right," he snapped. "You should be flattered, not giving me a hard time."

Her steady eyes revealed nothing in response to his words, but a vibration of energy came off her body, a low, silent humming that only Andres could have caught. His fingers stilled on the fasteners of the vest as she spoke.

"My job will be done when you're off this plane and still alive." A heartbeat passed as her gray eyes locked on his. "Trust has nothing to do with it."

ANDRES GATHERED his briefcase and jacket while Lena stood at the door of the plane and surveyed the runway area one more time. Her eyes went slowly over the buildings in front of her, but in fact, she wasn't really seeing them. The image coming to her instead was that of Andres and his hands. When she thought of him, she always thought of those hands. Other women might have noticed his trim stomach or the width of his shoulders or even his eyes as they'd stared at her, but not Lena. She'd watched his fingers move over the buttons of his blazer. They were long, his knuckles slim and well-formed, his wrists broad and strong-looking.

She'd noticed the rest of him, too, though. Above the collar of his pristine white shirt, the café-au-lait tone of his skin, that sweet, smooth color she'd always loved, was darker than before, the contrast of the material against his face and neck sensual and appealing. When he was under a lot of stress, he spent as much time as he could outdoors, playing baseball usually.

Beneath all the polish, though, he acted just as he always had—like a banked fire poised on the verge of explosion. She'd responded as she'd known she would, too, with the same mix of fascination and dread and anger he always created inside her. Nothing she could say to herself would make her heart stop crashing inside her chest. How could she do what she was supposed to do? How could she concentrate?

All she could think about was the last time they'd been together, when he'd shown up after the canceled wedding and told her about the special operation he'd had to run. She'd been a cop all her adult life and a good one; even though his distrust had hurt, she had understood the need for secrecy, the reticence to talk. But she was a woman, too. He'd broken her heart and destroyed her self-confidence. She could never forgive him for that.

As she always did when her thinking got too heavy, she turned to action, forcing herself to focus as she pulled her microphone closer. "L1 calling team leader. Package secure."

"Gotcha, L1. We're clear. Wait for final check then proceed."

They transmitted on closed channels, but when doing protections Lena insisted on maintaining as much security as possible. With a precise, calm voice, she checked on each of the team members, using the code they'd already agreed on. Everyone was in place and ready to move. When Ryan, the sniper, issued a final clear from his vantage point, they'd go. She looked over her shoulder, past Scott to where Andres stood.

He was giving some last-minute instructions to the woman who'd brought Lena his vest. His secretary, his assistant, his lover? Lena wasn't sure of her position, but she'd immediately known how the woman felt about Andres. Her adoration of him was obvious. It meant nothing to Lena, of course, yet she couldn't help but notice. When they'd been together, he'd continually attracted women. They couldn't seem to resist him.

Passing Scott, Andres moved to the front of the cabin and took up his position directly behind her. He'd donned his jacket again and the bulky vest beneath made his chest look vast. As he juggled his briefcase to his other hand, he bumped into her shoulder. *"Lo siento,"* he murmured. *I'm sorry....*

The Spanish was unexpected and somehow too intimate. She looked directly at him then, and in the closeness, all her senses, the ones she'd been trying to tamp down since she'd walked into the plane and into his presence, heightened, as if someone had turned up a volume knob until the sound was out of range. She could smell his aftershave, a scent she didn't recognize, thank

God, and even see the tiny flecks of gold imbedded in the iris of his right eye. She had on a SWAT jacket and vest as well, but the brush of his arm burned through the fabric like a lighted torch.

She couldn't physically step away; she was trapped between him and the door, but she pulled into herself and shuttered her expression, turning her face away from him.

Her coldness didn't stop him. Impulsively, it appeared, he reached out and drew a line down the side of her cheek. His touch was as smooth and sensual as ever and it left a trail of stunning memories behind. "Lena..." He gave her name the Spanish inflection. "Will you have some time for me later? To catch up?"

His stare was so black, Lena felt herself slide into its endless depths. She fought the sensation with everything she had in her, stopping the headlong disaster only at the very last moment. She spoke slowly, distinctly. "I'm here today because I have a job to do. And as far as I'm concerned, that job is the only reason I'll be seeing you again. I have nothing else to say to you and I certainly don't feel like going over old times."

"And if I disagree?"

Her pulse jackhammered, but Lena had trained herself well. She knew her expression was neutral. "Feel free to disagree all you want. I don't really care one way or the other."

His eyes danced over her face, searching it for something, and she felt the plunge begin again. Before his inexorable pull could drag her any deeper, her radio sounded, Ryan's voice in her ear. "This is G1. Area clear. L1 proceed."

She acknowledged the call, then spoke to Andres, heading off whatever his reply might have been.

"The stairs are going to be our most open point. Stay as close to me as possible and keep your head down. Don't look around. Just watch my feet and go where I go. Scott will be at your back. When we hit the ground, we'll walk directly to the car. If anything happens, fall down. Understand?"

At her imperious tone, his own voice sharpened. "For God's sake, Lena, I know what to do. I've done this before—"

"Good," she broke in. "Then do it right, and we'll all come out alive."

He started to reply, but at the last minute he snapped his mouth shut and jerked his head toward the stairs in an impatient let's-go motion. Lena caught Scott's eye, spoke into her headset then started down the stairs.

AS ANDRES FOLLOWED Lena down the steps, he told himself to calm down, to act as if he didn't care. It was an impossible order, though.

He'd never be able to do that, not as far as she was concerned.

When she'd made that crack about trust, Lena had been putting him on notice. There was no trust between them—not now. She would do her job but there would be no other contact. She wanted nothing to do with him. Nothing at all.

Forcing himself to ignore his response, he discarded Lena's instructions and looked around the tarmac, his stare quick and jumpy as it traveled over the jetway and to the buildings beyond. He saw nothing unusual.

To their right a mechanic in a set of blue overalls worked under the hood of a small Cessna, his tools laid out in a precise line at his feet. To his left, a man in sunglasses and a cap sat behind the wheel of a small motorized cart filled with luggage. In between them was the terminal, and through a wall of windows, Andres could see a group of passengers mingling and talking. Well-dressed and well-heeled, they matched the expensive designer suitcases on the wagon. They were probably waiting for one of the private jets that made up the majority of planes coming in and out of the airport.

By the time he finished his scan, they were at the foot of the stairs, and Andres took a deep breath, an unconscious sweep of relief hitting him hard. For the first time, he noticed the weather; the sunshine was almost blinding, the air warmer and softer than it usually was this time of year. Along the walkway, a row of sago palms swayed in the brisk breeze, their green fronds gleaming in the light.

A second later they reached a nearby SUV. The unmarked Suburban, painted black with darkly tinted windows, was so obviously a government truck it could have had the department's seal on the side. The back doors swung wide, and Zack Potter stepped out. Potter would be running the Destin office Andres was here to officially open. A former D.C. policeman, the handsome man looked more like a bodybuilder than a federal official. They'd been friends a long time and Andres respected him greatly. Except for Andres himself, no one could run the office any better. With Zack Potter in charge, the Red Tides's pipeline of drugs from Mexico to New York was about to hit a major roadblock.

Potter crossed the space between them and held out his hand, a wide grin splitting his face. "Casimiro! 'Bout time you got here." He nodded toward the jet. "Nice ride, too!"

"Let's save the greetings for later, gentlemen." Lena glanced in Potter's direction, then spoke quickly, her eyes studying the area around them as she motioned Scott to the other side of the car. "I need to get Mr. Casimiro inside, please...."

"Of course, of course!" Potter smiled again then stepped aside to let Andres pass. Lena stood at the door of the truck waiting for him.

He reached her side, threw his briefcase onto the seat, then turned to look at her. Just as in the plane, they were inches apart, her slim form backed up against the open car door, his body poised to get inside. Her gaze was serene and composed, the stone color of her eyes even more intense now that they were outside in the sunshine. It was crazy, but he had to try—and he wasn't even sure for what—one more time.

"Lena...*querida*..."

Again the Spanish. Lena couldn't believe it, but something curled inside her, a warm yearning for a time that was far behind them. The depth of pain that accompanied the craving surprised her, but she stiffened against it. She wasn't his sweetheart and hadn't been for a long time. How dare he use that word and that tone of voice? How was she supposed to deal with that?

Before she could form her angry reply, she caught an unexpected movement in her peripheral vision, a sudden motion that made her snap to, almost as if waking up from a dream. She glanced toward the area, already cursing herself for letting down her guard. Her profanity had barely cleared the air when the first bullet slammed into the Suburban.

A moment later, the second one came.

Beside them, Zack Potter collapsed onto the asphalt,

his scream dying as the bullet ripped into his neck. Lena stared at his still-jerking body, then she yanked her head up and cried into her headset for backup. As she spoke, she whirled and Andres's shocked eyes met hers. Grabbing his arms instinctively, she did what she was trained to do—she pushed him straight into the truck.

But he resisted her, and for one single second, they held on to each other, each trying their best to protect the other one first. Lena won—not by strength—but by doing the only thing she could. She went limp. Caught off guard by her action, Andres hesitated and that was all she needed. With a violent shove, she forced him down, then turned, thrusting herself in front of him.

The final shot was a direct hit. Lena crumpled without a word.

CHAPTER THREE

ANDRES REACTED instantly, old habits taking over as adrenaline kicked in. He grabbed Lena by the collar of her jacket and yanked her to him. Still trying to draw her weapon, she fought him futilely. "No," she gasped. "You go! Get in the car and leave!"

"Not without you!" They wasted a few more precious moments, then too weak to do anything else, she gave in to Andres and allowed him to pull her into the truck. Before he tumbled inside the vehicle with her, Andres sent a quick glance in Zack Potter's direction. The time to help his friend had passed. "Get us out of here," he roared to the driver. "Now! Let's go!"

The man needed no urging. The black SUV sprang forward, the tires squealing as he drove it down the sidewalk and straight toward a set of double gates. Only when she spoke again did Andres realize Lena had never released her grip of his arm. She pulled at him weakly, her voice fading but still urgent. "Stay down. We don't know where the shots came from."

Andres turned, but it was too late for her to hear his reply. Her eyes rolled back and she fainted without a sound. Her limp body started to pitch off the seat, but he threw himself on top of her and stopped her fall at the very last minute. Bracing himself, he fought the violent rocking of the truck and prepared for the crash of the vehicle as it went through the metal frame of the gate.

When it didn't happen, he lifted his head and took a quick glance. A figure in black, one of Lena's men, had swung back the iron grilles. The driver deftly maneuvered through the narrow opening, then bumped the speeding vehicle over the grooved tracks to a grassy swell just at the left of the runway. With the tires screaming even louder than before, the Suburban hit the pavement outside the terminal then turned right on two wheels. Within seconds they were on the main road into town, two black and whites escorting them, one front, one rear.

In the back of his mind, Andres realized what he had just witnessed. Lena had planned for this. She'd had a man stationed at the exit and an escape route in place.

The man behind the wheel said something about alerting the hospital, then spoke into a headset. "Let them know we're bringing someone in," he said shakily. His voice thickened as he answered an obvious question. "No, it's not the package. It's Lieutenant McKinney. She's been hit."

Beneath Andres, Lena groaned. He slid to the floorboard of the vehicle to give her more room, then he took a good look at her injury for the first time. The bullet had managed to go beneath her vest. It didn't look good. His mouth went dry.

"Where's the first aid—"

Before he could finish, the driver thrust a white metal box over the front seat. "There's bandages and tape inside," he said. "We'll be at the hospital in five minutes."

Andres ripped open the case and grabbed a roll of white gauze, but the material was woefully inadequate. It seemed as if blood was pouring from Lena. Yanking off his coat, he pressed it against the wound but the fabric was immediately soaked. He'd seen plenty of men shot, had even done the shooting himself more than once, but this was Lena, for God's sake. She groaned and a sick feeling rose up in his chest to block his breathing.

He slipped a hand beneath her head. She was going into shock, her skin pale and clammy, her body shaking on the leather cushions that were already slick with her blood. Her eyes fluttered open, and suddenly she looked smaller and more frail.

"Hang on, *querida,* hang on." His endearment slipped out naturally, just as it had earlier in the car. "We'll be at the hospital any minute. You can do it."

She spoke with great difficulty. "You...okay? Not hit?"

"Don't talk," he said automatically. "You'll lose more blood."

She ignored him completely. "Are you...okay?"

"*Sí, sí.* I am fine, now *por favor*—no more talking!"

She nodded weakly, her eyes closing once more, only to blink open again. "W-what about... Potter?"

"Don't worry about him. The others will take care of him. You just lie there and be quiet."

They bounced around a curve. She tried to bite back a cry but failed, her agony apparent. Helpless to do anything else, Andres screamed at the driver. "Take it easy up there, goddammit! You're hurting her!"

The man didn't respond; he simply added more gas, the black Suburban barreling down the highway, passing everything else in a blur.

"Andres..." She spoke his name softly, painfully.

He bent down, his heart suddenly plunging into a

frightening abyss. She was fading right before his eyes, growing obviously weaker as he held on to her. "Lena! Stay with me, okay? Stay awake!"

She lifted a shaking hand and grabbed his shirt. Her fingers were red and sticky with her own blood, but the strength in her grip was shocking. She pulled him closer, her voice a fading rasp. "I should have done a better job...shoulda checked better." Her lips were dried and caked, the words thick but the meaning clear. "I'm sorry, Andres, I'm so sorry...."

She was apologizing for saving his life? If there were *shoulds* they belonged to him, dammit! *He* should have been the one lying there bleeding, not Lena.

He leaned over her. "Lena, please! You *did* do your job. Don't get *loco* on me, okay? *¿Me escuchas?* Do you hear me?"

She nodded faintly, then she went still in his arms and her head fell back.

ANDRES DIDN'T KNOW which was worse: holding Lena's unresponsive body or handing her over to the medics at the hospital. Either way he felt helpless and totally out of control.

Three nurses and two doctors were waiting as the SUV wheeled into the drive-through by the hospital's back door. They shoved him out of the way and disappeared with Lena down the hall. He caught up to the gurney just as they turned it into a room and slammed the door in his face. All he could do was listen as someone screamed for X rays STAT and another voice yelled out for a chest tube. He vented his frustration by cursing in Spanish and waving his arms but his actions were futile. No one would let him inside.

Leaning his head against the mint-colored wall, a storm of emotion broke over him. Panic, anger, fear, guilt—every feeling he'd ever experienced erupted all at once. It was a tide he couldn't stop, a flood he couldn't control. In a useless attempt to stem the sensations, he raised his hands to cover his face, but all he did was make it worse as his fingers came into focus.

The creases in his skin were painted red. Red with Lena's blood. His horrified gaze fell lower. His pants, his shirt, even his shoes were crimson. He was covered with her blood.

He stared a moment longer, then he closed his fingers, his knuckles shining under the bright lights of the corridor as a rush of guilty rage shook him. Lifting his arm in one fluid movement, he slammed his fist into the wall. A hole appeared as a rain of green plaster cascaded to the floor.

His whole side went numb, but his mind—and his heart—cracked open wide.

THE DOCTORS and the nurses were talking. Their voices were hurried, but distinct, each word a perfectly formed entity that Lena heard, then saw. They floated above her, just out of reach in little cartoon boxes, as did the masked faces of the people nearby. She wanted to tell them she felt fine but everyone seemed too rushed to listen to her mumbles. She closed her eyes slowly, the lids fluttering down. The next thing she knew, she was at the beach. Jeffrey, the youngest of all her brothers, was chasing her into the tide, splashing her and calling her a baby, telling her about the monsters that were just offshore, waiting to get her.

She looked out into the emerald waves and shivered.

Monsters were out there, all right, but they weren't in the water. They were closer, closer than either of them had ever suspected. She shut her eyes and screamed, but no one heard her.

ANDRES HEARD Phillip McKinney long before he saw him, the man's unmistakable voice rolling down the hallway and bowling over everything in its path. Andres jumped to his feet and after a questioning glance, Carmen, at his side, stood as well. A moment later, Lena's father strode into the waiting room, his entourage following behind him as he plowed through the crowd of cops who'd begun to congregate after hearing the news.

Phillip had aged a bit, but not that much. His hair, always silver, was a little thinner and his step a little slower, yet his back was ramrod straight, his skin tanned and tight. The handmade suit, the polished shoes, the silk foulard tie, they hadn't changed at all. Expensive and flashy, they were essential to Phillip's presence.

At seventy, he was a still practicing attorney with personal injury lawsuits his speciality. His thriving partnership had given him the kind of wealth and power few men could ever achieve; he was well-known all over Florida and even in the nearby states.

Almost as an afterthought, Andres's brain registered the identities of the men surrounding Phillip. They were Lena's brothers, all older than her except for Jeffrey, the baby of the family. Bering, the eldest, waited anxiously just beside his father. On the other side of the old man was Richard, her second brother. Behind those two came Stephen, and finally, trailing, came Jeffrey.

As always, Jeff was a peripheral member of the group. Even though he worked at Phillip's law firm alongside his brothers, he was the black sheep of the family. Idealistic and sometimes naive to Andres's way of thinking, Jeff continually disavowed what he considered the other McKinneys' base materialism. He spent his vacations helping migrant workers and went his own way, a way that was usually the opposite of what Phillip McKinney wanted.

Which was exactly why Andres had liked Jeff and had called him to inform the family of the shooting. He couldn't stand the rest of them.

Shaking hands and greeting the officers, most of whom he seemed to know, Phillip McKinney was almost on top of Andres before he noticed him. He didn't have time to prepare himself, so instead a cascade of emotions, genuine and unedited, crossed his expression at once. First surprise then anger, and finally a wary edginess, all of which he hid as soon as he could behind a stony mask.

Andres stared back from behind his own facade. He'd never known if the old man was aware of the investigation he'd conducted against him or not. Regardless, they'd hated each other from the very moment they'd met. Phillip had told Lena that Andres wasn't good enough for her, but the real truth was a lot more complicated. Phillip had had Lena to himself since her mother died and he didn't want to share her, with a husband or anyone else. It was power and control and love, all mixed together.

Phillip recovered fast. "How is she?" Silky smooth and deep, his voice was his trademark. It now held a tinge of something Andres had never heard before. Fear? Concern? Love?

"Lena's in surgery," Andres answered. "The bullet

entered her body just beneath her left breast. They re-inflated her lung in ER, then took her into the operating room."

Phillip sagged. It wasn't a physical response, but just as Andres had caught the tremble in his voice, he saw this as well. Phillip seemed to falter a bit, to pull inside himself, then the moment passed, almost, it seemed, before it had happened.

He tilted his head toward the double doors behind them that led to the operating room. "How long have they been in there?"

Forever.

Andres glanced at his watch. "An hour and a half."

Bering spoke for the first time. He lived in his father's shadow, never quite measuring up, never quite making the grade. He compensated for this with a blustery attitude and a burning desire to replace his father in the practice. "An hour and a half? And no one's been out with an update?" He shook his head at Andres's obvious lack of status, then turned to Stephen. "Go find somebody who knows what's going on. Get a doctor out here."

Phillip nodded his approval and Stephen scurried off through the crowd. Wearing a self-satisfied expression, Bering said something about coffee and bustled over to a small kitchenette in one corner of the room, Richard going with him, offering help. Andres remained where he was, his black eyes meeting Phillip's blue ones with the coldest of gazes. Something passed between them. It definitely wasn't a truce—the war between them was too involved for that to ever happen—but the moment was understood by them both. This wasn't the time or place.

Jeff broke the tension by moving up to where Andres stood. He extended his hand, then his eyes widened as Andres lifted his own, now swathed in bandages. "You were hit?" Jeff asked in surprise. "Why didn't you tell us—"

"No, no. I wasn't shot." He dismissed the inquiry with a shake of his head. When Carmen had arrived at the hospital with fresh clothes for him, she'd taken one look at his hand and forced him to have someone take care of it. He'd bruised three knuckles so badly the doctor had insisted on wrapping them. "It's nothing."

Behind him, Bering and Richard returned, Carmen helping them distribute the coffee they'd brought. Earlier Andres had been annoyed by her presence. Now he was glad. She handed out packets of sugar, then she made conversation and kept things cordial. Andres was suddenly grateful; he wasn't sure he could have kept up the facade for much longer.

Stephen returned with the doctor a moment later. They stepped to one side, isolated by a bumper of space from the waiting officers. "They're still in surgery," the man said, holding up his hands as if to ward off their questions. He was young but looked exhausted, his jaw dark with stubble, his shoulders a weary slump beneath his pristine white coat. "I'm Dr. Maness, Dr. Edwardson's assistant. She's still operating. The bullet's currently lodged in the diaphragm behind the patient's lung on the left side. It nicked the lobe before it stopped."

His gaze went to Phillip, then on to the other men until it came to Andres. Despite Phillip's age and obvious status, the doctor seemed to sense Andres was the man he should be addressing. Andres hardly noticed this, though. All he felt was a rush of anxiety as their eyes met and locked.

"I'm sorry," the doctor continued. "You're just going to have to be patient. If you want something to do, then go downstairs." He let his gaze go over all of them this time. He wore thick glasses and his eyes were bleary and sad behind them. "There's a cafeteria...and a chapel."

ANDRES DIDN'T LOOK for either place. He certainly wasn't hungry and he'd given up searching for comfort from above a long time ago. Instead he went outside. He wanted isolation and some distance from the crowd upstairs, stopping first at the hospital gift shop to buy a pack of cigarettes. He hadn't smoked in as many years as he hadn't prayed, but the craving had hit him and there was nothing to do but satisfy it.

Cupping his bandaged hand around the flame of his match, he was lighting the first one when Carmen opened the door of the hospital's atrium. As she walked across the flagstones toward him, he jumped to his feet, his pulse suspended in midbeat. She shook her head as soon as she saw him and motioned for him to sit back down.

"There's no news," she said. "I just came outside for some air." She stared curiously at the cigarette between his thumb and forefinger. "What are you doing? You don't smoke."

He was angry at seeing Phillip McKinney, angry over Lena's injury and angry at himself. With a pointed disregard for Carmen's feelings, Andres unleashed the emotion and sent it flying toward her, his words scathing. "You don't know me that well, Carmen. Don't tell me what I do and what I don't do."

She blinked at his tone, and he immediately felt like a bastard. Instead of apologizing, he turned his face away from her and took a deep drag on the cigarette. The acrid smoke seared his lungs with a sting so painful it brought a wave of dizziness with it as well.

Without saying a word, she sat down on the concrete bench beside him. They weren't the only ones in the small, walled garden. There were other smokers who'd been banished, and they all wore the same worried expressions. No one saw the carefully tended flowers or heard the bubbling fountain. Andres studied a young man on the other side of the patio, his hand on the head of a young girl who was dancing a doll along the edge of a low concrete wall.

The silence between he and Carmen built and hung, then finally she spoke softly, almost reluctantly, it sounded to Andres. "This woman who was shot. Lena McKinney...you know her, don't you? From before. You didn't just meet today."

It took him a moment to decide how to answer, then he realized there was only one way. He had to tell her the truth; she deserved it.

"Yes, I know Lena." He looked at the cigarette between his fingers. "I know her very well."

"Why didn't you tell me before?"

"I didn't think it was important."

She shifted on the bench. He could feel her eyes on him. "You didn't think it was important?" She shook her head and smiled softly. "That usually means it's just the opposite."

"Carmen..."

She stopped him. "You don't owe me an explanation, Andres."

"No." He rose abruptly. "I do owe you that. At least." He took a final, death-defying drag on the cigarette, then crushed it under his shoe. He turned and looked at her. "Lena and I were engaged at one time. We were going to marry."

"To marry!" Her dark eyes widened in surprise. "You mean she was your fiancée?"

"That's right."

"Wh-what happened? Why didn't you get married?"

"It didn't work out." His tone defied her to ask for more information. "I went back to Miami."

"And?"

"And what? That was it."

"You never saw her again?"

"Not until this morning."

Carmen sat immobile on the bench, a pinprick of guilt stinging Andres as he looked at her. He should never have slept with her. She wasn't crying, but she looked as if she wanted to. Beneath her expression, there was a gentle dignity that made him feel even worse.

"Does she still love you?"

Back in the plane, Lena's gaze had held nothing but disgust when she'd looked at him, yet she'd protected him with her life and now she might have to pay up. Did that mean she loved him or had she just been doing her job? He didn't know...so he didn't answer.

"I guess that wasn't the right question, was it?" Carmen asked.

His hand suddenly ached, a striking, sharp pain that bypassed the painkiller the doctor had insisted he take. He cradled the injured fingers with his other palm. "What do you mean?"

"I should have asked, 'Do *you* still love her?'"

This time she waited even longer for his answer. When it was obvious he wasn't going to reply, she stared at him a minute more, then she stood and walked away. He watched her disappear through the hospital door, and after it closed behind her, he reopened the package of cigarettes and tapped out another one. When he lit the end, the match trembled in his hand.

TWENTY MINUTES LATER, the double glass doors opened once more. Dropping his cigarette, Andres jumped to his feet again, his heart pounding as Jeff McKinney crossed the small patio and came in his direction.

The nearby ashtray was overflowing with butts, and Andre's stomach felt sour and sick. With nothing else to do, he'd been on his cell phone ever since Carmen had left, making calls and getting as much information as he could about what had happened. It hadn't taken long and the news had started a train of thought Andres couldn't stop. But those thoughts fled now.

"The nurse just found us," Jeff announced as he reached Andres's side. "The doctor's finished the surgery and she's coming out to talk to everyone."

"Did she say anything else? How'd it go? Is Lena okay—"

Jeff held up his hand and stopped him. "I don't know any more than what I just told you. Let's go upstairs and see what the doctor says—"

Andres was heading for the door before the young attorney could even finish. Jeff caught up with him a second later, sending a quick glance at the phone in Andres's hand. "Did you find out any more details?"

Andres nodded grimly. Normally, he wouldn't tell a civilian anything, but Jeff was an attorney. He knew the system. "According to Lena's right-hand man—some guy named Bradley—the shooter never made it off the field."

"Who was he?"

"They don't know yet."

"And your associate?"

"Potter's dead."

They walked into the hospital lobby. "How'd this guy get in the airport?" Jeff asked. "With Lena in charge, I can't imagine—"

"Bradley wasn't sure, but he thinks the perp picked one of the baggage handlers and started a friendship. The bad guy had on the handler's ID and uniform and when they started checking afterward, they found the handler's body back at his apartment. Bradley thinks the guy might have hidden his weapon the day before when he visited his pal."

Jeff raised his eyebrows. "That's an awful lot to know so soon."

"I wouldn't expect any less from Lena's team." Andres spotted the elevators and headed toward them, still speaking. "Her sniper took out the shooter with a cold shot." He pointed to the base of his neck.

"Lena won't like that. She hates it when the snipers have to fire."

Andres met Jeff's eyes with a steady look. "I think she'll understand this time."

The elevator came and they both got in.

"Before you got here, Lena had said there might be trouble with some group named the Red Tide. Was he a member?"

"That's the assumption." Andres shook his head angrily and jabbed at the buttons as he spoke. "These *pendejos*—these Red Tide people—they're idiots. That makes them even more dangerous. We can't predict what they're going to do. They haven't actually done anything violent like this since—"

When Andres didn't continue, Jeff looked at him

then obviously thought better of whatever question he'd had in mind. The silent elevator rose slowly. "Why do they want you dead?" Jeff asked finally.

"Because I'm trying to stop them and have been for years. They're behind ninety per cent of the drug shipments coming through here. They finance their political activities—their little riots and rigged elections—with drug money. They tell the people they're fighting for freedom when what they're really doing is taking it instead."

"Drugs? I thought Lena said they were revolutionaries."

"That's what they want everyone to think. They're nothing but a bunch of thugs, though." Andres paused, the inevitable conclusion he'd come to while he'd been waiting forming itself into words. "They've gone too far this time."

The elevator pinged softly, announcing its arrival on the surgical floor. When the doors slid open, Andres held them back, but instead of walking out, he turned and looked at Jeff. His voice was low and soft. No one overhearing them would have even bothered to listen.

"Shooting Lena was the biggest mistake they could ever make," he said quietly. "I'll lock up every one of the bastards...or I'll die trying. *Ya están muertos.*"

Jeff stared at him, then nodded his head with a slow thoughtful movement. The Spanish needed no translation.

THE SURGEON came out moments later. She was a handsome woman, in her fifties, with graying hair and dark blue eyes that looked both kind and exhausted. She wore a set of green scrubs with her name embroidered on the left side. Laura Edwardson, M.D. Obviously recognizing Phillip as he held out his hand, she greeted him then nodded toward the rest of the group.

Her eyes stopped on Andres when she saw his bandaged hand. "You were the one who was with her?"

"That's right."

"She kept asking about you. Fought the anesthetic so hard I didn't think we'd ever get her out." Before he could reply, she continued. "She's in stable condition right now. The bullet clipped the lower lobe of her lung. We sutured that as best we could and put in a chest tube, but we're going to have to watch that area very closely. Infection can be a big problem in the lungs. So can pneumonia."

"We need a specialist."

She glanced at Phillip as he spoke. "That's exactly what I recommend," she said calmly. "In fact, I've already called in our thoracic man and our pulmonary man as well. Dr. Weingarten, the thoracic surgeon, assisted me in the operation, and he'll be monitoring her closely." She stood wearily. "She'll be out of the recovery unit in an hour. After that, she'll be in intensive care until we know we're clear on that lung. Once she's settled into ICU, one of you can see her then. *One* of you." She paused until all eyes were on her. "It's none of my business, but since she asked for Mr. Casimiro, I suggest it be him."

SHE WAS COLD, colder than she'd ever been in her entire life, and nothing but a jumble of sounds and impressions made their way through the bone-chilling numbness. Lena lay perfectly still and let the sounds wash over her. Eventually one stood out—a bubbling noise. She had no idea what it was or where it came from, but strangely enough she was breathing in rhythm with it. Other than that, she felt little. It was like being suspended in midair, as if nothing were touching her, nothing holding her down, nothing holding her up. She wanted to open her eyes but she couldn't. Her lids were too heavy and when she tried to speak, her tongue felt the same way. Someone had attached weights to it.

Out of the confusion another detail started to register. It was minor, but she concentrated on it and tried to magnify the feeling. After a moment, she put a name to it. Touch. Someone was touching her. It took another second to understand where the connection was being made and another second after that to name it. Her hand. Someone was touching her hand. She strained to respond, but her fingers wouldn't move, the command never making it out from her brain.

"Lena...*querida*... Can you hear me?"

The words were soft in her ear, soft and loving. They brushed her cheek with a feathery touch and a warmth she craved. For some unexplained reason, the Spanish made her feel good, too, made her feel as though whoever had spoken cared deeply, cared passionately. Who was talking to her like this? She could hear the emotion in his voice and the coldness faded, if only for a moment. When he spoke again, she fought the cloud of confusion that surrounded her, but it was too strong. It picked her up and carried her off.

The last word she heard was *querida*. The last thing she felt was a kiss.

CHAPTER FOUR

HER SKIN WAS the color of pearls, a luminescent ivory so pale and bloodless Andres felt as if he were looking through Lena instead of at her. Even her hair seemed to have lost its hue, the blond-streaked strands limp and dull on the pillow beneath her head. Only hours ago, he realized with a start, she'd stood before him on the plane, vital and beautiful. Now she appeared as if all the energy in her body had drained out, and with it, her life.

He knew this wasn't the case. The doctor had reassured him that Lena would be fine. Her wounds seemed grievous, but she'd recover; they weren't fatal. Andres couldn't help himself, though. Myriad tubes and lines snaked from her body to the control panel above her bed, and his eyes darted to the monitor situated there. Along with other functions he knew nothing about, the apparatus apparently tracked her heartbeat, a path of peaks and valleys being traced on the amber-colored screen. Each time the red line dipped, he held himself still until it jerked back up.

He'd thought she was awake at first, when he'd spoken in her ear, but now he wasn't sure. She lay motionless under the cotton blanket. All he could do was stare helplessly at her and feel his rage growing. It should have been him lying there.

Without warning, he thought of the night before the wedding, the last time they'd been together while she'd still loved him. He could even remember what she'd worn that evening. A dark-blue dress, clingy, sexy, with tiny sparkles all over it. She'd had sandals that matched, two straps of navy leather and little else. The shoes and the short hem had shown off her tanned legs and the color had deepened the gray in her eyes. The outfit wasn't her usual style, but she'd told him she'd seen it in a shop window in Pensacola and it'd made her think of him and of the Caribbean. She'd been so excited about the honeymoon she'd talked about it more than the wedding.

Lena moaned softly, a painful sound that sliced right into his heart. Andres leaned over the bed, taking her hand in his. Her fingers felt like ice and he rubbed them gently to warm them, wishing he could do more, but knowing he couldn't.

"I'm here, *querida...* I'm here."

FROM THE HALLWAY, there were windows into the patients' rooms and during visiting hours, the blinds were pulled back. Anyone passing by could see inside. Carmen watched carefully as Andres took Lena's hand. His movement was filled with emotion, his entire body straining with the effort of caring for her, listening to her...loving her.

It couldn't have been more obvious had he stood up and shouted it to the world, she thought. He still loved Lena McKinney. The part he held back from everyone else, including her, he gave to Lena and probably always had. Carmen felt a wave of anger and resentment wash over her. He'd taken advantage of her and she'd let him.

She stared, her bitterness etching its way deeper inside her psyche, then she turned away from the glass and walked down the hall.

TUESDAY MORNING, Lena woke up slowly. Her mouth was dry, her throat parched, but for the first time, her mind felt clear. Even though the nurses had already gotten her up and forced her to walk, for some reason, she was more aware of her surroundings than she had been previously. They'd pulled the chest tube, too, an unpleasant experience to say the least. She'd drifted through most of that, wishing she were somewhere else.

Her eyes followed the lines of the room until they came to the chair in the corner. She wasn't sure why, but she'd expected to see Andres. Instead, her father was dozing in the wingback, his head tilted against the padded side.

She studied him for a moment. She'd never noticed that his hair was so thin or his wrists so bony and white. Had her accident affected him that much or had she simply never taken the time to truly look? Shaken, she started to sit up, then gasped as a lightning strike of pain hit her lower chest.

The sound woke him, and Phillip rose immediately, his eyes widening as he saw her pain-etched face. He was at her bedside in a heartbeat. "Lena? Baby? What's wrong? Do you need the doctor?"

He hadn't used that term of endearment in years, and the sound of it now made her grin weakly. "Hey, Daddy..." she croaked. Each word was painful, each breath torture...but not as much as it had been. "Could I just have some water?"

He reached for a nearby pitcher and poured her a

glass, then helped her drink through the straw. "You look better," he said, staring down at her with a critical eye. "Are you sore? How's the incision?" The questions came as rapidly as a cross-examination. "Can you breathe all right?"

"Don't you have something better to do than sit here and bother me?" she asked hoarsely.

"Not at the moment, no."

After the death of Dorothea McKinney, Lena's mother, Lena and her father had become very close, each depending on the other for love and support. They'd grown apart through the years as Phillip had become too controlling, and the relationship had changed into a seesaw of love and manipulation. His violent opposition to Andres had pushed Lena away even more. But seeing him here now, sitting in her hospital room when she knew he had work to do made Lena feel like a little girl again, loved and protected.

The emotion lasted only a second. Sensing her regained strength, he spoiled the moment with his very next words.

"What in the *hell* did you think you were doing, Lena?" He knit his eyebrows together in one angry line as he set her cup back down. "You could have gotten yourself killed out there! And for what? I can't believe you let yourself do this—"

Lena tuned the words out, just as she did each time her father acted this way. He was the only person on the planet she let talk to her so disrespectfully. She would have crucified any of her team if they'd dared do the same.

After he ran out of steam, Lena defended herself. "I was doing the job I'm paid to do," she answered. "I'm a cop, Daddy. And I'll always be a cop."

His lips were a firm line, and she knew what part of the argument was coming next. He had begged her to go to law school, to join her brothers at the firm, but she'd wanted to be a policewoman. "Nonsense! There's plenty of time for you to go back to school. You could walk into the firm and be a partner in no time."

"Daddy..."

He ignored her warning tones. "You're too damned bright to waste your talents on that rinky-dink police force. You could do so much better. If I've told you once—"

"You've told me a thousand times," she interrupted, "and you *don't* need to tell me again. I know how you feel about it."

Her impudence brought out his old trump card. "Your mother would not have liked this."

The words usually wearied Lena, but somehow this time they did just the opposite. She pursed her mouth tightly, her lips the only part of her body she could move without causing pain.

"Then consider that *your* fault," she answered sharply. "You taught me there were things worth fighting for. *You* taught me the difference between right and wrong."

"The difference between right and wrong..." His stare was blue and piercing—Dorothea had been the one to give Lena the granite-gray eyes—and suddenly Lena understood they'd come to the heart of the argument. "Is that what you think you were doing when you saved Casimiro's life?"

He said the Spanish surname incorrectly. Time and time again, she'd told Phillip how to say Andres's last name, but he insisted on his way. Finally she'd realized he was deliberately trying to denigrate Andres by mispronouncing his name, and she'd given up trying to rectify the mistake.

He spoke in a biting voice. "If that's what you think you were doing—"

"I was doing my job," she reiterated.

Not that she'd done it very well, she thought to herself. Each time she'd woken, that had been her only coherent thought. *She'd screwed up. Big time.* No unauthorized person should have been anywhere near that airport, and if she had been paying attention to her work instead of Andres, she wouldn't be in a hospital bed now.

"Well, I can't believe you almost got yourself killed for the likes of him. He isn't worth the time of day, much less your life. I don't want you having anything to do with him, Lena." His voice rose stridently, as if he were winding up a case. "You can't trust him and he'll hurt you again. Do you hear me?"

"Everyone can hear you. But it doesn't matter one way or the other. I have no intentions in that direction, I can assure you."

"I'm glad to see you've finally gotten some sense about the son of a bitch because I don't care how important he is, the man's still a worthless bastard."

With the last word ringing in the air, the door of Lena's room suddenly swung open...and Andres stood on the other side.

Lena's eyes swept over the man in the doorway. Dressed in a navy suit, his chiseled shoulders filling the opening, Andres held a crystal vase of Brazilian orchids, their petals snowy white and curved against the somber color of his jacket.

"Am I interrupting?"

His voice was reserved, polite even, but he'd heard what Phillip had said. Something in the set of his expression told her this and she was assaulted instantly by a complicated storm of emotions. She spoke quickly before her father could reply. "P-please come in, Andres. You're not interrupting a thing."

He walked inside and set the vase down on the table beside her. The faint, sweet smell of the flowers drifted over Lena's bed. When they'd been together, he'd always brought her orchids.

"They're beautiful," she said despite herself. "Thank you."

When he didn't reply, she looked up. Andres and her father were locked in a staring battle, the tension so fierce between the two of them Lena could almost see the cloud of pressure taking shape over her bed. She wasn't surprised since they'd always disliked each other, but there was something different in the air this time. Something thicker, denser.

Surprisingly, her father looked away first. He reached for the briefcase he'd left beside his chair, and spoke— to Lena only. "I have to get back to the office. If you need anything, you call me, baby."

She accepted his kiss on her forehead then watched him go out the door. He said nothing to Andres. Didn't even acknowledge his presence.

Her gaze went back to the man she'd almost married. He stared at the closing door with a brow-marring frown that cleared only after he realized she was looking at him.

"What is it with you two?" she asked in exasperation.

"You don't really want to know."

"I wouldn't have asked if I didn't."

"Your father loves you," he said after a second. "Let's just leave it at that." He moved toward the window and looked outside before turning to speak again. "Tell me how you feel today."

"Better," she said automatically. His answer hadn't satisfied her. For a moment, she considered pursuing the topic, even though she knew Andres would say no more. Why on earth would there be even more animosity between the two men now? When Andres had left her at the altar, Phillip had gotten what he wanted.

"Better?" He raised one eyebrow. *"¿Verdad?"*

"Yes. I feel more clear, if that makes sense. Still sore, but more with it." She reached again for her water, but he did as well. Holding the plastic cup closer, his fingers over hers, he bent the straw toward her mouth. His touch was warm, his whole hand covering hers.

"I can do it myself," she said.

"I know that."

They stared at each other for a second, the same old sparks flying between them, heating her up. Lena took a deep breath and pulled the cup away. He acted as if it didn't matter one way or the other, stepping back from the bed with a neutral expression.

Lena spoke quickly in an effort to cover up her reaction to his touch. "Has the P.D. found out anything about the shooter?"

"They know for sure the guy wasn't local. All his identification papers—driver's license, ATM card, whatever— were fake and his prints aren't coming up at all. They're examining the recent flights from the islands. Washington thinks he was probably brought in for the job."

"Washington?" Lena didn't bother to hide the surprise in her voice.

"The FBI."

"But the local guys can handle this—"

"And they are. They sent the prints to the feds as a precaution, just to widen their investigation. The FBI has a better database."

"What about the weapon? Where'd it come from?"

"They don't know yet. The serial number didn't come up stolen."

She inched upward in the bed, holding back a groan as a dull ache began to throb along her incision. "Tell Bradley I want to see him. I need to know what the department's doing about all this and then I want—"

Andres leaned down as she spoke and put his hands on the mattress, stilling her movement. "You don't need to know anything, Lena. All you need to do is lie there and recover. Let the police department handle this. They're perfectly capable of being in charge—"

"But *I'm* in charge of the Emerald Coast SWAT team," she answered, bristling at his tone. "I may be temporarily out of action but I'm still the commander. I want to know what's going on."

"What's going on is that you're going to recuperate, and the P.D.'s going to investigate. That's all."

The response was typical Andres—Latin and arrogant. "In case you haven't noticed," she said slowly, "you have no authority here. I am responsible for this situation."

"I'm well aware of that fact," he said, surprising her. "But I understand something that apparently you do not."

"And that is?"

"You won't get well if you don't rest."

"That's my concern."

His voice was liquid and low. It rippled over her bed and made her pull up the blanket without thinking. "I care what happens to you."

"You don't have the right to care anymore," she said bluntly. "That time has passed."

"Maybe. Maybe not."

"No." She shook her head, his unexpected answer triggering something inside her. "There's no maybe to it, Andres," she answered. "Not anymore. When you left me two years ago, you left me. It's over and done with, and if you're thinking differently, then you're making a terrible mistake."

ANDRES DEPARTED a few minutes later, and the last of Lena's energy evaporated in the aftermath of their exchange. What was he doing? What was he thinking? If he was considering a reconciliation, he was nuts. The world would have to come to an end before she'd ever get back together with Andres. Ever. To make matters worse, her father would be so opposed he'd make life hell for her. He hated Andres still, maybe even more than ever. She didn't understand why, but that much was very clear.

She shook her head, her hair whispering against her pillow. No...Lena had given Andres her heart and he'd walked away. He'd never get another chance to do that.

LENA DOZED then fell completely under, sleeping so deeply that neither sound nor light could penetrate the almost coma-like rest. When something finally broke through and woke her up late that afternoon, she opened her eyes and was momentarily shocked. Her bed was surrounded by men in black. Automatically she did a head count. Every one of her fifteen officers was standing over her and grinning. She remembered a couple of them visiting when she was still groggy, but seeing them all together was truly surprising.

"Who's minding the store?" she asked, without thinking.

They laughed at her characteristic remark. Bradley, the designated commander since the shooting, stepped forward to answer. "We told dispatch to hold it down," he said, his voice a low-pitched rumble in the confines of the crowded room. He was a gentle giant—a huge black officer with gray frosting his close-cut hair. "Told 'em they couldn't be havin' any emergencies for at least twenty minutes...."

She eased up in the bed and winced. "And you think the bad guys are going to listen?"

"They'd better." From the back of the room, Peter Douglas, one of the rear entry men spoke up. "If they know what's good for them!"

Beck Winters stepped through the crowd to stand beside Lena's bed. He was one of the men she recalled visiting her, his very pregnant wife, Jennifer, in tow. He looked down at Lena now. "We really want you to hurry up and get back to work. Bradley's way too easygoing and we're afraid we might lose our edge without you around. Our workouts are going downhill and training...forget about it!"

"I *could* direct you guys from here. I don't want you getting fat and happy without me around...."

The men chuckled and looked embarrassed, but underneath their studied reactions, their relief at Lena's recovery was palpable. They respected her and even though she was harsh at times, they were proud of their unit. It went unsaid that no one wanted to lose a member, especially a leader. They were a family as much as a team.

"Since you're all here, I just want to let you know that I think you did a great job the other day," Lena said when the laughter died. "Things didn't go exactly as we planned, but once it went down, the whole team reacted perfectly. I'm proud of every one of you."

They murmured protests at her praise, but she waved their words aside. "I'm telling you the truth," she said. "Everyone did what was supposed to be done, and we accomplished our main goal. I think you should all be happy with your work."

They visited a little bit longer, then one by one the officers said their goodbyes and left. On duty twenty-four hours a day, the team trained and took classes when they weren't responding to calls. It was a difficult life, and hard as hell on their families. Sarah had to have performed a miracle for all of them to come in and see Lena at once. She watched them leave and thought about how lucky she was to have such a good group of people around her.

Beck and Bradley remained behind. She questioned Bradley closely about the situation. The team never investigated the call-outs that sent them running, but they always stayed on top of the cases. It gave closure to their actions and fostered a sense of accomplishment when the issues were resolved. Bradley gave her the same answers Andres had. Except for one important detail. Bradley was sure the shooter had been a member of the Red Tide organization. The weapon, his nationality, even his method—they all pointed to the group who wanted Andres dead.

Bradley left a few minutes after that, promising to keep her informed. As the door closed behind the huge officer, Beck turned back to her.

"You're looking pretty good." Towering over her bed, he was tall as a Norse god and just as imposing. His blond hair was cropped short, his muscles long and lean. They'd been co-workers for a long time, friends even longer. Lena would be the godmother to his baby when it arrived.

"I'm feeling much better," she said.

"When will you get back to work?"

She grimaced. "I'm not sure. They'll probably let me out in a few days, then the docs say I'll have a couple more weeks taking it easy before I can return. When I finally do get there, I may not be able to go out right off."

"You'll need to take care of yourself."

She rolled her eyes. "Please, I don't need anyone else giving me advice like that today. I've had more than enough."

He grinned, but his gaze held sympathy. "Your father?"

"No..." She cursed herself for saying anything, but it was too late to stop now. She had to explain. "Andres."

Beck's expression shifted. He'd liked Andres a lot, but he'd also been a witness to Lena's pain after the relationship was over. She knew his reaction to the news would be a mixed one.

"He's giving you advice?" was all Beck said.

"He gives advice to everyone."

"But are you taking it?"

She lifted her gaze to Beck's. His eyes were chips of blue ice, the total opposite to Andres's simmering black ones. "He told me I needed to rest," she said. "That I should let Bradley run the show and just worry about getting well."

"He's right."

"He also said he's concerned about me."

"Concerned, eh?" The blue gaze deepened. "And how do you feel about him? That bullet did have his name on it, you know. Does that bother you?"

"I have no feelings for Andres whatsoever. He no longer matters to me. I truly don't care."

Beck looked at her steadily as her last words died. "A simple no would have worked," he finally said.

She started to shoot back an answer, but nothing came. Beck was right, as usual. She should have just said no and left it at that. But when Andres was involved, she went over the top, one way or the other.

Beck left a little later and she eased over in the bed to stare out the window. She told herself her reaction meant nothing, but the words rang hollowly...even in her mind.

CHAPTER FIVE

AT THE END OF THE WEEK, Lena sat on the edge of her hospital bed and fidgeted as the doctor listened to her chest and tapped her on the back. "Another breath, please."

She drew in as deeply as she could, then let the air out slowly. She remained sore and uncomfortable but the piercing pain of the first few days had finally disappeared. She was ready to leave and had told the doctor so more than once.

After a moment of listening, the physician stepped away from the bed, her stethoscope in her hands. "I'm going to have Dr. Weingarten look at you this afternoon and if he agrees, then we'll discharge you." Dr. Edwardson's voice was full of warning. "But you may not go back to work for at least two full weeks, and I'd prefer that you waited longer than that. You need to give yourself plenty of time. Nothing strenuous for at least a month and a half."

Lena nodded, visions of her own bed, her own bath, her own set of sheets dancing in her head. She couldn't wait to get back to the rickety old house. A lot of confusing thoughts were parading through her brain, and she needed the solace of her beachfront home. She did her best thinking on the deck looking out over the water. And God knew she needed to do some thinking.

Andres was *still* in town and showed no signs of leaving. She'd asked him why he hadn't returned to Miami, but he'd simply given her his standard Latin answer, a shrug of his broad shoulders, and changed the subject. She couldn't figure out what he was doing and it was driving her crazy.

She pulled her hospital gown back up over her shoulders and focused on the woman beside the bed. "Thanks for everything," she said.

"You're very welcome." The physician slipped her stethoscope back into her pocket and smiled. "But try not to come back. We don't like repeat customers."

The gray-haired woman left a moment later, and Lena walked slowly to the door to follow her out. Her side was stiff and sore, but the more she moved, the better it felt. The physical therapist had shown her how to stretch and work her injured muscles, and twice a day she shuffled to the other end of the hospital wing for extra exercise. She began the long walk now, each step bringing her a little more flexibility.

Ten minutes later she was standing by the window of the ward housing the newborns. Somehow she always ended up here. Leaning her hands against the window, Lena looked at the babies.

There were only two today, one wrapped in a blue blanket, the other in pink. The day before there had been twins in another set of the beds, each bundled up in blue covers, their tiny heads fuzzed with black down, their legs and arms kicking in protest as the nurses tended to them. Lena had felt the old familiar longing deep inside her.

She wore a gun to work, but that didn't make her different from other women; she still wanted children, a husband, a home. She'd never told anyone how much she wanted children—in a SWAT team environment that subject didn't come up much—but she had confided in Andres. He'd assured her he wanted a large family, too, and she'd been thrilled. Imagining what their children would look like, she'd come up with perfect images each time. A little blond girl who looked just like her and a boy, all boy, of course, who was a miniature Andres.

After she and Andres had parted, Lena had set aside those dreams and had even refused to date for a long time. But Beck had started on her, and tired of his ragging, she'd given in and begun to go out again. There was no shortage of men when you worked with cops but none of them had provided more than passing entertainment. She'd dated Nate Allen, the police chief of Pensacola for quite some time, but she'd finally had to tell him it might be best for them both to call it off. He'd been terribly hurt, and she'd felt like a four-letter word, but what else could she do? The relationship had been doomed from the very start and she'd known it all along.

One of the babies started to cry. Lena couldn't hear the child through the thick glass, but she could see his open mouth as his face turned red and his tiny body began to shake in his bassinet. A nurse quickly appeared to soothe him, picking him up and patting his tiny shoulders. Lena watched for as long as she could stand it, then she headed back to her room.

LEANING AGAINST the doorway of the hospital room, Andres watched Lena walk down the hall. She didn't know he was observing her because she was completely focused on her progress. It was steady, but clearly painful as she took step after careful step on the spotless linoleum.

She'd lost at least ten pounds, ten pounds she couldn't afford to lose, and beneath her light-blue robe, her finely toned body looked thin and fragile. Even her face looked slimmer, her cheekbones more pronounced, her jawline finer. He continued to examine her until she finally felt his gaze and looked up. Her expression, a study in concentration, changed immediately to one of guarded wariness.

Andres started down the corridor, stopping only when he reached her side. He couldn't help himself; he took her elbow, his fingers wrapping around her arm. "Let me help you."

"Thank you," she said firmly. "But it's better if I make it on my own. I need to do it myself." She pulled her arm away from his touch just as she had the day he'd tried to help her with her water.

Her reaction stung even though it wasn't unexpected. Lena was the most independent woman he knew. "I guess it's true what they say...some things never change, no?"

Her eyes narrowed. "What's that supposed to mean?"

"You know exactly what it means." He spoke calmly, rationally even, but inside he was a wreck. "You never need anyone."

She gathered the collar of her robe and pulled it closer. "There's nothing wrong with being self-reliant."

"No, there isn't. But there's nothing wrong with accepting help, either. You might give it a try sometime, Lena."

Without answering him, she resumed her walking, her gait more stiff than it had been a moment before, a result of their conversation more than her injury. A brittle silence filled the space between them.

"I just talked with Dr. Edwardson." Digging up his patience, Andres tried to break the tension once more. "She told me she's probably going to release you this afternoon. I'll come back at five to pick you up."

Lena stopped again, so abruptly this time, he thought something was really wrong. There was, he realized a moment later, but not with her body.

"That won't be necessary. I can—"

"Don't be ridiculous, Lena. Let me take you home."

"You don't need to do that." She spoke through gritted teeth. "My father can drive me if I don't want to call a taxi."

They were standing outside her room, near the nurses' station. Andres could feel their curious looks on his back. He lowered his voice and spoke again, before Lena could protest further as he knew she was about to do. "Let's go inside, shall we?"

She glanced over his shoulder, then nodded, walking inside ahead of him. He caught just a whiff of almonds as she passed. She still used the same shampoo. The realization distracted him and that, in turn, made him remember the conversation he'd had a few hours before with his boss.

"Are you sure this is a good decision, Casimiro? Have you thought it through?" The director had sounded worried.

"It's the only choice I have. I'm not leaving here until I've stopped these Red Tide *bastardos*. They may try again. Why should I endanger anyone else?"

"You could go back to the office in Miami. I could give you twenty-four hour security with our guys. If we can get them up here, we can nail them."

"I have a better chance of baiting them from Destin,

of luring them in. There are good people running things down here and they can help me," Andres argued. "And as long as I'm here, I can take care of the operations that Potter was supposed to handle."

The director had dropped his voice. "Andres, you can stay there and do that—hell, you can do anything you want to—but do you understand the consequences?"

"I understand. I still need to stay, though—"

As if Andres hadn't spoken, his boss continued. "You're on the fast track. There are people in Washington keeping their eyes on you, but if you disappear in some backward Florida town just to run an ops shop, your name is not going to be one that gets brought up in meetings. As much as I'd like to see you get these assholes, I don't want you to sacrifice your career for it. Do you understand what I'm saying?"

Andres had let the silence build, then he'd spoken. "This is something I have to do."

The director sighed, a weary sound that told Andres exactly what kind of fool he thought he was. "All right then. You do what you have to do."

The words reverberating in his mind, Andres looked across the room to Lena. She stood beside the foot of her bed. In spite of her obvious loathing of him, he couldn't leave Destin. Not now.

He owed it to Mateo to deal with these idiots.

He owed it to Lena, even though she didn't know it.

He owed it to himself.

Holding on to the metal railing with one hand, Lena spoke with vehemence. "I'm not sure I understand what's going on." Her knuckles were white where they gripped the runner. "I want an explanation, Andres."

He stared at her and remained silent.

"Why are you still here?" Her voice rose slightly when he didn't answer. It held a tremble as well. "What about your job? Why haven't you gone back to Miami? And give me a real answer, this time, not some shrug."

He took a deep breath and prepared himself for her reaction. She wasn't going to be happy with his news. "I didn't know what was going to happen and that's why I haven't said anything. But I talked to my director today, and there's been a change of plans."

She didn't move, didn't even blink.

"I'm not going back to Miami, Lena. I'm staying here. Here in Destin."

Her mouth fell open then she snapped it shut. "You can't do that."

"Potter's gone and there's no one else available to open the office."

"There's got to be someone else. You're not the only hotshot in the Justice Department."

"Hotshot, eh? Is that what you think I am?"

"That's the rumor."

"But not the truth?"

"I don't know, but I don't care, either." She moved closer to him, as if her proximity would make her point stronger. "I do know one thing, though. There are other men who could run this shop. If you're staying here, you have a reason. A real reason. I want to know what it is."

"This feels like an interrogation."

"Call it whatever you like. Just give me an answer."

He stepped away from her then, putting some distance between them by crossing the room to stand beside the window. The afternoon sun had disappeared behind a bank of stormy fall clouds. They were rolling in from the east. He watched them for a few moments, gathering his thoughts. He should have known better than to try to protect her. She didn't need him and she definitely didn't need that.

"I want to catch these bastards, Lena," he said. Turning around once more, he faced her. It was the truth, after all. Part of it, anyway.

"We've never known where the main cell was. Because of the amount of drugs we're seeing locally and their attempt at the airport, it could very well be here in Destin. If I stay, I might force their hand."

"Force their hand?" Her voice was incredulous. "Don't you think they're aggressive enough as it is?"

"They've got to be stopped."

"And they will be. The Destin P.D. can do it."

"I'm not saying they can't. But if I stay here—"

"If you stay here, you'll just make things more difficult." Her jaw twitched angrily. "You know this isn't the way to get this done so why are you making it harder for us?"

"I'm not trying to do that," he said. "But I can't just walk away. Not now."

She stared at him. Her eyes matched the clouds outside, but as he watched, the dark gray grew even more wintry. "What happened to me is my concern. Not yours. It's part of the job and you know that as well as I do. I'll handle it on my own." Her mouth turned down, into a bitter line. "It's something I've grown accustomed to doing in the past two years."

As always, she managed, with one swift jab, to cut straight to the chase.

His abandonment had inflicted a wound on her that everyone saw, that everyone could comprehend. Until he could tell her the whole truth—and he didn't see that ever happening—the injury would never heal.

"We should sit down and talk." He would think of something to tell her. "There are things that need to be explained...."

She interrupted him. "All I want is to be left alone. If you're staying here out of some kind of misguided guilt, you're making a big mistake. You don't owe me anything, and I don't want you here."

He looked into her eyes and his chest tightened. He didn't have a choice. There was only one way he could answer her and only one thing he could do.

"I'm sorry, but you're not going to get what you want, Lena. I'm staying here. And you have nothing to say about it."

RIGHT AFTER LUNCH, Dr. Weingarten, the thoracic surgeon, came in and after looking Lena over again, released her with warnings about doing too much. She barely heard the doctor. All she could think of was Andres's news.

He was staying in Destin.

Why? Why now? Why did he have to come back after all this time?

Angrily grabbing the phone beside the bed, she dialed her father's office and asked for Jeff.

Her thoughts were still in a turmoil when her younger brother walked into her hospital room a half hour later to take her home.

They were halfway to her house, the windows of the Toyota down, the cold sea air washing in as they puttered down Highway 98, before Jeff took a chance and spoke. When they'd been kids, her temper had been legendary. She might have been the girl, but all her brothers had been scared of her.

He looked at her from across the seat. "What's going on? I thought Andres was taking you home. He told me last night he wanted to see if—"

"Andres Casimiro doesn't always get what he wants." Turning in the seat with a slight grimace, Lena interrupted her little brother, belatedly realizing she'd used the same phrase Andres had spoken to her a few hours before. "Did you know he's staying here?" she demanded. "To run the ops shop?"

Jeff's surprised expression revealed his answer before he even spoke. "I didn't know that," he replied after a moment. "But I guess it makes sense now that I think about it...."

"No, it doesn't," she insisted. "He has no business here. He said he wants to draw out the Red Tide, but that's ridiculous. We can catch those guys without him here."

Jeff steered the car around a slow-moving construction truck. "Of course, you can," he said. "But that's not really why he's staying and you know it."

A ray of sunshine had broken through the clouds and hit the water to their right. Lena had been watching the waves, but when Jeff spoke, she quickly swung her gaze back to him.

"Andres and I talked while you were in surgery. He said the men who shot you were *ya están muertos*. Does that give you a hint?"

Lena felt a sudden chill that had nothing to do with the open window beside her. "*Ya están muertos?* Are you sure?"

"'Already dead.'" Jeff nodded. "That's what it means, right?"

She didn't answer because she didn't know what to say. Those were strong words. What had fueled them?

She thought about it until they pulled into her driveway, Jeff carefully maneuvering around the ruts in the shell road to bring them right in front of the door. He killed the engine and looked at her. Faintly, Lena heard the waves hitting the beach. Other than that, there was total silence.

Her brother spoke. "He was really shaken up, Lena. I don't know if you know it or not, but he put his fist through the wall at the hospital. He almost broke three fingers. He was madder than hell and he still is. He wants to get these guys."

Her chest went tight. "'Getting these guys' is not his job."

"Well, he thinks it is."

She shook her head. "He's forgetting who he works for. The Justice Department doesn't investigate local homicide attempts."

"This doesn't have anything to do with who he works for."

She stared at Jeff. "What are you saying?"

"They shot you, Lena. Don't you realize what that means?"

She put her hand on the bandage beneath her blouse. "I think I've got a pretty good idea—"

"No. No, you don't. This is personal. It's got nothing to do with work. Andres still cares about you."

Jeff was so naive she wondered sometimes how he could actually practice law. He lived in a parallel universe, she thought. A perfect one where everyone lived happily ever after. "You're nuts."

"Am I? There are a thousand guys in Washington who could handle this office. Why him?"

As her brother repeated the very same words she'd said to Andres, Lena bit her bottom lip and remembered his answer. *I can't just walk away. Not after what happened to you.*

When she didn't answer, Jeff spoke again. "Lena, he still cares about you."

"No, he doesn't. He can't."

"If you'd seen him waiting while they were operating on you... He was a wreck."

"That doesn't mean anything."

Her brother waited a few seconds then he spoke again, almost with distraction. "Look, I know you two had a rocky time before, but Andres is not leaving until he finds the men responsible for your shooting." He gripped the steering wheel. "He won't go back to Miami until the job is done or someone stops him."

All she could do was shake her head. An hour later, Jeff left. She watched him drive away, his words in her mind. Deep, deep down, where she didn't go too often, she wondered if Jeff could be right, but as soon as she formed the question, she put it away.

Andres didn't still love her.

He couldn't.

CHAPTER SIX

CARMEN HAD ARRANGED the Monday luncheon, and the minute Andres walked into the restaurant, he wished he'd told her to have sandwiches delivered instead. He'd wanted to meet the office staff Zack Potter had assembled and give them the news that he'd be taking over, but he wanted to do it in a way that didn't upset anyone any more than they already were. The restaurant was packed. How was he going to talk to everyone in this setting?

Carmen read his mind as she saw him come through the door and into the noisy waiting room. Gently pushing through the crowd, she took his arm and pulled him to one side. "There's a private room in the back," she said. "It's quiet, and no one will bother us. In fact, just about everyone is there already."

He nodded and began to trail her through the restaurant, then he stopped abruptly. Carmen stopped as well, looking at him with a puzzled expression.

"Andres?"

Her voice died out as she followed his gaze. From across the busy dining room, Phillip McKinney had obviously witnessed their arrival and was making his way to where they waited. Each step was purposeful, and his stare never wavered from Andres's face.

When Andres had shown up at the hospital Friday evening to take Lena home, she'd already left. He hadn't spoken to her since but he had no doubt Phillip had whisked her away before Andres could get there. Her father probably wanted to gloat.

Andres watched the silver-haired man stride toward him. *Had* he arranged Mateo's death? *Was* he involved with the Red Tide? The hatred Andres had always felt for Phillip was as much a part of his life as breathing; giving up the investigation to prove Phillip's guilt had been one of the hardest decisions Andres had ever made.

Now, once again he found himself second-guessing that choice. Phillip might be older but he was no less the man he had been. If he wanted Andres dead nothing would be able to stop him. On the other hand, would he put his own daughter in danger to accomplish his goal?

It was all so twisted, Andres thought, so tangled up. Lena, her father...the past. From the minute Andres had seen her in the airplane, he'd felt himself drawn to her again. The emotional upheaval of her shooting had overshadowed his true feelings, but they couldn't be contained any longer. The decision to stay here had as much to do with her as it did anything. Andres wasn't the kind of man who'd try to fool himself into thinking otherwise. He still had to sort through everything and decide what it all meant, but Phillip was a complication he could have done without.

The attorney halted his progress directly in front of Andres, his expression bordering on the belligerent, his stance almost aggressive.

Andres turned to Carmen before Lena's father could

say anything. "Tell the group to go ahead and order their lunch. I'll be right there."

She looked uncertain, but he nodded toward the dining room. "I'll only be a minute."

She shot Phillip an unreadable look, then started toward the back of the dining room, her high heels clicking on the shining terrazzo floor. Andres faced Phillip. "What can I do for you to—"

"Is it true?" he interrupted rudely. "Are you taking Potter's place?"

Andres lifted one eyebrow. "You're either well connected or you've talked to Lena. Which one is it?"

Phillip answered the question by asking one of his own. "She knows?"

"I told her on Friday," Andres answered. "And yes, I am taking Potter's place. I'll be running the operations here, at least for a while."

Phillip wasted no time. "You stay away from my daughter. I don't want you around her. At all."

"I think that's a decision for Lena and me to make."

"You broke her heart once already. I won't have you hurting her again."

"She's a grown woman."

"Who's vulnerable and wounded. It was bad enough for you to show up in Destin, but to ask her to protect your sorry life—"

"Just a minute, *viejo*." Andres's voice went soft as he looked at Phillip with a cold expression. "You'd better watch what you're saying."

Phillip McKinney's blue eyes didn't waver in the sunlight pouring through a nearby window. "I love my daughter. I want you to stay away from her."

"Or what?" Andres asked, suddenly taking a chance.

"You'll 'take care' of things like you tried to before? It didn't work then, Phillip, and it won't work now. Save your breath if that's what you're doing."

"I was protecting her."

All at once, Andres realized they were talking about two different things. He'd been thinking of Mateo and the old man had been remembering the money. Andres had almost forgotten that issue—it'd been so insignificant to him.

He laughed. "You were protecting her. Of course. That's why you told Lena what you did." He smoothed a hand down his tie, then looked up, straight into Phillip's eyes. "You *have* told her, haven't you? That you offered me a half a million to leave her alone?" *And when that didn't work, you tried to kill me.*

Phillip flinched, his face taking on an uncharacteristic slackness. "She didn't need to know about that. And it...it's in the past now."

"And you want it to stay that way, don't you?"

"Y-yes. I do." He started to bluster. "There's no reason to tell Lena, and even if I did, it wouldn't matter. She'd understand."

"She'd understand...." Andres shook his head. "She may be your flesh and blood, Phillip, but you don't know the first thing about your daughter if you believe she'd understand that."

He reached out and put his hand on the older man's shoulder. Anyone watching them would think they were having a pleasant conversation, two old friends, maybe discussing an upcoming fishing trip. If they looked close, though, they'd see the hard glint in Andres's eyes. It was anything but friendly.

"Your daughter is a grown woman, Señor McKinney.

She's old enough, and smart enough, to make any decision on her own. Respect that for once and let her live her own life." He paused and let his words sink in. "If I were you, I'd worry about something more important than who my daughter was dating."

Phillip blinked and something undecipherable flashed across his face before he could hide it. Suddenly the whole conversation took on more meaning than it had before. Andres's gut rolled over once, then again.

"Nothing's more important than Lena," Phillip said.

"I hope you're telling the truth." Andres waited a second but Phillip stayed silent. "If you aren't, you'll regret it."

Phillip hesitated, then he turned on his heel and marched across the dining room. Andres watched him leave. Phillip was older, yes, and slower, maybe, but he still had a fire within him. He could prove dangerous yet.

Andres would have to watch his back.

LENA SPENT the first week out of the hospital regaining her strength.

She spent the second week going nuts.

Unable to drive, she'd been stuck at the house the whole time, nothing to occupy her but the television and family visits, most of which she could have done without. Her brothers and their wives had been sympathetic, but they lived such different lives from Lena it was hard to connect, especially with Bering. He was so far removed from who they'd been as children he was almost a stranger to her. He'd called once, alleging to check on her, but she'd suspected he had another reason, one she knew nothing about. He truly cared for no one; only money meant anything to him.

Lena finally turned to what she usually did for distraction; she went back to work, but only by phone. She had called Sarah so many times the information officer was having to think up things to talk to her about. Thank God Bradley did a little better. He took her twice-daily intrusions in stride and patiently updated her on everything the team was doing. The reports didn't really help Lena—all they did was make her more anxious to get back to work—but at least the conversations ate up a bit of the lonely time.

Saturday afternoon, puttering around on the deck, she suddenly stopped and stared out at the ocean. Was this what the rest of her life was going to be like? If she didn't marry and didn't have children, would she be living here and doing these same things in twenty years? Watering plants? Sweeping the floor? Counting the hours until she could go back to the station?

The thought depressed her, so she put it away and headed down the wooden planks to the beach as the afternoon drew to a close. She'd walked the stretch that morning already, but another mile wouldn't hurt.

She was halfway down the beach when she saw the blur of a large SUV speed by on the blacktop road that bordered the sand. She stood up straighter and shaded her eyes with one hand. Catching a quick glimpse of a tanned face and dark sunglasses, she instantly recognized the driver and the vehicle, and she knew the destination. Andres was behind the wheel of the Suburban and he was heading to her house. No one else lived down the lane but her.

She stood there, in the pale fall sun, uncertain of what to do, telling herself she didn't really want to see him. What did they have to say to each other that hadn't already been said? On the other hand, she was bored to tears and he could be a diversion.

She turned around to track the progress of the truck and within minutes, Andres appeared on her patio. She was the only person on the beach, and he spotted her instantly. Moving with his usual grace, he crossed the deck, then headed in her direction. Even as she told herself she shouldn't, she sat down on the sand to wait. Her eyes followed his approach, her heart suddenly thumping as she remembered Jeff's words the day he'd brought her home from the hospital. *Andres still cares about you.*

She'd given that pronouncement a lot of thought and she'd finally decided Jeff's interpretation was wrong. Andres's Latin pride had been hurt. He was staying to handle the Red Tide but not because he cared; he was going to deal with them because his macho sensibilities had been wounded. He'd been challenged and now he was going to take care of the situation. She and her injury were secondary to his motivation.

Jeff was definitely wrong.

"*Hola,* Lena. *¿Cómo estás?*" Andres pulled off his sunglasses as he reached her side, his voice smooth and low above the ocean's roar. Instead of his usual suit, he wore a pair of black slacks and a soft white sweater. The casual clothing made him look even sexier, and she responded to the pull, in spite of her best intentions. "How are you?" he repeated, this time in English.

"I'm doing fine," she said. "Just fine. No need to check up on me."

"I'm not checking up on you, Lena." Dropping to the

sand, he sat down beside her. "I came to give you some news. I just talked to Bradley and he told me the FBI had prints of your shooter. His name was Esteban Olvera. He was a known Red Tide member. Not really active in public—which may mean something—but a clear connection all the same. His last known address was out of Miami."

"Miami!" Her mind went into overdrive. "Then he left a trail. He had to in order to get down here. A flight, a bus ride—something he might have paid for with a credit card. We can find out who paid him—"

"The P.D.'s already ahead of you. They think he might had driven over from the coast. They've found an abandoned car at the Silver Shore Motel. They're checking on it."

"That's great! They haven't pulled the vehicle in yet, have they? We could stake it out and see—"

Andres held up one hand. "It's already been done, Lena. They have twenty-four hour surveillance on it."

"I want to call the captain. I need a copy of that report." She made an impatient gesture with her hand. "Do you have your phone on you—"

"Lena! It's being handled, all right?" He shook his head. "What's wrong? Don't you trust your department, either?"

"Of course I trust them! I just want to check on the situation, that's all." She stopped abruptly. "What do you mean...trust them, *either?*"

A gust of wind came off the surf and lifted his dark hair. He fingered it back above his brow. "Don't you remember your comment on the plane? I know how you feel about me, Lena."

She waited a second, her heart taking a jump at his

unexpected words. Andres wasn't the kind of man who faced a problem head-on. He eased around it, finessed it, worked it smoothly. At least he had in the past.

She met his eyes. "You gave me good reason to feel that way."

Shocking her again, he agreed. "You're right, but perhaps you should tell your father as well as me. He seems to think I could convince you otherwise."

"I have told him," she said impatiently. "What makes him think that's changed—"

Andres waved off her question, a glint of gold catching the last rays of the dying sun. He wore a ring with a family crest on it. He'd told her once it was the only thing he'd brought from Havana, his grandfather's legacy. "I don't know why Phillip thinks the way he does, Lena. But he warned me to stay away from you. I told him you were old enough to take care of yourself, but I don't think he bought it."

Lena tightened her lips, her jaw going taut as she remembered the tension between the two men at the hospital. That's all she needed—Phillip and Andres fighting over what *she* should do with herself. She ignored the fact that Andres had actually defended her and made a mental note to call her father later and give him hell.

"Neither of you really have anything to say about it, but you both seem determined to tell me how to run my life. Why is that?"

He stayed silent for a moment, then Andres shifted in the sand and looked at her, his dark eyes unreadable for once. "Maybe you *need* some help. I know that's tough for you to accept, but it is possible, isn't it?"

"No," she answered hotly. "It isn't. I've been doing

just fine without you. Your return, and your help, are the last things I want now. Two years ago things were different, but now..."

All at once, he seemed impatient with the subject. "Look, Lena, I know you're still angry at me for leaving you. I understand that completely. But believe this, I had no other choice, all right? As I told you back then, I *had* to do what I did. There simply wasn't any other option for me at the time."

She fought to cover up the hurt, but she didn't make it. Some of it slipped into her words, a bit more into her voice. He hadn't trusted her, professionally or personally, and the sting was still there. "I understand more than you think."

"No," he said bluntly. "You can't. It had nothing to do with you."

"Nothing to do—" Her mouth actually dropped open in amazement. "How on earth can you say it had nothing to do with me and keep a straight face? My God, Andres, do you really think I'm going to buy that?"

"You can take it or leave it, as you please," he said simply. "But it *is* the truth."

She scrambled awkwardly to her feet, her side protesting the movement with a quick stab of discomfort. Surprised by the force of it, she gasped and wobbled unexpectedly.

He stood instantly, his hands reaching out to steady her.

There was nothing she could do but accept his aid. If she refused, she'd fall down. She felt a moment's emotion as his stare, and his warm touch, registered. She didn't know what to call the feeling, but she knew one thing: she didn't want it.

"I'm telling you the truth," he repeated softly.

His voice held so much pain that she was suddenly flooded with the awful memory of the night he'd tried to explain. The look in his eyes, the anguish in his face, the hint of grief she'd thought later to have imagined. Had it all been real?

Of course not, she told herself immediately. If he'd felt that way, then why had he left?

She stepped back and spoke stiffly. "What happened back then is over and done with now."

"No. It will never be over, Lena. Not between us. It can't be."

Startled by his words, she looked up and into the dark well of his gaze. Once again she couldn't stop the deep longing, mixed with confusion and bewilderment, that came over her.

"Love doesn't die." The late sun lit his skin and painted it a deeper bronze. "It may change and take on different forms, but the emotions and feelings...they will always be there."

"Maybe for you—"

"For everyone," he countered before she could finish. "And if you were honest with yourself, you'd understand that and admit it." With his fingertip, he drew a heated line down the side of her jaw. His touch was gentle and her response frightening.

Averting her face, she looked out to the churning water. The waves were as chaotic as her thoughts, but she revealed nothing other than coolness as she spoke. "You hurt me too much, Andres. You didn't trust me professionally and you destroyed me personally. I can't trust you again. It just wouldn't work."

"Trust is different from love."

She answered automatically, the words not really

meaning anything to her anymore. "You can't have one without the other."

Turning her around until she was facing him, he stared at her until she was forced to meet his eyes. With a single finger he gently tapped a spot above her left breast. "This is where you love." Moving the finger to her head, he tapped again. "This is where trust comes from. They're two different things, *querida*. Very different. That's a lesson you should have learned by now."

SUNDAY MORNING Lena was more of a wreck than ever. She dialed Phillip several times to tell him to butt out of her life but he never answered, and finally she gave up and phoned his secretary of many years, Reba Dunn, at her condo. She told Lena he'd flown to Miami for a golf tournament and had yet to return. Reba usually went with Phillip on occasions like this, but she'd stayed home this time. A long-time divorcée, Reba liked her independence. She traveled often, her generous salary allowing her the best of all the exotic places. Lena had always liked her, but Reba's news wasn't what she wanted to hear right now.

Unable to blow off steam by talking to her father, Lena spent the rest of the day doing everything she could to forget Saturday's conversation with Andres. Her constant busyness didn't do a thing but leave her exhausted.

ANDRES WASN'T THE MAN he used to be.

Walking into her office on Monday, Lena couldn't put her finger exactly on the change, but she understood a part of it. He was more direct, more to the point. Her realization only complicated things, and all the emotions she'd been fighting since he'd arrived surged forward.

She cursed under her breath. She was still attracted to him, still felt the same old pull, and it was actually stronger than it had been before. Why, dammit? Why?

Everyone welcomed her back but before she could even sit down in her office, Bradley appeared in the doorway. "We just got a call," he announced. "I'm not too sure what's up yet but it's down on old 98. Destin P.D. has been on the scene a while and they can't seem to get things cleared up." He pivoted to leave. "I'll phone in as soon as I know what's going on—"

"No! Bradley, wait!" Lena moved from behind the desk, grateful for the interruption. A run was the only thing that would get her mind off Andres. "No phone calls. I'll come with you."

"Lena, please, this isn't necessary. You know what the doctor said—"

"Don't even try," she said briskly. "I'll stay in the War Wagon but I'm not spending the next six weeks sitting behind this desk. I can't."

He looked as if he wanted to argue.

"Forget it." Grabbing her jacket, she brushed past him and strode down the corridor. Sputtering at her pronouncement, Bradley ran to catch up. He didn't have another choice.

Thirty minutes later they reached the War Wagon, a remodeled Winnebago, parked two blocks from the small residential area near the beach. The camper contained an array of high-tech surveillance equipment plus the team's weapons, body armor and other major gear. Sarah manned the communications center anchored in the rear.

Sarah's fax machine was spitting out a document as Lena and Bradley entered the motor home. Bradley's size made the quarters feel even more cramped than they really were. He squirmed past the two women to take up a post near the front.

"What have we got?" Lena asked.

"It's the fourth house down." Sarah grabbed the fax and ripped it off the machine. "The tax rolls show that house is owned by a Robin Smith of Destin. We called and she said there were renters in it right now. A Mr. and Mrs. Paul Eliot."

"Mrs. Eliot's the one who made the initial call." Bradley stood at the front of the Winnebago. He was looking through the windshield with a pair of binoculars. The rest of the team was already in place at various locations around the house.

"Domestic disturbance?"

Nodding, Sarah answered, "Yes. She said he came in early this morning, they got into a fight, everything escalated. When he ran to the kitchen and grabbed a butcher knife, she fled to the neighbor's house and called the police. Now he's barricaded inside and won't come out. She's afraid he's going to harm himself."

Bradley offered Lena the glasses. She took them and scanned the area, but saw no movement inside or out.

"Is he alone?"

"As far as the P.D. knows, yes."

"Any weapons in the house besides the knife? Any guns?"

"The wife says no."

Lena handed the binoculars back to Bradley then turned to Sarah. "Get Mrs. Eliot on the phone." Slipping on her headset, she spoke quickly, locating all the team members Bradley had placed by phone on the way over—two men at the back of the house, two behind vehicles on the street, and the negotiator, Diego Sein. One of the two countersnipers available, Chase Mitchell, was working his way to the roof of a nearby church.

"Diego, have you talked to the guy yet?"

Lena's headset crackled as the negotiator spoke, "No contact so far. We've called, but he won't answer the phone. I've tried the bullhorn, too, but got no response."

"Keep trying."

"Will do."

Sarah reached over Lena's shoulder and handed her the phone. "Here's Mrs. Eliot. She was talking to Diego, but she went back inside, to the house next door. We're keeping her out of sight for now."

Lena pulled away her headset and took the receiver. "Mrs. Eliot? This is Lieutenant Lena McKinney. I'm the commander of the SWAT team. What can you tell me about your husband that will help us resolve this situation?"

Mrs. Eliot's voice trembled so badly Lena could hardly understand her words. The longer they talked, the worse it got. Lena thanked her for her help and handed the phone back to Sarah a few seconds later. "That was pointless," she said. "The poor woman's a wreck. What do we know about this guy anyway?"

Hanging up the phone, Sarah handed her a second fax. The blurry photo and accompanying information weren't encouraging. A repeat offender, Mr. Eliot had just been released from the local county jail for his most recent DUI offense, one of many. Lena passed the sheet to Bradley. "Another fine citizen..."

A voice spoke in Lena's ear. It was Chase, the sniper. "I'm in place."

Lena put a hand to her microphone. "Copy that, C1."

She glanced at the house down the street. The tiny frame home looked well tended and neat. A new paint job gleamed in the sun and a row of oleanders waved along the sidewalk. Someone who lived in it cared. Mrs. Eliot, obviously. Thank God there weren't any children at home.

"Do we have the mirrors?" she asked.

Bradley nodded.

"Floor plan?"

"A rough sketch," Sarah answered.

Lena pulled her microphone to her lips and ordered one of the officers into the Wagon. A few minutes later, Brandon Friest rapped on the door and entered the Winnebago. He'd only been a team member for a few months, but Lena had been impressed with him so far. He was training to make front entries—a very dangerous position—and had been begging her to let him see some action. He tried to hide his anticipation as he waited for Lena to speak.

She tilted her head to where Sarah stood. "You've worked with these, right?"

Sarah held two of the devices she'd already pulled from the back of the supply cabinet. Reaching for them, the young officer nodded. Long and narrow, they were basically sticks with mirrors on the ends. "They're simple. No problem."

Lena tapped the penciled drawing on her desk. "The wife drew this and the owner confirmed it. If you can get to this back window, you'll have a straight shot from the den into the hallway. From what she said, he's probably in there."

He nodded without saying a word.

"You take the mirrors and approach the house the best way you can. Call in after you're positioned."

He turned and strode toward the door.

"Brandon?"

He stopped.

"Be careful."

She watched him leave the trailer and jog back into position. In a few minutes he disappeared behind the house. Five minutes after that he called in.

"I got 'em." His voice was excited now, pumped.

"What do you see?"

"The perp's pacing in the hallway. No weapon in sight."

"Are you positive?" Lena's heart thumped. "Look closely, Brandon. Be certain. The wife said he had a butcher knife."

"I don't see anything," he insisted. "I'm staring straight at his hands."

"Look everywhere."

After a second, he spoke again. "Nothing."

Lena nodded. "All right, then. Keep an eye on him."

Two hours later they still had no movement. Diego had talked until he was hoarse and the man inside had yet to say a word. He continued to pace the hallway with almost manic concentration. His wife denied the possibility, but he had to be on drugs, probably meth.

They waited another hour and Lena knew she didn't have much more time. Three to four hours was the limit with one team. She'd have to switch men, a tricky operation at best, or move in. With the information they had, going forward seemed safe, a nonlethal solution that would work out best for everyone. She checked with Brandon one more time. He assured her he saw no weapons, no guns, no bombs, no anything.

Pulling her microphone closer, Lena outlined the

plan, a standard one for entry in a situation without weapons. A few minutes later, from her seat in the Winnebago, she watched the surreptitious movements of her men as they took their places. Brandon continued to monitor the suspect with his mirrors as another officer assembled the battering ram and a third one prepared the tear gas. Lena took a deep breath, then she gave the go-ahead and the team swarmed inside the little house, disappearing through the doorway.

No one was ready for what happened next.

CHAPTER SEVEN

THE SOUND OF gunfire echoed through the neighbour-hood, and pandemonium immediately erupted. Lena watched in horror then she and Bradley turned in unison and rushed to the exit of the Winnebago. She yelled instructions to Sarah as they tumbled out. "Get the standby ambulance out here now. And call for backup black and whites! Hurry!"

By the time they reached the front porch, it was over. A man she didn't recognize was on his back in the hallway, bleeding from a shoulder wound. His weapon, a .22 caliber pistol, was twirling in a nearby corner, obviously sent there by someone's boot. Lena's gaze caught the movement, then skipped over it to the opening to the living room. Another man lay there. He was stretched out, his arms flung to the sides. It was Brandon.

She ran to the young cop's side and kneeled beside him. "Brandon! Brandon! Can you hear me?"

He didn't respond. With her pulse roaring, Lena let her eyes go over his body, her hands following their path. She could see no blood, find no injury.

After a heart-stopping second, his eyes fluttered open. "I—I'm o-okay," he stuttered. "I took a hit but my vest caught it. I—I can't breathe."

Relief washed over Lena, leaving her weak. She sat down abruptly on the scuffed wooden floor.

Bradley bent over the other man. "This one's alive," he pronounced. "He'll make it." As he spoke, he glanced toward Lena, his expression suddenly alarmed. "You okay?"

Lena nodded. Her side was screaming and her head spinning, but neither complaint meant anything. All she could think about was how close to disaster the team had come. Another inch and she'd be talking to the widow of the officer lying beside her. They'd never lost a member—not like this—and she didn't intend for it to ever happen, either. Not on her watch. Closing her eyes, Lena fought the nausea that was threatening her now that she knew everyone was all right. She opened her eyes a second later and looked down at Brandon.

"What happened?" She wanted to shriek the question, but her voice was calm. "I thought you gave it the all clear. You said he didn't have any weapons."

"I—I thought so, too. I—I swear to God, Lena. I don't know where the gun came from...."

Patting his shoulder, she watched him struggle—to catch his breath and to accept what had almost happened. "It's okay, Brandon. I shouldn't have let you do this on your own."

Looking down at the flushed, scared face of the young officer, Lena tried to smile reassuringly. She wasn't lying. She should *never* have given him total responsibility. She should have let one of the more experienced men supervise him. Hell, she should have gone outside *herself* and double-checked.

He'd almost died, and it was no one's fault but hers.

ANDRES LEFT his office after work that evening and headed downtown to the SWAT team's offices. On the seat of the Suburban was the report from Washington on Esteban Olvera. Andres could have mailed it, he could have faxed it, he could have even sent Carmen over with the papers, but none of those options had appealed to him, and he knew why.

He wanted to see Lena.

Their conversation at the beach had left him dissatisfied. There was too much unfinished business between them, and though he knew it had to stay that way, he didn't like it. Maybe there was something he could say...

The drive didn't take ten minutes. Parking the SUV in the evening dusk, he entered the squat, concrete building. He'd been to the SWAT headquarters several times since arriving, talking to Bradley and making the various arrangements he'd needed for his own office, but the appearance of the place never improved. It looked and smelled like every government building he'd ever worked in. Bare and institutional, the station was located within minutes of some of the most expensive real estate in Florida, but no one would ever know that just from looking at it.

Andres passed a warren of cubicles before he got close to Lena's office. The area was deserted with not a soul in sight, but just as he'd expected, Lena was still there. He could hear her voice as he neared the back, and he knew instantly something was wrong. He increased his pace and rounded the corner quickly.

She was perched on the edge of her desk, a pained expression on her face as she spoke over the phone. Her windblown hair and disheveled appearance did nothing to lessen her appeal, but it did tell him one thing; she'd been on a call. Not sitting in her chair taking it easy, writing reports or reading training materials.

She'd been out.

His first response was anger. What in the hell did she think she was doing? Didn't she know she had to take care of herself? She hadn't healed yet, dammit. But when he heard her words, his irritation turned into concern.

"He'll be okay?" she asked. "Just bruises, then, no broken ribs or anything?" She nodded to herself. "Good, good...and the perp?"

She looked up at that point, as if sensing Andres's presence. Her gray gaze widened, and she beckoned him inside. Her motion seemed to hold reluctance, but he didn't care.

She listened a bit more and said, "All right. Thanks for the update. Please keep us informed." She hung up the phone and looked at him.

"What's wrong?"

She started to answer him, then stopped. Obviously upset and angry, she blinked furiously and turned away from him to stare up at the ceiling, cursing all the while. He crossed the office and pulled her around so he could look at her. Her gaze was tumultuous as she continued to fight her emotions, clearly hating the fact that he was a witness to them.

"¿Qué tal, mi amor? ¿Qué pasa?"

After a few moments, she tried to step away from him again but he wouldn't let her go.

"What's wrong? What happened?"

"We had a run." She looked shaky, not quite together. "It didn't go well."

"Was anyone hurt?"

"Yes. But not seriously."

He lifted a thumb and feathered it over her cheek. "Then what's the problem? This isn't like you, no?"

"I screwed up, Andres." She shook her head in a measure of misery. "Someone could have really been hurt, maybe even killed. I sent the men in when I shouldn't have." She gave him the details in a halting way. When she finished, she shook her head. "First the airport, now this... I think I might be losing it. Really losing it."

He waited a beat, then spoke harshly. "Don't be stupid, Lena!"

She jerked her gaze to his. She'd expected sympathy, words of compassion, and he'd given her this. It threw her off guard and that was exactly why he'd said it.

"Everyone makes mistakes. Remember what you said at the airport? *'I'm not perfect...and neither are my men.'* Those were your exact words. Have you forgotten so soon?"

"But I shouldn't have—"

He raised his palm again. "Are you listening to me? You. Aren't. Perfect. And neither is your team. Mistakes get made all the time. And many end up with worse outcomes than this." His eyes narrowed. "Trust me on this, Lena. You won't ever forget it, but it doesn't mean you can't do your job anymore."

He could tell his words reached her. It was a risk, but he'd had to take it to make her feel better. She took a deep breath and blinked twice, making the connection he'd known she would.

"This—this has happened to you?"

"Something like it." He paused. "Only much worse. I lost a man. It wasn't my fault, but I felt responsible."

"I had no idea."

"I did the best I could, but my best wasn't good enough. Someone else was ahead of me in the game and my man was killed. He wasn't simply an officer, either. He was my best friend."

"Oh, God, Andres. How awful! I didn't know...."

"You couldn't have known. It wasn't something you would have read about in the papers. I'm only telling you about it now to help you."

"Did you get the shooter?"

They were reaching thin ice, but he had to answer her questions. It would seem strange if he didn't. "No, I didn't catch him. For several months I investigated the man I felt was responsible—the man who paid to make sure it happened—but I found no proof. I had to let it go."

This time it was her voice that turned soft, the words a whisper between them. "You must have been devastated."

He looked up and noticed, for the first time, the tiny lines radiating from the corners of her eyes. Lines that hadn't been there before. Lines *he'd* put there. He reached out and touched them gently.

"I suffered another loss about the same time," he said. "I didn't know which one to mourn the most so I grieved for neither. It seemed best."

Her lips were fuller than they had been, he thought to himself, somehow more lush. Strands of her hair, a jumbled-up mess, gleamed under the lights. The silent, deserted office suddenly made it seem as if they were the last two people on earth, and Andres went still. No words were exchanged to break the quiet, but they continued to communicate. Her pain, his guilt. His regret, her anger. It flowed between them in a river of feelings and emotions.

Their lips met a moment later.

It seemed odd, he thought, how perfectly they fit together, how closely matched they were. She nestled under his arms and against his chest as if they truly were two halves of one whole. At the same time, her curves had changed since they'd been apart. Her body was harder, leaner, the muscles beneath his hands as tight and well-formed as his own, her strength more sensual and erotic than the softness of the other women he'd known.

Andres's desire took another leap as she opened her mouth to his. *This* was what it'd been like, he thought. *This* was what had always been between them. Their passion had been a thing alive, an entity they almost couldn't control.

In the back of his mind, Andres knew he should stop. This was a mistake. For one thing, they were in her office. They'd done rasher things when they'd been together before, but this was different...or it should have been.

More importantly, though, Lena was upset and seeking something that would erase the pain, something that would make her forget. She didn't love him as she once had and she never would again. He'd hurt her too deeply to ever hope for that.

His body didn't seem to care.

The heat between them only increased, her hands drawing him to her, a friction building between them that would quickly become impossible to control. He would have chastised himself for the rush, but it was obvious Lena felt the same way. Her kiss deepened and so did the moan in the back of her throat. Despite her words to the contrary it was clear she wanted him as much as he wanted her. Maybe that was why she'd pushed him away so much. If Lena did need him—for anything—nothing would be more scary to her, would it?

He didn't have time to think about the implication of the revelation.

The door to her office flew open unexpectedly. With a guilty start, they jumped away as if they were two teenagers caught necking on the front porch. Her T-shirt was halfway up her chest, and Lena scrambled to pull the black fabric down. She glanced at Andres. He ran a hand over his crooked tie and tried not to look too dazed.

Beck Winters stood on the threshold, his ice blue eyes wide open with surprise. He immediately began to back out of the room. "I'm sorry."

His resounding voice rumbled down the hallway and Lena flinched. It was bad enough that he'd seen. Did he have to alert everyone else, too? It was late, yes, but who knew who was listening?

"I didn't mean to interrupt. Why don't I come back later—"

"Beck—it—it's okay. Really..." Her words said one thing while her mind screamed another. Like hell, it was okay! What did she think she was doing? Had she totally lost her mind? She should have never let Andres into her office when she'd been so distressed. "Wh-what did you need?"

Beck threw a glance at Andres but said nothing. Instead, they exchanged some kind of silent message. She sharpened her voice and spoke again. "What did you want, Beck?"

His eyes came back to hers. "I was wondering if you'd heard from the hospital," he said calmly. "About Brandon."

"He's fine." She gave him the details. "I'd appreciate it if you'd pass the information on to everyone," she said briskly. "And tell them also we'll have a special debriefing tomorrow. At 4:00 p.m. sharp."

He nodded then gave Andres another look and stepped outside the office, closing the door behind him with a snap.

Lena counted to three, then she faced Andres. "I think you need to leave."

"Lena..."

"No." She shook her head. "Don't say anything. Just go."

His black eyes went darker then he drew his mouth into a narrow line. Without a word, he went out the door.

LENA SAT ON THE DECK that evening after her workout and watched the sun go down. It was a huge ball of orange and red and it lit the sky for miles, turning the water beneath to fire. The weather had changed again, and it was cold. She'd worn an extra sweatshirt for her walk, but in reality, the temperature had nothing to do with the chill she was feeling.

She was scared. Scared to death.

Half the feeling came from the call-out. Things could have so easily gone the other way. Brandon could have been killed. The shooter might have died. Civilians could have been wounded. It was only through God's grace that they hadn't suffered more casualties. If the suspect had had a better weapon, the damage could have been tragic.

She should have been more careful. The two most dangerous times during a call-out were at the beginning and at the end. If the setup wasn't perfect, the team could be spotted, leaving them vulnerable. And if the takedown wasn't done properly, it was just as dangerous.

Hostage takers regularly committed suicide by cop. Too frightened to kill themselves, often they'd "surrender" then raise their weapons and step into the resulting line of fire. Let a cop take the responsibility. Lena had seen more than one officer devastated by that outcome.

It was her job to see that didn't happen. She had to protect the citizens of Destin *and* her men. They depended on her to do the right thing. And she wasn't sure she could anymore. The incident at the airport and now this had left her shaken and unsure of herself. If she'd been concentrating on work instead of Andres, neither situation would have happened.

Andres. The source of all her problems.

She stewed about him for a while then accepted reality. She *wanted* to blame him for everything, but inside her heart, she knew he wasn't her problem. She was.

She'd been thinking about him long before the callout. He'd occupied her brain ever since he'd stepped off that jet. When he'd come into her office, he'd come at the worst possible time, too. She'd wanted his warm embrace, and his revelation had made her feel better. She was falling into his trap.

Blinking into the dying light, she thought of the other truth he'd told her, not with words, but by the way his mouth had felt and how his arms had molded around her body. He'd wanted her, just as she'd wanted him.

She shook her head and shivered, confusion filling her thoughts with chaos. The sexual spark was still there, but did that erase all the hurt, all the pain, that had come later?

The phone suddenly sounded inside the house, shattering her thoughts. Jumping up, Lena ran through the door and caught it on the fourth ring. Phillip's sonorous voice answered her breathy hello.

"Reba told me you called yesterday. She said you sounded upset. How are you feeling? Do you need anything?"

"Actually, I do need something." Tired and angry, she didn't bother to hide her frustration. "I need you to keep your nose out of my business. Andres told me about the conversation you two had last week, and frankly I didn't appreciate it."

Her father didn't say anything for a moment. "He told you about it? All of it?"

His words held a hint of unease, which surprised her. It wasn't his usual style. Maybe he understood, for once, that she could handle this one on her own. And maybe she was indulging in wishful thinking.

"He told me enough," she answered. "Dad, I don't need your help with this. I resent you talking to Andres about it, too. I'm a grown woman—"

He interrupted. "He's not good enough for you—"

"Stop right there."

He fell silent, and she continued. "You don't have to give me reasons to stay away from him, okay? I have enough of them already."

"I was only trying to help."

"No, you were trying to do what you usually do. Manipulate and control. But in this case, you don't have to worry. I'm not interested in Andres and I've told him that." She looked out the window. Night had come over the beach and all she could see was darkness. It reminded her of Andres's gaze and the way she'd felt when they'd kissed. She closed her eyes and shut out the view...and the memory. "He knows how I feel. And there's nothing else to say about it. Your help isn't necessary."

They spoke a few more minutes, then Phillip rang off.

Lena threw a frozen dinner into the microwave and tried to blank her mind. One thing keep intruding, and surprisingly, it wasn't Andres or the call-out. It was the hesitant way her father had spoken when she'd told him she knew of his conversation with Andres. His reluctance was very unusual, and the more she thought about it, the more she wondered what had caused it.

"I'VE POSTED the schedule outside." Winding up their usual Tuesday staff meeting, Lena spoke briskly even though she felt like hell. She was anxious and still reeling from the encounter with Andres. "I know Thanksgiving is coming up and I tried to give the family men first consideration, but even so, most of you will need to stay in town. I'm sorry I couldn't do better. If you have a problem with the roster, please come see me. Any questions?"

When no one spoke, she gathered up her notes. "All right, then, if that's it, we're finished." The sound of scraping chairs and low conversation took over. Relieved the long day had come to an end, Lena headed for the back of the conference room. Beck stopped her as she reached the door.

She'd managed to avoid him up to this point and had been hoping for a clean escape. It wasn't going to happen.

"I'd like to talk to you, Lieutenant. Do you have the time?"

She wanted to lie, but she couldn't. This was Beck. If the team was her second family, Beck was her closest brother. She waited a beat, then answered with a sigh. "C'mon back to my office."

He closed the door behind him as she rounded her desk and pulled out her chair.

"What are you doing?" he said quietly.

"I'm sitting down—"

"That's not what I mean and you know it." He waved a hand toward the corner. "I'm talking about what I saw in here yesterday. I've tried to figure it out and I can't." He shook his head. "You and Andres? What's going on, Lena?"

She met his bright, blue eyes, but said nothing.

"You were kissing him."

"No. He was kissing me."

"Right." A skeptical expression came over his features. "It certainly looked to me as if there was mutual participation going on."

"Well, what if there was?" she asked, suddenly defensive. "Would that be so awful?"

"I don't think so. I always liked Andres, but you're the one who said he'd never darken your doorstep again. I'd hate to see you get hurt as badly as you were before." He crossed his arms and waited.

She shook her head, unable to answer. Swinging her chair around, she fought the urge to remember, but her body took her back. The heat of him against her and the warmth of his mouth... God, how long had it been since she'd felt truly loved by a man? Too long. Way too long.

But he didn't love her.

Abruptly, she swung the chair back. "It was nothing. He came in here right after the Eliot situation, and I was upset. He was trying to make me feel better and it got out of hand. End of story."

Beck sat down in the chair in front of her desk and linked his hands over his chest. He stared at her and said nothing.

Finally, she spoke. "That was it, okay?"

"If that was it, then why are you so defensive?"

"I'm defensive because you're sitting there grilling me. Anyone would be."

He shook his head, his blond hair gleaming under the harsh lights of her office. "Are you falling for him again?"

"No! Absolutely not! That's crazy," she answered quickly. "I'm not falling for Andres, okay? He walked out on me. I wouldn't give him another chance if he was the last man on earth. My father hates him, he hurt me, there's too much bad history between us—"

"I don't need the list, Lena. I've heard it before."

"Then why are you in here, giving me a hard time?"

"I'm not giving you a hard time. I came in here because I thought you might want to talk about what's happening. I'm trying to be your friend." His blue eyes seemed to glow as he leaned toward her. "Let's be honest, Lena. In the feelings department, you aren't always on top of things, mainly because you don't want to be."

There was nothing she could say. He knew her too well. He stared at her and she stared back.

Finally, Beck broke the silence. "Lena—c'mon...if you *didn't* still have feelings for him, we wouldn't be having this conversation. You wouldn't care. Is it your father? Are you afraid of what he'd say—"

"Dad has nothing to do with this."

"Then what?"

She stood up and crossed her office to stand beside the window. "I can't care about Andres," she said softly. "I can't let myself."

"Why not? He obviously cares—"

She pivoted. "Beck, he doesn't give a damn about me, okay? He kissed me because he could. I let him. I wanted him to do it. I felt like shit and I needed to feel better any way I could." She paused to gather her thoughts. They refused to be corralled, though, and all she could do was be blunt. "The truth of the matter is that Andres doesn't love me...and I *can't* love him. It would hurt too much to go through all that again. And I don't intend to do it." She stopped, then spoke again a second later. "I *won't* do it again."

CHAPTER EIGHT

WHEN HE'D DECIDED to stay in Destin, Andres had told Carmen to rent a condo for him. He hadn't seen the unit at Oceania until the night she'd called and told him it was his. He'd moved into the furnished place right then and there. Stretching along the beach in an area known as Holiday Isle, the pristine white building was steps away from the frothy emerald water. It was a setting straight out of paradise.

But wasted on him. He rarely came home before nine or ten. Opening the office had turned out to be more complicated than he'd anticipated. And that wasn't the only thing he'd misjudged, either.

Coming home Tuesday night, he thought of the encounter he'd shared with Lena the week before. Truth be told, he'd thought of little else since it'd happened, and with every passing moment his irritation had only grown. The kiss had left him wanting more, but it clearly hadn't had the same effect on her. Tossing him out of her office had made *that* point obvious. All he'd wanted to do was make her feel better, to help her with her problem, and that was the thanks he'd gotten. He should have known better. She couldn't accept help from anyone. Not even when she needed it. Not even when she *asked* for it.

He threw his coat and briefcase to a nearby chair and strode to the wet bar in one corner of the den. Carmen had stocked it well, and he pulled a beer from the under-counter refrigerator and popped it open.

He searched his brain for something other than Lena to occupy it, and in two quick strides, he went back to the chair and snapped open his attaché. Maybe the re-port he'd just picked up would capture his attention. It'd come in late that afternoon, a detailed account of the sur-veillance being conducted on the car abandoned at the Silver Shore Motel. As soon as Andres had known he was staying in Destin, he'd informed the different agen-cies involved and asked for copies of their weekly sta-tus updates.

He skimmed over the written summaries then skipped down to the bottom of the page. He had to give the local P.D. credit—they were certainly thorough. Each shift had noted every car model, make and license that had passed through the parking lot. Thankfully it was a small motel. According to Bradley, it had a rep-utation for being the local hot-sheet place, but prostitu-tion wasn't a high priority in the area. Most of the renters were fishermen who didn't want better or retir-ees who couldn't afford nicer. There were only a dozen units, each a tiny bungalow. A strip of parking spots lined one side making it easy to see who came and went.

He flipped to the back of the folder, past the list of cars. A contact sheet of photographs had also been in-cluded. A date at the bottom of the first one told him the pictures had all been taken the day after the watch had begun. There were two more sheets for the two subse-quent days, then just the listings. Andres glanced at them then dropped the papers on the nearby coffee table.

He'd have Carmen run a check on the Dade County tags tomorrow. She'd been surly lately, which meant she'd point out the uselessness of the effort, but in the end, she'd do it. What else *could* they do?

Taking his drink, Andres wandered into the kitchen and opened the freezer. It was supplied as well as the bar. Frozen dinners. Gourmet meals. Anything he could ask for from soup to steaks. With his beer in his hand, he stood beside the door, the cold air whispering over him. He wasn't hungry. He wasn't thirsty. And he sure as hell didn't want to work.

He didn't want anything...but Lena. The feel of her in his arms was suddenly so real, so immediate, his body responded as if she were right in front of him. She'd thrown him out, yes, but she'd kissed him first. And Lena didn't do anything lightly. The encounter had to have meant something to her, too.

Shoving the freezer door closed with a crash, he reeled around to stare out the nearby wall of windows, a cloud of condensation wisping up to the ceiling as he eyed the dark and empty beach. For a few tortured minutes, he wrestled with himself, then muttering a Spanish curse, he gave up.

Slamming the still-full can of beer to the counter, he grabbed his car keys and left.

HER DOORBELL rang at ten.

Startled, Lena looked up from the news she hadn't been watching. She'd come home at eight and had a glass of wine with a piece of leftover pizza. With Bradley on call, she'd decided to have another glass as well. Because of her twenty-four hour status, she hardly ever drank, but it'd been a helluva week so far and it was only

Tuesday. She figured she deserved to unwind, and alcohol was the only way she'd manage it. Without the liquid therapy, her mind would continue to spin.

The bell sounded again and she jumped up from the couch. Grabbing her service revolver from the locked drawer beside her bed, she returned to the entry, the weapon tucked into the curve of her back, beneath the loose waistband of her sweatpants. With one hand on the pistol's grip, she flipped on the porch light—and stared in surprise.

Andres waited under the bare bulb. He looked irritated and out of sorts...and sexy beyond belief, his shirt crinkled and unbuttoned at the neck, his jacket hooked over his shoulder with one crooked finger. The shadow of his beard told her he hadn't shaved since morning and the turbulence in his eyes told her she was in for a rough time.

With unsteady hands, she threw the dead bolt and opened the door. He stood without moving and didn't say a word. Her heart began to thud with an out-of-sync rhythm, and all she wanted to do was pull him inside and throw herself at him.

But she didn't.

Blocking the door with her body, she spoke calmly and rationally. "Andres! What a surprise. Did you need something?"

"Lena." He said her name formally. His gaze was tempestuous, his words heavy with a Spanish lilt. "I want to talk to you, and I don't intend to do it out here."

She hesitated for a fleeting second, then told herself she had no other option. Operating out of habit, she threw the locks behind him after he stepped inside and flipped off the light as well, removing her gun to lay it on the table by the door where he'd already dropped his coat. The hallway was narrow and dark, and when she turned, he was right behind her.

He spoke bluntly and without any warning. "We have some unfinished business." Raising his arms, he placed his hands on either side of her head, trapping her between the wall and the door.

They weren't touching, but she could feel the heat rising off his body. A tremor of desire shimmered down her spine and into her legs, leaving her with the wish that she'd never opened the door.

"Unfinished business?" she repeated. "What would that be?"

"You know what I'm talking about. I'm here to complete the conversation we started in your office. The one that got interrupted."

"That wasn't a conversation." She licked her lips. "A conversation uses words."

She could barely see his expression, but it didn't matter. His voice—and his body—were communicating everything she needed to know.

"You used words," he said quietly. "But they didn't match what you did. We need to clear up that contradiction. Right now. Right here."

All she could think of was what Beck had said and suddenly she didn't know how to answer because Andres had told the truth. Her body felt one way but her mind felt another. And her heart? She had no idea in hell what it felt.

Without replying, she ducked underneath his arm and started down the hallway, but he grabbed her before she managed two steps. She stopped instantly, but he didn't release her.

"I want to talk about us." His fingers—those long, slim fingers she'd always loved so much—tightened on her arm. It seemed as if they were around her heart, too, squeezing just as hard. She let her eyes land on his and he spoke again. "Let's get it out once and for all, and end this charade. It's way overdue."

HER GRAY EYES darkened as his words penetrated. He was pushing her, and pushing Lena was not a smart thing to do. He didn't care, though; he had to know.

"I've told you how I feel," she said hotly. "I've made it more than clear. There's nothing else to say."

"Then which was a lie?" He made his voice soft and deliberate. "Your words...or your kiss?"

"I didn't lie to you. I don't lie to anyone."

He paused a second. "Not even to yourself?"

She stared at him, and in the tension-filled silence, Andres moved closer to her. She never wore perfume, a necessity of her job, but he could smell the scent of her skin. He knew it as well as his own. Even if he had wanted to resist, he couldn't have; like an expensive fragrance, it drew him in.

She parted her lips as if to say something, but he didn't give her the chance. He lowered his head, his mouth covering hers with an urgency neither could deny. If she shoved him aside or told him to quit, he'd leave at her command. It was her choice and she knew it, but he needed an answer, one way or the other.

She didn't stop him.

The only thing either of them cared about was the embrace and experiencing everything that went with the physical part of their relationship. *Everything.*

Kissing her passionately, he moved his hands up her arms and gripped her shoulders tightly. Then she groaned his name into his mouth, and that was all it took.

Andres backed her against the wall and pulled at her sweater. Without a murmur, she lifted her arms and let him tug it off, her fingers fumbling with the buttons on his shirt the minute her own garment fell at their feet. He helped her as much as he could, then he simply gave up and tore it off. A button pinged against the tile floor.

"Oh, Lena...*querida*..." He whispered her name as he buried his face in the sweet juncture between her shoulder and her neck. Her warmth was like velvet beneath his mouth, so soft and sensual he couldn't believe it. Had she always been like this? Had he known her secrets before and ignored them or had he simply put them from his mind realizing he could no longer experience them after he'd left?

Either way, he didn't care. What mattered now was only the moment. He nipped at her skin with his teeth, making his way up her neck with tiny bites of pleasure. She whimpered and spread her hands against his chest, threading her fingers in his dense, black hair. For a moment, they stayed that way. Then she moved again, her hands going lower to the zipper of his pants.

He didn't wait. He couldn't. Andres pulled her toward him, his lips against her breasts. She wore a white cotton bra, no lace or frills, and it was the sexiest piece of lingerie he'd ever seen on a woman. Slipping his hand behind her back, he undid the clasp and the garment fluttered to the floor. He covered her breasts with his fingers. They were as perfect as he remembered. Taut and small, and peaked with desire. Licking her nipples with his tongue, he spread his hands against the satin of her back then began to tug at her slacks.

In another minute, they came off and she stood before him—almost nude. Her white panties gleamed in the darkness and unlike her bra, they were silk. And transparent. Dropping to his knees, he leaned toward her and kissed her through them, then he opened his mouth and pressed his tongue to the fabric. She groaned as he went lower.

When they slid to the floor, she landed on top.

THEY MOVED to her bedroom an hour later. Andres carried her through the darkened house to the bed and placed her gently on the comforter. Their lovemaking resumed, but it took on a different quality. Slower, almost dreamlike now, he touched her gently, his warm hands and long fingers trailing over her face and limbs as if he were renewing memories too long repressed. She reveled in his touch and wondered how she'd lived the past two years without it.

She knew the answer. She hadn't lived; she'd been in a deep freeze with no emotions getting in and nothing leaving, either. She'd gone through the motions and finally convinced herself that what she was doing *was* living, but inside, as she'd known all along, she was fooling herself.

He stroked her stomach, his fingers brushing lower. *This,* she thought, was living. A man's touch warming her, his breath against her skin. Everything else was a sham.

Some time passed before he made his way back up her body and kissed her lips again. "You're so beautiful," he whispered. "So perfect. You make me homesick, *querida....*"

She reached out and put her hand against his jaw. His stubble was almost soft. "What do you mean? Homesick?"

Covering her fingers with his own, he shook his head. "I'm not sure I can explain *la isla....*"

Her heart swelled. When they'd been together before, he'd never talked about the island he'd left. She hadn't pressed, either. It was too painful for him, she'd always assumed. "Is it hard to talk about it?" she asked now.

"Sometimes, yes. But lying here with you, I'm reminded of the beaches, the long hot days, the laughter...everything good that I abandoned and can never get back." His eyes went to hers. "You would have liked *mi familia*. And they would have loved you."

She eased up on one elbow and looked at him. She knew so little. "Tell me about them."

"My parents were poor. They both worked hard, long hours. My mother was a day laborer at one of the big family *fincas*—farms—outside of town. My father fished. My only other relative was Tia Isabel."

Lena had met his aunt. Isabel Gaspar was still a beauty—elegant and long-limbed with transparent skin, silver hair and piercing, black eyes. Andres had paid a fortune to bring her out of the country and into America.

"Does she still live in Miami?"

He nodded. "I bought her a new condo in a nice highrise building a few years ago. The stairs in the town house were getting to her, and I wanted to see her somewhere safer."

Lena dredged up other tiny bits he'd told her before. "You didn't have any brothers or sisters, right?"

"That's right. I asked my mother once why not. I knew she went to the *santera* a lot and bought candles to light. I heard her praying at night while my father was gone on his boat."

"The *santera?*"

"A kind of priest," he explained. "A lot of Cubans believe in Santería. It's a mixture of African religion and

Catholicism. A *santera* helps you with everything, from getting pregnant to making someone fall in love with you."

"What did your mother say?"

"She started to cry. I never asked again."

Lena thought of her own four brothers then. "You didn't miss much," she said dryly.

"Maybe so," he answered, "but in Cuba, it's different. The larger the family, the more people to work. When my father was sent to prison, we could have used the extra hands."

"Your father was arrested?" She looked at him in surprise. "For what?"

"Arrested?" He shook his head wearily. "That implies justice, a trial, some kind of fairness. That's not how it works down there, Lena. They came to the house and took him away to *La Cabaña*. He was a political prisoner for almost ten years."

"So they released him?"

"No. He passed away in prison—which is unusual. Generally they let them out to die. They say the only way to escape *La Cabaña* is to go with the devil. It's almost a joke in Havana."

"It might be a joke but it isn't a funny one."

"No, it's not, you're right. There are three or four hundred political prisoners, as we speak, rotting in jails over there. For no good reason."

His eyes held so much pain, she felt the pangs herself. Reaching out, she pulled him closer to her. He'd never shared this with her before, never given her the heartbreaking details. She didn't know what to do except comfort him.

Accepting her embrace, he sought her solace, but in

a different manner. He was a man, and for him there was only one way to face the long-ago hurts. Reaching out— once more—for the condoms he'd placed on the night-stand, Andres wrapped his arms around her and rolled them both to the center of the bed where he began to kiss her all over again. Swept into his arms and into his anguish as well, Lena let him do what he did best.

FOR A MOMENT, Andres didn't know where he was when he woke up, then everything registered. Lena's motionless form sleeping beside him, the scent of their lovemaking still in the air, the quiet ticking of her bed-side clock. He glanced toward the luminous dial and read the glowing green numerals—3:00 a.m.

Slipping his arm from beneath her bare shoulders, he eased away and climbed out of the bed. When they'd been together before Lena had always insisted he go after they make love. She didn't want him to spend the night. Not before they were married, she'd said. It'd irritated him, but at the same time it was a quirk he'd found endearing.

As he looked down at her now, she murmured and shifted in the bed but she didn't wake up, the sheet falling to her waist at her movement. Her hair was a silken sheen against the pillowcase, the still-healing line of her scar a shadow against her paler skin. He reached out but stopped just short of touching it.

What had he done by coming here tonight?

Turning away from the bed and from his question, Andres went back to the entry and the pile of abandoned clothing. It was cold in the quiet, still house. He slipped on his pants and then thrust his arms into his shirt but he didn't bother to do it up; he couldn't have anyway. Half the buttons were gone.

He returned to the living room and was almost to the bedroom when he heard a clicking noise. It was coming from one of the huge windows off the deck on the rear of the old house. Immediately curious, he crossed the room and spotted the source of the sound. Lena had a row of pots sitting out on the covered deck, and each one held a single rosebush. The plant nearest the window was tapping the glass with its leaves, almost as if it wanted inside. His eyes, now adjusted to the dark, caught the subtle sway of the rest of the plant. It was covered in pale-pink blossoms, some open, some still closed. How she'd managed to get the rose to bloom at this time of year, he didn't know, but it seemed to be fate.

He opened the window and plucked the nearest flower. Going back into the bedroom, he laid the bloom on the pillow beside Lena's head, then kissing her softly, he turned and left.

LENA HEARD the front door shut and sat up in bed. As she moved, she jostled the pillow beside her and the flower Andres had left tumbled into the knotted sheets. She picked it up and brought it to her nose. Above the blossom's fragrance she caught a salty hint of the ocean and the lingering scent of his aftershave.

She'd awakened the minute he'd left the bed, but she'd kept her eyes closed, feigning sleep. She didn't know what to say to him or how to act; it'd seemed simpler to pretend she was still asleep. She heard him start his car, then she listened to the whine of the motor as he turned around in the driveway and headed away from the house.

She fell back into the wrinkled sheets and threw an arm over her eyes. She couldn't block the images, though. His body, his mouth, his hands... every last detail she'd spent the past two years trying to forget was now so fresh she could still feel them on her skin. Now there was something new to add to the mental scrapbook: his memories of his home. He'd shared his body with her before, but never his past. They seemed tied together even more closely than they had been before.

Why on earth had she unlocked that door?

CHAPTER NINE

ANDRES HAD ALREADY called twice by the time Lena made it into the office the next morning. She stood beside her desk and fingered the pink telephone slips, pondering what to do. She didn't want to call him back because she couldn't tell him everything she was feeling. His touch had affected her even more than it used to; she was reeling from the emotions that had taken place between them. Their relationship had always been a powerful one, but last night had gone beyond even that.

She knew only one thing for certain. They couldn't repeat what had happened. Not until she had things sorted out.

Her ringing phone saved her. Dropping the messages, she picked up the receiver, listened to Bradley's news of a call-out, then raced out into the hallway, grateful for the interruption. Fifteen minutes later, she was in a squad car heading due west toward Fort Walton with Bradley at the wheel.

A small community between Pensacola and Destin, Fort Walton had its share of SWAT calls. Most of the military people from Eglin Air Force Base lived within its confines or nearby, and the soldiers had the same problems a lot of young men did—too much energy and not enough money. They were highly trained and highly stressed and things sometimes got tense.

But this wasn't to be one of those times. Lena's cell phone rang before they could get on-site.

"Turn around," Sarah said calmly. "Everything's over."

Lena put a hand over her phone and looked at Bradley. "It's Sarah. She says to forget about it."

He raised his eyebrows and slowed the car.

"What happened?" Lena asked.

"It was a fugitive arrest, a parolee. The parole office hadn't seen him in about three months and they finally tracked him down. They thought there was going to be trouble, but the guy came out when his mother happened to show up. They took him down and everything's fine. The Fort Walton people will wrap it up."

Hanging up the phone, Lena explained and Bradley headed back to the office. The aborted call was a harbinger of what was to come. Missing reports, a canceled court appearance, two men out with the flu... Lena was exhausted by the time she finished the paperwork that had piled up on her desk and was shocked to discover it was 7:00 p.m. She pushed her chair back, rolled her neck, then the phone rang.

Jeff's voice answered her weary hello. "How you doing, Sis?"

"You don't really want to know." She put a hand on her side. Beneath her fingers, her scar throbbed.

"Sure, I do, that's why I'm calling. How about some Mexican food and beer? I'm heading over to La Paz. Come with me."

She considered his offer. Nothing sounded better than a cold Corona, but the reminders of Andres's calls glared at her from the corner of her desk. Two more had been added to the ones that had been waiting for her when she'd arrived. "Jeff, I'd love to, but you wouldn't believe the day I've had. I better head home and crash. I've got some thinking to do."

"Lots going on?"

"This and that."

"Have you found out any more about that Olvera fellow?"

"Not much."

"Doesn't that bother you? I mean, the guy shot you, after all."

"It's part of the job." Lena answered his questions with distraction. Thoughts of Andres made it impossible to concentrate on anything else. "Look, Jeff, I hate to cut this short..."

"No, it's okay. I understand completely. I'll call you next week and try again. How's that?"

"I'd love it."

"Great—we need to talk about Thanksgiving, too. You know, it's coming up."

Lena groaned. "Not again."

"Every year." She could hear the grin in his voice. "Dad called me yesterday to make sure I 'remembered' so you can expect your own summons shortly. Georgia Belle's getting wound up, too. I could hear her ranting and raving in the background when he phoned me."

Every year her father threw an enormous day-long party for Thanksgiving. It was basically a family affair but he also invited everyone from his law firm, including their children. His longtime housekeeper, Georgia Belle, grumbled about it for months before and months after, but she refused to let him cater it. It was her hams and turkeys, her pies and cakes, on the vast dining room table or no one's.

Lena hated the parties. Other than her brothers and their wives, she knew very few of the people who attended, and the ones she did know, she didn't care for. But her appearance was required.

As if reading her mind, Jeff spoke. "You will be there, right? Getting shot in the line of duty is no excuse, you know."

Lena had to laugh. "It almost might be worth it."

"You just don't know how to approach these things," Jeff responded. "I always try to find the most inappropriate date I can and that usually helps. Why don't you bring someone? Hell, bring Andres! That'd liven things up."

Lena responded without thought as she recalled the tension between Andres and her father. "Oh, no, Jeff. That's not a good idea, believe me."

"What's wrong with inviting him? It might make the party bearable. Otherwise, the poor guy's gonna be all alone. No one should have to spend Thanksgiving in a rented condo."

The image stopped her, especially after what Andres had told her about his family. Andres never said so, but surely he missed them even more on holidays.

"If you're saying no 'cause you think Dad will get pissed, that's probably true, but when has that prevented us from doing anything?"

Lena laughed again.

"If you're saying no because it might not be the right thing for you and Andres, then I guess I ought to butt out." In typical fashion, he then contradicted himself. "*Are* you two getting closer?"

Lena closed her eyes. Closer? Yeah, you could use that word to describe their changing relationship...and a few others, too.

"I don't know," she lied. "I'm just not sure it's a good idea to bring him to the house."

"Well, it's your call," Jeff agreed. "I'd certainly enjoy seeing him, but you know best."

Lena hung up the phone slowly, her thoughts confused and unsettled. A second later, right on cue, Andres walked into her office.

LENA LOOKED UP, surprise coming over her face. She wore her standard SWAT garb, a tight black T-shirt and slim black slacks, and she'd obviously had a rough day. He could see where she'd repeatedly run her hands through her hair and her lipstick was long gone. It didn't matter. A jolt of desire still went straight through him. It was the same kind of reaction he'd experienced when he'd first seen her on the plane, but this time it was even stronger.

He told himself he felt this way because of last night; his hands had caressed each curve and his lips had kissed all the secret places. His response wasn't simply physical though. Now it was emotional, as well.

But she hadn't called him back. His messages were spread across her desk like scattered leaves.

He paused on the threshold of the door. "Are you busy?"

"No, I'm finished. I was just about to go home."

They looked at each other with awkwardness. Andres knew what he wanted to say, knew what he wanted to do, but he had to tread lightly. He didn't want to scare her off.

"How was your day?" he asked. "I'm guessing very busy?"

She nodded, almost gratefully, he thought. "I was swamped." Lifting a hand toward her desk, she indicated the notes. "I'm sorry I couldn't call back."

"Don't worry about it. I figured you were tied up."

The superficial conversation dwindled into silence, and he walked over to her desk, stopping at the edge, close to where she stood. She let her eyes finally meet his.

"You have regrets?" he asked softly. "Over last night?"

His directness shocked her, he could tell. Shocked her so much she answered him truthfully. "No. I don't regret what happened."

"Good."

"But, Andres—"

He checked her words, putting a finger over her lips. "Stop there," he whispered. "Don't say anything else." Taking away his finger, he reached out and pulled her against him. She didn't resist. "I don't want to hear anything negative."

"How do you know it'd be negative?"

"Any sentence that starts with *but* is usually an argument I don't want to hear."

"But—"

"I know what you want to say, anyway." He ran his hands over her narrow back, feeling the taut muscles. "If you aren't going to say it was a mistake, then you want to tell me last night didn't mean anything. You want to say what happened between us was just sex and it won't happen again. You want to take away what we shared, and I'm not going to let you do that. When you opened your door, you opened your heart, too. Let's don't try to pretend you didn't."

"Last night *was* just sex—"

He shook his head. "No. Sex is *never* just sex. Not between us and you know it. It's never been that way with you and that's one thing you can't deny."

The look on her face told him he'd hit a nerve.

"Maybe not." Her hands, resting on his shoulders, tightened. "But I'm not sure where I want this to go, Andres. There are a lot of issues between us that we may never overcome."

He hated what she said, but he understood. He'd hurt her deeply, and any woman would be wary of him. If there was a way he could clear the air between them, he would, but not at the cost she'd have to pay. He refused to make Lena choose between him and her father.

She slipped out of his embrace and went to her window. Silent for a moment, she finally turned around. Her expression seemed uncertain, but when she spoke, she spoke impulsively, almost as if she were issuing herself a challenge.

"What are you doing for Thanksgiving?"

Her question took him by surprise. "Thanksgiving?"

"It's next week. Do you have plans?"

"Isabel is coming. She called and told me I'd bought her a ticket. She wants to see Destin."

Lena laughed. "Doesn't sound as if she's changed any."

"No, thank God, she hasn't. I haven't decided what I'd do with her, though. If you have any ideas..."

"Actually, I do. Remember the party, the one my father throws every year?" She shrugged apologetically. "It's kind of a madhouse, but it's required attendance for me. It's so huge you won't have to see him. Why don't you bring her to that?"

He couldn't help himself. He laughed out loud. "What an invitation! 'Please come to this party and you won't even have to see the host!'"

She grinned. "You'd be doing me a favor. And I think your aunt would like it."

Andres nodded. His *tia* did love to socialize, but underneath Lena's casual offer, there was more than a simple invitation. He knew it and so did she. Their eyes came together and the breezy exchange deepened into something more. He wasn't sure what, and she obviously wasn't, either, but they'd passed a certain point last night. Where they went from here depended on too many things to count. Maybe the invitation was a test.

If it was, Andres intended to pass.

"We'd be delighted to come to the party," he answered. "I'll phone Isabel and tell her to pack her best dress."

JEFF HAD CALLED it exactly right. As Lena headed out to the parking lot following Andres's departure, her cell phone chirped. She glanced at the display and saw Phillip's ID. For a moment she considered not answering. She wanted to think about Andres and the conversation they'd just shared. He'd asked her out for dinner and she'd turned him down. Accepting her answer without argument, something he would never have done in the past, he'd simply nodded.

But not before kissing her into oblivion. She'd watched him leave afterward, feeling breathless and more confused than ever.

She neared her car as the phone sounded again. Punching one of the small, lighted buttons, she said, "Hello, Dad."

"Lena, I'm calling about Thanksgiving. I want you to plan on being at the house by nine."

No "hello," no "how are you," nothing in the way of polite conversation. She juggled the phone and the armful of reports she was taking home to read, reaching out

to unlock her car door. "Thanksgiving?" she said inno-
cently. "Is that coming up already?"

"Don't be smart with me, Lena."

She threw the notebooks into her car where they
landed on the passenger seat then slid to the floor. Rolling her eyes, she climbed inside. "Dad, I'm thirty-five
years old. Don't talk to me as if I were twelve."

He ignored her answer as she knew he would. "All
your brothers and their families will come at ten. I want
you to come early so you can check on things. You have
a good eye for detail. Just like your mother did. I want
you there to make sure everything's been done right."

The unthinking demand, combined with the offhand
compliment and reference to Dorothea, was so typi-
cally Phillip that Lena shook her head. Carrot and stick.
Love and hate. Push and pull.

She answered him as she usually did, by agreeing to
what he wanted. "I'll be there, Dad." Starting her car,
she kept it parked and gripped the phone tighter. "But
I'm bringing a guest. Two actually."

"No problem. There'll be plenty for everyone. Who
have you invited?"

Her mouth went dry and she reminded herself of
what she'd just told him seconds before. She was thirty-
five, for God's sake. A grown woman. If he didn't like
who she was involved with, it was his problem, not hers.

"I'm bringing Andres," she said. "And his aunt. I'm
sure you remember her, Isabel Gaspar. She's a lovely
woman."

An icy silence built. She reached out and turned on
the heater.

"What are you doing, Lena? Mounting some kind of
petty rebellion just to upset me?"

"No." She answered serenely, and suddenly she realized her attitude wasn't just a ploy, she really did feel calm. If Phillip didn't approve, it wasn't important. What mattered most was what was happening between her and Andres. *That* was what she had to work out. "Jeff suggested it and after thinking about it, I asked Andres. He accepted the invitation."

"Are you telling me you're seeing this bastard again, Lena?"

"I'm telling you I've invited him to the house for Thanksgiving."

"That's not what I asked you."

"No, but that's the answer you're getting. If you don't like it, I'll uninvite him. It is *your* party. But I'd feel an obligation to have them to my place instead."

"And not come to the house."

"That's right."

He said nothing and in the quiet Lena repeated to herself the same question he'd just asked. What in the *hell* was she doing? She wasn't even sure she wanted Andres at the party, much less back in her life again, but here she was standing up for him. One thing made about as much sense as the other.

Her father spoke again. "This was Jeff's idea?"

"He mentioned it, yes. But I'm the one who asked Andres."

She switched off the heater. All at once, it seemed too warm.

"All right." Phillip seemed suddenly weary. "You can bring the son of a bitch, but I don't like it, Lena. I don't like it one damn bit. You're asking for more trouble and a broken heart to boot. When he hurts you again—and he will—you remember that I warned you."

REACHING FOR HIS fourth cup of coffee, Andres tried to focus on the reports spread out in front of him. He was sitting at the dining table of his condo, the sound of the ocean a distant murmur. He'd left Lena's office hours ago, but in his mind, he was back in her bed, his arms wrapped around her slender body, his lips buried against her neck.

Her invitation to her father's party had been completely unexpected, and Andres still wasn't too sure what it meant. From the way she'd given it, he decided she wasn't too sure, either. It seemed as if she were trying to judge where they were and what was happening between them by issuing the offer.

One thing was for sure. He'd made an important, if inadvertent, point when he'd told her what had happened between them wasn't just sex. Those gray eyes had widened and she'd blinked—in that funny way she could—telling him he'd expressed not only how he felt, but how she felt, too. She could try to deny it all she wanted; he knew the truth, and in her heart, she did, too. Their connection was as strong now as it'd ever been, maybe even stronger. No matter what secrets he kept from her, the bond would always be there.

He rocked back in his chair then stood and crossed the room to the balcony doors. Pushing open the heavy glass, he stepped out onto the patio. Tiled and bordered by a sturdy metal railing, it ran the length of the condo. He walked to the edge and stared out into the darkness, the sound of the waves louder now that he was outside.

Maybe it was time to tell her the truth.

And maybe not.

After a moment, he accepted reality; his speculation

was pointless. With a disgusted curse, he turned and went back inside, slamming the door behind him. He might as well get back to work and see if he could make any progress there.

He returned to the scattered reports. It took a while, but he finally managed to focus his thoughts, his fingers shifting through the papers until he found the ones he wanted. The notes from Carmen.

Using the cops' listings, she'd fed the license plate numbers and car models of the vehicles seen at the Silver Shores Motel into the database in Miami.

Three had been registered in Dade County. One was a rental, registered to a retired tailor from New York who'd come to Destin to fish. The second vehicle was a van owned by a man and his wife who were visiting relatives nearby. The final vehicle, the abandoned car Andres had told Lena about in the hospital, had been "borrowed" by a teenaged couple who'd run off to get married. Ultimately, none of the cars under surveillance had any connection to the Red Tide.

But Carmen was sharp. One local vehicle had been seen in the vicinity several times, she noted. Three times to be exact. The first time had been just after the surveillance had begun, the second time a few days later, early one morning. In the third and final instance, the car hadn't stopped but had cruised through quickly. Since it hadn't parked, the cops hadn't noted its presence but Carmen had. She'd studied the photo sheets. The vehicle had been captured passing through the parking lot just as one of the officers had snapped the row of parked cars.

She'd traced the number and make of the late-model silver Lincoln. It was registered to a business in Niceville, a small town just north of Destin off Highway 285.

AAA Bail Bonds.

The name meant nothing to Andres, and probably meant nothing, period. For all he knew the car belonged to a frustrated bounty hunter meeting up with a local hooker. Or maybe it was an unfaithful husband and his girlfriend coming together at the Silver Shores.

He tossed the report to one side and made a mental note. He'd call Carmen in the morning and tell her to track down the owners of AAA and see who they were. Most likely a dead end, but worth a try. The Red Tide frequently worked through legitimate businesses.

He went to bed an hour later. Lena was beside him, but only in his dreams.

CHAPTER TEN

SHE DIDN'T dress up often.

Standing in front of her closet a week later, Lena glared at the choices as if it were their fault nothing seemed adequate for her father's Thanksgiving party.

She ran her hand through the hangers one more time. She was taking so much time, she knew she'd be late, but she didn't really care. Selecting the right thing to wear meant more to her than Phillip's certain irritation.

The red jacket and skirt? Too businesslike. She only wore it to the various conferences she attended as a representative of the team. The black silk pantsuit? Too severe. It was her marry-and-bury suit. She pulled it out for weddings and funerals.

From the back row, something caught her eye and she pushed aside her jeans to get to it.

It was her navy dress. The sparkly one. The last time she'd worn it was the night before the wedding.

Her fingers closed around the hanger and she removed the gown. Holding it up to her body, she turned slowly and looked in the mirror behind her. The heat in Andres's eyes when she'd worn it that evening was something she'd always remember. Oh, she'd pushed it aside, of course, like she'd pushed away all the good memories of their times together, but it was there all the same. Waiting, watching, daring her to resurrect it.

Impulsively, she threw off her bathrobe and slipped the dress over her head. It was a little loose, because she'd lost some weight, but the sheath still fit.

Turning slowly, she studied herself in the mirror and ran her hands over her sides, smoothing the seams. The garment was more than just a dress—it held all the promise of what had been before them. Their life together. Their marriage. The unborn children that were sure to come.

Lena cursed softly. Andres had had to go to Washington for a few days and they hadn't spoken since he'd returned. But she didn't need to talk to him to understand that she was torturing herself. The past always replayed itself, one way or the other. If she let Andres in her life once more, it wouldn't be the good times that came with him—it'd be the bad. He'd make her love him again and then he'd leave her. Her speculations ran together, connected by a string of confusion. She didn't trust him and he didn't trust her and nothing had changed so why would it work now when it didn't back then?

She was crazy if she thought the relationship would be different now. Great sex didn't mean a damned thing. It was great sex and nothing else.

Closing her heart and shutting off her mind, she yanked the dress over her head and marched across the bedroom to the phone. She picked up the receiver, dialed his number and practiced what she'd say.

I'm sorry, Andres, but I think it'd be best for you not to come.... I'm sorry, Andres, but the situation has changed.... I'm sorry, Andres...but please don't come today. I don't want you there....

The phone rang emptily—he'd obviously gone to the airport to pick up his aunt. They'd go straight from there to Phillip's. Cursing once again, Lena hung up, her real message sounding only inside her head.

I'm sorry, Andres, but I think I'm falling in love with you again...I just can't let that happen.

RAMROD STRAIGHT and every detail in place, Isabel Gaspar was the first person off the plane. She wore her standard garb; a severe black dress and three-inch heels. Her hair was pulled back and twisted into a single bun, pinned at the nape of her neck. The model of a fashionable older woman, her appearance was almost Spartan until a huge smile warmed her expression as she spotted Andres. He realized at once how much he'd missed her the past few weeks. In Miami, they met at least once a month. He'd take her out to one of the nice Cuban restaurants she loved or shopping in one of the glittering malls. She'd raised Andres after his mother had died and it'd been her encouragement that had propelled him to leave Cuba. They were very close.

They embraced tightly, then she looked at him critically, her eyes going over his face. "You look tired," she announced, her Spanish fluid. "You're working too hard, I assume?"

He laughed and draped his arm around her shoulder. "I'm working like I always do."

She nodded. "Too hard."

In the luggage area, he grabbed her case then led her out the door to the parking lot. She tugged her sweater closer. "It's colder here than Miami."

"Destin is much farther north. And on the Gulf of

Mexico. But the water is spectacular. You'll love it. Emerald green and smooth."

They continued the casual conversation until they were in the black Suburban and heading toward Phillip's house. Then Andres felt her black eyes drilling his profile.

"So you're seeing Lena again, eh? I'm surprised she let you near her. You hurt her deeply, Andres."

Isabel knew the truth. He'd told her everything.

"I know, I know." He glanced toward her. "I didn't have a choice, *Tia.*"

She pursed her lips in disapproval. "Don't give me that. Everyone has choices."

He didn't try to argue with her; she'd win because she always won—and because she was right.

"Would you like to stop by my place and freshen up or go straight to the party?"

"Don't ignore me," she said sharply. "I'm not going to pretend your past with Lena does not exist. I'm too old for such nonsense."

He reached across the car seat and patted her hand. "No one could ignore you, *Tia,* believe me. I don't have an answer, that's all."

"Then perhaps it's time you find one. You're growing old, and so am I. Before I die, I want to sit in the sunshine with some little ones on my lap."

He laughed and draped his arm around her shoulder.

LENA PULLED INTO Phillip's driveway and angled her truck into the first empty spot she found, a narrow patch of pavement close to the sidewalk. The circular turnaround was already full of her brothers' Mercedes-Benzes and BMWs. Her Ford looked as out of place as Jeff's Toyota, which was in the street, next to the curb.

He hadn't even tried to park near the house. As she slammed her car door and locked it, she couldn't help but shake her head. What a metaphor for how they all related...

She started up the sidewalk and smoothed her dress, a dark-green silk that she'd dragged from the back of the closet in desperation. Her thoughts turned again to Andres. Why on earth had she invited him here today? She thought briefly of trying to call him one more time. It would be past rude at this point, though. He was due any minute.

By the time she reached the front porch, she could hear the crowd inside. With a grimace of distaste, she opened the door.

Phillip materialized just as Lena slipped off her jacket and hung it in the hall closet. For a while after Dorothea's death, her fur had dangled, abandoned in the back. Lena would sneak into the darkness and press her face against its satin folds, seeking some comfort from it. Phillip had found her there one day and the next time she'd looked for the coat, the garment was gone.

He brushed her cheek with his, then eyed her outfit in a way that told her she'd made a bad choice. "You're late," he said brusquely. "I wanted you here early—"

"I know what you wanted, Dad." Glancing in the mirror, Lena ran a hand through her hair and tried to tame it before giving up. "I'm sorry. I ran out of time."

He waved away her excuse, as quick to forgive as he was to criticize. "It doesn't matter," he said. "Lucy came and checked things out for me."

Lena held back a groan. Lucy was Bering's wife. Quiet, shy and totally cowed by her husband, she did exactly what he told her to, and since Bering's biggest dream was to move into Phillip's house, he made Lucy "help" Phillip every time he had the opportunity. Lena wasn't surprised at anything Bering did these days. He was definitely getting pushier, though. She didn't like his aggressiveness, but she kept her opinion to herself.

"How nice," Lena said neutrally, "that Lucy could do that for you."

Ignoring her reply, Phillip took Lena's arm and steered her toward a corner of the entry, deftly dodging two of her nephews who ran by, screaming at each other at the top of their lungs. They were Patty and Richard's, Lena noted, and totally out of control, as always. Patty was a stay-at-home mom who'd given up a lucrative law practice of her own to raise their children. She should have stuck with her torts.

"Is Casimiro still coming?" Phillip's hand tightened on Lena's arm.

"As far as I know, yes, he is."

"Well, I want you to know I don't approve."

Lena sighed. "I'm aware of how you feel."

"You have no idea how I feel, Lena." He clutched the baluster of the stair beside them, his knuckles going white. "None whatsoever—"

The doorbell sounded behind them, and Stephanie, Steven's wife, bustled into the entry, called by the tones. Competent and organized, she ran her home like the military one she'd come from herself. She nodded a quick hello to Lena. "Shall I get that, Papa?"

"Yes, please." He put his hand back on Lena's arm and dropped his voice. "All I'm trying to do is protect you, Lena. That's all. I love you and I don't want you hurt. There are things you don't understand about this situation. Things I should have told you."

Behind them, Lena heard the front door open. "I *do* understand, Dad, more than you realize. But I'm a grown woman now and I have to make my own decisions. That's the bottom line and—" She broke off suddenly, the noise of the arriving guests finally registering. Phillip's expression snapped closed and without a word, he turned and left. Lena whirled and met Andres's eyes.

Her pulse began to thunder before she could control herself. He wore a black double-breasted suit with a white shirt and a gleaming red silk tie. All she could think about was the time they'd spent in her bed.

He crossed the marble floor and kissed both her cheeks, his lips warm as they brushed her skin, his hands reassuring as they took hers. He said nothing, but led her back to the front door where his aunt stood.

"Mrs. Gaspar! How wonderful to see you again." Lena smiled at the older woman and accepted her kisses, too. "Did you have a good flight?"

"It was very good, thank you." Her voice, heavily accented, was quiet and refined as she looked around the entry. "What a lovely home. It was nice of you to include us today."

"I'm glad you could come."

Lena looked cool and collected and incredibly beautiful, the deep green of her dress the perfect complement to her hair and eyes. He wanted to take her into his arms and kiss her until neither of them knew where they were. But he couldn't.

Lena stepped closer and took Isabel's arm. With their heads bent together, the two women walked toward the living room. Andres watched them go and wondered what he'd done by coming here. He didn't have too long to think about it as Jeff entered the hallway and greeted him.

"So you made it!" Jeff shook Andres's hand. "You're a brave man."

"Brave or stupid? I'm not too sure which, my friend."

Jeff laughed. "Sometimes that's one and the same, you know. At least with my sister, it is. And I have the scars to prove it."

He rolled up the right sleeve of his sweater. A small white line bisected his forearm. "That's where she caught me with the business end of a sword we weren't supposed to touch." He pushed down his sleeve and pointed to his chin. "And this is where she got me with a tennis racket when I was fifteen. It's a good thing I went off to school when I turned eighteen. I might not have survived much longer."

Andres chuckled. "Phillip did nothing to protect you, eh?"

"Protect me?" Lena's brother made a scoffing sound. "Lena could have killed me and Dad would never have noticed. The only time he paid any attention to the rest of us was when he took us hunting, and I had to get a twenty point buck with one shot before he even acknowledged me." He shook his head. "Lena was always his favorite."

Jeff was clearly joking, but just beneath the surface, Andres heard a touch of sibling rivalry. It was no secret, even though their relationship was a perplexing labyrinth of love and hate, Phillip had always favored Lena over the boys. And the other brothers over Jeff. He *was* at the bottom of the hierarchy no matter how it was viewed.

As if realizing he was getting too close to the truth, Jeffrey abruptly dropped the subject and steered Andres into the crowd, introducing him to everyone. The crush of lawyers from Phillip's office and their families relieved Andres from saying little more than hello to Lena's other brothers, although Bering had enough time to send him a particularly nasty look. Jeff stayed by his side as if he understood the potential awkwardness of the situation. But he couldn't stop the inevitable. Phillip met them near the back of the room, close to the French doors that led to the garden.

"Go check on the table, Jeffrey." Phillip didn't look at his son as he spoke. He only stared at Andres. "I want to talk to Mr. Casimiro."

Andres felt Jeff hesitate, but there was little he could do other than comply. He eased back into the crowd and left them alone.

"Let's step outside," Phillip said. "I don't want to be overheard."

Andres followed the old man into the weak fall sun. They crossed a slate-covered patio and stopped just before the steps that led down to the pool. Crystal clear and shimmering, the turquoise water looked cold and uninviting. Andres folded his arms, raised his eyebrows, and waited for Phillip to speak. He was angry and about to erupt.

The explosion came quickly.

"I want to know just what in the hell you think you're doing." Phillip's blue eyes held fire.

"Attending a dinner party?" Andres ventured.

"That's not what I mean and you know it. Don't give me that innocent act, dammit."

Truly mystified, Andres shook his head. "You must be losing it, Phillip. I have no idea what you're talking about."

"Save your bullshit, I'm not buying it." He reached

inside his coat pocket and pulled out a pink phone slip. "I have proof and if you don't cease and desist, I'm filing on you, make no doubt about it."

Andres reached out and took the note from the lawyer's fingers. The scribbled notation told him little other than the fact that Carmen had called Phillip's office last week. Puzzled, Andres shook his head. "I don't know what this is about, Phillip."

"You're having this woman harass me for no good purpose."

"Harass you?"

"That's right. She called my offices last week and insisted on talking to me. When my secretary refused, she somehow managed to obtain my private number and called me directly." His face flushed. "I know you're behind this, dammit, so don't act so naive."

Andres frowned. "What did Carmen want with you?"

"You're telling me you don't know about this?"

"That's exactly what I'm telling you."

For the first time, Lena's father looked hesitant. "She wanted information about some of my businesses," he answered. "I hold primary interest in a number of concerns besides the law firm. Investments I've made through the years. I haven't been active in some of them for quite some time and in others, never." He narrowed his eyes, his irritation returning. "I told her to go to hell and that's the same message I have for you."

"I have no idea what she was doing, Phillip."

"You expect me to believe that?"

"It's the truth." Andres shrugged. "Believe what you will."

Phillip turned and looked out over the pool. He

thought quietly for a moment, then he glanced at Andres again. "We go back a long way."

Andres waited.

"And you're sleeping with my daughter."

The words ignited Andres's own anger. "That's personal and none of your business! You have no right—"

"I may not have the right, but it's the truth." A ray of sunshine hit his silver hair and highlighted the wrinkles pulling down his face. "Don't try to tell me you aren't because I know. I can tell just by looking at her. And I know where it's probably going to lead, too. I'll fight it every step of the way, though—make no mistake about it."

"You're jumping to conclusions, *viejo*."

"Say what you must," Phillip answered, "but I disagree. That's why I need to know the truth once and for all. If you're investigating me—*again*—let's put the cards on the table and get the evidence out in the open."

He knew.

A wave of shock rippled over Andres at the revelation. Phillip *knew* Andres had investigated him for Mateo's murder.

"I want to know, Casimiro. I want the truth." He focused on Andres's face with all the intensity of a time-tested interrogator. "You tell me right here and now why you have so many questions about AAA Bail Bonds."

ISABEL SAT QUIETLY on the sofa and nodded as Lena explained to her who the various guests were. When Lena finished, Andres's aunt spoke softly. "You have a large family. How nice for you."

Lena immediately remembered Andres's words about his mother. "It can be nice," she said with a smile.

"But you know how brothers and sisters get along. I'm closest to Jeff, but sometimes the others get to me. Did you have that problem?"

She smiled gently. "Of course. Yolanda, Andres's mother, and I had our disagreements. It was just the two of us, though. We had no brothers or other sisters. We would have loved it if there had been more, but now I guess it worked out as it should. I could never have left the island if I'd had relatives still there."

Lena nodded. "Was it difficult for you to leave?"

"Not in terms of going, no. I'd had my fill of what they were doing—still do—to the people. And of course I wanted to be near Andres since he's the only one I have left." Her dark eyes turned soft. "I do miss the island itself, though. The warm winds, the blue sky, the green water..."

"Andres loved it."

"Oh, yes, he did. When he was a little boy he said he would never leave. That he would grow up and be a fisherman just like his *papá*. Every day he would go out on the boat with Angelo. It made Yolanda nervous, but she said nothing." Her voice sharpened. "My sister was a good Spanish wife."

Lena looked at Isabel curiously. "What do you mean?"

"She never said anything to Angelo that would make him unhappy. She existed only because of him." The older woman pulled a lace-edged handkerchief from the inside of her sleeve. Folding it twice, she twined it around her fingers. "It cost her her life."

"Her life?"

"She dared to complain when Angelo persisted with his activities with the underground. He quickly told her it was man's work and to stay out of it so she did. Then he was arrested. He rotted in prison for ten years while she pined away. She needed him to live. When he died, she followed shortly."

Isabel looked across the room, but Lena knew she wasn't really seeing the crowd. "She should have been a stronger woman," she said softly. "She should have needed him less and depended on herself more. She had a child she should have lived for. Instead, she died and I raised him." Blinking, Isabel seemed to come out of her past. She turned to Lena, reached out and patted her on the knee. "She should have been like you, *chica*. An independent woman who needs no one but herself."

Lena protested without thinking. "I'm not that self-assured, Isabel, believe me. I may have a tough job, but I also have more than my share of self-doubt."

"Andres doesn't think so. He sees you as totally independent."

"He always has."

"Why do you think so?"

"I don't know," Lena replied. "He sees the outer me and assumes it's the inner me, as well. Deep down, I'm as shaky as the next guy, but I can't let that out."

"Because of your job?"

"That's part of it." It was Lena's turn to look across the room. Her father was holding court, telling one of his stories to a crowd of attorneys. She nodded toward him. "The rest of it goes back to my childhood, I suppose. After my mom died things changed. I wasn't the youngest, but I was the only girl, and if I showed any kind of weakness or neediness, it was pounced on by my father *and* my brothers. I *had* to be independent to survive. It became my habit, I guess. My protective armor. I think I simply picked a job that matched my attitude."

"So you always must be the strong one, yes? Never let them see you cry?"

As Isabel spoke, Lena thought back to the conversation in her office the day Brandon had been hurt. She'd told Andres how she felt, confessed to her self-doubt. She'd allowed him to see her true emotions.

And he hadn't mocked her; he'd understood completely. He'd understood, then he'd comforted her, in just the right way, and finally he'd kissed her. She'd let down her guard and needed him, and he'd come through for her in the best possible manner.

It was a realization that would stay with her for the rest of the day.

CHAPTER ELEVEN

SITTING AT THE dinner table an hour later, Andres glanced down the expanse of mahogany in Phillip's direction. Clearly feeling the heat of the stare, the attorney turned his head sharply and glared back.

Although he hadn't revealed it, Andres had been shocked by Phillip's question on the balcony, the pieces of the puzzle clicking into place with alarming alacrity. "I can't answer questions about current investigations," he'd replied automatically.

"Then you *are* investigating me?"

"I didn't say that. Don't twist my words."

"I'll twist any damn thing I want to," the old man had said angrily. "And when this is finished, it'll be your neck."

Andres reached for his wineglass and felt a stare of his own. He didn't have to look up to know it came from Lena. She'd seen him reenter the living room a few minutes after Phillip, and going to his side, she'd wanted to know what they'd been talking about.

"The usual," he'd said laconically. She hadn't accepted his answer, and even now he could sense her curiosity from across the table.

It hardly mattered. Connecting that Lincoln Town Car to AAA Bail Bonds meant connecting Phillip McKinney to the Silver Shores Motel. And the Silver Shores

Motel meant one thing and one thing only to Andres. The Red Tide.

He couldn't believe Carmen hadn't told him what she was doing. She knew nothing, of course, about his prior investigation of McKinney but she should have recognized the importance of this information. He'd tried to call her early this morning, but she hadn't answered. Why hadn't she said anything about this to him last week?

The rich wine suddenly felt heavy on his tongue. Carmen still had family in Havana, and many times they'd discussed the situation—the unstable atmosphere, the uncertainty of life on the island. She'd voiced opinions about the political upheaval there, but he hadn't listened that closely. Now he wished he had. Could she somehow be involved with the Red Tide? God, if she was, it meant she had conned Isabel and Andres both. What was she doing?

What was Phillip doing?

Andres looked down the table again. Ever since Mateo had died, he'd wanted to connect Phillip McKinney to his best friend's murder. Now he had a concrete link between McKinney and a known member of the organization—Esteban Olvera. Not just any member, either, but the one who'd been sent to kill Andres. He should be overjoyed but he wasn't. He simply had more questions than ever before, the most important of which he hardly dared to consider.

Wrapping his fingers around his goblet, Andres turned his head again to meet Lena's puzzled eyes. There was something special in her gaze, and all at once, he accepted the fact that Phillip *was* right about one thing. Andres did love Lena.

He loved her as much as her father hated him.

SOMETHING WAS bothering Andres.

From above the flickering candles, Lena stared at him, pretending all the time that she was listening to the woman at her left. Intense and way too focused, she was one of Phillip's young attorneys, and she was doing her best to ingratiate herself to Lena. She had no idea Lena was ignoring her.

He'd been fine before he'd gone outside with Phillip. Lena peeked toward her father. He was deep in conversation with one of his partners but as she watched, he turned in her direction. It wasn't her he was trying to see, though; it was Andres, she realized a moment later. Andres raised his eyes, and an arc of tension stretched between the two men. Lena felt caught between them in more ways than one.

She decided right then and there she was going to get to the bottom of their problem, one way or the other. She'd insist one of them tell her the truth and if he didn't, then she'd go to the other. Enough was enough.

A second later, Lena's pager, tucked into the pocket of her dress, began to vibrate. Excusing herself, she reached down and pulled it out. The code number it displayed sent her abruptly to her feet. Her father looked at her with an inquiring glance.

"I have to go," she announced. "I'm sorry, but it's an emergency." She dropped her napkin on her chair and headed out to the hallway. Andres met her in the center of the entry as she jerked her coat from the closet.

"Let me drive you," he said, reaching for his own jacket.

She automatically started to decline then she stopped. She'd have to change clothes. If he drove her, she could switch in the car and be there even faster. "That would help," she said. "But what about Isabel—"

"I asked Jeff to drop her by the hotel. He said it would be no problem. And someone from the office can get the SUV and drop it at my condo."

She nodded. "All right, then, let's go."

Their footsteps echoed on the marble as they strode out the door. Fifteen minutes later, they were speeding down Highway 98 in Lena's truck. From the back, Lena grabbed the spare uniform she always kept in a bag, then began to peel off her panty hose.

Andres glanced across the seat, his black eyes gleaming. "This could be interesting."

"Keep driving." Her voice was muffled by her dress as she yanked it over her head and quickly replaced it with a black sweatshirt. "I want us to get there in one piece. You, especially. I have some questions and I want some answers."

"I've had enough questions from McKinneys today, *por favor...*"

She retrieved her boots from the rear floorboard and a pair of socks. "That's exactly what I want to ask you about. What were you and my father discussing outside, Andres? The tension between you two is unbelievable."

"He wanted some information about a case. Something I'm working on. I couldn't tell him, of course, and that made him mad."

"A case? The only thing you're working on is the Red Tide thing, right? What would he want with—"

"Our office has more than one investigation going on, Lena."

She stuck a clip in her mouth then used both hands to pull back her hair. Holding the strands to one side, she reclaimed the clip and secured it at the back of her head. "Tell me more," she demanded.

"Tell me where to take you. I'll fill you in later."

"Fill me in now." She took out her beeper and read off the address.

He ignored her demand, his reaction immediate. "Are you kidding? About that address?"

"No." Puzzled by his voice, she shook her head and looked at the flashing window again. "That's the number and the street. 1990 Gulf Shore Drive, Number 403. It's a condo complex. Someone saw a guy going into one of the units then they heard shots. The P.D. came but the intruder apparently started shooting back and they can't get any closer." She stopped. "What do you know about the building?"

"That's Emerald Towers South." He glanced across the seat, his eyes going dark. "That's where Carmen lives. In Number 403."

LENA JUMPED OUT before Andres had the vehicle fully stopped. "I'll call you after I know what's going on—"

"No way." Andres put the truck in park, then climbed out as well. He slammed and locked the door, staring at her from over the hood. "I'm coming."

"Andres! You can't come. This is a SWAT operation—"

"And I'm Justice with an employee who might be involved. I'm coming, Lena."

It was futile for her to argue. With a curse, she turned sharply and headed toward the Winnebago down the street. He followed right behind her.

As they entered the War Wagon, Bradley glanced up. He nodded as Lena explained Andres's connection to

Carmen. Sarah Greenberg stood in the back and listened as well.

"Give me all her personal information," Sarah demanded. "I need to know everything I can about her."

Andres and the young cop began to talk as Lena grabbed the headset Bradley held out to her. "Tell me how this started," she said.

"As a cluster-screw, basically," Bradley answered, shaking his head. "Resident calls the switchboard an hour ago and says she thinks her neighbor's been shot. She saw the woman's boyfriend go into the condo, then she heard something that sounded like gunfire a few minutes later. The P.D. happens to have a unit down the street. They're here in seconds, they come up the elevator, knock on the door, and shots are fired—through the door—no warning whatsoever. Instead of going in, they take cover and now we're stuck. It's a miracle no one was hit."

Lena felt her gut tighten. Reaching for the binoculars, she focused on the fourth floor of the high-rise building in front of them. This was her worst nightmare. For years she'd worried about something happening in one of the densely packed condominium towers that dotted the beach. The majority of them had a single elevator with stairwells at both ends. If he had enough ammo, a hostage taker could hold off an army for days. The people at risk would be the closest civilians.

Bradley seemed to read her mind. "The neighbor who called is a widow who lives by herself on the right side of 403. On the left are renters. Two families from Texas—two couples, five kids. There are five other residents on that floor. We got out the two nearest the stairwells but we're afraid to move the rest."

"Keep them where they are for now." She dropped the glasses and spoke into her headset. "Check in, please."

The men answered in rotation. Two in each stairwell. One beside the elevator. Diego on standby in the lobby. The telephone wasn't working inside the unit. He'd been up once and tried the bullhorn but no one had answered.

Behind them, Sarah spoke up, a phone in her hand. "The unit above 403 is empty," she said excitedly. "I just talked to the management firm. We can get guys in there."

"Do it."

Bradley spit out instructions into his microphone. Listening to the conversation, Lena heard the men respond. They were already prepared and had the mirrors with them. In seconds, they'd be above the unit and with any luck, able to see inside.

The radio continued to crackle softly as she glanced to where Andres stood in the back of the bus. Underneath his calm demeanor, she could tell he was worried. For a single second, she felt a flash of jealousy; Carmen was gorgeous, they worked together closely. From the first time she'd seen the woman on the plane Lena had known how she felt about Andres. Did he know, too? How did he feel about her? The widow had mentioned a boyfriend....

"She has two kids." Andres answered Lena's unspoken questions. "She's divorced." Pausing for a second, he seemed to think about something, then he spoke again. "She doesn't have a boyfriend."

"Well, she's obviously seeing someone," Lena said. "The neighbor must have seen the guy coming and going if she's calling him a boyfriend."

"I don't know about that. But I do know she was not dating anyone here." He paused, then spoke again, almost haltingly. "She was checking on some things for me about the Red Tide case. Following a lead I didn't know anything about. I just found out she was doing this tonight."

An uneasy feeling came over Lena. "What kind of lead?"

"A local tie-in," he said tensely.

Before Lena could query him further, a voice came through her headset, speaking quietly. Her attention immediately left Andres and she focused on the words, her fingers pressing her earpiece closer.

"We're in." It was Scott. "Linc is going to the balcony to drop the mirrors."

"Easy, Linc," Bradley spoke urgently. "You can hear those balcony doors open from below."

"Ten-four."

Unlike Brandon, Linc was a seasoned veteran; he knew what he was doing. Lena turned back to Andres, her voice tense. "Surely there's something else you can tell us, Andres. Anything—"

"I've got him." Linc's voice broke into Lena's headset. Something in his tone alerted her, and all at once Lena forgot about Andres.

"I can see through a crack in the drapes. They're parted just a bit. He's by the front door, looking out the peephole."

"How many?"

"Just one."

"What about the woman?" Lena felt Andres's eyes on her face as she spoke into her mike. "Can you see her?"

The answer was professional and curt. "She's on the couch. She's dead."

Lena dropped her gaze. "Keep your mirrors steady and hang tight."

She pulled back her mouthpiece and looked up. Andres read her expression, then pivoted and cursed. Bradley and Sarah stood by quietly. Lena tilted her head toward the front of the bus. They moved past her, and she went to the rear of the narrow aisle, where Andres waited, his head bowed.

Feeling guilty for her earlier jealous thoughts, Lena put her hand on his shoulder. "I'm sorry." Andres shook his head and said nothing. "Had she been with you a long time?"

It took him a second to answer. "About a year, more or less. She was a friend of Isabel's and that's why I hired her. Her kids—" He stopped and cleared his throat. "Her kids are staying with her father while she's working here. I'll call him when this is over. I have the number."

"Do you want me to do it?"

"I will. Their father works overseas, and Carmen's dad will have to track him down." He raised his head and stared out the window. "This is all my fault."

She spoke automatically. "This isn't your fault, Andres. Don't say that."

He turned around, his expression tortured. "Yes, it is. Trust me, Lena. If I hadn't—"

He stopped himself abruptly and Lena felt a knife twist inside her. What kind of feelings had he had for Carmen? Was she in Destin to work for him or did their relationship go deeper?

"L1, we got trouble!"

Lena yanked her mike toward her mouth, but Linc was speaking again before she could say anything. "The patio doors just opened downstairs. He's standing by the railing and—goddammit, he's climbing up. Shit! No, man, wait... No—"

The cop's voice broke off abruptly, and in the background, Lena heard a scream. Then silence.

"L1?"

"I'm here, Lincoln." Lena gripped the mouthpiece with her fingers as Andres moved closer to her. "What happened?"

"He just jumped! I guess he was trying to make it to the balcony below but he missed." She heard the wind whistling into the cop's mike as he obviously leaned out to look over. It made for an eerie sound. He finally spoke again, his voice weary. "Call for the wagon. He's dead."

IT WAS AFTER midnight by the time they wrapped up the scene. From an out-of-the-way spot nearby, Andres watched Lena direct the various men and handle the debriefing. He'd already called Carmen's family. Sarah had dealt with the news media. They'd descended on the condos immediately, their microphones thrust before them, the anchors made up and ready. Even now, looking through the crowd, he could spot the print guys still hanging around, hoping for another tidbit. The television crews had left a little after ten. They'd done their live remotes for the late news then disappeared. The dead man had no identification on him and without that, the reporters no longer appeared to care.

What did it all mean? Andres wondered emptily. If Carmen had been involved with the Red Tide, where did that leave them now?

If she hadn't been connected to them, the questions were even more confusing.

Lena navigated the crowded parking lot, lifted the yellow crime scene ribbon at the edge, and came to Andres's side. She threaded her hand through her hair, her face wearing a look of total exhaustion.

"Come home with me," he said suddenly. "My place is one block over. It'd take half an hour to go out to your house."

She shocked him by agreeing.

They pulled into his complex five minutes later. He thought briefly of telling her his suspicions about Carmen, then he swallowed his words. He had to be sure before he threw out an accusation that serious. Lena stayed silent during the elevator ride up to his floor and remained that way until they entered his unit.

Stepping inside, she looked around. "Very nice."

"Carmen picked it out." He regretted the comment the minute it was out of his mouth. It seemed to thrust them both right back into the horror.

Lena simply nodded and headed to the back, the obvious direction of his bedroom and bath. He heard the sound of the shower running, and fifteen minutes later she came out, wrapped in his bathrobe. She walked directly to him and stood so close he could smell the shampoo she'd used, so close he could see the drops of water still hanging on her eyelashes. She looked younger and even more vulnerable. She spoke huskily, as if the words hurt. "Were you sleeping with her?"

It took a moment for him to understand, and another to form his reply.

"What makes you think I was sleeping with Carmen?"

"I'm not sure that *is* what I think," Lena replied. "But something's not right here. What is it?"

He put his hands on either side of her face. Her

skin was moist and warm. "I wasn't sleeping with her...."

She nodded, her expression easing minutely.

"But I had."

She stiffened and started to pull away, but he refused to let her go. His hands on her shoulders, he held her in place. "I'm not going to lie to you, Lena. You asked me so you're getting the truth."

Her eyes filled with pain. "Right. And next you'll tell me it was a mistake, and it only happened once."

"It was, and it did." He tightened his grip. "It should never have happened."

"You're a grown man. You're not married. It's all right."

"No, it's not." He rubbed his thumbs over her arms, the silky robe too thin to hold her heat. "I shouldn't have slept with her...because I still loved you." He paused. "I love you now. I always have. And I always will."

Lena felt her heart stutter to a stop.

Dropping his hands, he stepped back as he spoke, his expression angry. "I wanted you but you weren't there and she was. That doesn't make it right—in fact, it makes it worse—but that's the truth. When I realized it, I told her it wouldn't happen again, and it didn't."

"You love me?" Lena repeated the words stupidly.

"Of course I love you!" He pushed his hands through his hair. "My God, Lena, you couldn't tell that the other night?"

"I thought it was just..."

"Just sex? I told you already that wasn't the case. Do you really think so little of me?"

"I didn't know!"

Abruptly, he drew her to him. She could feel his fury as she raised her hands and put them on his chest.

"How many times do I have to say it? It's never been just sex between us, Lena, and you know it. Every time I touch you, every time you touch me, something happens between us, something that goes way beyond the physical. It's what makes our relationship work, it's what holds us together, even when we've been apart. Surely you know that by now."

His words and his intensity shook her. "But I thought—"

"You don't have to think about it, dammit. You do that too much. You *shouldn't* think about it." He flattened his hands on her back, his accent intensifying. "Just love me back. That's all you have to do."

She parted her lips to speak, to say something although she didn't know what, but he lowered his mouth to hers and began to kiss her. It was a needy kiss, a demanding kiss, a kiss that told her more than any words he could have said.

And God help her, she kissed him back.

He dropped his hands to her buttocks and pulled her closer, almost lifting her off the ground. She responded by wrapping her arms around his neck, the feel of his hair soft beneath her curling fingers. Moaning into his open mouth, Lena knew she was lost once more. Set into motion, the passion between them took on a life of its own. Nothing could have stopped it. She didn't care if he'd slept with Carmen, she didn't care what kind of issue existed between him and her father, she didn't care that he'd left her with a broken heart.

Just as before, the last time they'd made love, all that mattered was the moment. The feel of his skin, the smell of his body, the touch of his hands.

He picked her up and carried her to the rear of the

condo, to the bedroom she'd passed through earlier. It was lined with a bank of windows and they looked out over the Gulf. The water was so black and endless she couldn't tell where the glass stopped and empty space began. A storm of vertigo came over her at the sight, and Andres's touch only added to the sensation. He peeled back the robe that she wore, then dropped it to the floor, his own clothes quickly following as dizziness took hold of her.

They swayed in the darkness for one long moment. Not touching. Not breathing. Simply staring at each other, a heartbeat's distance apart. She wondered if he could tell what she was thinking—that none of their past ever mattered during a moment like this—then she knew that thought wasn't important, either. Andres was Andres and she would always love him. It was her destiny to have him in her heart.

He reached out and brushed the edge of her jaw. His touch left a path of heat all the way down her cheek to her lips. She turned her head and took his thumb into her mouth, sucking gently. His eyes burned in the darkness; she could feel their energy and taste his desire.

"You love me," he whispered. Pulling his thumb away, he rubbed it over her lips, then glided his nail over her mouth. The edge felt sharp and it escalated her desire.

She nodded slowly.

"Tell me," he demanded. "Say the words. Let me hear them come from your mouth."

She stood quietly for a moment. When she did speak, her voice was so strained, it didn't even sound like her. "I love you." Another woman *was* speaking, she thought in a daze. How on earth could she—Lena—be telling Andres she loved him? It didn't make sense.

"Show me," he demanded. "Make me believe it."

Without hesitation, she reached for him. The kiss lasted forever, then she dropped her mouth to his shoulder, then his chest, then finally lower. A few minutes later, he gasped and brought her to her feet. "If you keep doing that, I'm not going to last too long."

"How long you last isn't important." Her eyes met his in the darkness. "What counts is what you do with the time you've got."

"Then let's not waste any more of it."

CHAPTER TWELVE

WHEN LENA WOKE in the early dawn, Andres was still beside her. Gently, she touched his shoulder. As always, his lovemaking had left her both drained and fulfilled.

He stirred under her fingertips, and she realized he'd been awake all along. Turning his head against the pillow, he looked at her. "I love you," he said simply.

She closed her eyes against the feeling that came over her at his words, but the emotion was too strong to fight. All at once she was back where she'd been before, imagining life with Andres, a family, a home.

Everything she'd always wanted with the man she'd always loved.

She continued to fight the images just as she had ever since he'd left her, but they managed to get past her defenses and slip into her heart.

The bed shifted and she opened her eyes. Andres was watching her, his head propped up by one hand, his expression barely visible in the darkness of the room. He touched her face with a gentle caress. "Lena..."

Her name always sounded different coming from his lips.

"Andres..."

He smiled and let his hand drop to the tops of her

breasts. Raking a fingernail across her skin, he sent shivers up and down her spine.

"You're so beautiful," he said. "So perfect."

She laughed lightly. "Me? Perfect? I don't think so, but I love to hear it. Tell me more."

"Why tell you?" He bent his head and dropped a kiss where his touch had been a second before. "When I can show you instead?"

"I have to go to work in a bit," she protested. "And I didn't sleep at all."

"You slept at least an hour."

She groaned. "I need more than that, please... and it's going to be a long day. It always is after a call-out."

She felt him tense and wished immediately that she hadn't brought up the subject. It was too late though, the words had already escaped. She eased up in the bed and started toward the edge. Andres stopped her, his hand on her arm.

"Don't leave."

She couldn't resist. Allowing him to bring her closer, she relaxed against his chest and he wrapped his arms around her. Together, they stared out over the water. The faintest line of red marked the eastern sky.

"Lena..." He said her name again, then she felt him hold his breath.

She waited and for some reason, held her own.

Inside the circle of his embrace, he turned her slightly, so he could see her face. "Lena...I want to ask you something. Something very important. But I don't want you to answer me, okay? I want you to think about what I'm going to say then, later, I will ask you again. You can tell me your reply at that point. *¿Está bien?*"

"This sounds scary." Trying to keep her voice light,

she laughed nervously. "I don't know if I like the rules, either."

He smiled, but his eyes were serious as they caressed her face. "Just don't answer now, that's all I ask."

"Okay, okay..." She nodded her acceptance.

He took her hands between his and lifted them to his mouth where he kissed her fingertips, one by one. For a moment, he stayed quiet, as if he were gathering his thoughts, then he raised his gaze and spoke over the top of their joined hands. "I love you, Lena, and returning to Destin has made me realize that fact even though it was something I wanted to fight at first. It's not anything that will ever change, though. You can blame my Latin nature for saying this, but I know that we were born to be together, no matter what. I hope that you share these feelings with me, *querida,* and I would like to know if you would again consider marrying me."

In the silence that suddenly filled the room, the bottom of the world fell out. Lena tumbled into the hole it left, her mouth dropping open in shock. She'd expected something important, but not this. Never this. Andres immediately reached out and covered her lips with his fingers.

"No," he said. "Say nothing now. I want you to let out your feelings, allow your emotions to decide this one for you. I know we have some problems, but they can be vanquished. We have enough love to conquer them and anything else that might come our way." He cupped her chin with his fingers. "I thought I could live without you, but the truth is, I can't. I love you and you love me. You said so last night. If we share that, surely we can work out our problems, no?"

"Andres, I—"

He kissed her into silence.

When he finished, he put his finger over her mouth once more. "For once, please, just listen to what's in your heart, *querida*. Don't think—just hear what your heart says—it will tell you what to do."

ANDRES GOT DRESSED and left a little while later. In his pale-blue robe, with her hair blowing in the early dawn's breeze, Lena stood at the front door and watched him walk to the elevators. He came back twice and kissed her each time, loath to have her out of his arms, then finally he left, driving away in his SUV, which had been delivered the night before. Both of them were reluctant to lose sight of the other, but neither had known what to do after his proposal. Especially Lena. Her eyes couldn't have gotten any larger or her body any more tense. Clearly he'd shocked her.

Which was all right. He'd shocked himself as well.

Leaving the complex, he rolled the truth over in his mind, the truth he'd come to accept some time during the night. He would never stop loving Lena, no matter what. The situation with her father, the details behind the wedding that had never happened, even Carmen's death—they were all tragedies, yes, but the truth couldn't be denied. They *were* meant for each other.

He reached the main highway in a few minutes and headed straight for the hotel where Isabel was staying. He'd called her last night with an apology for leaving her at the McKinney house, but had told her little else. Now she had to hear the grim truth about Carmen, and he wanted it to come from him, not some newscaster. Knocking on the hotel door, he waited for her to answer.

Fully dressed, Isabel opened the door a second later,

a mug of steaming coffee in her hand. His aunt looked surprised but pleased to see him. "Andres! So early.... Come in, *por favor,* come in."

He stepped inside and kissed her smooth cheek. Her skin was fragrant with lavender, the scent she always wore. "I'm sorry to bother you like this even before breakfast, but—"

"No, no, it doesn't matter." She went to the mini-kitchen in one corner of the room, poured another cup of the strong black brew and brought it back to him. Their eyes met as she handed him the china mug, and this time she saw the darkness in his gaze.

"What's wrong?" she asked immediately.

He didn't mince words; his aunt was a strong woman. "It's Carmen San Vicente," he said. "There was a terrible accident last night."

Isabel put her hand to her chest. "Oh, no. Is she hurt?"

"She's dead, *Tia.* I'm sorry."

"Oh, no...oh, dear..." Crossing herself, she sat down on the edge of the bed. "What happened?"

He gave her the basic details, leaving out the worst of it. "We don't have an ID on the killer yet."

"Do her children know?"

"I called her father last night."

"Oh, those poor babies."

He let her talk a little more, then he asked the question that had been on his mind since talking with Phillip. "*Tia,* do you know much about Carmen's family back in Cuba?"

"I knew them well."

"Tell me what you know, please."

She didn't ask him why, she simply began to talk. Twenty minutes later, he was more confused than before. If there was anything—anything at all—in Carmen's past that might make her a friend of the Red Tide, Andres had no idea what it might be. Maybe she simply hadn't had time to tell him about the lead yet. Maybe he was looking for what wasn't there.

Then why had they killed her?

The answer to his question came so swiftly he knew it had been there all along. He'd never *really* suspected her. Carmen had been killed for asking about things she shouldn't have. They'd *had* to stop her.

Andres could think of nothing but Phillip McKinney's angry expression the day before.

Promising his aunt he'd return and take her out for lunch, Andres left the hotel and went straight to his office. Going into the small cubicle where Carmen had sat, he looked through her desk and files, but he could find nothing that looked suspicious. A quick check of her computer told him even less. If she'd made notes on her conversations with Phillip she must have kept them at home. He'd seen nothing in her condo last night, but her killer could have destroyed them. After he tortured her to make her tell him where they were. Andres closed his eyes against the image but that action alone was not enough to erase the picture. He'd seen the body.

Leaning back in the desk chair, he stared out the window toward the parking lot, his thoughts growing cold. If Phillip had had Carmen killed, she was his second victim. And an innocent one at that. She'd simply gotten too close, linking Phillip to the motel where Olvera had stayed. Was that enough to make the old man kill her or had she known more? It made no sense that she'd found out something and held it back from Andres, but he'd known of stranger things to happen during the course of an investigation. He'd have to go back and track down everything she'd done, repeat all her actions. It was the only way he'd know what she'd been doing.

LATE FRIDAY AFTERNOON, Lena finished the debriefing and dismissed the men. Their mood was quiet, and underneath it all, she could sense the disappointment many of them felt. She discerned it because she felt the same way. There was no good explanation for Carmen San Vicente's murder and the killer's identity remained a mystery. The detectives were working on the case now, and eventually they'd know who he was, but in the meantime the lack of information only served to frustrate.

Deep in thought, Lena made her way back to her office. She didn't know which was more upsetting right now—her personal life or her professional one. Both were in such an uproar, she felt as if she were caught inside a tornado. Spinning and spinning, no control, no end in sight.

Andres's proposal had been so unexpected, she was still reeling. There was only one thing she was glad of and that was the fact that he hadn't wanted her to answer. She had no idea what to say, no idea what to think about the feelings storming inside her.

Her phone was ringing as she stepped into her office.

Her father was on the other end, and Lena dropped into the chair behind her desk. This was all she needed. He was probably mad because she'd had to leave his party and wanted to let her know about it.

"Your run made the ten o'clock news." Throwing her off guard, his voice was subdued. "I watched it after the party. The woman who was killed, she was Andres's assistant, wasn't she?"

Lena pitched the file she'd been holding to the top of her desk. "Yes, she was. Did you know her?"

"I'd met her once." He seemed to hedge, then went on. "She was stunning."

"She *was* an attractive woman."

"Any leads yet?"

"None that I know of." Lena gripped the phone. Her father wasn't usually this attentive to her work. "Why are you so interested?"

"No particular reason," he answered quickly. "I was just surprised, that's all. Her association with Casimiro then her death. It seemed...unusual, don't you think? Did he say anything about her?"

"She was his assistant, Dad." Lena shook her head. How far would Phillip go? Did he really think he could make her believe Andres had something to do with Carmen's unfortunate murder? "He felt badly about it, of course. He said she was involved in a case he was working on, but that was all. He couldn't say more because he didn't know more. And I believe him," she added for good measure.

"Of course you would." His voice turned bitter, but instead of pursuing the issue as she would have expected, Phillip surprised her again and dropped the subject. "Did you have a good time at the party? I wish you could have stayed longer. Jeff disappeared right after you did, too. Something about a girlfriend. But he came back, at least, to take Andres's aunt home."

"I didn't finish the case until midnight, Dad," she said automatically. "The party was over by then. But I want to know what you and Andres were talking about outside on the balcony. When he came in, he looked—"

"It was business," Phillip interrupted. "A case I've got going that the Justice Department might impact."

"A case?" Her voice revealed her suspicion.

"Down in Miami," her father answered impatiently. "You don't know anything about it, Lena."

He was lying.

As sure as she was sitting in her office, holding the phone against her ear, he was lying. But there was nothing she could do about it. Confronting him would only make things worse. He'd get his back up and she'd never find out.

What would he say if he knew of Andres's proposal?

Phillip returned to the topic of the party, and she let him talk, her mind focusing once more on the question that faced her. When he started to say goodbye, she realized she hadn't heard a thing he'd said. Which was just as well, she decided, hanging up a second later. He'd been so imperative at the party, she'd almost been relieved to get the call-out. She could only imagine the blowup that would occur should she decide to marry Andres. Did she really want to put up with that? She twirled a pencil on her desk and shook her head. She couldn't let her father's reaction keep her from marrying the man she loved.

The thought startled her into stillness and she dropped the pencil. She really did love Andres, she realized suddenly. She'd said the words last night, but the emotion hadn't hit her until this very moment. She *did* love him, and if that was the case, then her answer was simple, wasn't it? There was no good reason *not* to marry him. Sure, they had problems, but everyone in a relationship had problems. No one's love life was simple.

But he left you, a little voice whispered. *If he did it once, he'd do it again.*

Before she could start to argue with herself, a shadow fell over her door. Raising her eyes, she was almost grateful to see her brother standing on the threshold. The annoying voice in the back of her brain sputtered into silence. "Jeff! What are you doing here?"

"Hey, Sis." He stepped inside then took the nearest chair, dropping his briefcase to the floor as he sat down. "I had to come downtown to see a pro bono at the jail. Thought I'd stop by."

She nodded approvingly. Jeff was the only one of her brothers who took not-for-profit cases. Phillip grumbled every time Jeff handled one of the nonpaying clients, especially the criminal ones. The McKinney law firm wasn't a charity agency, he would say. Someone has to help people with no money, Jeff would always reply.

"I just talked to Dad," she said, grimacing. "He's on a tear, as usual."

"About what?"

"You name it. The party, us, Andres...I should blame his bad mood on you. It was your idea to bring Andres to the party. Where was the bad choice you threatened to show up with?"

He grinned. "I chickened out. Your inviting Andres created enough of a stir, anyway. Was the old man upset about anything else?"

"Other than Andres, not really," she said. "Same-old, same-old. You know how it is."

"I'm afraid I do." He shifted in the chair. "Tell me about the call-out. I heard some of it on the news. The woman was Andres's assistant, wasn't she?"

Lena nodded then told her brother the same thing she'd told her dad. "Andres was very upset," she added.

"I'm sure he must have been."

For a few seconds, Jeff studied her from across the desk, then he spoke. "You guys are getting serious again, aren't you?"

She kept her expression neutral. "Why do you ask?"

"I tried to call your place last night. No one answered."

"And that told you we're getting serious?"

He shook his head. "No, that told me you weren't at home, at least at 2:00 a.m. The look on your face is what told me you're getting serious."

Suddenly uncomfortable, Lena rose and stepped to the window. After a second, she turned slowly. "He's asked me to marry him."

"And your answer was?"

"I haven't given it yet."

"But you're thinking about it?"

"Yes. I am."

He stood then, too, and walked over to where she waited. She looked up at him. His eyes were blue, like Phillip's, but she couldn't read the expression in them. "I think you should say yes," he said, surprising her. "You should say yes, move to Miami with him, and have lots of babies."

She laughed suddenly.

"He loves you, Lena. He's always loved you."

"How do you know that?"

"I can just tell." He shrugged. "Don't you remember right after you got shot? I told you then that Andres loved you and you didn't believe me. Do you believe me now?"

She looked back out the window, her voice low and quiet when she spoke. "I have to, but I'm just not sure I want to."

THE BEACH WAS COLD that night, cold and lonely. From the house, Lena headed down to the dunes and past them to the shore, her feet tracing a route she'd taken a thousand times before, probably more. Ever since she'd been old enough to walk, she'd crossed these sands and gone to the water when she needed to think. And she needed that more tonight than she ever had before. She had a tremendous decision in front of her, one that would affect the rest of her life. She'd made the choice once before and been hurt so badly, it'd taken months to recover. Now she was facing it again.

She stood at the edge of the wet sand and watched the waves come in. Their white, foamy tops glowed in the dark. Flashes of silver, just beneath the surface, gave away the presence of amberjack and flounder. Over the water, as if it were scripted, a silver moon rose slowly. Its pearly reflection rippled and moved on the surface of the sea, coming in and going out with the pull of the tide.

She'd half expected Andres to show up, but after Jeff had left her office that afternoon, the rest of the day had been quiet. No one had called or stopped by. The team had been busy with training lessons and Lena had concentrated on them. Eventually, she'd gone out to the shooting range, the feel of her weapon in her hand the only thing that seemed real. She'd fired, time and time again, the targets moving, her mind whirling. When dark had slipped up on her, she'd been shocked to look down at her watch and see how much time had passed.

Now here she was. Thinking about her past and contemplating repeating it. The images of the last few weeks shot through her brain in rapid succession, each almost too vivid to bear as she relived them. Seeing Andres for the first time. Feeling the bullet hit her. Making love with him again. The look in his eyes when he'd proposed.

Everything mingled in her mind, but two thoughts stood out. She loved him. But she didn't trust him.

Lena sat down abruptly in the sand and closed her eyes for a second, her thoughts unexpectedly assailed by memories of her mother. Her death had left Lena lost. She didn't know how to act or what to do. After all, who was a child without a mother? It'd taken Lena months to learn to believe in her father. He'd been an unknown entity at the time, a shadowy figure in her life who'd been present but not really there. Forced by Dorothea's death, father and daughter had come to know each other and build the trust they'd needed. The connection between them was convoluted and not always pleasant, but Lena knew one thing for sure. Phillip had always done what he considered the best thing for her; he had her faith in that and therefore he had her love.

Trust. It was the foundation of everything.

Lena opened her eyes and stared out at the water. She'd told Andres before she didn't trust him, but until this very moment, she hadn't really thought about what that meant. Trust was what she'd had but lost when her mother died. It was the knowledge that someone would be there for you, always.

And if they weren't, there had to be a good reason—a damned good reason—for their absence.

Lena groaned in the darkness, the sudden, awful truth so painful as it hit her she could hardly breathe. She had never believed what Andres had told her about the night he'd stood her up. She'd accepted his excuse wrapped in a fog of pain and denial, because that was the only way she could keep living. But in her heart of hearts, she'd never been sure.

If he'd lied to her and there hadn't been a special ops that night taking him from their wedding, it meant he didn't love her. If the ops *had* taken place and he'd simply chosen *not* to tell her about it, it meant he didn't trust her.

Neither choice was acceptable.

Suddenly, from somewhere down the beach, beyond where Lena sat, she heard the sound of children laughing. Staring into the darkness, her eyes adjusted and then she saw them. A family. A mom and dad with two little girls. They were flying a kite, the white triangle as pale and ephemeral as angel's wings in the inky darkness above them. Lena watched as the children jumped up and down, the strong breeze from the sea catching their long hair and whipping it into their faces. The father handed the string to the taller child. The kite dipped up and down then she passed it to the smaller one. It took a tumble before that little girl handed it back to her father who played out the line and sent it back toward the stars. He wrapped his arm around his wife while the children danced around them.

Lena stared at them and felt her heart expand. She could have this. She could have the husband, the children, even the stars above. All she had to do was reach out, take them, and bring them closer to her. All she had to do was say yes.

But she couldn't.

Not until she knew the truth.

CHAPTER THIRTEEN

IT WAS A LONG and torturous weekend, and Monday wasn't much better. The day crawled by. When six o'clock finally came, Lena was more nervous than she'd ever been in her life, but she headed straight for Andres's office. She hadn't been there before and it took longer than she expected, the traffic inching along in the early winter evening. By the time she located the building and found a parking spot, her heart felt as if were going to implode.

He was sitting at his desk, talking on the phone, when she walked inside. With an abrupt goodbye, he ended the conversation, hung up the receiver and came quickly to where she stood.

In his dark eyes she read his desire. He wanted to pull her into his arms and kiss her but he didn't know how she'd react. Obviously deciding to do what he wanted regardless, he reached out and brought her close. She didn't resist. Through the starched white shirt he wore, she could feel his warmth, his strength, and she melted against him. Their lips met in a long, deep kiss, his mouth soft but insistent against her own, his touch demanding as he pressed his case the best way he could.

It was a kiss that would have swayed any woman.

After a second, he leaned back and looked at her as

she struggled with the emotions raging inside her, the ones that were tearing her in a dozen different directions.

"I've come to give you an answer." She gripped his shoulders with her hands. Beneath her fingers, his muscles were tense.

He said nothing, but he didn't need to. They each knew how important the moment was, how it would affect the rest of their lives.

She blinked, then plunged ahead.

"I want to marry you, Andres. I really do. But I have to hear the truth first. I have to know why you left me at the altar before I can make up my mind."

ANDRES STARED AT HER and tried to keep his demeanor flat and emotionless. Lena stared back. This was his worst nightmare coming to life before his eyes, but he could tell it wasn't an easy moment for her, either. Smudged beneath her eyes were dusky shadows and her mouth was outlined by tension.

"We've been over this, Lena," he said carefully. "I told you what happened when I came back and tried to reconcile with you after the wedding."

"Tell me again."

"I don't think this is necessary—"

"Then my answer is no." Her gray eyes were tortured as they met his. "I have to be able to trust you. And I don't right now. I didn't realize how important that really is until last night, but the more I thought about it, the more I understood. I can't marry you without trusting you."

"But I love you!" he said. "You love me! That's enough."

"No, it's not. Not for me."

His chest went tight, as if he were being pressed between two metal plates, and he took a step backward. Away from her.

"I'm afraid that history will repeat itself," she said sadly. "That I'll give you my heart and you'll leave me again."

"That won't happen."

"How do I know for sure?"

"Because our circumstances are completely different. What happened then *can't* happen now. I've explained this already."

"No, you didn't explain anything," she said. "You gave me a tale about a special ops and told me that was all you could say." Her jaw tightened. "I don't believe that's the truth—at least not all of it."

"This is crazy," he said harshly. "Why drag this up now?"

"Look, Andres, I'm a cop. I take care of business first and worry about why later. When you left me I was so devastated I accepted what you told me because I didn't have another choice. I had to close my eyes and keep going. But you told me to feel, not to think, and your aunt said something similar at Thanksgiving. Last night I let my emotions out and for the first time I realized, deep down, what it really meant not to trust you."

She took a deep breath. "I can't pretend the past never happened. I just can't do it, not without knowing you won't leave me again. Otherwise, I'll spend the rest of my life worrying every time you walk out the door."

"Lena, I promise you—"

She shook her head and stopped him. "If what happened was a special ops, you should have explained," she said resolutely. "I would have understood the situation, no matter what. Were you afraid I'd jeopardize the mission? If you were, then—"

"That wasn't the reason. You're a good cop, Lena. One of the best I've ever known."

His compliment went ignored.

"Then if it wasn't a professional decision," she said quietly, "I can only come to one other conclusion."

He looked at her.

"You don't really love me. And you never have. You made up the story just to avoid the wedding."

"No!" He spoke with such unexpected force, she stumbled back. Reaching for her, his fingers found only air.

He dropped his outstretched hand back to his side and softened his voice. "I love you with all my heart, Lena. You are my life. You're the very reason I live. You're everything that's good and strong and perfect."

She started shaking her head before he finished. "Don't lie to me—"

"I'm not," he insisted. "I've lived through ten kinds of hell but leaving you when I did—knowing you were waiting for me at that altar when I couldn't get there—it was the worst. You *have* to believe me when I tell you that."

He heard her take a tiny breath—almost a sigh—and something unsaid passed between their hearts. He could feel it; a flutter, a warmth, a brief moment in time. The sensation might have given him hope except for her expression.

"I do believe you," she said finally. "I actually do...but that isn't enough. I have to trust that you won't leave me again after you've made me love you. And I don't. Not with what you've told me."

Andres struggled, a huge heartache building inside him. He'd never wanted Lena to have to pick between her father or him. He'd had to make that kind of gut-wrenching, life-changing decision when he'd chosen freedom over staying in Cuba, and it'd been the hardest thing he'd ever done. He'd always wanted to protect Lena from having such a dilemma.

But suddenly he realized how wrong he'd been.

He hadn't been protecting Lena—he'd been protecting himself. She would ask him for proof and he had none. She'd do what he'd always feared the most. She'd abandon him as he had her.

How could he have been so blind? He sighed heavily. "If I tell you the truth, you'll leave me."

"I'll leave you if you don't."

The words fell like stones at his feet. After a long moment, he nodded sadly and began to speak.

"WHAT I EXPLAINED before was what happened," he began, "but I didn't tell you everything."

Lena's pulse began to throb so hard at the base of her neck, she knew Andres could probably hear it, as well as see it.

"I couldn't tell you," he said, "because you wouldn't have believed me. You still won't."

"That's for me to judge."

He didn't answer her. Instead, turning away from her, he went to his desk and pulled something out. When he came back and handed a piece of paper to her, she saw it was a photograph. The tattered black-and-white snapshot showed two little boys sitting in a beat-up rowboat that was half buried in the sand. They were both dark-haired and poorly dressed, about six years old. They looked as though they didn't get enough to eat.

"That's my best friend, Mateo Aznar, in the back of the boat. And that's me, in the front."

She raised her gaze to his in surprise. She'd never seen a childhood photo of Andres. She focused once more on the picture, and the image of the little boy he'd been so long ago stole her heart. He had eyes that were way too old.

"I lied when I said the only thing I took out of Cuba was my grandfather's ring." He nodded toward the photo. "I took that snapshot, too. We were inseparable. We were like brothers. I loved him."

Her mouth filled with sand, making it hard to speak. "Loved? Past tense?"

"Mateo is dead." His eyes went flat. "He was murdered the night of the wedding."

Lena saw life and death every day, but something about the way Andres spoke now put his harsh pronouncement into a different perspective. She reached out for the chair behind her, and when her fingers felt the arms, she sank down into the seat. "What happened?"

He took the photo from her hand and walked back to his desk. Slipping it inside the center drawer as if he couldn't stand to look at it any longer, he spoke.

"After I joined Justice, Mateo helped me. He became a source of information. A spy, if you will. He fed me everything he could about the Red Tide, and I passed it on. The day you and I were to marry he called me and told me the Tide had found out about him. They were searching for him even then, and as soon as they could find him, they were going to kill him. He was hiding, but didn't have much hope. He begged me to try a rescue."

Andres turned his face away from Lena, his profile all lines and hard edges. "I left the minute I could and flew to Miami to rent a boat. I went to the island that night to try to get him, but the Red Tide knew about our rendezvous. They killed him as he swam toward me."

Stunned into silence, all Lena could do was stare. "This was the operation you told me about, wasn't it?" she finally asked. "The one where you lost your friend and felt responsible for it?"

He nodded once. After a second, she spoke softly. "Why didn't you tell me all this, Andres? My God... Surely you knew I would have understood."

He turned slowly. "I couldn't tell you, Lena. It was too risky."

"Too risky?" She stood, confusion sweeping over her. "What do you mean? Did you think I'd tell the authorities you were going to Cuba? C'mon, Andres, it's illegal, yes, but surely you didn't think I'd—"

He shook his head. "That's not it."

"Then what?"

"There was someone else involved. Someone here in the States."

His voice was remote, his demeanor cold. She'd never seen him like this before. It scared her.

"I don't understand...."

"Money had been coming into the Tide in small amounts, but a larger payment was made. A payment for something specific. Mateo had proof of the payments but they went down with him." He looked at his desk as if gathering his thoughts. Or maybe his courage. When he raised his eyes, they were even colder. "We didn't know what the money was for."

Lena felt a shadow pass over her, then he spoke again. "But we knew it came from here. From Destin." He paused. "Specifically, from your father's office."

She looked at him dumbly and simply repeated his words. "My father?"

He nodded.

"What are you—" Licking her lips, she stopped and tried again. "Are you saying—"

The second time was no better. How could she ask a question when her brain couldn't process the information he was giving her?

He took pity on her and answered what she couldn't ask. "He wanted me out of your life, Lena, and he used the Red Tide to do it."

"That's insane." It was the only thing she could say. Andres had clearly lost his mind. "My father would never do something like that."

"I know this is difficult for you to believe, Lena, but I'm telling you the truth. I wouldn't lie to you about something this important, I promise."

"Are you saying he got involved with a terrorist group just to keep you from marrying me?"

"No. I'm telling you he was involved with them all along and when it was convenient, he used them to try to get rid of me. I was getting closer to him, closer to proving my case, and he was going to have to do something soon. The night of the wedding gave him the perfect alibi. No one would be able to pin the deaths on him because he would be in Destin, and everyone would know that."

"But why? Why would he be involved with people like that? What's the motive?"

Andres shook his head. "I don't know. All I can tell you is that he has a client named Pablo Escada. Escada is into drugs and around here drugs mean the Red Tide. It's a connection, that's all I can say. I can't explain more. Only your father can do that."

She shook her head.

"Mateo wasn't the only one under fire that night. The men who shot him tried for me, too. I was wounded, but I made it back to Miami."

"This is outrageous," she countered hotly. "Where's your proof?"

"I told you—Mateo was bringing out records that he felt would seal the case, but they went down with him. I couldn't recover his body."

He looked at her steadily. "After I came back I investigated your father for months. There was nothing to link him and the Red Tide but Escada. I hate Phillip, Lena, but I'm not an idiot. I wasn't going to bring charges if I couldn't back them up."

She felt a small tick of confusion. She'd heard cops recount stories a thousand times and the way Andres was talking, the way he was presenting the facts, felt so right, it was scary. That wasn't enough, though. She couldn't believe him based on that—not when everything else sounded so bizarre. "I can't believe this, Andres—"

"I know." He spoke simply. "I didn't want to tell you before because I was afraid it'd make you crazy, that'd you'd be torn between believing me and listening to your father. Then I realized the truth. You're Phillip's daughter, yes, but you think like a cop. You'd look for evidence and look for proof." He held out his hands. "And I had none..."

His words died, and she understood immediately what that meant. "But you think you've got some now," she said incredulously.

"It's what Carmen was working on. I believe she might have found a link between Phillip and Esteban Olvera."

Shaking her head, Lena wanted to cry, but she wouldn't allow herself the luxury. Her throat stung with the effort. "You're kidding yourself, Andres. My father would never put me in any kind of danger—"

"Your getting shot was an accident, Lena. That sniper was aiming for me."

"Of course he was! And there's no way in hell you can tie my father to him, either."

He stepped closer and started talking about a car. She let him speak, her mind catching the details, but refusing to accept them. "Save your breath," she said finally, interrupting him. "This is just crazy. Absolutely crazy."

He fell silent and they stared at each other. After one long heartbeat, Lena realized there were no more words between them. There was no more...anything.

She turned and walked to the door of his office. As her fingertips closed around the doorknob, she knew she had to ask one last question even though she knew the answer would be a deception, like everything else had been. Pivoting slowly, she let her eyes meet his for the last time.

"How could you do this to me?" she said quietly. "How could you come back here and make me fall in love with you all over again—knowing this lie was between us?"

She was afraid he might cross the room, that he might come to where she was and try to convince her with his mouth, his arms, his eyes. But he made no attempt to move. In the end, she realized he didn't need to touch her. She could feel the force of his words, of his truth, from across the room. It hit her with a strength that almost made her sway.

"I love you," he said simply. "I've never *stopped* loving you. Nothing means more than that."

She wanted to believe him so badly, she felt ill with the need inside her.

Instead she opened the door and left.

LENA DROVE directly to Phillip's office, but by the time she got there, the windows were dark and the building was closed. There was no one inside.

She got out of her car anyway and strode up to the etched-glass doors. She wanted the facts and she wanted them now. There was too much at stake to wait. Raising her fists, she pounded on the heavy glass. She wanted to smash the glass—to smash something—into as many tiny pieces as her life was in at this moment. The doors didn't move, of course, and nothing even remotely dramatic happened. After a second, she stepped to the side and beat on the windows but the building stubbornly remained dark and no one responded.

She wanted to cry, but she'd been holding in her tears since she was nine years old. What good would it serve to let them out now? She walked back to her vehicle, her heart bruised and heavy.

Inside the truck she started the engine, but before she could reverse out of the parking space, a sudden thump at the back of the vehicle made her slam on the brakes. Wincing, she swung her head around to see Bering standing beside the curb. Huffing from the jog he'd made between the office and the parking lot, he'd obviously slammed the fender with his fist to get her attention.

"Oh, shit..." He was all she needed right now.

His face red, his eyebrows woven into an angry scowl, her brother rounded the vehicle to stand beside her door. He was talking before she could even lower the window.

"What on earth are you doing, Lena? I saw you from the window upstairs. I had clients in my office, for God's sake! I had to take them out the back so they wouldn't see my sister acting like a crazy person on the front steps."

Any of her other brothers, especially Jeff, would have asked what was wrong. Not Bering. "I'm looking for Dad," she answered stonily.

"Well, he's not here. He's in Atlanta. He's on a case over there."

She nodded and put the truck back into reverse, then suddenly she had another thought. She braked and looked at her brother. "I need to know something. About the firm."

"What?" he asked suspiciously.

"Do you represent a guy named Escada? First name, Pablo?"

His expression immediately froze. "Why do you want to know that?"

"It's important," she answered. "Just tell me—"

"I can't. That's privileged information—"

"Oh, for God's sake, Bering, get real! I can look up the goddamn case myself tomorrow morning when the courthouse opens, but I need to know right now! Did the firm represent him or not?"

"Don't you curse at me, Lena Marie." He pursed his mouth tightly, and she knew she had lost. "I'm not telling you a thing. You're a cop! You should know better than to even ask. Wait until morning and find out for yourself!"

She started to ask him more, but he made a huffing sound of disapproval then headed toward the office. He was moving quicker than he'd been when he'd come out to the car. When he got to the sidewalk, he shot a quick glance over his shoulder then scuttled back into the office. She cursed again. Why had she even tried?

She made the trip home without even thinking about what she was doing. She was almost startled when she realized she was in front of her drive. Turning into the curved shell road, she parked the truck and killed the motor. The resulting quiet was unbroken and complete, the only sound she could hear was the roar of the waves coming from behind the house. With leaden feet, she went inside.

The phone rang just as she opened the front door. Thinking it might be Sarah, Lena threw her bag to the table in the entry, hurrying into the living room. She grabbed it on the third ring.

"Lena, sweetheart, it's Isabel. Can you talk with an old lady for a few moments?"

Dropping to her sofa, Lena closed her eyes and rubbed them, gripping the phone. "Of course, I have time for you, Isabel. I'm not too sure you'll want to talk to me, though. It hasn't been a good day."

"I'm sorry to hear that." Isabel's voice was soothing and kind, a lilting balm to Lena's frazzled soul. "Tell me about it. What made it so bad?"

The urge to unload, to cry and to let out all her raw emotions was overwhelming and almost too big to fight. Lena struggled with the yearning and finally managed to get herself under control. What good would it be to tell Isabel everything? She loved her nephew like the son he almost was to her; he'd be the one she'd defend and understand.

Lena opened her eyes. Maybe he'd already called Isabel. Maybe that was why she was calling Lena.

"Andres and I had a fight," Lena said cautiously. "Do you know about it?"

"Oh, dear...oh, dear..."

Lena knew immediately Isabel hadn't spoken to Andres.

"No, no. I know nothing. I simply called to chat. What happened?"

"He asked me to marry him—"

"Oh, *Dios mío*..."

"And I turned him down."

It was Isabel's turn to be silent, and Lena could only imagine the thoughts spinning through the older woman's head.

"I am very sorry to hear this," she said finally. "I love you, Lena, and having you in our family would make me very happy. If it isn't meant to be, though, it's not meant to be."

Lena's throat closed. It took her a moment to speak. "I'm flattered that you feel that way. I think a lot of you, as well. Unfortunately, though...there are problems. Problems I don't know how to deal with."

"Is there anything I can do, or would I just be an old woman meddling?"

Lena shook her head, even though, of course, Andres's aunt couldn't see her. "You would never be a meddler. But I'm afraid there's nothing anyone can do. Andres has said some things, made some accusations, that I simply can't accept. About my family."

"I'm so sorry."

"I am, too." Lena looked out the bank of windows that made up her living room wall. An empty blackness, as stark and desolate as her future, stretched beyond the other side of the glass. No husband. No lover. No children.

"Would it make a difference if I told you how much he loves you?"

"There's too much between us now, too much that's not good. The things he said were—" She stopped, her throat going tight.

"Oh, Lena...our hearts aren't always connected to the rest of our body, you know."

"Wh-what do you mean?"

"Your heart...your brain... You and Andres react so differently. He feels first and then thinks. You think first and then decide if you can feel. It's just like Yolanda and Angelo."

Lena and Isabel had discussed Andres's parents only last week but it seemed as if it'd happened a year ago. "I hear what you're saying, Isabel, but this time I think you're wrong. I am feeling this with my heart. And that's the problem. And I simply can't accept what he had to say. The emotions are there—but the facts aren't."

"Is that so important?"

"Facts are the only thing we have to go on, Isabel. There isn't another way, no matter how I feel." As she spoke, she got the sudden feeling that Isabel knew exactly what they were talking about. Andres had told the older woman his suspicions of Phillip.

"I understand, *chica.* You have to live your way. We all do. Remember this, though..." There was silence on the other end of the phone. "Andres loves you very, very much. He wouldn't have said what he did unless he had good reason. You might want to think about that and ask yourself what that would be."

CHAPTER FOURTEEN

ANDRES LOST the rest of the week. He ate when he was supposed to, worked at what was before him, went to bed when the clock struck midnight. None of the activities registered, though. He was merely going through the motions of living, a paralyzing numbness taking over because he couldn't bear to face what had actually happened.

His aunt's telephone call caught him at his desk on Friday evening.

"I'm worried about you," she said. "I think you should come home." They'd talked once briefly and he'd told her about Lena. Isabel had been sympathetic but beneath her words there had been a kind of unspoken censure he wasn't sure he understood.

"I can't," he replied without thinking. "I have work to do."

"And are you really doing it or just sitting there, staring out the window?"

He blinked as her words hit their mark.

"Come home," she said, not waiting for his answer. "Come just for the weekend if nothing else and we can talk."

He refused once again and they spoke for a little while more, but by the time he got ready for bed, Andres decided Isabel might be right. Some time away from Destin, away from the presence of Lena's ghost in his bed, was probably a very good idea. He reached for the phone on the nightstand and called the airline, booking a flight for the next day. There was no real need for him to stay in Destin Saturday and Sunday, and he'd made so little progress in trying to figure out what Carmen had been doing that it was depressing.

Maybe his heart wouldn't be so numb in Miami.

He turned out the light and lay down on the bed, feeling the lie crumble as the darkness came over him. He would feel the same no matter where he was, and he knew it as surely as he knew the sun would come up tomorrow. He was incapable of hearing anything but the truth since he'd realized his denial about Lena. Without it to protect him, he couldn't deceive himself about anything anymore.

In the days since their confrontation, truth after truth had descended on him. He'd had no idea how much he'd depended on something other than reality to sustain him.

He'd always thought he could make Lena love him again.

He'd always thought they'd marry.

He'd always thought Phillip McKinney was guilty of murder.

How many of those *facts* weren't real? Like the other certainties he'd realized were false, Andres couldn't bear to consider the answer.

He went to sleep and dreamed of Lena.

LENA WOKE UP Saturday morning, rolled over in the bed and covered her head with the pillow. It'd been a helluva week—a nightmare of a week—and she really wished she could just lie there and sleep until it was all over. The only problem was she was afraid it would never be all over. She couldn't stop thinking about Andres's accusation against her father. It had consumed her. She'd returned to Phillip's office Tuesday but Reba had confirmed Bering's information, saying Phillip wouldn't be back for at least two weeks. Lena had considered calling him, but this wasn't exactly something that could be discussed over the phone, especially since she knew Phillip would go ballistic. Bering's evasiveness had bothered her the more she'd thought about it, too. What did he know about the situation he wasn't telling her?

And if all that wasn't enough, Isabel's words continued to haunt Lena. When he'd been on the force, Andres had been an excellent policeman, and his hunches were usually good ones. He was emotional, yes, and depended more on his instincts than Lena ever would, but he wasn't a man who jumped to conclusions. If she thought about it logically she had to admit he wouldn't have felt the way he did about Phillip unless he'd had good reason.

But he had no proof.

Lena went round and round in her thinking, but she kept returning to the very same points. Phillip could be obnoxious and pompous but he wasn't a criminal. She remembered some of the men who'd come to their home, before Phillip had become so successful, when she was just a kid. They claimed to be his friends from college who jokingly said he'd sold out as he made more and more money. But to think he'd support a terrorist organization was simply bizarre.

Lena made a vow. Monday morning, she'd start her own investigation. She'd get someone discreet working on it, maybe Sarah. There were too many questions in the air, too much chaos. Andres hadn't found the truth, but maybe he didn't know where to look. He was investigating *her* family, after all. She should know where the skeletons were, right?

Feeling slightly better with a decision made, Lena climbed out of the tangled blankets to stumble into the bathroom and wash her face. In exactly one hour she had to be at the range. She was supervising a training exercise for a small police team from Alabama. They wanted to start a multicounty SWAT team like the Emerald Coast's and needed to know more about the requirements. Lena frequently ran classes like this and usually she enjoyed them. Today that wouldn't be the case.

She was on-site twenty minutes later. Beck had volunteered to help, and he was setting up a table of weapons as she pulled up, his white-blond hair shining in the sun.

"You look like hell," he said as a way of greeting her.

"Thanks for the compliment." Lena looked over her sunglasses and braced herself for more.

It didn't come. Instead, he nodded toward the other end of the firing range from where they stood. "You have a visitor."

Automatically assuming it was Andres, Lena caught her breath and whirled around. But instead of Andres, her father waited. He stood off to one side, near one of the picnic tables under the trees. He looked thin, Lena thought with a start, thin and old.

"He was out there when I arrived." Beck ran an oiled rag over the barrel of the gun he was cleaning. "Said he'd called the station, and they'd told him you were coming here this morning."

"That's strange...." Lena shook her head. "I thought he was in Atlanta. I guess Reba told him I was looking for him, but why didn't he just go to the house?"

Beck shrugged. "Can't answer that. He does seem a little preoccupied."

Feeling uneasy, Lena headed toward her father. She called out as she neared and he looked up and waved.

It was a halfhearted gesture and only served to increase her anxiousness. She reached the shady spot a few seconds later. "Did you get my message?" Not waiting for an answer, she continued. "I want to talk to—"

"Whatever it is, it's going to have to wait." His voice was gruff. He looked so exhausted he almost seemed ill. "I've got something I want to tell you first."

She felt an alarm go off inside her. "Are you all right? What's wrong?"

"What makes you think anything's wrong?"

"Well, you could have just called me, for one thing," she said. "And for another, you're supposed to be in Atlanta."

"Bering called and told me you were looking for me. I decided I'd better get back."

"Why?"

"I wanted to see you."

"Here?"

"I wanted neutral ground. It's always a better place for confessions."

Before she could react to the startling word, Phillip reached over and took her hand. Following her mother's death, Lena had sorely missed the physical closeness she'd shared with Dorothea. Each time she'd tried to climb into her father's lap or hold his hand, he'd gently, but firmly, pushed her away. She'd finally learned not to even ask for it. Only in the past few years had he managed to bestow the occasional affectionate gesture. But his touch felt ominous now, and she almost winced.

Moving to the table, he pulled her with him. He sat down on one side and she took the other, his eyes bright and steady as they met hers. "I want to tell you about something that I did. A while back."

Her pulse jumped.

"I'm not proud of what I did, but for the thousandth time Reba has pointed out to me that you're a grown woman. She called me an old fool and told me she wouldn't have anything else to do with me if I didn't tell you the truth."

Lena felt a tiny shock wave break over her at the way he spoke about his secretary. Her mind continued to spin but it landed on this inconsequential detail. It almost seemed as if she couldn't bear to focus on the important part.

"Why would you listen to Reba when you've never listened to me?"

"She's been with me a very long time," he answered carefully. "Reba and I have grown...close over the years. I respect her advice." He shook his head almost ruefully. "Actually, I *have* to—she's relentless if I don't."

Lena stared at him in amazement. "You mean you and Reba..."

He looked at her with wry amusement. "I may be old, Lena, but I'm not dead." His voice dropped. "Reba's a beautiful woman, inside and out. And I was only forty-five when your mother died. I didn't want to be alone forever."

When Dorothea had passed away, he'd only been ten years older than Lena was right now. Surprised, she said, "I never thought about it before...."

"That's because I didn't want you to," he told her stoically. "I could never have replaced your mother, and I didn't want you kids to have to adjust to another woman in the house just because I needed someone. Reba understood. The arrangement fit her fine." He glanced down at his left hand and twisted the gold band he'd always worn. Lena realized she'd never wondered about that, either.

Phillip looked up from his wedding ring. "I didn't come here to discuss Reba, Lena. I came here to tell you something else."

Beneath the table, she laced her fingers nervously. Her mouth was too dry to even swallow.

He spoke without preliminary. "I came to tell you that I tried to bribe Andres to leave you when you two were about to marry. I offered him half a million dollars to walk away from you and never come back to Destin."

After the few days she'd just had, Lena wouldn't have thought it possible for her to experience another shock. *Wrong.*

"You what?"

"I offered him money not to marry you." He held his hands out over the table, then dropped them. "He turned me down. Then he walked away. I was so happy to see the last of him I didn't give a damn why he did what he did, but that doesn't make what I did any less wrong. I shouldn't have done it and I'm asking you to forgive me."

Lena let the words roll over her. Then she attempted to connect the accusations Andres had made with this latest news, but the two wouldn't come together.

"You offered him money," she said slowly, "to leave me...."

"I thought I was protecting you, Lena. I thought Andres wasn't the man for you and I wanted him out of your life any way I could arrange it. As I said, I'm not proud of what I did, but I did it out of love."

All she could think was one thing: what if Andres had told her the truth? She swallowed hard as the thought played out to its logical end. Was Phillip telling her this now because he had more to confess? She started to ask him directly, then thought again. Direct wasn't the best way to deal with her father.

Especially, a little voice in the back of her head whispered, *if Andres is right.*

"And you're telling me this because Reba wanted you to?" she asked slowly.

He seemed hesitant, but he answered, "I'm telling you this because it's haunting me, and Reba knows how badly. She's worried about my health. When you got shot, it nearly killed me, Lena, but it made me realize life is too short for the foolishness of lies. I would have never forgiven myself if you'd been hurt more seriously...or worse."

She licked her lips. "But the shooting wasn't your fault...."

"Of course not! But what I did was wrong. I tried to get Andres to leave you and he did. Whether or not I was responsible for his departure is beside the point. The result was the same...your heart was broken."

"Oh, Dad..." Lena looked above her father's head. She blinked several times, then met his gaze. She knew instinctively he was telling her the truth.

Still she had to pursue it. She was, after all, a cop. She framed her question as carefully as she could. "After you offered him the money and he turned it down, did you try any other way to get Andres out of my life?"

A line formed between his silver eyebrows. He was clearly puzzled. "I didn't have to. He never showed up at the wedding and that was that."

"Are you sure?"

"Of course I'm sure." He looked at her with some of his old impatience. "What are you implying?"

"I'm not implying anything. But a few days ago, Andres asked me to marry him."

She had to give him credit. Phillip didn't react at all. He simply stared at her.

"I told him no," she said. "Not unless he explained why he stood me up."

His eyes went wary. "And did he?"

"He told me he had to go back to Cuba to rescue a friend. The friend was killed, though. By the Red Tide."

She told herself she didn't see it, but it seemed as though Phillip blanched.

"Tell me more."

She gave him as few of the details as she could. She couldn't come right out and reveal Andres suspected him—to say that much went totally against her training as a cop, but she told him what she could. As she talked, she studied his face. He absorbed each point as if preparing for a case. He didn't seemed surprised by anything she told him, and a heavy coldness settled over her, despite the morning sunshine.

She finished her brief explanation. Phillip didn't move, but something in his expression changed and she knew before he spoke he had figured it out. He knew exactly what she *hadn't* said: that Andres believed Phillip was the man behind everything.

"And did Andres say who supposedly funded all this? Terrorism doesn't come cheap, you know."

"He said the money came from the States," she hedged.

His face stayed as smooth as the table between them. "Did he have proof?"

"His proof went down with his friend. At the time, it was all he had."

"At *the time*. Are you saying—"

"He's found another link."

Phillip's eyes jerked to her face.

"He thinks there's a local tie to Olvera," she said. "The man who tried to kill me."

Her father closed his eyes and stayed motionless for several long moments. Finally he opened his eyes and locked them on her face. When he spoke, his voice was strained in a way she'd never heard before.

"I didn't want Andres in your life, Lena. I thought I knew what was best for you, and it wasn't him."

A giant hand began to squeeze her throat.

"But I didn't do what he obviously thinks. I swear to you on your mother's grave. I didn't set up the attempt on his life. And I would never, ever do something to endanger you. I love you."

Lena was sitting down, but she still went weak. "Then who did? Who paid the Red Tide back then? Who's paying them now?"

His jaw tightened, then he relaxed it, so deliberately she could see the muscles move. "I have no idea."

She looked at him sharply. She didn't like the way he spoke and her suspicions rose. "Are you sure—"

As if propelled by an unseen hand, he stood suddenly, his expression imperious, his attitude defensive.

"Of course, I'm sure. Andres is simply trying to discredit me. But he's way off-base."

She opened her mouth to reply, but fell silent as he rounded the table to come to her side.

"God, I'm sorry, baby." He dropped both his hands on her shoulders. "I'm sorry. All I ever wanted was to be a good father—to you and your brothers—but I've screwed it up royally. Your mother is probably standing in heaven shaking her fist at me."

Lena met her father's regretful stare, the complex, confusing nature of their relationship coming sharply into focus once more. How could she love him *and* hate him at the very same time? She couldn't answer, but she knew one thing: she couldn't be mad at him. Not now. Somewhere in the telling of the story, she'd seen the man he really was. Lonely. Worried. Doing the best he could. How could she blame him for what he'd done? It'd had no impact on Andres's decision anyway.

Feeling even more adrift than ever before, Lena put her arms around her father and hugged him for a long time.

THE MIAMI AIRPORT was as bright and colorful as always but Andres walked down the corridor in a fog, not seeing the overhead replica of the Wright Brothers' airplane, not hearing the dozens of Spanish dialects, not even noticing the ever present drug dogs and their handlers.

He grabbed a taxi and went directly home. His house felt empty and smelled stale. The lone ivy his aunt had insisted on giving him had died a slow death, its leaves now brown and shriveled. He clicked on the air-conditioning and then the television but the emptiness was overwhelming. He'd gotten accustomed to the sound of the waves back in Destin and the silence here was simply too thick. Unable to bear it, he took a quick shower, called Isabel, and headed for her high-rise.

She met him at the door with a kiss, then led him through the small condo to her balcony. The whole place was redolent with mouthwatering smells wafting out from the kitchen. Andres recognized the main one—she was cooking *lechón asado*—a classic Cuban dish of shredded pork with lemon and garlic. Underneath that aroma, he caught a whiff of cilantro and black beans. She'd made all his favorites. For dessert there would be flan and hot Cuban coffee, served in tiny cups that were hardly needed. The bitter brew was so strong it could stand by itself.

They reached the balcony and Isabel slid back the doors. She was on the fourteenth floor and Biscayne Bay shimmered in the distance, the evening sunlight cutting diamonds on the bright-blue water. As he settled into a patio chair, she poured him a drink from a pitcher sitting on a nearby silver tray. Bacardi, mango and pineapple juice with just a hint of dry vermouth. The drink went down easily and she refilled his glass a moment later.

They sat in silence for a while and let the alcohol do its job.

After a bit, he spoke.

"She won't talk to me." He didn't have to say Lena's name. They both understood. "I've tried to call her several times and I went back to the house twice. She wouldn't come to the door."

"Did you expect something different?" Isabel spoke in Spanish. The words sounded less harsh but their meaning wasn't.

"No," he said. Holding his aunt's crystal goblet up to the dying light, he shook his head. "I suppose I didn't."

"You hurt her. Again."

"She wanted the truth."

"Of course she did. Any woman would. You should have given it to her the minute you came back from Havana."

"You know I couldn't do that. It would have totally jeopardized my investigation."

"But you did it now."

"I had to," he answered. "And it hardly matters anyway. The case is going nowhere."

She looked over at him, her eyebrows rising in surprise. "But you told me Carmen had linked Phillip—"

"Apparently she did. I can't duplicate her steps, though, and without solid proof..." His frustration boiled over and he cursed soundly. "I can't believe it, *Tia!* I *know* Phillip McKinney is behind this—I know it! Yet everywhere I turn, I reach a dead end."

"Maybe you're trying *too* hard. Sometimes the answer is obvious, but when you get too wrapped up you can't see it."

He shook his head. "Not possible."

"But Lena loves you. Knowing that should make anything possible."

"I thought it would—that's why I asked her to marry me—but I'm not so sure anymore. About that and a lot of other things as well."

"Lena's love for you is something she can't shed. It's like her skin." His aunt drilled him with a stern, unforgiving stare. "It's the same for you. You may live to be a hundred, but you will never forget her, no matter what."

His aunt's words disturbed him, and Andres turned the conversation in a different direction after that. Ordinarily stubborn about such things, she seemed to sense his need and allowed him to fill the rest of the evening with idle talk. They lingered for a long time over their meal, the food as filling and rich as the smells that had greeted Andres when he'd first arrived. Finally, after he dried the last gold-edged coffee cup and put it in the cabinet, he turned to his aunt and gently gathered her into his arms. Her frailty always surprised him when he hugged her; her strength was so tangible he forgot it wasn't physical as well.

She smiled up at him. *"Te amo, chico...."*

"I love you, too, *Tia*." Switching to Spanish as well, he smiled down at her, thinking how lucky he was to have someone like her. Their relationship was a special one. "Thank you for listening to my problems this evening. Do they make you weary?"

She reached up and patted his cheek. "No, no. Of course not. I'm worried about you, though."

"Don't be. I'll work it out somehow."

"And Lena? Will she work it out, *también?*"

"I don't know." He heard the sadness in his voice and didn't bother to hide it. "I'm afraid we may never be together."

"It would be a shame to waste the love you both share. It's too rare for that."

"I know, but I've broken her heart too many times. I wouldn't be the man I am unless I did what I've done, though. I've spent all my life protecting people, trying to do the right thing." He paused. "To live as you raised me."

"Are there no exceptions?"

"If Lena's father is a criminal, I can't look the other way."

"Even if it means sacrificing your love for her?"

His gaze went over his aunt's head, to the window

and the darkness beyond. Somewhere out there, Lena was as angry and confused as he was, and neither had the power to make those feelings go away.

He thought about the issues all the way back to Destin the following day, but the truth stayed the same, and so did he.

CHAPTER FIFTEEN

ANDRES WENT STRAIGHT from the tiny Destin airport to his office Sunday night. There was nothing waiting for him at the condo. He might as well get some work done.

He dropped his briefcase at the table where Carmen had worked, then he walked toward the back, to his private area. But he stopped midway and turned to look at the empty chair. In Miami, he'd visited Carmen's family. Her children, a boy, five, and a girl, seven, had been quiet and subdued as Andres had talked with their grandfather. They were beautiful kids and they'd studied him silently with huge brown eyes identical to Carmen's. In their stillness he'd sensed their pain and confusion. Their mother was gone and no one could change that. Luis, Carmen's father, had cried when Andres had handed him the small box of things he'd gathered from Carmen's desk. The rest of her belongings, from her rented apartment, would be shipped, he'd told the older man, but Andres had brought some items she'd obviously cared about. A snapshot of her father and the children. A rosary. A birthday card she'd bought for one of the children but hadn't had time to mail.

Andres had escaped as soon as he could.

Retracing his steps, he returned to Carmen's space and sat down. He'd gone through everything too many times to count, but he'd found absolutely no clues of what she was doing or why. Despite his earlier efforts, Andres let his brain drift over the well-worn path one more time.

Carmen had traced the silver car that had been seen at Olvera's motel to AAA Bail Bonds.

Phillip McKinney owned AAA Bail Bonds.

All the employees who had access to the car had rock-solid alibis as did Phillip himself. Andres had verified that fact with Jeff as soon as he could following Carmen's death. Jeff hadn't asked any questions in return, either. He was the kind of lawyer who knew that sometimes it was better *not* to know more.

But Andres couldn't shake the idea that he was missing something obvious. When he figured out who had been behind that wheel, he would know who'd hired Olvera. It was just that simple.

It was just that difficult.

He worked at Carmen's desk, lost in thought, for two more hours. Finally, scribbling on a yellow pad she'd left in her center desk drawer, he began to take inventory of the points he knew for sure. Not his suppositions, not his feelings, nothing but the facts. Phillip's association to the bail bond company. His ties to Pablo Escada. The past in all its stark detail. Andres compiled the list then drew the lines to connect the names and times.

The process was similar to one he'd experienced when he'd looked at a hidden image in a puzzle book once. The abstract drawing had been made of squares and diamonds, but as he'd stared, something else had made itself visible. Slowly, almost maddeningly, a second image began to emerge here as well. The picture wasn't one Andres could even recognize at first and then, as it became more visible, he refused to even consider it. The closer he looked, though, the more clear it became. He couldn't deny it. No one could.

His mind reeling with the revelation, he threw his notes into his briefcase, hastily locked the office and ran outside. He had to find Lena. That was all he could think.

He had to find Lena.

SUNDAY NIGHT came too fast. Lena needed more time on the beach, more time by herself, more time period...to think about everything that had happened. Her father's admission about his attempt to bribe Andres was something she was still trying to absorb. Had Phillip really thought Andres would take money to leave her? He should have known better if he had.

Getting ready for bed that night, Lena stood in front of the mirror and brushed her hair. None of what had happened to her in the past few weeks made any sense at all. Her life had been turned upside down. She'd have the wedding dream tonight, she just knew it. Every time things went nutty she had the damn dream. Tossing her hairbrush to the countertop, she muttered an expletive and got in bed.

In less than ten minutes, she was marching down the aisle.

ANDRES HAD BEEN shot before, but the bullet that ripped through his left shoulder as he walked out of his building was so unexpected, so unbelievably startling, he simply didn't understand what had actually happened.

Gasping, then reeling backward, he dropped his briefcase and crashed into the wall behind him. The pain was instantaneous, a hot, black wave that exploded in his body and threatened to overwhelm him. He slid down the stucco before he could stop himself, a red trail marking his progress as his shirt snagged the roughened texture of the wall.

His breath rasping, his mind spinning, he was still for only a second. Immediately his old training kicked in, and he scrambled sideways to get behind a nearby planter. He had no idea where the shooter was, but he wanted his .38 in his hand. The lightweight pistol, in a leather leg holster, was only an inch from his fingertips, but it felt as if it were a mile. Crying out with the pain, he bent until his fingers wrapped around the cold wooden grip, the unexpected scent of pine mulch from the nearby planter reaching him as he yanked out the weapon.

The revolver was a five-shot Smith & Wesson he'd bought off an ex-CIA man, but before Andres could even think about where to aim, a second report rang out over his head. He sprang to his left with an agonizing lurch, the gun in his hand no match for the high-speed, long-distance rifle being used against him. He half ran, half stumbled toward a low wall that fronted the building itself. It'd give more cover than the planter...but not much. Just as he reached the three-foot ledge, the sniper shot once more. Whoever he was, he had a helluva aim and a damn good weapon.

But still he missed.

The window behind Andres exploded and the taste of fear filled his mouth. A second earlier, and it would have been his head instead of the glass. His shoulder screaming with pain, Andres turned, thinking he could retreat now, back inside the building through the broken window. The shot had gone high, and he saw the glass had come from a section too far above him to be reached.

There was no way he could get back inside, and no way he could get to his car.

He was trapped.

COMING UP from the nightmare was like swimming to the top of an endlessly deep pool, but the ringing phone insisted she make the journey. Groggily, Lena reached for the portable receiver with one hand and the clock with the other. It was 2:00 a.m. She'd only been asleep for a couple of hours.

"We've got a problem."

Bradley's deep voice boomed from the other end of the line, and all thought of sleep fled. Lena was fully awake before he finished speaking. "What's up?"

"We just got a report of a sniper at an office building off Highway 98."

"A sniper?" She waited for more information, but Bradley stayed silent. Was she missing something? "I don't understand. Are you saying some idiot with a gun is taking potshots at civilians for no reason? At 2:00 a.m.?"

"Something like that."

"How'd the call come in?"

"We don't have all the details yet. I think someone driving by saw something. Dispatch sent a black and white then a second-shots-fired call came in from the same location and they decided a regular unit would just be another target. They sent the run to us."

Cradling the phone between her shoulder and ear, Lena jumped out of the bed and grabbed the pants and shirt she always kept nearby. Stripping off her night-gown, she pulled on her clothes. "What's left to know?

Get Alpha Team out there right now. Call Diego, too. It's probably useless, but he might be able to do something."

Without missing a beat, she juggled the receiver to her other ear and reached for her boots. "Get Sarah working on the neighborhood, too, and see if she can get something on the area. What's the address?" She snatched up her SWAT jacket and was heading toward her entry when she realized Bradley hadn't answered.

"Brad? Are you there? I'm going out the door...."

He was the calmest man Lena knew. He was the person she'd want beside her in any kind of situation. He never got rattled. When he finally spoke, she stopped. Because all at once he sounded upset.

"Well, that's the problem, Lena. That's why I'm calling...."

She was at her front door, one hand on the phone, the other on the doorknob. Later she marveled at how composed she sounded. Her voice was as smooth and flat as ice but just as thin, her heart suddenly beating inside her chest so hard it hurt. "What is it?"

"The office where this is happening...well, it's Andres's office, Lena."

Her lungs went tight and she suddenly couldn't catch her breath. "Have you tried to reach him?"

"We called his office *and* sent a unit to his condo. No one answers at either place."

"Have you located his vehicle?"

"Sarah did that first thing." She heard Bradley swallow. "His Suburban's in the parking lot...at the office."

They spoke a few more minutes, then Lena hung up the phone. She told herself to stay calm, to stay focused.

The advice went unheeded.

Two seconds later, she flew down her driveway on

two screaming tires, the left side of her truck hanging in the air as she careened around the corner. She felt the jolt as the tires hit the highway's pavement and dug in, but she gunned the engine, driving through the darkness half-blind with fear.

Accusations shrieked through her head. She *should* have insisted Andres have a guard all this time. She *should* have made sure no one got close to him. She *should* never have let him out of her sight.

This was all her fault.

The road was a blur as she hurtled through the night.

HIDDEN BEHIND the wall, Andres crouched down as far as he could. He had no idea where the shooter was located, but with the right angle, he might easily be able to aim over the short brick enclosure. Andres held no illusion of safety. He couldn't depend on the P.D., either. He thought he'd seen a black and white at one point, but they'd disappeared and rightly so. They would have been pinned if they stayed. He could only pray SWAT had been called. For the moment, though, he was on his own.

With his shoulder on fire and bleeding, he turned to assess his location.

The enclosure was small. No more than six or seven feet in circumference. To the left of the front door was a mirror image of where he hid. Every morning and afternoon, the building's smokers huddled here. There was room for about five people, but from the butts on the ground, it seemed as if a legion of them came out to smoke. Over the coppery smell of his blood, Andres caught the stale scent of tobacco. It reminded him of the last time he'd smoked. When Lena had been shot.

He held his breath, then chanced a look over the wall. The mental snapshot burned into his brain as he fell back down behind his cover. There were countless places a sniper could hide: a tall apartment building directly across the street, a corner grocery to the right, a closed flower shop on the left. He suspected the apartment, though. It afforded the best view.

But it was his own parking lot that gave him the most pause. There were three vehicles in it, besides the black Suburban. Andres closed his eyes and positioned the vehicles in his mind. His SUV in the front, to the left. A red Firebird to the right. A green Jeep in the back.

And a silver Town Car by the curb across the street.

As if spurred on by the realization and not his sudden movement, blood began to pour from his wound. Andres cursed roundly into the darkness and clamped a hand over the wound. It was hell to be right after all this time.

He only hoped the truth wouldn't die with him.

LENA KEPT a steady conversation going with Bradley as she sped toward the scene, giving him instructions and getting minute-by-minute updates. The War Wagon was dispatched with record speed and set up two blocks away from Andres's office. She drove straight to the site, dropping her cell phone and the link to Bradley only when she had the team in view. Slamming the truck to a stop, she parked with two wheels on the curb and two in the street, then jumped out and sprinted toward the gathered team members. Bradley noted her entrance then turned back to the men to help distribute the gear. As she reached them, Beck came to her side.

"What have we got?" She reached for the headset he

handed her and tried to keep her anxiousness from her voice. "Any news?"

Beck's eyes met hers in the darkness. "Nothing so far. Sarah's inside still trying to find Andres. She's running the tags on all the cars parked for two blocks around here, and she's contacting the other tenants who have offices in the building. We were waiting for you before we deployed."

She turned to the nearest man. It was Brandon. "Get me a jacket and a helmet," she instructed. "I want night vision goggles, too."

Beck put his hand out at once and stopped Brandon. "Lena, you can't do this," he said sternly. "You need to stay in the Wagon. You haven't recovered fully."

"I'm fine." Her demeanor was even and so was her voice as she glanced back toward the younger cop. "Go get the gear."

He started off again but once more Beck stopped him, this time with a growl. "Just a minute—"

Brandon halted his progress, but he looked askance at Lena. She *was* the commander.

"Stand down, Brandon," she said. "Lieutenant Winters and I need to talk." The younger cop took two steps backward and locked his hands behind his back. His gaze was in the distance but his ears were almost twitching.

No one ever contradicted Lena.

"What in the hell do you think you're doing, Beck?" she asked softly.

"I'm trying to save your butt," he answered. "You aren't ready for this and even if you were, that could be Andres caught up there. You can't think straight when he's involved."

"That's not true. And I'm fine."

"No, you're not," he said, each word deliberate. "You're upset, you're shaking, and you're going to make decisions you shouldn't if you command this operation."

She glared at Beck in the darkness and remembered Brandon's near miss all those weeks ago. Beck had a point, but suddenly she knew she'd handle this situation just as she had the last one, and would the next one and still the one after that.

She was a cop.

She had to put aside her personal life and all that entailed because lives depended on her ability to do so. She'd accepted that principle when she signed on, but she hadn't understood exactly what it meant until this very moment.

Now she did.

The awful clarity was overpowering and far-reaching. Suddenly, she understood the terrible dilemma Andres had faced when he'd gone to rescue his friend. Everything he was, everything he stood for, had come to a head with that call. He couldn't have done anything but try to save his friend, then afterward deal with the man responsible *and* the backlash. She would have done the same, even knowing her own father could have been involved.

She turned to the young cop behind her. "Get that gear and make it fast." He fled immediately then she looked up at Beck. "I'm a cop," she said quietly. "I'll make the decisions I have to and worry about the consequences later. Nothing is more important than that."

Beck's eyes held stony judgment. They were friends but she was also his boss and until this moment that relationship had never been tested. He read something in her gaze, however, something Lena suspected hadn't been there before. He nodded once, then turned away.

SILENCE ECHOED in the empty streets.

Andres was getting weaker by the moment and he had to do something fast. A plan formed in his mind as he gripped his gun and turned to stare at the window behind him. He hand-packed his own ammo, and it was powerful. One shot might be enough to shatter the thick, tempered glass. He could hit a lower pane, then crawl inside and escape through the back of the building. He'd be exposed while leaping inside but that was better than sitting here and bleeding to death. There was someone out there trying to kill him and he had to find out who.

He didn't give himself time to think about it. Andres popped up then immediately dropped and rolled to his right. Just as he wanted, the sniper responded a heartbeat later. He was a good shooter but not experienced enough to recognize the ploy. Lifting his pistol with his good hand, Andres fired quickly into the glass. The window shattered and he crawled through.

He found the nearest hall and ran toward the rear, the closed doors of all the offices silent witnesses to his flight. Stumbling blindly, he finally spotted a dim red light signaling an exit. He increased his speed and hit the door with one shoulder to sprint outside. Turning right at the corner of the building, he doubled back and disappeared into the darkness. Two seconds later he was across the street and where he needed to be.

GEARED UP and ready to go, Lena studied the map someone had thrust before her. She thought for a bit and discussed the situation with Bradley, then together they decided on a plan. They explained the deployment to the men who asked few questions; they trusted her with everything, including their lives. After a second communications check, she raised her hand and sent them out. They jogged silently down the two blocks toward the office building and within ten minutes, everyone was in place.

From her position, Lena lifted her night vision glasses and peered through the lens to the building beyond. It sprang into focus and what she witnessed made her tremble.

The ground in front of the building was littered with glass. The team's spotter had reported more shots fired just before the men had gone out. There was no sign of anyone at the moment, but someone *had* been there. He'd left a trail of blood. Her hands shook as she swept her gaze from left to right. He'd clearly been hit coming around the building and had fallen backward. She could see where he'd crashed against the wall and then slid down, a solid patch of red splattered against the stucco, just about shoulder height.

Dropping the binoculars, Lena pulled her microphone toward her mouth. "Call for an ambulance, Sarah. I think we're going to need one."

Sarah replied immediately. "Ten-four. I'll get one on the way."

She didn't want to look any more, but she had to. With even shakier hands, Lena raised the glasses once again and picked up the trail.

More blood was smeared across the sidewalk, and she followed the horrible streaks until they disappeared behind the low wall that fronted the building.

Was he still there, lying behind the wall, suffering?

Or had he already died?

CHAPTER SIXTEEN

As soon as Andres entered the apartment's garage, he remembered the building was empty. It was under renovation and he'd seen the trucks coming and going without even thinking about what that meant.

It was the perfect place for the shooter to hide; Andres would have picked it himself. The third or fourth floor, he'd estimated earlier. Good angle, quick getaway, a corner unit to see as much as possible. The whole setup felt right, and his intuition had yet to let him down.

He studied the empty garage, his shoulder going numb, black dots swimming in front of his vision. If he'd had any sense at all he would have holed up inside the office and called for backup, but he hadn't wanted to waste the time, and more importantly, he wasn't going to risk anyone else's life.

The thought renewed his energy, and Andres forced himself to press forward.

Lena wanted to scream but she spoke quietly into her microphone, calling out the code names for Cal Hamilton and Jason Field, the rear entry men. She couldn't risk approaching the offices from the front, and everyone knew why. They'd seen the blood, too. "Are you guys in place? At the back door?"

Both men answered in the affirmative. Before Lena had even gotten on-site, thanks to Sarah's hard work, the team had floor plans of Andres's building from the city inspector. They hadn't been able to find the manager, though. They had no keys.

"How's it look?" Lena asked anxiously.

Cal spoke for both of them. "Seems clear at this point. The back door's pretty protected. I think we can work our way up there and slip inside."

"Go ahead," Lena instructed, "but keep me informed."

She pressed her mike closer and spoke again. "R1, this is L1. Come in, please."

A calm, collected man whom Lena considered one of the best on the team, Ryan replied immediately. "This is R1."

"Any idea where the shooter might be?"

"Negative for now. All we know is what's most obvious—he has to be in front. If he shoots again, I might be able to triangulate his position and give you some idea, but anything else at this point would be a guess. I wasn't in place when he last fired."

"Go ahead and guess." Her mouth was almost too dry to form the words. "It'd be better than nothing right now, and nothing is all we've got so far."

"Give me a second. I need a better angle myself."

She waited in the tension-filled silence. Because she knew where each man now was, Lena imagined that she could see them. One behind the stand of palms near the left side of the building. One crouched behind a hedge that lined the western side. One in the parking lot. She was fooling herself, though, and she knew it. With their camouflaged faces and black clothing from top to bottom, no one could be spotted without infrared gear.

They had come across bad guys with that kind of equipment, but something told her this one didn't have it. He would have already been shooting if he did.

Ryan Lukas broke into her thoughts. "There's a building across the street," he said. "It's an apartment. Have Sarah call the management and see if there are any empty ones facing the offices."

Before he finished speaking, Lena relayed the message. She then checked in with the rest of the men. Each one answered quietly, but there was tension in their tones. A fellow cop was in trouble and they didn't like that.

Lena settled in to wait.

And to pray.

ANDRES MADE HIS WAY to the rear entrance of the apartment building, stepping over construction trash and trying to stay quiet. There was only one door. The lock had been jimmied, and the door itself was propped open with a chopped-off brick.

Easing past the opening, he stood quietly for a second and let his eyes adjust. The entry was cavelike; for a moment he could see nothing at all, then a darker square slowly took form to his right. It was another door, this one wide-open. He edged toward it and stepped inside, the stygian blackness claustrophobic. After a second, he realized he was in the stairwell, just as he'd hoped. With nothing but his feet to guide him, he began to go up.

The only sound he heard was his own harsh breathing and his pulse as it rushed through his body. His left arm and shoulder had no feeling at all now, and that whole side of his body was useless, a weight that was only slowing him down. He clutched the .38 in his right hand and thanked God he'd been hit on the left side.

Panting with the effort, he made it to the third floor. A quick survey and he knew it was empty. The fourth floor was the same. He was beginning to get worried by the time he reached the fifth floor. But the door from the stairwell to the hallway was propped open just like the one downstairs had been. Andres slipped into the deserted corridor. There were four doors between where he stood and the unit at the end. Each was painted a dark blue with brass numbers decorating the front. Each was closed, except the last. Gliding down the passage, he made his way to the end where he stood before the final doorway.

If he'd still been a cop, Andres would have called out, then knocked on the door, but he wasn't bound by those laws. The only thing that mattered now was Lena. He prayed she'd understand. He lifted his leg and kicked in the flimsy wooden barrier.

The man at the window rose in shock, his face revealed by the street lamp outside. Confused and incredulous, he jerked up his rifle to shoot, but Andres was faster.

With one last ounce of effort, he raised his weapon then aimed and fired. The man before him pitched to the floor, and a heartbeat later, Andres crumpled as well.

"THE APARTMENTS are empty." Sarah's voice sounded in Lena's ear. "They're being remodeled, and all the renters were kicked out about three months ago. The manager says he can—"

"*Quiet!*" Lena silenced Sarah with the command and at the same time ripped off her headset. She'd heard something while Sarah was speaking. Something that sounded like gunfire.

She strained to listen in the darkness, her pulse pounding so loudly it was impossible to hear more. The headset in her hand began to squeak and she quickly put it back on. Beck spoke this time.

"I heard it, too," he said. He had stayed with the Wagon to coordinate. "That was gunfire."

"Check in," Lena ordered. "Who's out there? What's going on?"

One by one the men responded. No one had fired his weapon. Ryan spoke when they finished. "I think it came from the apartment, Lena. I saw a flash."

She whirled and faced the building behind her. The windows were black and unnerving; they stared back at her with blank resistance. Grabbing her mike, she spoke curtly. "Scott, you and Hamilton get over there. Check out each entrance then call in."

"Ten-four."

Two shadows detached themselves from the darkness then disappeared again. Lena only saw them because she'd placed them herself. She had no idea where they were now or which direction they'd taken; they'd be in place before anyone else would know where, either.

In the waiting silence, she refused to think about Andres or what was happening.

An endless minute passed, then two more. Scott Brody's voice finally sounded. "The front door's secure. There's a chain linked through the handles. No one could get in or out that way. The back has been propped open, though." He said something in a muffled voice about a flashlight, then he spoke again. "Linc says there are two sets of prints in the dust. Two people have gone up there, and I'd say they're still there, unless they came down a different way."

Lena measured her breathing. In and out. In and out. "What do the prints look like?" she asked calmly.

"I'm no expert," Scott said, "but one set looks like hunting boots to me. About a size eleven maybe? I'm not sure about the others. They're smooth with a heel. The same size, I'd say."

"Do you see anything else?"

"There's blood," he said. "And lots of it. It's fresh."

He continued to speak, but Lena heard nothing more. A sudden buzzing in her ears blocked all her hearing. She brought herself under control, but it wasn't an easy task.

"Can you follow it?" she asked thickly. "The blood..."

"Oh, yeah." The cop's voice was matter-of-fact. "I'd say probably we won't have to go too far, either—he's losing too much of it to keep going for long."

Lena grabbed her microphone as if it could steady her. "Cal, you and Jason get across the street. Back them up."

"What about us?" Scott asked. "You want us to go up or wait?"

"Hold your position," Lena ordered. "I'm on my way."

THEY WERE HUDDLED at the doorway, waiting. Lena alerted the four men before she made her approach, then she darted to where they were poised. They explained the layout of the building and waited for her to tell them what to do.

It didn't take long for her to assess the situation. There was only one way they *could* do it.

She looked at the blood, a chill settling in her heart, then she lifted her gaze to the expectant men. "Okay, we'll do this in twos." She nodded at Scott Brody, on her right, the cop who'd been her backup the day Andres had flown in and she'd been wounded. "Scott and Linc go first. I'll go next, then Cal and Jason follow. That way we'll have coverage front and back."

The strategy was one they'd practiced a thousand times. They nodded as she continued.

"We'll stop on each floor and do a quick sweep, but for God's sake, stay alert. Obviously we're dealing with someone who knows his way around a gun."

All four men acknowledged her warning with serious looks, then they turned toward the stairs, Scott and Linc, the two more seasoned vets, leading the silent team into the kind of hell they knew best—the unknown and the deadly. The dark couldn't have been more thick, and Lena's heart couldn't have beaten any faster.

On the fifth floor they found them both. One dead, one alive.

One her lover, one her brother.

CHAPTER SEVENTEEN

ANDRES KNEW when they found him.

He felt Lena's hands on his chest—her sweet, soft hands—ripping off his shirt, her nails raking over his skin, her touch brutish as she tried desperately to get to his wound. He opened his eyes as cold air brushed against his bare skin. He couldn't move his left arm, and his right felt as though it were tied to the floor. Despite this, he tried to wave her off.

She captured his fingers with hers, and in an eerie echo of him, she said, "No...no, Andres. Don't move—be still! The medics are on the way."

"God, Lena...what are you doing here? Go...go away." He struggled to get the words out. "Please, please don't...don't look—"

She spoke as if he'd said nothing, and then he wondered if he had gotten the warning out or simply imagined giving it voice.

"He's dead." Her voice cracked. "Wh-what happened, Andres? What in the hell just happened here?"

"J-Jeff was the one behind everything, Lena." With each word, Andres felt more blood leak from his shoulder, but he had to speak. The pain in Lena's voice was much worse than what was happening to him. "He was the one sending money to the Red Tide. N-not your father."

He felt his sight ebbing, a darkness intruding on the edge of his vision. He was going into shock, his blood pressure dropping. "I'm sorry, Lena...I didn't figure it out until tonight.... I read Carmen's notes and saw Jeff had defended Escada. I-I was coming to tell you. He knew I was close.... He had to stop me himself. He—he couldn't risk another miss...."

Lena bent over him, and he smelled the scent of her skin. It seemed strange, lying in the dirt and the blood, to catch that hint of sweetness.

"Oh, God, Andres..." Her voice broke completely. He could hear her stop and draw a breath of her own. It was ragged and filled with agony. "Oh, God...this is all my fault! I should have known. When you told me about Dad, I confronted him, and he acted so strange. I could tell something was going on, but I didn't understand. He must have guessed! He suspected Jeff all along, and he was protecting him...."

Through the growing murk of his vision, Andres summoned his last bit of strength to look at Lena. She was holding a flashlight, the beam weak and unsteady but strong enough to reveal her face. She was covered with camouflage makeup, dark-green streaks mixed with black. Her T-shirt was torn on one sleeve and her gorgeous hair was matted to her head. She'd never looked more beautiful or been more precious.

He'd love her forever.

STANDING IN the center of her brother's tiny apartment, Lena looked around her, nothing but dead silence and dusty air keeping her company. After many hours of work, the forensic team had left. The investigators had departed shortly after that. She'd wanted to stay at the hospital but the doctors had told her there was nothing she could do, so she'd left Andres in their hands. She'd arrived in time to get a quick report from the lead man, a report she now wished she hadn't heard.

How could she have been so blind? How could she have missed what Jeff had become?

With grief and disappointment weighing her down, she walked slowly across the living room and stood in the doorway of her brother's bedroom. He'd pushed the bed against one wall and lined the rest of the room with cheap metal tables. Their surfaces were covered with a jumbled mess of books, writing tablets and various magazines. The investigators had boxed up and taken out over a dozen different notebooks. One quick glance at their pages had told them everything: Jeff's long-standing connection to the Red Tide. His idealism taken to madness...his excruciating need to prove something to Phillip that even he couldn't articulate. He'd filled hundreds of spiral-bound pages with every detail.

Tacked to the drywall above the tables were photographs. The investigators had left them after videotaping the room. Their content made no sense—there were movie stars, pages from war books, even drawings Jeff had done himself. One in particular caught Lena's eye. She crossed the room and took out the pin holding it to the wall.

It was a pen-and-ink sketch. The details weren't perfect, but she had no trouble recognizing herself and Jeff. He'd drawn them—as children—on the beach right outside her home. They couldn't have been more than seven and five. She sat down heavily on his bed, the paper crackling between her fingers.

Why? Why had he done this?

Hot, stinging tears filled her eyes and overflowed, but no answer came with them. It seemed impossible that Jeff had been able to live a double life with no one being aware of it, but obviously he had. It'd started with Pablo Escada's trial. He'd handled it for the firm, his notes full of excitement at the possibility of doing something "worthwhile." Lena had stared in disbelief as the investigator had shown her that passage. Escada had recruited Jeff with talk of a revolution and a better life for the poor of the islands. And Jeff had fallen for it completely.

She looked at the drawing in her hands, but didn't really see it, her breaking heart filled with sorrow. Convincing Jeff to join the Red Tide would have been an easy task for Escada. Jeff had always been the one on the outside, the one who didn't fit in. He hadn't known what he was really getting into, though. The little boy who'd chased her into the waves then warned her about the monsters had found them himself.

Feeling older than she was, Lena pushed herself up from the bed and went to the small closet in one corner of the room. Someone had left the light on inside. Reaching around the corner to the switch, something caught her eye on the floor. When she bent down, she realized it was one of Jeff's notebooks. Dropped or simply missed, it'd been left behind.

She stood there for a moment and trembled. The little bit she'd been shown had been painful enough; could she stand any more?

But she did what she had to and opened the cover. The hate-filled message jumped out at her, the vitriolic words scribbled so hard the ink had gone through to the next page. She skimmed the first page and went on to the next. She read until the writing was blurred by new tears.

Jeff had hated Phillip beyond all reason. He'd done everything he could to make Phillip look guilty, while trying to keep Lena safe.

She lifted her eyes and blinked, remembering his attempt to save her. He'd told her to marry Andres and move to Miami and have babies. In his tangled confusion, he'd wanted her away from everything, and possibly Andres as well. The notes trembled in her hand and a tear fell to the opened page, smearing the ink.

"I can't handle another screwup like the last one," he wrote. "I'll have to do the job myself. I like Andres but I can't risk hurting Lena again, and she'll show up. She loves him too much not to be there. I'll have to take care of this myself. He can't stand in the way of what I have to do. Eventually she'll forgive me."

She closed the notebook and a sob caught in her throat. Of course she would forgive him. He'd been her brother and always would be. She had loved him; they'd shared more than just a mother and father.

She'd forgive him, but she'd never understand.

ON THE PATIO OF Phillip's home a week later—a lifetime later—Lena stood with her back to the door and the crowd that had gathered. She was still numb, numb and angry, a paralyzing grief too breathtaking to even describe filling her heart and mind. They knew no more now than they had the first day, but she'd read more of Jeff's diaries. With each word, she'd felt worse.

She tried to shut out the noise behind her, but she couldn't. The crowd was too big, the sound of their chatter too deafening. None of these people had really known her brother, she told herself. A second later she realized the irony of that thought. She hadn't known him, either.

Wrapping her arms around herself and shivering in the cool winter breeze, she stared out over the lawn.

The worst part had been telling Phillip. She'd tried to make it as easy for him as she could. She'd actually lifted the notebook she'd found—even though it was technically evidence—and stashed it at her house. Later, if necessary, she could "find" it and turn it in. Why did her father need to know how much Jeff had hated him? How he'd done everything in his power to set Phillip up and make him look guilty?

As if her thoughts had conjured him, Lena heard footsteps behind her. She turned to find her father walking toward her. He looked even more frail than he had before, and she wondered if he could survive this.

Without saying a word, he came to her side and put his arm around her. They stood quietly, each lost in thought, then he spoke.

"I'm sorry, Lena. I'm so sorry all this happened. I've been the worst father in the world."

"That's not true, Dad." Lena turned and met Phillip's watery blue gaze. "You did what you thought was best."

"I never thought Jeff would actually try to hurt anyone or I would have—"

"You weren't sure. You didn't have proof. What could you have done?"

"At the very least, I should have told you my suspicions. You're such a good cop, I guess I thought you were invincible.... I just assumed you could always take care of yourself, no matter what."

Lena couldn't believe her ears. Her father had actually said she was a *good* cop?

"But I'm a blind old man and a foolish one, too. Just after you were shot, Bering and I discovered money was missing from the firm. He knew Jeff had handled the Escada case and began to put it together. When you came looking for me, he called me in Atlanta and told me because we were afraid you might find out we'd been investigating Jeff. I had gone there to talk to another lawyer, a woman who'd done some work for Escada."

Lena remembered Bering's startled look when she'd asked him about Pablo Escada, his reluctance to talk to her that day. It made sense now.

Phillip gripped the railing of the balcony. His hands were spotted, the veins large under the papery skin. "I even put an investigator on the case. We were doing all we could but Jeff didn't give us enough time. I couldn't accuse him without being sure."

He looked toward the pool, his eyes unfocused.

"Jeff was the only one who seemed to care. He did the pro bono work and handled the cases no one else would. We gave him a hard time for what he did. I didn't understand...."

"None of us did, Dad. Don't beat yourself up over it. You were trying. We just didn't know who he was."

Footsteps sounded on the patio behind them, and in unison, they turned. Andres walked slowly toward them, his left arm bound against his chest, his black hair gleaming in the weak winter sun. He'd only gotten out of the hospital the day before and they hadn't had a real chance to talk since everything had happened. There had been too much confusion and too many details to handle.

Lena wondered now if they hadn't talked because they didn't know what to say to each other. He was pale beneath his tan and there were shadows behind his eyes, but his ever present aura of sensuality and power radiated toward her as persistently as it ever had, maybe even more so. Her heart jumped inside her chest and begin to knock painfully against her ribs.

Phillip spoke first. "Hello, Andres."

Andres appeared to pull his eyes from Lena's face with an almost physical effort. He turned to Phillip and nodded, but he didn't say a word.

Phillip stared straight back. Lena could feel the tension between the two of them just as she had before, but now—at last—she understood. Phillip had suspected all along that Andres was getting closer and closer to the real culprit behind the Red Tide. He'd been afraid for his son.

Her father spoke abruptly, spitting out the words as though he wanted to get them out before he could change his mind. "I owe you an apology, Andres. If I hadn't been so stubborn, there are people who might be alive instead of dead. I don't know what to say except I was wrong, and you were right. I'm sorry for everything that happened, although I understand that's no excuse."

Lena watched as Andres shook his head, one thick lock of his black hair falling over his forehead. She was sure her father didn't see what she did; the way Andres's eyes changed and filled with pity.

"You don't owe me an apology, Phillip. I'm the one who should offer the apology. My suspicions of you were unfounded. I'm sorry for suspecting you. The truth is Jeff would have done whatever he wanted to, regardless of what you did. He was past the point of logic."

"My son just tried to kill you. He had your best friend and your assistant murdered. He almost killed Lena. Are you telling me you can forgive him all that? I'm not sure I can...."

Lena reached out and put her hand on her father's arm. His voice was agonized.

"It's not my job to forgive anyone," Andres replied quietly. "But I understand the situation. Jeff wasn't thinking straight. If he had been, he would never have done any of those things. That's all I can really say."

"I don't understand," Phillip said, shaking his head. "I just don't understand."

"Jeff didn't think there was any other way," Andres answered. "He *had* to have Carmen silenced. She was getting too close, just as I was. As for Mateo, I don't think Jeff even knew I was involved at that point. He was sending the Red Tide money and that was all. They found out about Mateo somehow and used Jeff's money to bribe the right people and have him killed. It had nothing to do with me. Nothing at all...."

They spoke a bit more, then finally, a few minutes later, Phillip left to tend to his guests. Andres moved closer to where Lena stood. He smelled like soap and fresh air. She couldn't resist lifting a hand to place it on his cheek. "How do you feel?"

He put his fingers over hers and squeezed gently before taking his hand away. "I think I'll be all right."

"You think?" Andres wasn't a man who used qualifiers.

"It all depends," he said.

"On what?"

"On you."

She stayed silent. She didn't know what to say.

"I left you at the altar. I accused your father of being a criminal. Now this...I don't know where to begin to heal the hurts between us, Lena. I don't know if you can forgive me."

"I love you," she said softly. "There's nothing between us that time can't handle...and nothing to forgive."

His gaze was black and unfathomable. "You told me

before you couldn't trust me, that you weren't sure I wouldn't leave you again. Do you still feel that way?"

Her throat ached with the effort of answering him. She wasn't sure she could explain herself. "Oh, Andres... When I was outside the office building—when I realized that you'd been hit—something happened inside me. All I can say is that suddenly I understood why you did what you did, and the truth is I would have done the very same thing."

"But Jeff—"

She stopped him. "Andres, you didn't have a choice. And I understand that completely—I'm a cop. I'll miss my brother the rest of my life and there's..." she faltered, her voice turning thick before she could control herself and start over. "There's always going to be a hole in my heart where I loved him. But the man you had to shoot wasn't the person I knew. He wasn't my little brother. That hurts so deeply I can't even explain it. He was my brother, but he was a stranger."

She blinked the tears back, her eyes filling anyway. "You aren't like that. You're exactly who you say you are. And you live the principles that mean so much to us both. You're going to be the one who gets me through this, Andres. I couldn't do it without you."

"Are you sure?"

"Absolutely. If you hadn't done what you did, I wouldn't love you. And that's what it all boils down to. I love you and I always will. I know that with my brain *and* with my heart. For once, they're in total agreement."

She expected him to say something, something that would make everything all right between them once more, but he managed to surprise her even so.

He reached out and cupped her cheek with his free hand. "Does this mean you'll marry me?"

Without saying a word, she put her arms around him and pressed herself against his chest with care. She could feel his heart beating between them—or maybe it was her own.

He responded by bending his head and kissing her deeply. When they broke apart a few moments later, she looked into his eyes and answered him once and for all, full of the knowledge that she was doing the right thing.

"There's nothing I'd like better than to be your wife, Andres." Her voice broke as she uttered the words, and then her tears flowed freely. She spoke past the ache in her throat, past the stinging release. "I'd be honored to be your wife. Now and forever."

He nodded with satisfaction and drew her close once more. As the sea breeze blew through the palms, they kissed again and dreamed of their future together.

EPILOGUE

LENA MCKINNEY stepped onto the red-carpeted aisle of the flower-filled church, the solemn strains of the "Wedding March" drifting above the crowded pews.

All the guests were watching her and she knew what they were thinking—Lena McKinney was *finally* getting married. Her single years were behind her, and now she was with the man she loved. From beneath her lacy veil she smiled with silent satisfaction, then all at once, the realization hit her.

It really was happening! They were actually getting married!

Andres smiled and held out his hand and Lena walked toward him to take his fingers in hers.

His warm grip was as real as the rest of the moment. Ten minutes later they were husband and wife.

Everything you love about romance...
and more!

Please turn the page for Signature Select™
Bonus Features.

Bonus Features:

Researching a Romance
Novel 4

Behind the Scenes
Kay's Favorite Places in
Destin Florida 8

Recipe 12
Seafood Casserole

Sneak Peek 14
NOT WITHOUT PROOF
by Kay David

BONUS FEATURES

the GUARDIANS

Researching a Romance Novel
by Kay David

It's all in the details...

Have you ever found a glaring mistake in a novel and felt disgusted? Well, I have, and let me tell you, it's even worse when you're the one who wrote the book!

4 Romance enthusiasts are sharp-eyed readers and very few errors get past their steady gazes. If you've ever considered writing a book yourself, romance or otherwise, one of your first considerations should be your research. Here are some tips to get you started.

- The Internet is your friend. Every detail you could possibly need to know is available to you on the Internet. The only hitch is you have to know where to look. This involves search engines like Google or AskJeeves. If you don't know what I'm talking about, get the book *The Internet for Dummies*. You have to know your way around to get where you're going.

·Beware of the Internet! (Yes, I know. I'm contradicting myself, but it's okay.) Verify the legitimacy of the sites where you get your information. Many colleges and some high schools now have their students submit papers through the Net, and a search engine may turn these up. Do you want to base the details of the architecture of Kathmandu on the opinion of a sophomore attending Kansas State? I didn't think so. Make sure your sites are reliable.

·Read as much as you can. Fiction, nonfiction, biographies. All of these will help you see your situation through a different set of eyes.

·Find someone who works in the same profession as your character and bug them to death. Go to work with them, if you can, and keep your eyes open for the little details that will make or break your story. If you're writing about a quilter, does she have calluses on her thumb? If you're writing about a doctor, when does she sleep?

·Whether you're putting your characters in a foreign location or a nearby town you haven't visited before, a trip is the best way to obtain the details you need to make your setting a rich one. How does the place smell? What does it sound like? Are the locals rich? Poor? What kind of attitude do they all have? These are the particulars that will put your readers into your characters' shoes.

•If you can't actually get there, rent a video. National Geographic produces wonderful travel videos that are always accurate and enjoyable.

•Ask other writers. It's amazing to me the careers most writers have experienced before becoming writers. Chances are great that in your circle of friends or your RWA chapter, if you belong to one, there are folks who may be familiar with the career or lifestyle you need to know all about. If they weren't biochemists, for example, in another life, they probably know someone who is.

•Double-check your information. No, triple-check it. If your research turns up an answer to one of your questions, make sure you get that same answer somewhere else, as well. Tailor your details to your setting, but be aware that in other situations a different case might hold true. The rules in one police station may not apply to the station one town over.

•Remember, in the end, that you are writing fiction! You can invent your own town, your own rules and your own characters, but if you place your story in a particular setting, try to make it as accurate as possible.

Marsha Zinberg, Signature Bonus Features Editor, spoke with Kay David in a café in the fall of 2004. 🐚

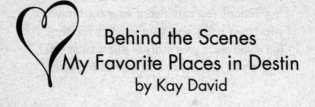

Behind the Scenes
My Favorite Places in Destin
by Kay David

Destin, Florida, is one of the most beautiful places I've ever seen. The white sand beaches, the pure emerald waters, the unique little communities—the town has so much to offer it's really difficult to pick what to do next when you're visiting. I've narrowed down my choices, but it wasn't easy!

Since eating is always at the top of my agenda, I'll talk about restaurants first. Destin has an overwhelming selection of excellent restaurants, and finding one that fits your budget is no problem. If you want to have a special night out I would recommend either the Flamingo Café or the Marina Café. Both are located on Highway 98 and are easy to find, but once you're inside and staring at the menu, the choices become much more difficult. Both places have wonderful seafood dishes and spectacular views of the Destin Harbor area and beyond. Any special occasion can be celebrated at these two restaurants. I know, because I've done so.

If you want a more casual atmosphere but still desire seafood, I'd suggest either Pompano Joe's or AJ's Seafood and Oyster Bar. You can dine inside or outside at both and the food is so fresh you won't believe it.

Ethnic food sounds better? Try Café Grazie for Italian or La Paz Restaurante & Cantina for Mexican. I always hit both when I'm in town.

Are you full now and need some exercise? My favorite way to burn off calories is shopping, and Destin has plenty of that, as well. There are wonderful small and unique shops throughout town, but if you're looking for the mega-experience, head straight for the Silver Sands Factory Stores. Every manufacturer you can possibly think of seems to have an outlet here, and the selection—and prices—will amaze you. Plan on spending several days if you want to go into every store, and wear your most comfortable walking shoes, too. The shops are air-conditioned, but the complex is an outdoor one and it's very spread out. There are places to eat here, as well.

If you've spent all your money and need a quiet day next, the beaches of Destin are legendary. The Emerald Coast, as it's sometimes referred to, has the clearest water I've ever encountered anywhere, and that includes the Caribbean. You can't park on the beach, so if you're not renting a condo near the waterfront you'll have to locate one of the public parking areas. In addition to the beach in Destin itself, there are several other nearby places you should check out. Rosemary Beach is nearer Panama City than Destin, but the drive is worth it. If you're heading that way, be sure to stop at Seaside, another interesting community on the way. The houses that line the narrow streets are million-dollar babies, with the entire area designed to resemble an old-fashioned hometown. Blue Mountain Beach is also on this road, and it's a lovely, peaceful area where the only other living thing on the beach might just be a seagull.

If you want to head west out of Destin, toward Pensacola, there are many gorgeous parks, some on the barrier islands themselves. You might have to pay a toll or two to cross onto the islands, but last time I checked the price was very reasonable and the scenery was definitely worth the cost.

If you're not lucky enough to have a relative who lives nearby and you need a place to rest your head at the end of the day, I'd recommend renting a condo. You can find them in any and every price category, from the most luxurious to the most economical. If they're located directly on the beach you'll pay more, but again, I think it's worth it. When you pull back those drapes in the morning and see the diamonds sparkling off the water, you'll be glad you paid extra. Every condo I've ever stayed in has a wonderful balcony of some sort, and there's nothing like sitting out in the morning sun and contemplating what you want to do with the rest of your day in Destin. My favorite is Oceania, but I've stayed in many different ones and have never been disappointed. FYI, if you can go in the winter, the rates are lower—sometimes half as much as they are in the summer. Many of these units are available for monthly rentals, too. If you have the time and the resources to lease one for a month, call me! I'll come and visit.

I grew up on the Texas Gulf Coast, and while I don't want to knock my own beautiful state, I must say Florida's coast is simply outstanding. If you have the opportunity, visit my favorite places. By the end of your trip, I'm sure you'll have your own list, too!

Kay's Seafood Recipe

As just about anyone who knows me will tell you, I'm not much of a cook, but fortunately I come from a family where that particular talent abounds. Since Destin is world famous for its delicious seafood, I'm going to share with you my Aunt Dorothy's world-famous crab casserole recipe.

AUNT DOROTHY'S CRABMEAT CASSEROLE

2 cups crabmeat (1 lb)
4 tbsp butter, melted
2 tbsp flour
1/2 tsp salt
1/2 tsp dry mustard
1/2 tsp paprika
1 dash nutmeg
1 cup milk
2 tbsp parsley, chopped
1 tbsp lemon juice
1 cup soft bread crumbs (homemade)
2 tbsp butter, melted
2 medium onions, chopped
1/2 medium bell pepper, chopped
Celery to taste, chopped
1 cup bread crumbs, store bought

Flake crabmeat and set aside.

Melt 4 tablespoons butter and stir in flour, salt, mustard, paprika and nutmeg. When blended, add milk slowly, stirring over low heat until mixture thickens and boils.

Stir in parsley, lemon juice and soft bread crumbs.

It tastes a lot better eaten on the beach!

Sauté vegetables in butter until soft, then combine two mixtures, gently adding crabmeat.

Put in 1 1/2-quart baking dish and sprinkle with store-bought crumbs mixed with a little melted butter.

Bake at 375° F for 10 minutes or until golden brown.

Here's a sneak peek...

14

NOT WITHOUT PROOF
by
Kay David

In the high-stake business of hired assassins, a hero can be deadly....

PROLOGUE

February
Houston, Texas

THE DIAMOND WEIGHED almost ten carats.

Resting on the desk, the gem was round and cut precisely, the fifty-eight perfect facets reflecting the low light overhead with an amazing brilliance. The color was just short of summer butter, delicate enough to give the stone a treasured elegance, yet bold enough to triple its value.

The three men sitting around the desk were whole-sale diamond dealers, people who made their living selling and buying intrinsically useless pieces of carbon that were worth thousands sometimes hundreds of thousands, of dollars. None of the three seemed particularly interested in the diamond at the moment, though. They were discussing something much more compelling.

They were discussing murder.

Outside the high-rise office building the weather matched their conversation. A February northerner had blown in that afternoon, dropping the temperature from fifty-five to thirty-two in the space of an hour. Texans were accustomed to drastic weather changes, but this one had been unexpected, and when the wet roads had become icy, the streets and freeways had turned into battlegrounds, the SUVs and pickups morphing into deadly weapons. Houstonians liked their ice in tall glasses splashed with Scotch. They didn't know how to handle it beneath their tires.

"I told him to be careful, to keep his eyes sharp. There is evil in this world," the dealer in the center said solemnly. "But did he listen to me, an old man? No, of course not." He patted his yarmulke anxiously, aligning the small black circle with nervous fingers. His name was Ami Leonadov and he was seventy-eight years old. He was the one who'd brought the diamond. Tilting his head toward the empty chair at his left, he spoke with sadness. "C.J. was a good friend for many years. For him, I would have wished a better death."

"How much do you think he told them?"

The second man, Luis Barragan, spoke in English just as Ami had, but it was not the native tongue of either. Barragan had flown in from Mexico City, his home, that morning, and he was weary, his accent heavy.

Before Ami could say anything, the last man, silent until now, answered for him.

"Anything would have been too much! Anything!"

His voice was harsh, and the other two stared at him. They were embarrassed by Joseph Wilhem's bluntness and considered him obnoxious, but they had needed his money. Of the four of them, Joseph had the most to lose—or win. He lived in Argentina now, his family all refugees from the wrong side of Germany, another fact Ami and Luis tried to overlook.

"We should have our wills in order," Wilhem said in disgust. "We're walking dead men."

Luis Barragan sent Ami a frightened look. The older man made a calming motion with his hands and shook his head imperceptibly. "You are overreacting, Joseph, just as you always do. C.J. was murdered by thieves. They robbed him and then they killed him. He told them nothing because there was no need."

"How do you know this?" Wilhem's expression was suspicious. "If it's gossip, I don't believe it."

"I talked to the police and the IDDA," Ami replied.

"The IDDA?" The German's voice went up another notch. "They're involved?"

"Another dealer called them." Ami shrugged. "He was scared—I think it must have been that new fellow on six—and they may send someone to help the police as an added precaution. The IDDA want their dealers safe as well as their stones."

The majority of diamond brokers in the building, and around the world, obtained their goods from a privately held New York firm, the International Diamond Dealers Association, mainly because they had no other choice. The IDDA more or less controlled the supply of diamonds, from the ground to the diva's finger.

"The police told me his death was the work of a heartless *farbrecher,* a criminal, nothing more. C.J. would have had no reason to bring up our plans while he was being robbed. The act, as horrible as it was, had nothing to do with us."

"And what if it wasn't just a thief?"

"No ears but ours have heard what's been said in this room. The project is safe," Ami replied. "You see too many ghosts."

"That's because they're there!" His face flushing a deep red, Wilhem rose abruptly, his hip hitting the edge of the desk. The furniture was sturdy—Ami's wife had brought it with them from Russia aeons before—but the desk moved under the force of Wilhem's anger, its legs scraping across the cheap linoleum with a nerve-etching screech. The diamond rocked with the movement, then rolled to one side, reflecting light against the opposite wall.

Ami stood slowly. He wasn't as tall or imposing as Wilhem. He enjoyed eating too much and in his slippers he reached five-six, maybe five-seven. He had the advantage over the other man, though, because he was the one who'd brought the deal to the table.

"If you want out, Joseph," he said in a dignified

18

voice, "please say so now. We cannot proceed if we do not all agree."

The Argentinian frowned, as if he were actually considering the question, then he shook his head, just as Ami had known he would. "I don't want out," he said gruffly. "But I *am* worried."

"Don't you trust me? Is that it? Have I not reassured you enough? Have you not seen with your own eyes? What is there to fret over?" He held his hand out toward the yellow diamond. "The stone is everything I promised it would be, no?"

His words hung in the air between the three of them, and one by one they turned to the diamond. They each stared at it until Luis, soothed by Ami's calm manner, chuckled nervously and spoke. "It *is* everything you said, Ami, *and* it isn't."

The tension broken, Ami smiled indulgently at his friend's simple joke, then he patted Wilhem on the back. "Very soon we're going to be rich old men, Joseph. Relax and accept your future."

"When I know for sure that I will have a future, then I will accept your advice." Wilhem's expression was dark, his voice even more so. "Until that point, I wait and see. If you two are as smart as you think you are, you will do the same. Otherwise we might be joining our old friend C.J. long before we're ready."

CHAPTER 1

April
Somewhere in California

THE RINGING PHONE cut through the silence of Stratton O'Neil's run-down beach rental like a Stryker saw on high.

Stratton didn't move. Sitting in a deep armchair, staring at the waves as they rolled in, he listened to the sound with a detachment one notch short of depression.

The machine kicked on, his message played and a woman's voice filled the room. He'd listened to too many people for too many years. The need had left him, but the habit was still intact, and her grating accent was a detail he noted without thinking. New Jersey coast, he thought indifferently as she spoke. But trying for upper East side.

"This is Lucy Wisner with IDDA in New York. Mr. O'Neil, please call as soon as possible. You've been recommended to us by a former client and we're in need of your services. This is a matter of some urgency, so please contact us quickly." She read off four telephone numbers, then hung up.

Lucy Wisner had called twice before and left messages, begging him to phone her. Stratton had no idea who she really was or what she wanted, but he knew one thing for certain—she was a liar. None of his former clients would have given his name to anyone, unless it was to warn them to stay as far away from him as they could. He hadn't worked in almost two years.

And he had no intention of ever doing so again.

He drained his coffee mug, then set it down on the floor. His hand hit the bottle of Jack he'd dropped there the night before, and he picked up the whiskey and held it in front of him, the setting sun giving it a warm amber glow.

For the past two years he'd kept the bottle close. The seal was intact, but he harbored no illusions. At some point he'd break down and open it. He knew himself too well to think otherwise.

The phone rang a second time.

The accent sounded from across the room. "This is Lucy Wisner again. I forgot to give you the cellular number of my assistant. His name is Daniel—"

Stratton put down the bottle and picked up the phone, his irritation finally overcoming his lethargy. "I don't want the number of your assistant or any of the other numbers you've left here, lady. Leave me the hell alone," he said without inflection, "and don't call here anymore." He started to punch the off button, but he stopped when her pleading voice sounded again.

"Mr. O'Neil? Stratton O'Neil? You actually answered! I need to talk to you—"

"Why?"

"We want to hire you." She answered swiftly, as if she were afraid he was about to hang up. Which he was. "A valuable member of our organization—"

"What organization?"

"IDDA," she replied. "The International Diamond Dealers Association. We broker diamonds to wholesalers all over the world. One of our dealers in Houston has been murdered and we were told you could help—"

"Told by whom?" He interrupted a second time.

"That's confidential information. I can't tell you."

"That's just fine," he said, "because I can't help you. I'm no longer in the 'helping' business."

"Please let me send you a first-class ticket, Mr. O'Neil. Our offices are in New York. We'll pay you just to come talk to us."

"You aren't going to pay me squat," he replied, "because I'm not going to New York or Houston or wherever you said you're from. I'm not going anywhere but to hell and I don't want my progress slowed. Don't call here again."

"WHAT DID he say?"

Lucy Wisner looked up from her desk and shook

her head at the man leaning against the door to her office. In his custom-tailored suit and two-hundred-dollar haircut, Ian Forney looked exactly like what he was—the successful CEO of a multinational business with sales in the billions.

He was her boss and her lover, and she despised him.

"He won't come," she said in a dismissive way. "He's not interested."

"Did you offer him money?"

She narrowed her dark eyes, intentionally making them as hard and shiny as the pear-cut diamond she wore on a chain around her neck. "You heard me, didn't you? I told him a ticket was on its way, but he didn't give me the chance to explain."

Ian smiled. "He'll come."

"What makes you so certain? He sounded as if his mind was made up."

"Maybe it is, but when he sees the check, he'll un-make it."

"Money doesn't motivate everyone, Ian."

"Of course it does," he answered easily. "The trick is to figure out the *right* amount. Once you do that, you can buy anyone."

She arched one eyebrow but stayed silent. She was afraid that if she spoke she'd say something she'd regret. Ian was so full of himself he made her sick. When they'd first hooked up, she'd thought he was different, but he wasn't. He was a carbon copy of every self-centered, egotistical bastard she'd ever known.

He dropped his gaze to the neckline of her blouse, then slowly brought it back up. "Trust me on this one, Lucy. We can buy Stratton O'Neil. He's a washed-up, has-been failure. He's a loser, and the organization he worked for fell apart because of it."

"What kind of business was it?"

He laughed coldly. "I wouldn't call the Operatives a business, sweetheart, unless you consider death a product."

Lucy felt herself blanch, but she didn't blink. "What are you saying? Are you trying to tell me these people were mercenaries or something?"

"'Or something' might cover it," he answered. "Until he went wacko, he and his buddies made a living from killing third-rate dictators and inconvenient drug lords on the q.t., mostly in South America where those kinds of things can be more easily accomplished. Our precious government used them on occasion as well, but only when they had plausible deniability. You do know what that means, don't you?"

"I'm well aware of the definition of plausible deniability," she said coldly, "but what I don't believe in are assassins."

"Fine," he said petulantly. "But that's exactly what the Operatives are."

"If that's the case, why didn't we hire them to begin with?"

"Haven't you been listening? They're no longer in business because of Stratton O'Neil's incompetence." He hesitated. "But they wouldn't have worked for us regardless. They don't kill just anyone. According to my source, their targets have to deserve what they're getting."

The office fell silent as they both considered the meaning of his words. Lucy broke the silence. "So what did this guy do that was so bad?"

For the first time since their conversation had begun, Ian looked uncomfortable. "They wouldn't tell me, but I got the impression that whatever it was, it must have been pretty unbelievable."

She made a scoffing sound. "You're crazy, Ian. This is fantasy-land stuff, not to mention illegal."

He sneered, his attitude back in place. "Illegal, oh, my God! You're right! We wouldn't want to be doing anything illegal now, would we?"

Her anger rose another degree at his mockery. "How do you know all this, anyway?"

"I just do," he said smugly. "And that's all *you* need to know. Stratton O'Neil has a price. I know what it is and you just doubled it. He'll take the job and he'll do just what we want. A month from now, our little situation will be solved."

"I'm not sure I agree."

"Well, that's your problem then, isn't it?" Ian

straightened his cuffs. "Because I know I'm right. I have it on excellent authority that he's the perfect man for us. No one can screw up a job better than Stratton O'Neil, and that's exactly what we need."

...NOT THE END...

Look for NOT WITHOUT PROOF *in stores July 2005 from Signature Select.* ✎

26

If you enjoyed what you just read,
then we've got an offer you can't resist!

Take 2 bestselling love stories FREE!

Plus get a FREE surprise gift!

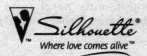